The Convict
AND THE
SOLDIER

JOHN P. F. LYNCH

Published in Australia by Sid Harta Publishers Pty Ltd,
ABN: 46 119 415 842
23 Stirling Crescent, Glen Waverley, Victoria 3150 Australia
Telephone: +61 3 9560 9920, Facsimile: +61 3 9545 1742
E-mail: author@sidharta.com.au

First published in Australia 2016
This edition published 2016
Copyright © John P. F. Lynch 2016
Cover design, typesetting: WorkingType (www.workingtype.com.au)
Cover Design by Luke Harris
Cover picture by permission of the National Library of Australia, Canberra
Tucker, E., *Relief guard arriving at a prison hulk, Deptford, 1821*, Ref. an5576207

346pp

The National Library of Australia
Cataloguing-in-Publication Data
Lynch, John P. F.
The Convict and the Soldier
ISBN 978-1-877059-95-7 (pbk)
    1.   Convicts — Fiction
    2.   Soldiers — Fiction
A823.4

To my mother, Evelyn Ida Lynch (nee Keogh) —
a true daughter of the Australian bush

Contents

Foreword

I feel privileged to be asked by a fellow Legatee, John Lynch, to write a foreword for his book, *The Convict and the Soldier*, when it is republished by publisher request.

The book is set in the mid nineteenth century. This is a very interesting time in history to set a novel in the conditions prevailing in the Terra Australis colonies.

The book's title may at first lead to a potential reader assuming that this is just another book dealing with the First Fleet, the challenge of the New South Wales colony to feed itself, and the British Army and local troops to keep order.

But *The Convict and the Soldier* deals with a crucial period of colonial development. Transportation, which has provided much of the necessary labour to till the land and farm sheep, has ceased in some colonies and its days are numbered in others.

The colony of Victoria has already broken away from its parent to the north and is about to gain representative government. It was the discovery of gold during that time that was to have such a material effect on the communities. Suddenly, there was an injection of wealth and successful gold miners were able to underwrite the construction of solid brick or basalt buildings, many of which have stood the test of time and still stand today.

The novel's story begins in Ireland, a country that had endured a long history of being bled by its English neighbour, of potato famine, poverty and evictions by English landlords of those peasants who could not pay their rent.

Michael Keogh comes from a relatively well-off family. He is a skilled shipwright. He comes in difficulty with the law when he assists a felon to escape the country. Without much evidence he is declared guilty and sentenced to transportation to Van Diemen's Land, now of course Tasmania.

Michael was hence the convict. John Hall is the soldier. Commissioned in an English regiment that is charged with supporting the constables in the execution of the unjust laws that stood at the time, He becomes embroiled in a situation created by his commanding officer and, although discharged from a courts martial without a decision, John Hall decides to leave the army and seek a new life in the Antipodes.

Just to add spice to the story, we find that John has become besotted with a member of the Keogh family, Maeve, and they pledge to be married but not before John has become successful in the colonies.

The author, who has travelled extensively, including five times to Ireland, describes in some detail for the benefit of the reader, the conditions in Ireland and then the long sea voyage down south.

With our modern way of life, where milk does not come from cows, but from the dairy produce shelves in the supermarkets; where the trip to Europe can now be flown in less than 24-hours; and where the pace of life touches on the frenetic, it is most useful for the author to describe with some feeling the conditions of living as they were then.

Michael and John arrive safely in Hobart Town, one as a convict, the other as a free passenger. Life on the ship is well described. John of course is free to travel in Van Diemen's Land, but Michael must first escape from the boat building to which he was put to work as a convict.

The book then takes us north from Hobart Town to Bass Strait, our two heroes having become skilful sheep shearers and

Michael is forever putting distance between him and re-arrest. At this stage a reader will be so fascinated by the book that he or she will not be able to put it down until Michael and John achieve their respective goals. For John this would be success as a colonist and being reunited with Mauve and a happily married man. But it is hardly likely that either will escape frequent challenges to their health and freedom with many pages yet of the book to be enjoyed.

Graham J Farley,
OAM RFD ED
B.Com B.Ed M.Ed
Colonel (Rtd)
Headmaster Braemar College 1976–1996

Introduction

The Colony of New South Wales was originally populated by people from England, Scotland and with the majority coming from Ireland. These people travelled to Australia for various reasons; some were free settlers, some military men and many others were convicts. Their voyages, at times, were not always of their choice. The legal system and the politics of the time were often the basic causes for many injustices, which resulted in changing their lives forever. Fortunately, many of these people made a success from their adversity and became respected citizens in the New Colonies of Australia. This story is based on the experiences of some of those people.

John P F Lynch
OAM KSJ J.P.
"Woodlea"
Romsey
AUSTRALIA

The Families

THE KEOGHS

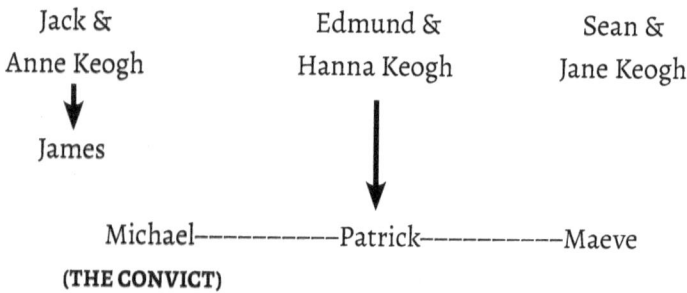

Jack &
Anne Keogh
↓
James

Edmund &
Hanna Keogh
↓

Sean &
Jane Keogh

Michael———————Patrick———————Maeve
(THE CONVICT)

THE HALLS

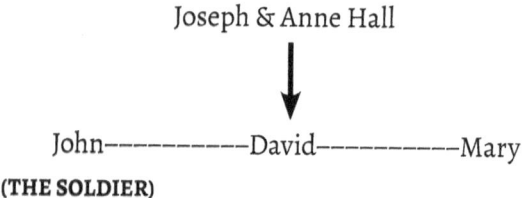

Joseph & Anne Hall
↓

John———————David———————Mary
(THE SOLDIER)

THE LANGS

Paul & Victoria Lang
↓

Frederick

CHAPTER I

Troubles in County Clare

—

he young man sat staring out to sea. Through the rolling mist he watched a three masted barque sailing parallel to the coast line. It would soon turn to port, to tack south–west, en route to America across the vast and treacherous Atlantic Ocean. *The bad weather and heavy seas would test both man and vessel*, he mused. He knew this area had claimed many ships. Ships of the Spanish Armada had floundered there. They would turn too soon after rounding the northern coastline of Ireland, on their trip south back to Spain, and were forced onto rocks by the strong westerly winds. *What secrets did the waters hold?* he pondered.

As a youngster, Michael Keogh had often come to the Cliffs of Moher. He always found that the solitude and starkness of these remarkable cliffs, that rose over six hundred feet from the sea, had allowed his mind to think more clearly.

The cliffs had been there since time forgotten, their sheer cliff faces providing a natural haven for millions of birds that nested in crevices. Its only distraction was O'Brien's multi-rounded tower up on the North Point. Stark against the skyline it could be seen for miles around, without a tree to interfere with the view. The surrounding area was strewn with small rocks and patches of grass, and sloped inland to a long row of large boulders with patches of colourful flowers occasioning the peaceful scene.

But now his thoughts wandered.

His birth place was within a short walk from there, two miles north west of the town of Liscannor in County Clare. His father was Edmund Keogh, whose cottage could be seen from the cliff, several hundred yards behind where he now sat. It was hidden from the road by large boulders. His forefathers had lived in the area for hundreds of years, when their original property had been over twenty acres. However, with the Keogh family's division of the land over the years, little now remained to be farmed by his father. What did remain was not yielding much corn or wheat and other produce was only of average quality. Fortunately, their two acres had not been challenged by the local British landlord, who regarded the small area on the cliffs as unproductive and, as such, insignificant.

Three weeks ago he had received a letter from his Aunt Jane, his father's sister-in-law, advising him that his father's health was poor and he was having difficulty working the farm. The words sent a shiver down his spine for he knew the land must be worked or his father would end up struggling like so many others.

Michael had only arrived home yesterday from his uncle's boat yard. His uncle had needed him to stay to help build Hookers, small river boats, but he knew where his duties lie and had packed up his belongings.

He had walked most of the way home carrying two small three legged stools. They were popular seats as they were easier to sit on regardless of the level of the cottage floor. Each time Michael had returned home he had taken an article of furniture, courtesy of his uncle. His uncle allowed him to build them in his free time, from the wood off-cuts at the boatyard.

If only he had the freedom of the gulls gliding up and down the cliff face on the westerly winds. What should he do? He had returned to his childhood home to help his ageing widowed father. To help him to do what? He was the oldest of three children; his brother, Patrick, was three years younger than him and his sister, Maeve, who was the youngest of the family, was five years younger than Michael.

Their mother, Hanna, had died shortly after Maeve was born and they had spent the following years being reared by his father and their Aunt Jane, who lived at the next farm. Her husband, Sean Keogh, had gone to America in 1848, lured by the Californian gold rush. He occasionally sent home money which helped to give Aunt Jane a reasonable living standard for the times they now lived in, but his money could not be relied on.

Michael remembered his childhood years with warmth. He had enjoyed the love and care typical of the poor Irish families. He remembered the singing, the fiddles, the bodrums and dancing the Irish reels. How could one forget this part of his life?

Patrick was now seventeen and was away working in Queenstown, or to use its Irish name — Cobh, in Cork Harbour. He was also learning to be a shipwright, building and repairing boats. This was normally the port from which both the immigrant ships and the transportation ships with Irish convicts sailed to Australia.

Patrick had told him the ships were being used as floating jails in Cork Harbour. The disgraceful and filthy conditions on the ships and the cries of the convicts being flogged were known to all who lived near the docks and shipyards. Patrick had said how these sounds sometimes played on his mind, disturbing him greatly.

Maeve still lived with Aunt Jane. Together they spun wool and made clothing material, shawls and bandle linen cloth as well as running the small farm. The other three Keogh family farms were not being worked as their ground had been contaminated by the imported American potatoes.

His father and Aunt Jane had wanted to sow their relative's farms after two families had fled overseas and the third moved on for employment but they had left hurriedly and could not be contacted.

Fortunately, each Keogh family had learnt the rudiments of reading, writing and arithmetic, including Gaelic. Secretly their parents taught them in accordance with family tradition. The Keogh families were an exception in Clare, as few families had had any education at all.

Their two families were both surviving, they were not poverty stricken as were the majority of the tenant farmers who had grown corn, wheat and potatoes, and had been required to surrender the corn and wheat to the landlord for their rent. The tenant farmers needed to survive on the potato harvest only. The dreaded Corn Law had killed millions of the Irish population, due to the requirement to ship all the corn out of Ireland for foreign trade.

Michael became aware of a dog barking behind him in the distance. He glanced over his shoulder and saw his father walking towards him. His dog was running here and there, seeking a hare or some other wild life hiding in the grass or between the rocks. His father was now slightly stooped and carried a shillelagh to assist him with walking in the rocky fields.

Michael's father, Edmund wore his normal thick flannel trousers and shirt, together with a sheepskin coat and a similar skull cap. Heavy leather hob nailed boots completed his outfit. His wife had made several of pairs of trousers and shirts years ago. They had lasted well and would last for a few more years still. Any farmer who kept sheep eventually owned a sheep skin coat and cap. The boots were excellent for walking on farmland but were a risk on cobblestones. In town he wore his second pair of shoes which were more suited to the paved streets.

The dog reached Michael first and sat beside him, looking up at him waiting to be patted. The Irish Red Setter was a good dog, somewhat lively but obedient and good company for his father.

Michael's father sat beside him, looking out to sea. His face showed his age and the strain of the life he lived. He was still determined and proud.

Michael asked him to share his thoughts.

He looked at him and said, "It's good to have you home."

Michael said nothing.

His father continued, "We should go and visit your Aunt Jane and perhaps go to the Kilrush market."

Michael liked Aunt Jane; she was the closest relative he had apart from Uncle Jack at the Kilrush Shipyard. "Yes, anytime you wish. I'd like to see her again." He had always felt comfortable in her presence.

The waves were growing larger with white water aplenty. The wind was starting to increase in strength and the temperature seemed to be dropping. Michael suggested that they return to the house, calling out to the dog as he rose from his seat and stretched his arms out.

Walking back to the house required one to be careful where they stepped. Rocks of all sizes were everywhere and it was easy to twist and injure an ankle. It was only when they were within fifty or so yards of the house that the ground was level and there was a grass path. On one side there were two small separate patches of corn and wheat; the crops looked healthy as they waved in the strong wind. On the other side of the path some herbs, turnips and onions were sown with small green shoots now starting to break through the soil. Several hardy fruit trees had been established. These were harvested in October then preserved and stowed in the attic.

The three areas were about seventy yards by forty yards, each fenced by dry rock walls. The south side of the house had two small enclosed pens. One pen was for the sheep and the single goat. The other pen was for some chickens. Just over an acre could be used as arable land. The rest was too difficult to clear of rocks but could be used for grazing.

As Michael walked back with his father, through the tough terrain that was their farm, he wondered how his family had made a living from this land for so long. They had, and now he had somehow to ensure that they continued to do so.

They decided to visit Aunt Jane, a walk of some three hundred yards. She had known he was returning but she was unaware that he had arrived as yet.

It was the local custom to take some food when visiting another's home. His father picked up two turnips and two corn cobs and passed them to Michael to carry. They proceeded up a short steep incline of some two hundred yards. Upon reaching the top they stopped and looked north out across the start of the Burren. County Clare was a land of contrasts with its southern green grasslands and the northern barrenness of the Burren. It was a spectacular sight but also forbidding with its starkness.

The county was bordered on the south by the River Shannon with good grazing land but as one headed north the countryside changed dramatically until it reached the Burren with its limestone slabs. The Keogh land bordered the southern end of the Burren which was a mixture of some grassland and limestone. Caves were abundant in the area, some small and others quite large; big enough to hide a man or many men. It was said that they were used by the rebels for hundreds of years and yet few people knew of them. The Keogh's knew all the land's secrets but did not speak of them to anyone outside of the family.

While the Burren was unproductive to a farmer it had a

beauty of its own. At midyear, colourful rock roses, holly trees, maidenhair fern, hawthorn plants and geraniums grew between the cracks and crevasses. As a boy Michael had wandered these hills with his dog and had explored the limestone caves which had been carved out by the water run off through the porous rocks over many centuries. It had been a carefree but lonely life.

Michael stopped reminiscing when the dog started barking and ran down the hill to the cottage on the creek. The dog ran to his aunty standing at the gate waving to them. His father had walked on and had nearly reached the cottage gate. A smaller person now joined his aunt, whom he recognized as his sister, Maeve. She was now sixteen years old, taller and had developed the body of a young woman since he had seen her last. His sister ran to meet him and threw her arms around his neck and kissed him. He put his arms around her, swept her off her feet and spun her around.

She was in tears and laughing delightedly. He put her down lightly and turned to Aunt Jane and kissed her fondly on both cheeks then stepped back and looked at them both. They were a picture of happiness and health. He was proud that they were successfully weathering these dark times with determination.

His father looked on, smiling and nodding his approval of their joy at seeing Michael again.

Michael had not been home for nearly a year. He had meant to visit them but had grown fond of life in Kilrush with his friends and did not wish to be committed to farm life. He felt guilty whenever he thought about his attitude to the farm.

Aunt Jane filled a can with water and suspended it from a hook on a bar over the fire in the hearth. She placed the turnips and corn in the boiling water together with a small cut of meat. She took down her willow pattern plates made by Minton. Some had small chips around their rims but they were still precious to her. They had been a present from her husband in better days.

Michael preferred them to the metal dishes at his father's home. They showed a female touch to the home, something that was missing in his father's house.

It was a basic but pleasant dinner and all enjoyed the comfort of companionship with each other in her cottage. The cottage had three rooms and her woman's presence was evident everywhere. It had Burren geraniums in a rockery outside her front door and small curtains on the windows.

Aunt Jane had some of Michael's handmade furniture and wall cupboards. She had polished the wood with tallow until they had a deep brown colour with a flat polished look. This look, together with curtains on the windows, made for a very pleasant and homely interior.

At sundown Michael and his father bid goodnight and walked back to their home, enjoying the silence and solitude of their little piece of Ireland; thanking God for what little freedom they had, which others could never attain.

Michael's father's home was similar to Aunt Jane's, only smaller. It consisted of two separate rooms with a loft on a side wall. The walls and floor were made of a collection of stone, limestone slabs, sandstone and black shale pieces, sealed with a mixture of mud and ground sandstone. It had a roof of bog oak timbers, bracken and reeds supported by wooden support bearers. Regardless of how well the reeds were packed the roof leaked during heavy weather. There were two multi-paned windows on the eastern side of the house looking towards the road and a two-panelled stable type door situated between the windows.

Inside, stone seats were placed around the fireplace. The loft had an assortment of wooden home-made beds with sheepskins sewn together to serve as a base. Scattered around the main room were two small tables, several stools, some cupboards on the walls and a food box. A long, well-made box was kept hidden under his father's bed and his deceased mother's spinning wheel stood silent in the corner. Metal cups and plates with other cooking utensils hung from wall hooks over the hearth. A hip bath tub was pushed almost out of sight under a table.

Inside the door were a row of hooks holding a variety of farm utensils — sections of rope, a bridle, several hare snares, a whip, wooden buckets, an oilskin coat and hood, shears and a bag of general tools. Outside the cottage and on the south wall, was a wooden lean-to shelter which held various farm tools, like shovels and rakes, safe from the elements.

Michael and his brother had slept in the open loft across from the hearth and enjoyed the warmth from below — if they had sufficient wood.

The Keogh's were humble but they felt secure.

On this visit home, Michael had walked past the remains of a home and recalled an incident he saw there several years ago. At the time he had been travelling with his uncle who had stopped at a crowd of people two miles out of Kilrush to see an eviction. It was brutal and efficient. The tenant family was dragged out of their hovel by the constables with the army standing by observing the incident. The police had used a tall wooden tripod with a large rock suspended on a rope and swung the rock to strike the building. It was flattened within a few minutes. The constables let the family free and then marched off, leaving them shocked and bewildered at losing everything. Michael had been only seventeen years old but the memory had stayed with him. Only last year, he had heard stories of dead being buried by the dozen in the same area. He dreaded walking through there now.

The house was quiet when Michael and his father arrived home. He looked around the main room, comparing it to his aunt's house. His eyes found his father's bed. He could just see the box almost hidden underneath.

When Michael came home last year, his father became quite secretive one evening and asked him to sit down and listen carefully as he had to tell him something which no other living soul knew.

He started their conversation by saying, "Our forefathers were not always farmers. Several centuries ago, one of our antecedents, Captain Daniel Keogh, was an Irish aristocrat, appointed as an aide to General Owen Roe O'Neill and served with him in the Irish Army. In 1646 they fought a battle against Scottish marauders."

He continued, "The battle was at Benburb in County Tyrone. It was a major battle; the Irish Army had five thousand infantry and four hundred cavalry, and the Scottish Army had six thousand infantry and eight hundred cavalry. The Irish moved faster than the Scottish Army under Colonel Monroe and General O'Neill routed the enemy. The Scottish Army lost three thousand while the Irish lost only seventy-two. Colonel Monroe fled the scene, leaving his coat, cape and sword. General O'Neil gave Captain Keogh Monroe's sword, coat and cape.

"The General told Keogh to retire from the field, to return home with these trophies and ensure they were kept safe and secure, as he had no intention of handing them over to British officials. Keogh returned to Clare and hid them in a cave in the Burren where they remained until Captain Daniel Keogh revealed their hiding place on his death bed. Since then they have been handed down to the eldest son of the Keogh family."

His father stopped and looked at his son and could no doubt see the excitement in his features. He rose from his chair and pulled the box out from under the bed. It was dusty but still one could see that it had been well made. It was about four feet long and two feet by two feet. Two thick metal bands were hinged and shaped around the box with a large bulky lock through a hasp and staple. His father unlocked the box, gently lifted out the purple cape and opened it to reveal a magnificent distinctively engraved sword and an ornate senior officer's cap. They were still in very good condition after two hundred years. The oilskin multiple wrappings had sealed its contents and together with the tightly sealed box, they had done a very good job of protecting the treasures. They had effectively sealed them; there was no corrosion and the material was not faded, and surprisingly, had no smell of mildew.

Michael stared in admiration at them.

After a few minutes his father replaced them in the box, locked it and then pushed the box back under the bed. He walked to the window and looked out. "You are the next in the family line to be the keeper of the box when I go to God. Guard it well." The he lay down on the bed and soon started to snore.

Michael went to bed and lay there thinking of the exciting life Captain Daniel Keogh must have had. Little did he know that he had been badly injured in the next battle and then lived out the rest of his life as a cripple in this very area.

O'Neill. Where had he heard that name before? His brain kept thinking over and over again. Yes, he remembered. His mother used to sing a song to him as a boy:

"Owen Roe, our own O'Neill
He treads once more our land!
The sword in his hand is of Spanish steel,
But the hand is an Irish hand."

How could he have forgotten those stirring words?

Michael shook his head, pushing the past away. But try as he might the words kept echoing in his mind.

9

Sunrise signalled the start of his daily jobs, the same jobs he had done during his boyhood. First he lit the fire in the hearth, if it had gone out during the night. Fire wood was generally collected the previous day and stacked inside near the fire to help dry it out. Then he filled the water can and boiled the water over the fire. Next was a trip to the goat pen for some fresh milk. His hands would sometimes sting with the coldness of the dew-filled air in winter. Today was fortunately mild. They normally only had two meals a day. Today the first meal would be a corn and turnip broth with a cup of milk. His father shared the milk with Aunt Jane and Maeve. Maeve would walk down later to collect their milk.

His father had woken up and had gone outside, probably to the privy, which was a small wooden shed that they moved from time to time whenever a new hole needed to be dug.

When his father returned, Michael poured out two ladles of broth and two mugs of milk. They sat there in silence staring into the fire. His father had bought the goat which supplied their milk and he also had two ewes from which he bred a few lambs each year. They shared the cuts with other farmers and vice versa to ensure the meat was eaten before it spoilt. They also had a few chickens which supplied them with eggs. Their small section of land had a pocket of good soil and they managed to grow corn, wheat and turnips. His aunt still managed to grow some potatoes and some wheat and she also had two ewes.

Other farmers further down the road, sometimes net fish and would share them if the catch was good.

They were surviving much better than some of their neighbours. The dog sometimes caught a hare or a bird and this would be immediately stripped and cooked. He remembered his mother cooking over the open fire with a large pot on a rod sitting in two metal forks, turning it by hand.

Fortunately water was plentiful. There were large ponds of good clean water throughout the district and Aunt Jane had a small creek in the corner of her property. They were sometimes lucky and caught eels in its clear waters, too. Good quality watercress grew plentifully and often enhanced a meal.

¶

Michael had been home for two weeks and had finished clearing and planting the turnips and corn. He had also helped Aunt Jane sow the wheat and potatoes. The sheep and the goat had been shorn, and now there was little to keep him occupied. He pottered around doing small repairs to the roofs of both cottages. He moved the privy and repaired the pen fences.

He was looking forward to having a visit to the local town market at Kilrush, about fifteen miles away, where every month a large market was held. The Keogh family would carry shawls and bonnets, corn or meat to trade for salt, tea and food spices. In the past sometimes their aunt had lent them her donkey and cart. It was a diversion that they enjoyed. Their life was a life of poverty but others were much worse off than they were.

Kilrush was a seaport and market town. It was situated on the north shore of the Shannon River estuary fifteen miles from the mouth of the river and on a creek to which it gave its name, making it convenient for trade and export. The principal streets were well paved and flagged, and centred by the market square. There were factories producing nails, soap, tanning of hides, meat slaughtering and salt. Fishing and oyster dredging was a prime source of income for many families. The fleet consisted of about twenty Hookers boats.

Michael was familiar with the town. He had often walked down the main street past its two banks, its constabulary and courthouse, across the stone bridge down to the Cappa Pier and the customs house to the sea wall.

Michael spoke to his father about a trip to the market for both of them, but his father declined. He then decided to speak with Aunt Jane and perhaps take Maeve with him in the cart. Aunt Jane agreed for her to travel with him, to the delight of Maeve who rarely went to town.

At daybreak the following day they were ready to depart with all their goods on the cart. Maeve was dressed in her auntie's best dress and wore her leather shoes. Both items of clothing were for special occasions only. Michael wore a new shirt given to him for Christmas by his uncle's family, clean serge trousers and polished boots. They looked a smart couple. They started off with Michael leading the donkey and Maeve riding in the cart.

This didn't last long as they soon reached the bottom of a steep ascent, Maeve walked also to ease the load on the donkey. It was a pleasant day and they sang a few ballads to each other's enjoyment. His sister had a pleasant personality and he mused she may marry before Michael! After an hour or so they stopped for a short time for a drink of water and a corn cob to eat. They passed some suffering families but it was not as bad as it had been a year or so ago. Some husbands stayed on at their tenant farms rather than leave and had sent their families to the workhouse to declare themselves widows or orphans rather than have them starve at the farm.

It was nearly midday when Kilrush appeared below them. Michael and Maeve became just another farming family looking for a buyer for their goods.

Michael had been warned to avoid the constabulary and the local Dutch Vandeleur family flunkeys. Both were prone to baiting the Irish and subsequently were not only hated but shunned as much as possible.

They went to the town square which Michael knew well and started shouting their wares. All the shawls and bonnets sold quickly, then a sheep skin, then the dozen eggs and by the late afternoon the turnips were sold.

They now had several shillings to do their buying. First they purchased salt, soap and, finally, some cooking utensils and nails. They decided to see the Cappa Pier Harbour and visit his uncle's ship yard to allow Maeve to see him as they hadn't met for a few years. Several war ships were unloading, so they left the cart and donkey tied up at the start of the pier. They walked down it to stand and watch the soldiers coming ashore with their equipment and horses.

Local drays were being loaded with ammunition boxes. Together with several field guns, which had been dismantled, they were now swung ashore on the ship's davits. It was orderly and precise; obviously these soldiers had been well trained. The horses were fine specimens and, after being washed and curried by their riders, they were then saddled and bridled with highly polished leather gear. Several Special constables were on hand lounging against a warehouse wall, watching in a detached manner. Michael and Maeve could hear the sergeant giving orders.

A young British officer stepped ashore. The sergeant approached him and advised the progress of the unloading and asked for further orders.

The officer could see that they would be at least a half hour before they would be ready to proceed to their barracks.

"Ensure that the quartermaster has removed all the equipment from the ship's holds and check that the equipment is securely tied onto the drays. That is all." The officer then went aboard the ship and spoke to the captain who was standing watching the unloading.

"I wish all the cargo was unloaded as quickly and as efficiently as is being done now. Good job!" said the captain.

The officer thanked him for the compliment he had extended to his men. "Sergeant, assemble the platoon," he called out.

The horses were being led forward to be mounted when one reared for no apparent reason. A constable came forward, and ordered Michael and his sister to move quickly out of the way of the platoon. He pushed Maeve on the shoulder, she stumbled and fell to the ground.

Michael turned, saw what happened and challenged the constable not to mistreat his sister.

The constable sneered, "The likes of you should not even be here."

Michael angrily retorted, "The likes of what?"

Other constables started to come forward, contemptuous looks upon their faces.

The British officer saw what had happened and stepped forward to help Maeve to her feet.

"Are you hurt, miss?

She shook her head, suddenly embarrassed.

The officer turned and faced the constables; his face showed his anger. "What do you think you are doing?" he asked.

The constables stepped back as one and looked decidedly uncomfortable under the glare of the British officer. He said further, "You owe this young lady an apology." He looked at the senior constable.

The constable hesitated until he realised that the Platoon Sergeant and two other ranks had moved forward. He replied without feeling, "My apologies, young lady, for my constable's action."

The officer replied, "Rubbish, the act was deliberate! Get your men out of here!" The constable turned and ordered his men into line, then marched them off.

Michael could see by the stiffness in the constable's shoulders that he was angry — very angry.

The officer turned and said to Maeve, "Lieutenant Hall at your service, miss. I trust that you are unharmed."

Maeve blushed. She had met few men in her young years and this officer was most dashing, tall and gallant. "Thank you, sir, I am unharmed."

Michael stepped forward and offered his hand to Hall. "Allow me to introduce myself— Michael Keogh and my sister — Maeve Keogh."

Lieutenant John Hall took his hand, noting the strength of the man and his strong chin and deep gaze. *This is one determined man*, he noted. He then turned to Maeve and offered his hand to her. This time he noted her blue eyes and dark red hair, similar to many County Clare women. She spoke with a delightful, shy Irish brogue. *This young lady is beautiful!*

Michael broke into his thoughts. He was thanking him for his intervention. John Hall now had no doubt that, but for his intervention, Michael Keogh would have taken on the constable, regardless of the consequences.

A voice called out Michael's name. Turning he saw his Uncle Jack approaching, rather aggressively asking, "What's the problem, Michael?"

Michael explained briefly and this calmed his uncle.

Lieutenant Hall was unaware of the depth of the Irish feeling towards the English, and was puzzled at the man's aggressive behaviour.

Jack Keogh thanked the officer for helping his nephew and niece and apologised for his initial attitude towards him.

Lieutenant Hall saw his sergeant approaching and he advised them he had to leave as they were late now, and it would be dark before they reached their barracks. He waved goodbye to

Michael and Jack and then turned to Maeve. They looked at each other and bid their farewells each silently hoping they would meet again.

Michael and Maeve retired to Uncle Jack's home. It had been a long day, eventful and tiring, but Michael and Maeve made the most of it. They sat around the warm fire and chatted away, answering questions about their father and Aunt Jane and how the farms were producing. They in turn asked after Uncle Jack and his family's health and the boat yard business. All was fine and the day finished with a delightful meal of fresh fish with potatoes and corn, followed up with a cup of hot tea. After dinner Maeve went to bed early.

Michael and his uncle remained up, talking of the progress of the boat yard. The business was good but at times the government officials became difficult. Bribes had had to be paid to one or two of them or else they would have created trouble with his workforce, some of which he had been forced to employ by the all-powerful and notorious Vandeleur family.

"Any chance of you coming back to work in the next couple of weeks?" asked Uncle Jack. "There's two new boats to build."

As his father's farm had been sown, the sheep cleaned and the general repairs carried out, Michael agreed to be back at the boat-yard ready for work. He thanked the Lord that he had an uncle with a good business. The Keoghs could not complain about their good fortune. Michael sat quietly thinking of the past.

He recalled, in 1837 at seven years old, he had been sent to Kilrush to his Uncle Jack's home to be schooled. Jack was a boat builder and could afford to see Michael educated and then apprentice him as a shipwright. His uncle's house was larger and sturdier than the farm. It had smooth plastered walls, four rooms, a thatched roof and two lofts, one of which was where he slept. It was much larger than the farm's two rooms and mud and rock walls. His move to Kilrush was a complete change of lifestyle to Michael.

He missed his mother, father and brothers and had rarely seen his new sister, Maeve, after her birth, but Aunt Anne and James, their son, also aged seven, made him very welcome. He soon became a member of the family. His schooling had consisted mainly of arithmetic, and reading and writing, both Gaelic and English. The Gaelic lessons were taught both secretly and privately by the local priest. The priest had a small wooden church back from the road. It had been built in the days of the Penal Laws when churches were not to be visible to all and sundry.

Michael had found town life interesting and it enabled him to make friends, such as Barry Daniher, the son of a ship's captain, who sailed mainly in Irish waters. They had sat next to each other at school at one of the several long table with long bench seats and scratched away on their slates with nails. They had even helped each other in some school fights. He enjoyed school even though the punishment for misdeeds was cruel — a leather strap on the fingers in winter was very painful.

When he turned ten, he went to the shipyard after school and helped in the shaping of the timbers and had gradually been taught the rudiments of the shipwright craft, so that when he left school he would be productive, although still learning.

The ships his uncle made were mostly small vessels, suitable for trading in the estuaries and local ports. They carried a mix of passengers, livestock, farm produce and trade goods. The ships had only the upper deck and two or three split cargo holds. Generally they had only a foresail and mainsail. Michael would often sail on board the ships being delivered to new owners, sometimes with Captain Daniher, and eventually learnt to sail and navigate between the local Irish ports.

Life had been uncomplicated and carefree under his uncle's

mentoring. Michael caroused with his friends and had even saved some money.

He remembered all of these days with his uncle and his family with fondness. It was now late in the evening and time to sleep, ready to return home early the next morning.

¶

Next morning, everyone was up bright and early. Michael and Maeve were ready for their long trip back to their homes. Breakfast consisted of corn, bread and a cup of milk. They fed the donkey, which had been stabled from the weather, and strapped on the cart. They bid farewell and thanked their uncle for his hospitality before heading north down the main road, waving until they vanished over the hill. They passed the outskirts of the town and the Government offices from where the British authorities ruled the country in every aspect of Irish life. Its large paddock was full of gigs, carts and drays of all kinds with their owners queued already for its opening and the due process to be administered.

Out of the corner of his eye Michael saw two constables looking at him, pointing and nodding. He looked straight ahead and tried not to feel intimidated, more for Maeve's sake than his own.

They rode over to him, greeting him with "Good morning."

Michael acknowledged their greeting without stopping. They rode on but they left him with the feeling he would see more of them in the future. They continued north for some hours before stopping at a small store to eat and to feed the donkey. The weather was kind with a gentle wind and the blue sky appeared every so often through soft white clouds.

The road still had Irish 'unfortunates' heading into Kilrush carrying their meagre belongings, or pushing a small barrow.

If only the Corn Law had been rescinded earlier and the corn had been allowed to remain in Ireland, how different would this scene be now?

Michael and Maeve arrived home late afternoon with their purchases. They delighted both Aunt Jane and their father with the success of their trip. They all agreed it had been a pleasant family visit and passed on the news from Uncle Jack's family. Michael did not share with them the incident with the constables as it would only worry his aunt on their next visit to market.

After they had finished relating all their news, Michael said, "Uncle needs some help at the boatyard, so I've agreed to go back for a while. I'll be leaving in the next two weeks."

His father and aunt said nothing, only nodded their acceptance. Michael's father had expected that Michael would be soon be returning to Kilrush.

For the next several days, Michael busied himself around the farms looking for jobs to do, to ensure that he had done his best to assist both his father and aunt, as he now felt responsible for them. He asked Maeve if she could put up some curtains and improve his father's home interior. It had been deteriorating ever since his mother's death. It needed a woman's touch. Michael killed a lamb, butchered the carcass, tanned the hide and melted down the fat. He made some candles by pouring the tallow into some tins with a stick wrapped in a cloth in the middle of the tin.

He felt content and now spent time walking Laddie, the dog, for a few hours each day. The dog was obedient and the words 'Sit,', 'Seek' and 'Set', together with a hand signal would get an immediate response. After much difficulty he managed to teach him to 'Guard.' The dog would stand, growling, and show his teeth. He would miss Laddie when he returned to Kilrush.

Michael and his father awoke to the dog barking furiously. Michael lit a candle and picked up his father's shillelagh, calling out, "Who is it?"

A voice answered, "I need help. The constables are after me!" Michael opened the door and stepped back, letting the man enter the room. He appeared exhausted and almost fell onto a stool when sitting down.

They looked at each other, sizing each other up.

Can I trust this man? Michael thought. He asked, "Why are you being chased?"

The stranger answered, "I escaped from the constables after they arrested me for assault. I hit a constable who tore up my pamphlets. Can you hide me for a day or so?"

"I can't hide you here. We only have these two room,." Michael looked at him closely and asked, "What did these pamphlets say?"

The man pulled a crumpled piece of paper from his pocket and handed it to Michael.

Michael read it aloud. "All Free Irishmen are called to a meeting of the Free Ireland Party at the junction of the Kilkee and Kilrush roads on the first Saturday of January at Noon." He paused. "You will probably be charged with sedition as well," said Michael.

"No matter, I'll be transported or hanged regardless, if I'm caught."

Michael paced the floor. He knew the risks associated with assisting rebels. If caught, he would be sent to be transported to a penal settlement and his family would be persecuted.

"What's your name?"

"I think it is best if you do not know," the stranger replied. "But what is yours?"

"Michael Keogh and this is my father, Edmund," he answered.

Michael made up his mind. "I am willing to trust you. I just hope my judgment is correct." Michael told his father to go back to bed and to forget everything that had happened tonight. He then put on his jacket and said to the stranger, "Follow me."

The two men and the dog walked out into the night. Michael turned north, heading towards the large limestone rocks silhouetted in the moonlight. The night was cool and calm and they were able to walk quickly. He kept looking over his shoulder and watched the dog to see if it was reacting to anything he may not have noticed. If the stranger was guilty of his said offences, the authorities would certainly be looking for him.

They continued walking for an hour until they came to a rock about six feet high, surrounded by several smaller rocks of four feet diameter. Michael said, "Take off your boots and climb to the top of the large rock and lift back the bracken. You will see a hole that you will be able to slide into. You only need to slide down five or six feet, release the bracken to allow it to fall back and you will be in a cavern big enough to sleep in. It is part of a long cave but you will still have some moonlight entering. Stay there until I return tomorrow night."

¶

Noon the next day, the dog started barking furiously. This was unusual as their home was set back and out of sight of the road. People only came for a reason, not by accident.

Michael heard the hoof beats and the clink of saddle irons. "Come out now! Hurry!"

Michael stepped out into the yard and saw several constables led by the senior constable he had clashed with at the docks. They stared at each other for a few moments.

The senior constable said, "Where is he? He came this way. We know he's here."

Michael asked, "Who are you talking about? There is only my father and myself. Search the house if you wish."

The senior constable signalled his men to search the house. They soon returned, shaking their heads. He looked at Michael and said, "He is in this area and we will find him. Then we will be back for you." The senior constable turned and rode back to the road with his constables trailing behind him in single file.

Michael wondered who this rebel was and why he was wanted so desperately by the authorities. He then decided that the rebel must be moved, but to where and how? He started to rationalise what to do. The rebel must leave Ireland, but from where to where? From Galway or Cork? He had sailed to Galway several times on delivery trips on new ships. A few ships sailed to America from there. The majority of ships to America sailed from Cork. Perhaps that would be the port on which the authorities would focus and carry out most of their search.

Each time Michael had visited Galway there had always been American sailing vessels at anchor in the harbour. Galway would be a better chance for the stranger not being discovered. Once the rebel was aboard an American ship he would be safe from the British authorities. Michael made the decision. But how to move and hide him? He knew the Kilrush docks inside and out. He could move him at night to the docks and then leave from Kilrush to Galway. Decision one was made. But the big problem was to get him from the Burren to the Kilrush Docks. He needed to have a complete plan to convince the rebel before he went to the cave later that night.

Michael looked out the window and he spotted Aunt Jane's cart. Could this be the answer to the problem of moving the rebel? The cart was about six feet long and five feet wide. The axle was bolted onto two large blocks and these blocks in turn were bolted to the box of the cart. Could a man be stowed on the top of the axle? Michael guessed the rebel was about five feet six inches in height. If he made some straps for the rebel to fit his arms and legs into and he rested his buttocks on the axle, it might work. He could fill the cart with hides which would hang over the sides providing more coverage as well.

He walked up the hill and down to Aunt Jane's cottage to start to fit the straps. It did not take long. He then loaded the unwashed sheep skins into the cart and left some hanging over the sides. All that had to be done was to hitch the donkey to the cart. Decision three now made.

Michael now had his plan. He busied himself collecting a food package of corn cobs, turnips, some cured meat and water. He decided to get some sleep and leave when the moon was high. He slept soundly but was awoken by the dog shuffling around the room and quietly whining. He peered through the window and could see nothing, but he believed the dog knew something was amiss.

He had made up his mind and was determined to get some sustenance to the rebel tonight. But he needed to be careful. He picked up the food, opened the door and closed it, leaving the dog behind. He headed up towards the road, the opposite direction from the cave. He could sense he was being observed but he kept walking. He had nearly reached Aunt Jane's cottage when he heard her young black bitch yap and run down to him. He picked her up, turned at right angles and continued to walk in a circle into the Burren with the wind in his face.

After a few minutes, Michael heard a dog bark. He had guessed correctly. The constables were following him with dogs. He hid behind a boulder and waited until they came in sight. When they were almost on him, he let the bitch go. She took off in a direct line for home. The police dogs got her scent and took off after her in the dark with the constables trying to both keep the dogs quiet and not fall over the rocky ground. The bitch, which was in season, took shelter in a deep dry rock fence, safe from the dogs. Their bewildered keepers were looking for a person hiding in the rocks; they couldn't see the bitch!

The moon was suddenly hidden by cloud. This gave Michael a chance to move into the shadows of several large rocks bordering on a section of bracken. He then moved into a gap between a rock and some of the vegetation and remained motionless, looking out across the clearing. He stayed like this for around ten minutes and, seeing no movement, he started walking again towards the cave. It took him almost half an hour but he reached there safely.

Michael climbed the rock, pulled back the bracken and dropped down to the cave floor.

"I was starting to get hungry. I'm pleased that you are back. It's a bit lonely here," said the rebel.

Michael had left the bracken pulled back and they could see each other in the dim night light. He explained his plan to get the rebel first to Kilrush then to Galway and finally to America. "You'll need to bargain with a captain of one of he American ships, but I think it will work."

The rebel said, "I can get money in Galway or New York; that will not be a problem. All American ships have at least one Irishman in their crew. I'm sure he would go ashore and meet with my fellows. When can we leave?"

"Now," said Michael.

The two men walked quickly to Aunt Jane's cottage. Dawn was breaking with a dull cloudy day promising the possibility of a little rain. The roads would probably get greasy but hopefully no bogs would confront them on the Kilrush road. Michael quickly hitched the donkey and together they walked to his father's house.

His father was standing at the doorway fully dressed, a determined look on his face. He had guessed what Michael had planned. "Michael, I'll be doing the driving. The constables will give you a hard time and you will both be caught," said Michael's father. His logic could not be argued with; he was right.

The rebel crawled under the cart and slipped into the straps. "Alright?" asked Michael.

"Aye," said the rebel. Michael started walking and was about two hundred yards up the track before his father got the donkey moving at a slow pace.

Michael mused, *With the low clouds it will be quite dark by the time we arrive at the docks.*

There was a following wind and they travelled for two hours before they saw anyone and that person happened to be a friend of his father. The friend decided he would travel alongside them. Michael was comfortable with this.

After another hour they could see a group of people gathered near a small cottage. There were several constables and a squad of soldiers in attendance. It was a dreaded eviction about to take place. These events were the scourge of Western Ireland and had made the Irish populace hate the English.

Michael was still two hundred yards in front of the cart and made a point of ensuring the constables saw him. He stopped near them looking at the officers doing the eviction. These constables had been in the group at the dock. They made a few remarks and approached Michael, commenting on Maeve. He eyed them but was not drawn into an answer.

By this time the cart had passed and was heading to Kilrush at its normal pace. Michael then heard a voice call his name and, turning, he saw Lieutenant Hall walking over to him.

He greeted him. "Good morning, Michael, my compliments to you. May I enquire as to your sister's health?"

"Good morning, Lieutenant. My sister is in good health and I shall pass on your regards."

Michael and the Lieutenant moved away from the crowd. Lieutenant Hall lowered his voice and said, "I find these evictions deplorable but I have to stand here and watch. This is an abomination of both our societies. I have advised my father and he is trying to raise the issue in Parliament, but it may take years to change these laws. I pray something is done soon."

The noise of a crash made them both turn in the direction of the cottage. They witnessed the roof being pulled apart by ropes attached to the main beam and tied to the harnesses of two draught horses. Within five minutes the cottage was no more. Michael couldn't stand the sight. He bid goodbye to the Lieutenant and abruptly turned and took his leave. He was boiling inside, but what could he do? He walked on after his father who had made good time and was now heading to the docks. So far, so good!

Another hour saw the cart passing the market and on the dock road at the check point with the guards.

"Stop," a voice called out.

With his heart pounding his father stopped.

The caller rode up. "Are your skins for sale?"

"Yes, of course. Will you be here in the next two hours?" was his response.

"Yes, I will expect you." The guards looked on idly and did not search the cart as the skins were now stinking.

Edmund was shaken but he continued on until he was inside his brother's wood storage shed, heaving a sigh of relief that the trip was over. The cart stopped and the rebel crawled out — pale, stiff and unable to walk. Michael arrived and helped the rebel into a large shavings bin. His father immediately went back to the waiting skins buyer and sold all the skins, returning with several shillings. Why not? His father felt good. The excitement had invigorated him. He looked ten years younger. He had had a great day having struck a blow against the British rule, as well as making a few shillings.

The rebel was delighted with the success of the first stage of his escape and wanted to commence the Kilrush to Galway voyage as soon as possible. Michael went to the office and looked at the planned delivery dates of the next boats. It was bad news — no new boats were scheduled to be completed for a month. They were still being built. Michael then remembered this was why his uncle wanted him back at work.

He thanked his father and bid him farewell. His father responded by giving him some shillings for his coach fare back from Galway. Michael then went to the repair yard and checked the work coming and going out. In two days' time a small hooker would be leaving for a small fishing bay just north of Galway Bay. Michael had seen the owner before — a Mr McBean. He had repaired McBean's boats in the past but had not met him personally. Michael decided to offer himself as a crewman and see what response he got before he broached the matter of passage for the rebel.

Michael was lucky and soon found the boat owner in a nearby tavern.

As he approached him, McBean looked up and nodded. "Hello, young Keogh, what can I do for you?"

"May I speak with you in private, sir?" McBean led him to a small room off the main bar. Michael started hesitantly. "Do you need any crew to deliver your boat tomorrow?"

"Yes, I need a forward hand. Are you offering to crew?" asked McBean.

"Yes. Could I bring along a friend as well?"

The owner looked at him deeply. He had heard of the rebel

the authorities were seeking and he was now suspicious. McBean could not afford to get mixed up in such business and responded, "I'll tell you what you can do. You and your friend can deliver the boat and you can take my nephew, Jaime Neyland, with you. I know you two know each other from your school days. You will sail on tomorrow's tide and pick up Jaime at the West Point. Deliver the boat to where he tells you. Can you agree to this?"

Michael looked at him in astonishment. McBean had not only made up his mind on the spot but had decided how the trip would be done. "Yes, we will be there."

Michael walked back to the shed, delighted with the plan. He and the rebel would sail directly to Galway Bay to find an American ship once the rebel was aboard, then he and Jaime would sail to the nearby fishing village. He told the rebel of his plan and advised him that they should get some sleep as they would go to the boat at daybreak.

¶

Dawn showed a clear sky with a light north-westerly breeze. They slipped the boat quickly and quietly, helped by his uncle's workmen. His uncle did not know he was in Kilrush — the less involved the safer the venture. Michael unfurled the jib sail which instantly filled and pulled the small boat out into the harbour waters. They had a mainsail but he would not use this until he had picked up Jaime and was out in the open sea. They had a leisurely sail downstream looking at the Indianmen and the majestic Ships of War anchored in the middle of the harbour.

West Point soon appeared off to the starboard. Michael pushed the tiller over to steer the boat towards the sandy shore onto which he would beach the bow.

A man about his own age appeared and walked quickly towards them, raising his arm in greeting. Michael waved back. The boat touched beach, then Jaime jumped aboard. After pushing the boat back from the shore with the oars, they turned and shook hands. Michael introduced the rebel — still no name was forthcoming.

Jaime was an experienced sailor and took over the tiller, calling for the mainsail to be raised. They were soon clipping along at a good rate. They would be at Galway Bay by early evening and then planned to sail slowly around the ships at anchor in harbour searching for an American vessel. The wind was increasing in strength but from the same direction, Jaime decided to reef the mainsail as they were still making good time.

They stayed out to sea and did not turn towards land until the sun was setting. Both Jaime and Michael knew the coastline landmarks and easily identified Galway Bay. The wind strength did not abate until they were at the entrance of the bay. They had made good time to be there at sundown.

The men could see the town lights and the ships riding at anchor. The tide was running in causing the ships to have their bows to the open sea and into the northwest wind. Jaime decided to sail only on the jib to slow the boat to make it easier to read the ships' names and home ports which were painted on their sterns. They had sailed past five ships when Michael saw the name 'Nantucket — New York' on the stern of a large vessel. They sailed around the ship and then started a long slow approach level with the Nantucket's port side. A boom was out with a painter and a small dinghy attached. Jaime instructed the rebel to jump into the dingy, when told to do so and then climb the rope ladder. Farewells and thanks were made but the rebel remained nameless!

The boat continued its slow speed parallel to the Nantucket's port side hull.

"Jump!" said Jaime. The rebel jumped and stumbled. He nearly fell out of the dingy but managed to grab hold of the rope ladder and climb to the deck where two sailors approached him and led him away. The rebel was now on his own. Jaime pushed the tiller over as Michael raised the mainsail.

Jaime and Michael headed out of the bay and turned north, making good speed. Within half an hour they reached the fishing village and had completed their voyage. It had been a long few days and Michael felt exhausted.

Jaime took Michael to an inn where there was a coach stop. They had a few ales and a meal and Jaime stayed with Michael until he was to board the coach.

As he was being farewelled and about to board Jaime said to him, "I am almost certain that our rebel was Brendan Devine of the Free Ireland Movement. If he was, we are now famous. But don't tell anyone or we will get a free sea trip in irons ourselves — to the Australian colonies or worse."

When the coachman invited the passengers to board, the ladies were naturally helped to their seats first and, of course, got the best seats. When Michael boarded he was offered a seat between two rather portly elderly ladies. The ladies both dozed but unfortunately one had a chest complaint and she wheezed rather loudly for the next two hours. But at least being wedged between them Michael was saved from some of the discomforts of the swaying of the coach. The coach trip was rough, it pitched and rolled worse than any ship on which he had sailed and landed hard. He had hoped to get some sleep on the way back to Kilrush but that was impossible.

He thought of the comment Jaime had made about the rebel's possible name. Brendan Devine was a very well-known name for his Free Ireland Movement but would he risk his life to deliver pamphlets? He had not been to County Clare before, so maybe this was his way of reaching more Irishmen and at the same time showing his dedication in an attempt to encourage more of the populace to the 'freedom cause'.

The coach continued bouncing and banging for the next two hours. There was a stop for a change of horses and time for a welcome ale, a bite to eat and a stretch of one's legs. Then they reboarded the coach and continued on to Kilrush.

Michael looked at his fellow passengers and wondered who they were and what their thoughts were on the future of Ireland — if any. He wondered how many other Irishmen had been involved in similar escapades as he and his father. He had heard stories of the dramas in Dublin with the resultant transportation of Irish political activists. He wondered where Ireland was heading.

They were close to Kilrush now and Michael could see the buildings in the grey of the dawn. He started to sleep; the road had become smoother as they were close to town.

Michael awoke to hear voices calling out to the coach driver. "Stop in the Queen's name." The passengers on the coach immediately became wide awake, clasping their valuables; a hold up by highwaymen was uncommon in this part of Ireland, but not unheard of.

The call came from a group of constables and soldiers. They asked all passengers to alight and stand in a row alongside the coach. It was Michael's nemesis, the senior constable again. He was shorter than Michael but larger around the waist. His loose pistol belt exaggerated his ample girth. The constable walked along the short line of passengers and asked each their name and why they were travelling so early in the day. All had legitimate reasons.

Then came Michael's turn to be questioned. The senior constable stood very close and virtually spat his questions at him.

Michael said that he had delivered a boat to a fishing village and was returning home.

The senior constable knew Michael was a shipwright and a capable sailor as well. Could he be telling the truth? He asked, "What were the names of the crew?"

Michael replied, "Jaime O'Laughlin. He operated the boat on behalf of his uncle."

"Anyone else?" he asked.

Michael replied, "You only need two to crew a Hooker fishing boat."

The senior constable looked at him and walked away, then turned back to him. "I know that you're a party in this rebel escape and I intend to get you."

This worried Michael as he could see this situation could now be levelled at his father, sister and aunt and that they could be made to suffer.

On his arrival in Kilrush Michael went to his uncle's home and told him he was ready to work again.

His uncle queried him as to what he had been doing; he knew Michael had sailed the Hooker north.

"It is better that you do not know."

His uncle looked hard at him and then nodded his agreement.

¶

Two weeks later the search for the rebel was still continuing. The authorities were convinced that he was still in the area as they did not believe that he could have got past the guards manning the roads and docks at either Kilrush or Liscannor. Michael, with his uncle's blessing, decided to return home for a few days. He was still concerned at the possibility of the senior constable causing trouble. How right he was!

As Michael reached the crest of the small road to his home he saw the constables and some soldiers at the side of the house. The constables were arguing with his father, while the soldiers looked on. When they saw Michael approaching them, the constables stepped back a few paces. His father was angry but in control of his emotions; he had formed a hatred of this senior constable and intended to stop him from causing his family any more grief. Maeve had told him of the dock incident of a month or so ago. When Michael confronted the constables, his father quietly moved to the back of the house and walked away.

Michael asked the constables, "Why are you here?"

The response was, "We want to know where the rebel is."

"Well he is not here, is he?" Michael replied.

They argued like this for ten minutes or so, until suddenly a constable called out, "Look there, a man's running towards the rocks."

The senior constable said to a nearby constable, "Hold this man," pointing to Michael. Together with three of his group, he ran off in the direction of the rocks.

The man stood on the large rock and then vanished from sight.

When the constables reached the large rock it took them some minutes to find the entrance. They climbed up and then all slid down behind the brambles into the dimness of the cave. They stood wondering what to do next while their eyes became accustomed to the gloom.

Michael knew it was his father they were chasing and he thought he knew why. The cave was about a hundred feet long and opened out to the side of the cliffs immediately around the corner. If you were not careful you would step out into the Atlantic Ocean. There were a few steps where one could climb up onto the open grassland six feet above but it was a very dangerous, short climb and was not very obvious without being shown.

The constables heard a voice in the cave but it was unclear

what was being said as it was in Gaelic. One of the constables said, "It's the rebel," and started running towards the light of the opening.

The senior constable ran forward and pushed him out of the way. "Follow me." He wanted this rebel who had caused him so much embarrassment and abuse from his commander; he was determined to be the one who captured him. He was running confidently now that his eyes had adjusted to the gloom. The voice was nearer. *Soon I'll have you,* he thought. He turned the corner and saw the opening.

The senior constable tried to stop; managing to grasp hold of some bracken on the wall at the cave opening but the second constable was right behind him and ran into him. The senior constable started to fall and grabbed the second constable's belt. They both held there for a second and then fell through the cave opening to the sea below. Their screams reached the other two constables who immediately halted. Cautiously they looked around the corner and saw no one.

The two constables looked at each other and then bolted back along the cave to the large boulder, climbed out and ran back to the other constables to tell them what had happened. The constables were dead and so was the rebel. They had just vanished through the opening into the sea.

The constables lost interest in Michael and released him. Then they mounted their horses and rode off to the road to report back to their commander at Kilrush.

Michael could see his father walking back from the cliffs looking most grim. Not a word was said by either of them but they each knew what had happened. The senior constable would not harm the Keogh family again.

The local paper praised the heroism of the constables for their tragic deaths while pursuing a dangerous Irish rebel who was also reported as killed. After this the town settled down to a level of normalcy again. Some of the landlords were going broke and sold their holdings to other landlords who knew even less about farming than the previous landlords. Meanwhile the evictions continued. Although not as many as at the previous rate but they still continued.

Michael spent more time at home. He and Maeve still went to market and made a point of passing the military barracks each trip. It was no coincidence that Lieutenant John Hall was in attendance at the market during their visits.

¶

Maeve and John Hall were now on first name terms and had formed an affection for each other.

Michael's father had recovered his interest in life, and this Michael was glad about. The two farms had sufficient crops and Aunt Jane had started receiving some money from her husband in America.

The evictions were distasteful to all decent folk. Many of the town people who had steady employment, however lowly paid, had relatives who had been evicted, and felt guilty as they were unable to assist them with their meagre money. The famine was still affecting the Irish although some harvests were fruitful.

Michael was on his way to another market when he again had occasion to witness another eviction. This eviction was incredibly poignant as there were eight children in the family. The new senior constable, Smith, was a little man scarcely five feet two inches in height, but with an arrogance twice his size. He normally remained on horse, giving orders like an army officer on the field of battle. He always seemed to have his constables running hither and thither, whilst achieving very little.

On this occasion, the farmer had been manhandled out of the house with several of his children holding his legs. It was a pitiful sight. The woman was holding a baby and was begging the constables to release her husband. She promised that they would leave without causing any trouble. The senior constable lifted his foot from the stirrup and pushed her over with his boot. Both the woman and the baby fell to the ground. The Irish crowd was incensed by this cowardly action.

Michael who happened to be standing next to her grabbed the bridle and tried to pull the senior constable from his horse. The rider's bravado left him immediately and he tried to ride through the crowd. His horse reared and threw its rider. The crowd moved back and stood staring at the senior constable as he lay on the ground with his uniform soiled, cap awry and a gash on his forehead.

When the other constables moved in to rescue him from a potential crowd attack, Michael moved to the rear of the crowd. He realised what he had done. The senior constable remounted and looked around for Michael, his dark eyes filled with rage but unable to see him, he then refocused his attention on the family being evicted.

Michael managed to slip away in a dray cart of a friend. He went home somewhat shaken. He knew that one of the crowd would tell the authorities who he was and where he lived. He did not have long to wait.

The next morning up rode a detachment of constables and soldiers, led by Colonel Lang. Lieutenant Hall was with him.

The colonel took charge. "Michael Keogh? People like you disgust me. You ignorant Irish peasant. You're a blot on the face of the earth." His face was as red as his tunic. His professionalism was completely forgotten; his tirade went on and on.

Until the senior constable said, "I would like to arrest him now."

The colonel nearly had a heart attack. "Don't interrupt me when I am speaking, do you hear?" No one spoke. When the colonel realised that they were all looking at him, he gave an embarrassed, "Yes, of course you can."

Michael asked the colonel, "Why am I being arrested?"

The colonel said, "Don't you know? Constable, haven't you told him? I thought you said he was a dangerous man. The only risk I can see is the dog asleep at his feet."

The constable pulled a sheet from his pocket and read, "Michael Keogh is charged with interfering with the lawful duties of a constable in that he grabbed hold of a bridle and caused the horse to unseat the constable."

Michael asked, "Does it say why?"

The senior constable did not answer. He placed handcuffs on Michael's wrists and then tied them to his pommel. He ordered his constables to search the house. The constables found the Keogh's treasure box and brought it out into the sunlight.

"Open it," ordered the colonel.

They prised the hasp lock open to reveal the oilskin covering the cape. After unrolling the oilskin, they unwrapped the cape and saw the magnificent sword and cape of Colonel Monroe.

The colonel immediately decided he would have these treasures. "I am claiming these articles for and on behalf of the Crown. Lieutenant Hall, take possession of the box, if you please."

Michael stood there in shock. It was his responsibility to retain these treasures for the Irish people. Now the hated British Army had confiscated them. He felt angry and ashamed. Colonel Lang waved his arm and the troop turned to follow him. Lieutenant Hall had dismounted to see to the closing of the box with two of his troopers.

Michael walked all the way into town tied to the constable's saddle. He was thirsty, hungry and tired, by the time they arrived at the barracks. They placed him a small cell in which he could hardly stand upright. At sundown they gave him a mug of water, a piece of bread and dry meat. Michael had no idea what they intended to do with him. Would he be brought before the magistrate here or be sent to Limerick, Cork or Galway. Another question — when? Nothing moved fast in the justice system of Ireland so he resigned himself to a long wait. How wrong he was! Two days later he was brought before the Kilrush Magistrate whom he knew by sight. The hearing was set for the following week, giving time for witnesses to be located and ordered to appear to testify.

Michael was lead into the old bluestone building at the beginning of proceedings. He wrinkled his nose at the damp musty smell emanating from the tattered carpet. He looked around noting the magistrate's large desk, and a smaller desk in front of it for the clerk. The prosecutor and the defence counsel desks were immediately in front of the public seating. Over on the side wall was a small boxed-in section where he was lead to; two constables sat either side. There was a jury box, but today it would not be used; indeed it rarely was. The witnesses were sitting on a bench seat outside the courtroom in a long draughty hall, waiting to be called.

There were bench seats for the public that could hold around fifty people and another twenty could stand at the back of the courtroom. It was a very spartan building.

Even the magistrate had an air of days gone by. He wore the traditional wig and gown, however, each had lost its original colour. He was a long lean man, bald and with a strong, set jaw. He walked to the bench, and took his seat. As he looked around, one could sense his demeanour — one of authority, lacking compromise of any sort — and it set the tone for the day.

Michael's trial was full of apprehension for his family and

friends who had known him from his infant days. All his family was in the court room. He could see the severe frown on his father forehead and Maeve's tearful face. It made his heart heavy to know that he was causing such grief to his family and he could only hope that it did not cause them any problems after whatever sentence he was given.

The Magistrate opened proceedings by having the charges read. Then he asked for the plea — guilty or not guilty. Michael declined to answer.

The prosecutor called the first witness — Senior Constable Smith. He called three times and after receiving no response he advised the magistrate that the main witness was not in court. The magistrate adjourned the proceedings until the following day and told the prosecutor to find the senior constable or issue a warrant for his arrest.

The next day was no different. The senior constable had vanished. He had not been seen in Kilrush for over five days. The magistrate was in a dilemma. Obviously something had happened, but what? He decided to proceed with the case so the prosecutor called each constable who was present at the incident in turn. Two of the constables said that they had seen the defendant grab hold of the horse's bridle. The defence counsel asked them if they knew why the defendant had grabbed the bridle. One constable admitted he saw the senior constable kick a woman with a child in her arms.

The magistrate summed up, "I am convinced that an offence has been committed. The authority of the law officers cannot be interfered with for any reason." He made no comment about the reason the offence had been committed.

The magistrate noted that the young man in the dock looked strong and was a shipwright. He had received a letter that very morning advising that Tasmania was seeking convicts. The other Australian colonies were trying to stop the Colonial Office from sending more convicts, except Perth, in the west. The magistrate made up his mind.

He ordered Michael Keogh to stand. He then read his verdict. "You have been found guilty of unlawful interference of a constable performing his duty. You are hereby sentenced to seven years penal servitude in Van Diemen's Land."

The Keogh family sat there stunned. Would they ever see Michael again? It was 1853 and Michael was now twenty-two years old. What did the future hold for him? Only time would tell.

CHAPTER TWO

Deceit in the Army

he Hall family had been residents in the Cumberland district for over nine centuries. They were descendants of the robber bands that had inhabited the Hadrian's Wall district after the Romans had left the British Isles. They were Yeoman farmers and had owned land in the Lazonby district for generations. Their land had excellent soil for both agriculture and livestock farming, as it was bordered by the Eden River.

The district was well known throughout England for its quality food production. The river meandered its way through the farm lands heading north to the sea via Carlisle, the principal county city. Further to the west there were magnificent lakes, unsurpassed for their beauty in all of the British Isles. The local winters were cold but the summers were mild, ensuring that the countryside was always green.

John Hall knew much of the Cumberland country. He often visited his local relatives and travelled with his father, who had extensive property holdings in the area.

He was born at his father's Brackenshire Estate, three miles from the village of Lazonby. His sister, Mary, was five years younger and David was nine years his junior. His father, Joseph, had hired a tutor to teach the children; she was also their bookkeeper.

His childhood had been happy. His mother doted on her

children and his father kept a balance with his sternness. His mother had two live-in servants — a cook and a nanny. This help allowed her to spend considerable time with the children during their formative years. She used this time wisely to ensure that they were educated in formal manners, tidiness and personal presentation. Their mother's efforts helped them later in their adult life and careers.

John started riding when he was six years old, after his father gave him a pony for his birthday. He became a proficient rider in a short time and delighted his father when he rode at the local agriculture shows. His father would sit among his friends with an ale in one hand, pointing out his son to anyone who would listen with the other hand.

John enjoyed being with his sister and brother regardless of their age difference; they were a very close family. Their tutor devoted considerable time to each of the children and was pleased with their progress. John had attained a commendable level in his reading, writing and arithmetic studies. It was now time to move to his next level of education as advised by John's tutor.

It was planned that when the Hall boys' reached ten years of age, they would attend Carlisle Boarding School and then go to Manchester University. John had been a quiet and studious child and continued to be somewhat reserved when he was sent to the Carlisle Boarding School. He found boarding school unsettling, primarily because he had never associated with many boys of his age before.

Fortunately the teachers were skilled at handling this common problem for new students. They arranged table games in the evening and moved students from table to table each night. After two weeks nearly all the new students had settled into school life and had found a good friend or two. John made two friends — George Nickle and Owen MacLean. Both boys were sons of serving military officers, whose families were from the Eden Valley district. Owen MacLean lived only twenty miles from John's home. His father Colonel MacLean was well known. He had built Lazonby Hall. George's family lived in Carlisle.

The school expected each student to perform to the best of his ability. They were assessed each term, prior to returning home with a sealed report for their parents. Many students were shocked when their parents opened the reports but this lead to them striving harder from then on.

John passed all his examinations without being a spectacular student but he was considered to be a potential achiever. At the end of his boarding school years in 1847 he received a very good final report and both he and his father were delighted to find that he had been recommended for university entry.

John joined Manchester University in 1848 and stayed until 1850. He found university life more relaxed and soon realized that success was entirely due to the result of efforts. Performance was not monitored as it was at boarding school. He heard of some students had repeated a first year level subject, for three years! It was only when he went to university that he started to show his leadership ability. He excelled in science, military history, and politics and became known for being very capable at debating. He had entered the university with no idea of career, but gradually found himself becoming interested in obtaining a commission in the British Army.

His friends, George and Owen, had followed him to university. Although, they followed different careers; George was studying law and Owen, civil engineering. He was surprised that neither of them was interested in a military career.

John decided to major in military history and, with his father's agreement, obtained his commission. He was posted in 1851 to a military training school near Aldershot in Southern England.

His knowledge of military history gave him a distinct advantage over most of the other young officers and helped him achieve high marks.

John enjoyed the field exercises with gunnery firing and training manoeuvres with their platoons. He showed aptitude in moving his platoon into both defensive and offensive positions.

John kept to himself; most of the other officers were from the aristocracy and behaved as such. He would not have been surprised if some of them did not complete their training. Some were totally incompetent. Their titles and money were of no help in the training field where they could not hide their performance from their peers no matter who they were.

During a cannon field firing exercise, John saw an example of this total lack of concern or interest from his fellow trainee officers. This cannon firing exercise was conducted only by the trainee officers; no troopers were involved. The cannon team consisted of four men. Their first step was to line up the cannon on its target. Second, they had to place wedges firmly both in front and behind the wheels. The breech was opened, the ball inserted, the cartridge case in place then the breech block was closed and locked.

The team next to John was to fire their cannon first. This trainee team went through the drill and duly fired the cannon, but one of the back wedges was not in place. The cannon erupted with a loud explosion and it bucked backward, skewing to the right. The cannon ball hit a building, shattering the roof and one wall. The trainee officers stood there for a few seconds and then started laughing, slapping their thighs.

John and his team stood there looking at their extraordinary reaction, after the stupid and potential disaster that they could have created. The trainee officers appeared to treat the incident as a joke. They did not consider that someone could have been injured or even killed.

The senior training officer strode over, a furious look on his face. He ordered the officers to line up and then marched them to the barracks; they still wore smirks on their faces. An investigation was held but the resultant decision was kept quiet. Two of the trainees left the training school the following day, one of them was the nephew of a duke. The remaining two were assigned to different teams.

John's father presented him with an outstanding gelding. He was tall and jet black, with a high step. The horse handled the noise of the cannons and quickly learnt to stand still after a brief exposure to the smoke and gunpowder. The horse was, without doubt, the best horse John had owned and was destined to remain with John for many years. He named it Duke, due to its regal stance.

His time at the training school went quickly and graduation day soon arrived with all the officers keen to hear their orders. They had received their training course results and John was pleased to see he had achieved excellent results in every subject. The Commandant had recommended him for further promotional training at the end of his first posting.

On the day of the big event the officers were all attired in their dress uniforms. They looked smart in their red tunics, tall hats, white breeches and highly polished black leather boots. They were mounted on their steeds, which were all standing reasonably still. John thought that the horses sensed the importance of the occasion. The band started up with a rhythmic military tune. They rode down the parade ground in line and then the command 'Eyes left', saw them saluting the commanding officer on the podium. After a circuit of the parade ground the new officers halted and dismounted. The commanding officer marched down the line. Assisted by his aide, he handed each officer his personal sealed letter. They saluted him before they received their letter and saluted him afterwards. They all remounted and left the parade ground in single file. Immediately they reached the stables and dismounted they opened their letters.

John was to report to the Kilrush Military Barracks in Ireland within four weeks. A travel warrant was included with his orders. *Where is Kilrush*, he wondered?

John went back to the barracks to pack his equipment. He would leave for home tomorrow; he had a long ride in front of him. He would send most of his equipment and clothing ahead by coach and only carry a minimum for the four day trip. The next morning he reported to the commanding officer's aide, to bid him farewell. He said goodbye to his fellow new officers who had yet to depart. It had been a demanding course and now he was pleased to be free. He would be on the open road and able to relax for the next few weeks.

He was now twenty-one years old and ready for a new career, wherever it may take him. He looked forward to seeing his family again, particularly his father.

He rode out of the barracks and, after reaching the main road, he picked up the pace continuing until noon when he reached a small inn. A short break for both rider and horse and he headed north again.

The countryside was covered with green paddocks and flowering shrubs along the roadside. The sun was shining frequently through the clouds. It was a pleasant day and he hoped it would continue for the next few days. Riding in the rain was not very agreeable to one's person or temperament.

After three days the ride became monotonous and boring. The country had not changed but the sun had thankfully shone each day. The road was in good condition and he was frequently passed by coaches with the drivers cracking their whips and urging the four-in-hand on and on to their next change of steeds. He had stayed at some rather dubious inns and spent most of the night worrying about Duke being stolen. John had used his chain and locked the stable doors but he still had restless nights.

¶

Finally John was near Penrith and close to his home. He would arrive by nightfall. Duke was standing up to the trip very well. John would put the horse out to pasture for the remainder of his stay at home to allow him to fatten up and get his glossy coat back. He needed a good curry combing and reshoeing.

"Mr Hall, sir," called a voice from behind him. John looked back at the man. It was Jack Keane, his father's senior farm supervisor. "Hello, sir, I didn't expect to see you today." Jack had been in town collecting bags of grain for this season's planting.

"Hello, Jack, how are you? I've finished my training and I'm home for some leave."

They decided to ride back together. They arrived home late in the afternoon. John put his horse out before coming into the house to be greeted by the family. They were all both surprised and delighted. John's family had known he was coming but he wasn't expected until the following week.

His father was the first to welcome him home. They shook hands, and John handed him his 'Commission as an Officer and a Gentleman — Lieutenant John Hall' and his letter of posting. His mother then hugged him and kissed him on the cheek. Mary kissed him and hugged him, which he happily returned. It was a happy moment. His brother, David, was at boarding school.

After he was settled the family sat down to dinner and chatted about the farm, friends and local events. John sat and listened. He enjoyed these spontaneous discussions. He knew he was now home with his loving family. He had not said one word about his military training experiences. That could wait until tomorrow. Tonight was for family news and local topics.

¶

John slept until nearly noon. After a good bath, he dressed and was in the dining room in time for lunch. Only Mary was at home. His father and mother had gone into Lazonby for food stocks and to lunch with some friends. Mary and he chatted. She had a new pony and was enjoying her lessons from the tutor, together with her sewing and embroidery tuition from her mother.

Mary's enthusiasm was infectious. John could not but help laughing with her. He was also surprised at how she had grown. She was sixteen years old and was now a young woman, not his little sister anymore.

Her tutor had let Mary have the afternoon free from studies to allow her to entertain her brother. They walked down to the river and along the bank towards Lazonby. The river was broad and flowed fairly slowly. There were black swans and a few multi-coloured wild ducks on the water. Out in the middle was a punt, being poled by a young man, a lady lazing in the bow with her hand trailing in the water. Birds were plentiful and contributed to the picture by chirping and flittering here and there. It was good to be home amongst all this serenity.

His sister had put her hand in his and was chattering about

a girlfriend she had in town. John wasn't really listening. He was enjoying the walk and suggested that they walk all the way into Lazonby. He had not been into the village for several years. They continued for another hour and finally reached the main street. Lazonby was a typical English riverside village with a few shops, an inn, a farrier, a church and a cemetery. The majority of the small two storey houses on the winding main road were made of bluestone, some centuries old. The Halls' had several relatives living in the village but he wasn't interested in meeting them just yet. He just wanted to walk with his sister.

Suddenly he saw a face he did want to see. It was Owen MacLean. They saw each other at the same time; both waved and shouted greetings. They slapped each other on the shoulder and said in unison, "What a surprise! How good to see you."

John introduced Mary and they decided to go to the tavern's dining room and talk about their careers. Owen had begun his legal training as an articled clerk in Carlisle and was finding it both challenging and satisfying.

He said, "I'm thinking of going to Australia when I'm qualified, at the end of next year. I have my father's wander lust but not his desire to serve in the military."

John said, "Well, I'm off to Ireland in three weeks. I wonder where we will next meet, now that we will be on the opposite sides of the world." He continued, "Have you heard from George since he left university?"

"Yes, he went to London to work with the City of London."

Mary had finished her tea and was looking a little bored. Owen noticed. "I must apologise and excuse myself. I should go now as I'm leaving for Carlisle on the coach within the hour." He looked at Mary. "It has been my pleasure meeting you, Mary. Good bye to you, John." He nodded.

John and his sister both stood up and John responded, "Good

bye for now. I trust providence will allow us to meet again." John's gaze followed his friend as he departed up the hill to the Coach Inn.

It was time to return home. The sun was low on the horizon and John guessed it would be dark by the time they arrived. They walked briskly and in silence as they were both busy with their thoughts. John was thinking of his forthcoming journey to Ireland and Mary was considering her chances in the Women's Agriculture Gymkhana Event next week. Dinner was ready to be served when they arrived with the dogs signalling their return amid a chorus of barking and yelping.

9

The three weeks passed swiftly and it was soon time to take up his posting in Kilrush. John prepared, not only his equipment, but also himself for his journey to Ireland. He was unsure what to expect for the start to his military career. Also what was Ireland and her people like?

Duke had been groomed and reshod. He looked a little overfed but was glossy and spirited.

On his final night at home John had dinner with his family and friends. It would likely be a while before he would get a chance to come again. John had an early night and left in the rising dawn. Both his mother and father had stiff upper lips but Mary shed some tears with their farewells.

He was moved himself but did not delay his departure and rode off into the early sunrise. He looked back to see his father still standing there gazing in his direction. John gave a quick wave and cantered Duke down the road. He was due to report for duty in three days at Liverpool Barracks.

When he arrived in Liverpool and presented his credentials

to the commanding officer of the Liverpool Barracks, John was instructed to report to the officer of the day for his travel orders. The orders he received were similar to his instructions from the military training school. He was to proceed on the first available vessel with a platoon of foot soldiers.

John met with his men and advised them of the orders. No doubt they already knew; John knew the troops always had a good spy service. A shipping agent had arranged for them to sail on the next tide, so they immediately proceeded to the ship, loaded their equipment and embarked for Kilrush.

The weather was bleak but the ship made good time down the Irish Sea with the following icy northerly winds. The seas were choppy and the sea spray did not encourage visits on deck. John spent considerable time with Duke helping keep the horse calm. They had put the horse in a semi-sling to ensure he did not fall.

When the ship turned west along the Irish coast the seas abated as the land was sheltering the ship from the worst of the winds. John went on deck when they turned north towards County Clare. The coast line was most forbidding, with sheer rocky cliffs dotted with inlets, all with similar terrain. Very little farm land was in sight. A few small fishing villages came into view over the waves when the ship heaved. Even with the rolling seas several fishermen were out braving the waters to obtain their catch. He mused it must be a most difficult life to endure. He counted his blessings for his fortune to be born into a comfortable life.

They turned into the river and the captain pointed out Kilrush to him as they sailed towards the town. It was the biggest Irish town he had seen to date. The wind had dropped and this allowed the ship to soon be moored alongside the dock. He gave his troops an hour to stretch their legs before commencing the unloading.

The first cargo ashore was Duke. He was flighty and difficult to handle for a few minutes but soon settled down. The unloading was soon underway and John saddled Duke in the interim.

A disturbance on the dock caught his eye. A young woman had just been pushed to the ground by a constable and a tall man was challenging him. Several other constables approached them and the scene looked like getting nasty.

John stepped forward. He checked that the lady was unhurt and then turned to the constable and said, "What are you doing? You owe this lady an apology."

The constable hesitated, looked around at his men and then saw the troopers coming forward. "My apologies, young lady, for my constable's action."

John ordered the constables to leave. The military held the ultimate authority and the constables knew it. John introduced himself to the young Irish lass who had the delightful name of Maeve and the tall man who was her brother, Michael. Maeve was a beautiful girl with a captivating Irish brogue. They exchanged brief farewells before John left to report to his troop. He was pleased that he had stepped in to assist the Irish couple. Perhaps they would meet again. He certainly hoped so.

John ordered his sergeant to move the men out, with the drummer beating marching pace. He led out of the docks, with his sergeant next, followed by the troopers then the Mounted Horse. Finally the carts brought up the rear. They were an imposing sight with their red coats and white flannel trousers, black polished boots and tall helmets. They headed up the main street, passing through the market and up the hill to the barracks.

The sentry saluted Lieutenant John Hall as he led his men into the quadrangle. John then positioned them into formation, dismounted and was escorted by another lieutenant into Colonel Paul Lang's office, the commandant. He marched up to the desk where the colonel was still sitting. He waited at attention for the colonel to acknowledge him.

John sensed that this was not going to be a warm welcome. He was right.

The colonel looked up. "What gives you the right to interfere with constables doing their duties?"

John was dumbfounded and responded, "My responsibility as an officer and a gentleman, sir."

The colonel grunted, "Umm." *This was no ordinary officer.* He stood up and said, "Welcome, Lieutenant Hall. I'll inspect your men." John stood back and allowed the colonel to pass. He noticed that he had a slight limp.

The inspection proceeded without incident or comment. At the end, the colonel answered his salute and walked off.

The other lieutenant had been standing there watching him. He smiled and offered his hand. "I'm George Russell. You're relieving me. I and twenty of the Regiment are heading home for leave and then off to the Crimea. Anywhere is better than being here. I hope you can handle your time here better than I did; I found it very depressing."

The sergeant dismissed the men and they were shown to their new dormitory by the duty corporal. George Russell took him to his room and had an orderly collect his travel chest for him. The room was around eight feet square with a tall cupboard and a small window. The walls were thick so the temperature would not be extreme inside the room. *This room will be comfortable,* thought John.

Dinner time would be soon so John unpacked his mess uniform, then went to the wash room to refresh himself before dressing for dinner. He walked into the officers' mess and over to several other officers standing at the bottom of the table. There were seven officers and he was pleased he was not the junior rank. There were two subalterns.

Colonel Lang walked in quickly and immediately sat down. The others waited to see where he wanted John to sit. He signalled John to sit at the opposite end of the table. This started chairs being shuffled to accommodate the rest. He had George sitting next to him and on the other side were two Line officers — William Brown and David James. This made him feel comfortable. The colonel called for the Royal Toast and asked John to propose it. They all rose and John said, "To her Majesty the Queen."

"To the Queen," they all responded.

John waited for the toast to the regiment and was most surprised when the colonel ignored this tradition.

John was pleased with the meal; it was more sumptuous than normal mess dinners. He commented to George who shook his head.

"Don't say anything about the food."

John decided he needed to have a long talk with George before he left the regiment. There were obviously some things that were done differently here to what he was used to. After the colonel left they all retired for the night but not before John asked George to spare him some time the next day.

Subsequently George took him on a familiarization ride around the district which was the perfect time to glean information about the regiment from him.

George started, "The colonel has seen little service other than a short stint in India. Tragic really. He had his horse shot from under him. It fell on him and broke his leg on the first engagement. He was then sent back to England. He's had several postings in areas of civil disorder, such as here, but no actual theatre of war since India. However, he did not give up hope and applied to go with the regiment to the Crimea but he was rejected. You brought the letter on your ship."

John said, "Bad timing, eh?"

George went on. "His wife is a problem, so be careful. Don't be on your own with her if she has been drinking. The colonel knows but doesn't seem to care.

"Another issue is the eviction of the Irish tenant farmers. It's hard to tolerate the distress these families endure. We only attend to ensure that the government officials and constables are not attacked. Regarding the food in the mess, it's alleged that the colonel and the Commissioner of Constabulary have a black market deal going in return for turning a blind eye to custom fraud. So you say nothing; it's a no-win situation for you. I intend to say something when I'm back in England. You see, I'm a nephew of Lord Russell." They continued riding around the outskirts of the town. It was a pretty place with the river and sea views and the green rolling hills. He was to find out later that further north the scene changed dramatically. They completed their riding in time for dinner.

The colonel sent for him on his return. John hoped that this meeting would be more pleasant than the first one but didn't expect it would be. He knocked and a voice said, "Enter." He saluted and then removed his helmet.

The colonel immediately started talking. "Hall, I will not have friction between the constabulary and the regiment. We have built up a good relationship over the time I have been here and I will not have a young jumped up upstart like yourself jeopardising it. Do you understand?"

"Yes, sir," John replied.

"Good. Dismissed."

He was glad of George's briefing, otherwise he would have tried to defend his action and would have made matters worse for himself.

Obviously the colonel and the commissioner were close to

each other. Well, John Hall wasn't going to get involved. He would now be very careful indeed how he handled any problems with the constabulary.

�‍ꝯ

George and his troopers were formed up ready to depart. John bade him farewell and a safe journey. The drummer started and with George's sergeant's, "Quick March," the troop moved out past Colonel Lang, who was taking the salute. John was on his own now; only two of the other officers were line officers. The other officers were assigned to the hospital, quartermaster stores, administration and the colonel's aide. His duty required that, accompanied by a troop of soldiers, he would attend a schedule of evictions escorting the constabulary. John would travel often, so he and his troop always carried camping gear and food.

John had seen the Keoghs several times during his trips and had stopped to say hello. The Irish did not shun the military as they did the constabulary. The Keogh's drove past the barracks on their way into town and on the way back to their home. He guessed they enjoyed discussing the weather and other mundane topics with him.

Michael and Maeve always stopped or waved when they saw him.

The evictions were occurring at a regular rate and they were causing John some anguish. He had written to his father, who knew some politicians. Perhaps something could be done to stop this abomination. At one particular eviction he saw Michael Keogh and spoke with him about the situation. Michael became so upset that he had abruptly turned and left.

ꝯ

One morning not long after his arrival, the colonel addressed the morning parade, which was unusual. He announced that the regiment was going to help apprehend a notorious rebel who had escaped while being arrested. It appeared that one Irishman had struck a constable and then escaped. The commissioner was furious at the humiliation. The whole town knew of the escapade. The colonel wanted the three line officers — Brown, Hall and James, with their troopers, to cover three sections of the district. John selected the coastal area and had the troop mounted and set off by noon the same day. They made good progress and were at Liscannor by late afternoon. He had the sergeant set up camp on the harbour. They would operate from there.

John wanted to see Michael and, if the occasion arose, Maeve also. He selected Trooper Miles to accompany him; he knew he could trust him. He was also from Cumberland; his uncle worked on the Hall's farm. They quickly rode north, across the green fields and only moved to the road when they started to see rocky ground ahead. It was getting dark when they arrived at Michael's home. Dinner was being cooked and the waft of beef greeted them.

Michael and his father came out to greet the two riders and invited them to share their meal. John and Trooper Miles had some food which they gave to Michael's father who was doing the cooking.

John said, "I need to talk with you."

"Let's walk," answered Michael.

They headed up the hill towards Maeve's home. "I don't know if you are mixed up in this rebel business but I have to warn you; I'm here to search for him. I'm speaking to you as a friend now but tomorrow I will be here as a soldier."

Michael just said, "I would expect nothing less from you."

They kept walking so that John would not have to ask him about Maeve; he could ask her himself.

The barking dog brought Maeve outside. She laughed happily when she saw John.

"It's good to see you. Come in. Can you stay long? What are you doing here?" she asked without stopping.

"Yes, I can stay for a short time. I came to see Michael about a small problem."

Aunt Jane made tea for them after which she and Michael went to the kitchen. Aunt Jane had been preparing dinner when they arrived. This allowed John and Maeve to sit on the porch by themselves. Their talking was interrupted when Michael interrupted; they had to go back for dinner at his father's house.

Aunt Jane said, "We will bring our dinner and we can all dine together."

They managed to fit into his father's cottage and had a very enjoyable evening. Too soon Maeve and Aunt Jane had to leave.

John and Trooper Miles had to be back at Liscannor before dawn to start a structured search up the coast to the north. They asked if they could sleep indoors near the fire for a few hours and would then head back down the main road.

They arrived back at the camp as the sole trooper on guard was boiling water for tea. John unsaddled his horse and placed the saddle on the ground. He rested his head on the saddle seat and slept until the sergeant shook him by the shoulder to waken him.

The whole camp was awake and having a meal of boiled corn and bread. Not long after, the camp was packed and ready for a day's riding along the coast of County Clare. They spread out across the fields, moving northwards in unison. The dry stone fences were low but the horses easily jumped them.

Some farmers watched them as they slowly continued their search. The farm dogs barked but kept away; they were not used to large horses. The search was fruitless but John had his orders. He expected it would take another four or five days to reach the Burren at this pace.

They eventually reached the Keogh properties. He could see Maeve and the puppy at the corn patch. She looked to be busy checking the cobs. Perhaps she was hoping he would ride over eventually — he hoped.

At noon he decided to stop for a meal. The troopers quickly dismounted and arranged the food and drink, then tendered to their horses. They removed the saddles and watered them before giving them their feed bags.

John signalled for Miles to go with him as he intended to visit Maeve. After a long hard ride they arrived at the farm. She saw them coming through the window and started to prepare a meal for them. She invited them inside the cottage but Miles declined and sat outside chatting with Aunt Jane.

Time moved fast and in no time he realised that he should return to the troopers and continue his duty. After bidding farewell they rode back and found that the sergeant had the men ready to move on again. As they moved on, John wondered what he should do; he was genuinely fond of Maeve but their backgrounds were so different. If he pursued her with the object of marriage, what would his family think? And did it really matter what they thought — it was his life! What of his career as an army officer? He was close to his parents and would not want to cause them any unhappiness. The situation needed more thought.

They rode on but only flushed out hares, not any rebels. When they reached the Burren he sent a report back to the colonel asking for further orders. John received an answer which was scathing and vindictive, accusing him of incompetence and lack of vision. The letter had only criticism and no new orders.

He sent his courier to seek the other two field officers to enquire what new orders they had received.

Lieutenants William Brown and David James both wrote back that they were also out of favour with the colonel and had received no further orders. John decided to return and advised the other officers of his intention. They replied to him that it would be best if the three of them returned together, due to the colonel's attitude, otherwise the first to return would incur his wrath and possibly have their career ended.

Two days later they assembled a few miles from the barracks and rode through the gates in formation. They formed their troopers, line abreast, in front of the colonel's office and then the three officers marched into the building and asked the aide to advise the colonel they were here to report.

The colonel came out of his office in a rush, panting, his face red. "What are you doing here? You should still be searching."

Lieutenant Brown, the senior officer responded, "We are reporting for further orders, sir."

"What further orders?" asked the colonel.

"We each wrote to you requiring further orders," Lieutenant Brown replied.

The colonel turned to his aide and looked at him enquiringly.

"With respect, sir, I told you of their requests," the aide said.

The colonel then remembered that the aide had handed him three letters. He had only focused on the lack of success of their searches and he had ignored the main content of the letters. He turned abruptly and went back went into his office, slamming the door behind him. The three officers looked at each other and then the aide, who shrugged his shoulders and returned to his desk.

The colonel did not attend the mess dinners for several nights. He seemed to have other things on his mind. He was constantly pacing the quadrangle with his arms behind his back, and looking at the ground.

John was soon to find out why, when a small coach entered the barracks. The coachman went into the colonel's office and returned, the colonel following him. He opened the door and out stepped Mrs Victoria Lang. She paused, looked around — posing, no doubt — and then offered her hand to the colonel who graciously bowed to her. It seemed totally out of character, compared to the colonel's normal behaviour. The woman was tall, slim and well dressed, refined perhaps, although her voice had a touch of the Cockney accent. Her dress was expensive but more suited to evening rather than the day time. John's mother and sisters dressed for dinner so he was aware of the expected standards of the gentry. Her hair was dark while her complexion was pale with red cheeks. Rouge powder perhaps?

He watched as the colonel and an entourage of troopers carried her luggage to the colonel's quarters. So this was the dreaded Mrs Lang of whom George had warned him. The evening dinners might now be more interesting. John was glad that he sat at the far end of the mess table.

Mrs Lang did not appear in the mess until the next night. The colonel arrived on time and stood quietly in the corner talking with his aide. Mrs Lang arrived late much to the embarrassment of the colonel. She seemed oblivious to her lack of protocol. She had been married to him for over twenty years; it appeared to be a deliberate slight on the colonel and indeed the mess. It was not appreciated by the other officers. She sat herself next to the colonel in the seat normally occupied by his aide. After such a bad start to dinner, John expected that things would improve.

After the Royal Toast she asked why the Regimental Toast was not performed. The colonel was thunderstruck. He sat there for a short time and then stood and proposed the Regimental Toast.

The meals were being served with a distinct lack of communication at the table, when Mrs Lang said, "You, there, what is that medal you are wearing? The colonel doesn't have one."

She was looking at Lieutenant Brown who felt quite embarrassed and was reluctant to reply but had little choice. "It was awarded to me during my Indian service."

She continued, "Why do you have it?"

"I would prefer not to say, madam," he said.

"Oh, well, it's only a medal. Maybe they will give one to Colonel Lang one day." The table went quiet. Mrs Lang sensed that she had said something wrong and turned to her husband. "Did I say something I shouldn't have?"

The colonel rose from the table and took his wife's arm. He nodded to the officers and the colonel and his wife left the mess. The table remained quiet for a few moments.

General chatter soon commenced, without reference to what had happened. John felt sorry for the colonel but not for long. The colonel knew very well the mistake that his wife had made. Lieutenant Brown was known throughout the military for his bravery in India. He had rescued two of his men, after killing five Afghan tribesmen. The Indian Medal was actually an award for bravery. Events such as these were not for idle talk when dining in the officers' mess — especially by women. His wife should have known better than to discuss military awards. Such was the introduction of Mrs Virginia Lang to the officers of the regiment.

The officers' wives felt that it was their duty on behalf of their husbands to organise a luncheon for the colonel's wife. Little did they know of the faux pas she had committed. The wives had continued on their merry way so as to be seen as supportive of her as the commandant's wife. They had obtained use of the mess through the colonel's aide. John was not going to say anything about the events; he was not going to be caught in any non-military politics. If the husbands did not tell their wives of her indiscretions, he wasn't about to.

The luncheon started happily enough and all were pleased with the rapport between them all. Mrs Lang drank a wine or two and became somewhat vocal and quite loud. She was critical of her husband accepting a posting in this outlandish place, even though she had yet to venture from the town precincts. Her attitude was one of a pompous overbearing bore, the type of person most officers' wives avoided.

She was not the only such person in the British Army. The afternoon then degenerated into, "Please excuse me. I have another appointment." The colonel's wife soon decided she ought to leave, as the conversation had become very one sided.

She walked across the quadrangle and saw Trooper Miles unloading a dray. As it was a warm day he had removed his shirt. She said to him, "Come to my quarters in one hour. I have furniture to be moved."

Miles was somewhat surprised but not without caution, as he knew the commandant was in Limerick until the next day. He pondered his situation and thought, *Maybe I'm being concerned for no reason.*

He duly went to the door of the commandant's quarters. Mrs Lang opened the door and greeted him, the smell of alcohol on her breath. She stood back and ushered him in. "I want this bureau to be moved into that room and the chest in there to be brought into this room." Miles lifted the bureau to the first room and then picked up the chest and carried it into the next room, which he soon realised was a bedroom.

He placed the chest on the floor and then looked up to see the colonel's wife leaning against the door, her dress removed. She was wearing only a petticoat, which was completely undone exposing her breasts. She was indeed a magnificent woman.

She said quite simply, "Roger me or I will have you flogged." Miles was not completely surprised at this offer as he had guessed that such a situation might happen. She lay down on the bed and opened her legs, looking at him eye to eye.

He had rehearsed an answer and said, "I was shot in the privates in the Afghan war and I am no more, the doctor knows."

She looked at him and went white with rage. She could not threaten to charge him with rape if he didn't 'Roger her', if what he said was true. "Get out!" she shouted.

Miles' last vision of her was a set of bouncing breasts, a red face and an arm raised in anger. Much as he would have wanted to 'Roger her' he could have been signing his death warrant if he had been found out.

Miles told John what had happened, as he was worried it might have repercussions at a later date. John decided that Mrs Lang must go. She would be trouble for someone and soon. He had got to know the regimental doctor quite well, and with what the doctor's wife had already told him of the luncheon and now, with the story from his trooper, he decided to enlist his help.

The doctor listened as John suggested that perhaps Mrs Lang might become ill and need to return to England quickly. The doctor nodded and said, "Forget what you have said to me; this conversation never happened." The doctor had served at Waterloo as a youngster and knew army intrigues and how to handle them.

Within two weeks Mrs Lang was declared ill and the doctor advised her that she must return to England for treatment. She left without fanfare of any description. Indeed the mess celebrated her departure when the colonel was absent.

However, he was also celebrating, not just because his wife was leaving, but because his son, Frederick, was soon to arrive for a short visit to County Clare.

John received a letter from his father who said that he had had talks with two local members of Parliament. They stated that Lord Russell had initiated an inquiry into the Kilrush Custom Service and had already sent two members of the Foreign Service to County Clare to investigate the allegations. Whose allegations? Lord Russell's nephew's perhaps, Lieutenant George Russell!

John only became aware of the arrival of the Foreign Service officers when he received a hand delivered letter asking him to meet with a Captain Walker at the Oak Arms Tavern. He went to the tavern dressed in civilian clothes and asked at the bar for Mr Walker, who was sitting in the corner of the bar with another man. Both looked educated and had the appearance of men of action. As it turned out they were both Reserve Navy officers and unknown to army personnel. He accepted their invitation to be seated, with Mr Walker introducing the other man as Lieutenant James. They came straight to the point. They had two missions, first the investigation of the alleged fraud with the local customs service and locating those involved. Secondly, the more contentious case of the evictions of tenant farmers.

To start, what did he know of the customs fraud? He related what George had said and the standard of the food at the army mess. John explained that he was more familiar with the evictions situation than the fraud allegations. The navy officers said they intended to work backwards with the fraud allegations, starting with the colonel and barracks quartermaster. Then they would investigate the Commissioner of Constables. Mr Walker dismissed John and said that they would be in contact with him at a later date.

John continued with his normal duties of evictions and seeing to the safety of the government officials and the constables. The new senior constable was as bad as the previous one with his excessive brutal treatment of the Irish tenants. John had to accept the situation and, indeed, be seen to be supportive of these evictions. Maybe one day he could do something to correct the injustice. He heeded the colonel's warning and was careful of his relationship with the constabulary.

He had heard Michael had fallen foul of the constables and he made sure that his troopers were ready if the constables were heading for the Keogh's property. That day soon arrived. He had been advised by Lieutenant Brown, who had seen the list for the week. John reported to Colonel Lang and advised him of the day's mission.

The colonel said, "Wait, my son and I will join you. He loves riding and needs to see the country." The colonel's son was a college youth, eighteen years old and an avid horseman. He had brought his own pony with him and exercised him daily. He had shown he was a capable young rider.

The colonel's son used one of the jail cells to stow his ample supply of riding equipment. The youth ran to the cell and quickly collected his saddle and bridle and soon had the horse saddled and bridled. They rode out up the north road. When they reached the crest of the road down to the Keogh's property they dismounted and waited for the government officials and the constables to arrive. The day was slightly overcast, light wind with a mild temperature. Within a few hours events would occur that would change the lives of three families forever.

The government officials arrived first and the constables a few minutes later.

Colonel Lang approached the government officials and the constables and asked, "What is to happen here today?"

The senior constable replied, "We are here to arrest a dangerous Irish agitator who is suspected of aiding a rebel to escape. He also struck a constable, sir."

The colonel drew himself up and said, "These people must be taught a lesson. Follow me."

The cavalcade rode to the Keogh cottage and virtually surrounded it, such was their numbers.

Michael came out and looked at the group. The colonel immediately went into a tirade against the Irish tenants, their children and that they were a blot on human society. He went on and on until the senior constable asked if he could now arrest the man.

Michael asked him, "Why am I being arrested?"

The colonel asked in surprise, "Don't you know?" He looked at the constable. "I thought that you said this man was dangerous. All I can see is a man with a dog asleep at his feet."

The senior constable pulled out a sheet of paper and read, "Michael Keogh, you are charged with interfering with a constable in the performance of his duty in so far as you grabbed his horse's bridle causing the constable to be dislodged." He then placed handcuffs on Michael's wrists and tied him to his saddle pommel.

John watched in silence.

The constables were then ordered to search the cottage. They returned with a long box with a hasp lock; this was easily broken with a bayonet. They lifted out the oilskin bundle and laid it on the ground. The oilskin was slowly unfolded, revealing a cape wrapped around the cap and the magnificent sword of Colonel Monroe.

The colonel could not believe his eyes. He asked for it to be handed to him and withdrew the sword from its scabbard. The excellence of the engraving was obvious to all. Colonel Lang ordered them rewrapped and to be placed back in the box. "I am claiming these articles for, and on behalf of, the Crown. Lieutenant Hall, take charge of them, if you please." Colonel Lang was going to have the treasures to keep by fair means or foul. The colonel rode away with the troopers, except for two who stayed with John.

John dismounted and walked over to collect the box, just in time to hear the senior constable ask for a torch to fire the cottage.

He was shocked and immediately walked over to him and whispered, "See those two troopers over there? They are marksmen and if you torch this cottage they will shoot you dead within the week. Do you understand?" He looked directly into the constable's eyes for several seconds then turned and picked up the treasure box.

The constable stood riveted to the spot. He had just heard his potential death warrant; the officer meant what he said. He took the torch and plunged it deeply into a water cask.

John's troopers tied the box to the back of a spare horse and then headed back to the barracks. The box was placed in the steel cage which was in the middle of jail. It took three keys to access the two jail doors and the cage.

The jail's inner section had a guard in attendance day and night. It contained arms, ammunition and unclaimed valuables, together with the barrack's cash holdings.

Colonel Lang wondered how he could get the treasure from under the guards' watchful eyes. To rob the steel cage was impossible. Lieutenant Hall had chosen well.

The investigation had progressed without alerting the ring leaders. The colonel and his quartermaster both admitted to obtaining cheap foodstuffs but they denied wrong doing in anyway. However, the colonel was unaware that the roster of patrols around town was being given to the customs officers, as was the constables' roster. The customs officers would only smuggle illegal or tax free goods ashore at times when there was no patrol in the area.

The foreign service officers had instructed both the colonel and the commissioner to keep to the roster system but also to secretly send out random patrols without notice. On the third night the patrols nabbed ten people, three of them customs officers, bringing goods ashore from a vessel in harbour. The colonel and the commissioner were disciplined for their lack of supervision and ignoring suspect goods. The quartermaster was dismissed from the service. The experience of the navy officers with the way smugglers operated had paid off. One matter was now cleared up.

John met with the Foreign Service officers again, advising him they had prepared a report on the eviction situation. The report would be handed to the secretary of their department.

¶

The colonel decided to take his son to see another eviction of tenant farmers. John could not understand why he would subject a youth to these horrific and barbaric scenes.

The troop left early on a wet and drizzly morning.

No one could be looking forward to this day, John thought.

The government officials and the constables were already waiting. When they saw the troopers arrive, the officials started to read the eviction notice.

John was surprised that there was such a large crowd for a dismal day like this. He wondered why and he had his men assembled to be ready in case of trouble; he sensed it in the air.

The first man came out peacefully but he could hear a ruckus from inside. Suddenly three angry men ran out, fighting with the constables. The crowd surged forward and surrounded the fighting men.

The colonel rode straight into the crowd, his horse knocking people over and trampling them. There were screams of pain and fright.

John ordered his men to dismount, and draw swords. Each second trooper moved in to surround the colonel and get him out of the melee. John led the charge running forward, grabbing hold of the colonel's horse's bridle. He pulled the horse out with his men surrounding the colonel and him. The other waiting troopers had drawn swords and ridden forward upon John's command. He rallied his troopers to help extricate the constables from the fighting. The government officials had run to save themselves and stood with the colonel and his guard.

The crowd moved back when they saw the troopers advancing. The constables were battered and bruised.

The senior constable came over and asked John, "Why did the colonel charge the crowd? We could have controlled them."

John could not answer. He was as surprised as the constable at the colonel's action. John rode back to the colonel. "Are you alright, sir?"

The colonel just looked at him, said nothing then rode off with his son who had been sitting there, white faced, staring at his father.

The troopers remained behind until the government officials and the constables had completed their distasteful task. The constables were angry; several of them had been injured, together with a number of the Irish family members and friends. They knew this Irish family would resist being ejected from their home and they were prepared for trouble. There was no need for the colonel's rash action.

John checked with the senior constable to see if he felt comfortable with the troopers leaving. No doubt the commissioner would want an explanation from the colonel.

The colonel sat in his office looking out over the river estuary. He'd had enough of Ireland and Irish people.

He thought back over his three postings to this country. His career was going nowhere, particularly now that he had been rejected for service in the Crimea. His actions early today still shocked him. He just could not understand why he had acted so irrationally. He knew he was an angry man but not irrational! It was time he applied to return to England and have a more predictable army posting.

But these things didn't just happen; he needed a plan. The plan would have to include obtaining the trophies captured from Colonel Monroe and now stored in his barracks. He opened his desk drawer, removed some sheets of paper and started to write.

§

A ship was due to arrive from Portsmouth on Saturday night, carrying ammunition. John had been charged with the movement of the consignment from the docks to the barracks. He knew the town well enough now to be able to plan the best and safest route to cart the ammunition.

On Sunday morning, the cargo would proceed directly along the river road and straight up the main road of the shopping centre leading to the barracks. He was not too concerned about Irish rebels causing trouble. The speed of operation was the key to success. The security was such that the cargo would be moved from the ship as soon as the ship anchored and taken directly to the internal steel cell.

The trooper knocked on his door and advised that the ship would anchor within the hour. He quickly headed to the docks and organised the barges to move to the ship to ready for the ammunition to be off-loaded. The wharf booms were out and their operators started lifting the cargo onto the carts as soon as the barges were tied alongside. Within two hours of the first load being lowered onto the barges from the ship, the entire cargo had been loaded onto the carts and was moving along the river road. The trip was slow and cautious, with troopers alongside the carts alert for any trouble.

Dawn was breaking and John wanted to be back in the barracks by sun up. They continued up the main road through the barrack gates. They all heaved a sigh of relief when the gates closed behind them. The three entrances to the steel cell had already been opened to expedite the storage of the ammunition. John, together with the quartermaster, counted the boxes as they were unloaded and carried into the steel cage. The count was agreed and they each signed a duplicate waybill.

When they were finished, John walked into the steel cage. Something wasn't right? He scanned the cell and only after checking every corner did he realise what was amiss. The treasure box was gone!

He said to the guard, "Where is the box?"

"The colonel took it," the guard responded.

John ran from the cell and went looking for the colonel. He found him having breakfast.

"Where is the box, sir?"

The colonel put down his drink and looked directly at him. "I have put it in number one cell. The ammunition is more important and we are running out of space."

"But the security risk is much greater in an ordinary cell. I'll make room for it in the steel cell," John stated.

"No, it stays there. I want no arguments. You will hold the only key," said the colonel.

John knew he now had a problem and did not like the situation in which he had been placed. He went back to the cells to check the guard. Just to be sure he opened the box to check the contents were still there, too.

This cell also had the colonel's son's horse riding equipment. How many keys were there? It was hard to believe that there would only be one key for a jail cell. He discussed his dilemma with Lieutenant Brown who was second in command by seniority. Lt Brown agreed there could be a problem with security, so they decided upon a formal security procedure.

ꧏ

The commissioner of constables had not accepted the colonel's explanation why he had charged the crowd when his men were arresting the Irish tenants. He had written to his commanding officer in Wiltshire, the regiment's headquarters, about his dissatisfaction with the colonel's behaviour and lack of concern for the safety and authority of his constabulary. They had been friends but the commissioner now blamed the colonel for his association with the customs fraud.

The commanding officer's reply was non-committal with only, "Trusting you may work well together."

ꧏ

The colonel's son's visit was nearly at an end. He was due to return to boarding college and the colonel was busy arranging for the shipping of his son's horse and riding gear to travel on the same vessel.

John was assigned to travel to Galway to courier confidential documents and would be away for a few days. He and Miles left in the early morning and planned to stop at Maeve's to say hello. It was a good day for riding and they made good time.

He was pleased to be away from the colonel, who was totally unpredictable these days. Lieutenant Brown knew the colonel from his days in India and was able to tolerate his behaviour better then John and James.

John was pleased to reach the Keoghs' properties and wanted to see how Michael's father was faring. He need not have worried as Maeve's father was bright and breezy.

"Michael will survive and do his duty," said Edmund.

John did not understand what he meant by 'duty'. He wondered if it had anything to do with the treasure box. He rode on to Maeve's and was pleased to see her smiling face. When he dismounted she gave him a big hug. He was delighted with her show of affection and returned the hug. He felt like kissing her but was still unsure of Irish culture. He and Miles stayed for lunch then mounted and proceeded north to Galway. It had been a long ride and after they delivered the document, they headed south again and booked into a tavern for the night.

The British Army had no presence in this district. Hence, they were not greeted with any accord and both could sense the enmity of the Irish. How he wished life could be different, particularly if there was to be a future for both he and Maeve.

They left early the next morning on their return trip and, after a brief stop at the Keogh's, reached the barracks in the afternoon. He was advised that the colonel was at the docks seeing his son off to England.

John felt a nagging sense of dread. Would the colonel's son leave without his horse equipment? He ran to the cell. The guard was still there doing his duty. John unlocked the cell door and then opened the box. It was empty. John sat down in shock.

All the horse equipment was gone, too. The colonel had lied. He ran out of the cell, colliding with Lieutenant Brown in his haste.

"John, what's wrong?" John quickly explained the situation as he hurried to the stables. They mounted their horses and raced to the docks. They could see the colonel and his aide waving to a ship that was getting under way. The ship's anchor had been weighed and its sails were being unfurled.

The colonel saw them coming and took the belligerent stance of a guilty party.

They dismounted and saluted. No one said a word for a few moments.

Then the colonel said, "Well, why are you here?"

John spoke, "The treasures have been taken."

The colonel took the high ground. "They were your responsibility. Find them."

"Sir, you advised me that there was only one key," John answered.

"We will continue this discussion later today." The colonel turned away and looked at the ship sailing down the estuary. The two lieutenants mounted their steeds and rode back to the barracks to sit outside the colonel's office.

A short time later the colonel returned from the docks. "Show me."

They walked to the cell and John unlocked the door and opened the empty box.

The colonel looked down at the open box and then up at John. "How do you explain this? You have the only key."

"Sir, your son collected his riding gear when I was in Galway at the Yorkshire Regiment delivering Courier Mail," John replied.

The colonel looked at him. "Anyone could have collected it for him days ago."

Lieutenant Brown now spoke up. "The guards have to record the name of everyone who enters the cell."

"Show me," said the colonel.

Lieutenant Brown went to the guard's desk and lifted the lid which had a sheet of paper pinned to the inside. He looked at it and stepped back for the colonel to see. Lieutenant Brown then removed the paper and placed it in his pocket. The colonel went red in the face and started to pant with anger.

He had seen his son's name listed as the last person to enter the cell and it was dated yesterday, when Lieutenant Hall was in another county. How could he deflect the blame and get himself out of this mess? He had asked his son to smuggle the contents in a horse blanket. The treasures were now on the way to England. The colonel walked from the cell and then went to his quarters.

The two lieutenants looked at each other and then walked to the mess to sit down to decide what to do next.

The next day the colonel called both Lieutenant Hall and Brown into his office and with his aide as a witness, he read. "Lieutenant Hall, I am charging you with dereliction of duty in so far as you allowed treasures of the Crown to be appropriated by persons unknown." The room went quiet. The colonel was trembling; he knew he had taken a path from which he could not escape.

"By your leave, sir, we know that your son was the last person who entered the cell with a duplicate key," said Lieutenant Brown.

The colonel replied, "Gentlemen, please leave." His aide stayed and when the door was closed he said, "Have you thought this through? Hall is very well connected and he has Brown's support."

When the colonel did not answer, his aide then left the room to seek out the two lieutenants. He found them sitting under a tree, relaxed but not angry. He shrugged his shoulders and sat with them. They had forced the colonel into a corner and now had to decide the next step. Surprisingly, John felt that a door had opened.

John could resign in protest and this would bring the charge to the attention of the regiment's commanding officer in England. He could then fight the charge to clear his name. He knew that if he stayed in the regiment and brought down the colonel, his career would be over. No other senior officer would trust him.

§

John rode slowly down the road to Maeve's cottage. He had given a lot of thought to what he would say and how to say it. He knew it would upset her but she must be told. Aunt Jane saw the horseman approaching and at first she didn't recognise him, as he was not in uniform. She called to Maeve that John was there.

Maeve stopped spinning the woollen yarn and went to the doorway. After the normal greetings, he asked if Maeve would walk with him. They were both nervous now. They walked towards the cliffs not saying a word. When they reached a low log overlooking the sea, John asked Maeve to be seated and sat beside her. He slowly told Maeve what had happened. He spoke accurately and precisely. He did not waste words. She listened intently and believed that she understood the anguish John was enduring.

When he finished he looked at her and asked, "I hope this doesn't alter our friendship." He still felt badly over what had happened to Michael. Although he knew she realised that he could have done nothing to stop his arrest.

Maeve turned to him. "Nothing will alter my feelings for you."

His heart lifted with this knowledge. He continued, "I must resign and return to the regiment headquarters to clear my name. I will then decide my future and I want you to be part of that future."

Maeve stood and looked down at him, suddenly shy. "I am only a simple Irish farmer's daughter."

He stood up and put his arms around her. "Yes, I know but I'm in love with you and I want you to be my wife. Who, or what you are, is of no concern to me. I just want you." He surprised himself with his burst of words. It was not supposed to happen like this, but it had.

Maeve laughed happily. "Yes, yes, yes." She flung her arms around him and kissed him. He responded, showing his deep love for her.

"Let's see my father; I'm sure he will give his consent." They walked to her father's farm and found both he and Aunt Jane there. She had guessed something important was to happen.

John spoke first. "Sir, I wish to marry your daughter. May I have your consent?"

Maeve's father looked at John for a few seconds, then stepped forward and shook his hand. "Welcome to the Keogh Clan."

Aunt Jane then kissed them both.

John explained his problem with his military charge and that it might take some time to resolve. But it had to be done.

He walked Maeve back to her home and advised her he would seek the first boat to England. He would write often to keep her informed. He gave her his father's address in Cumberland and asked her to write to him via his estate. They sat talking for a while, promising they would wait for each other, regardless of how long it took. They kissed, then John rode back to the town.

When John reached the town he went to the docks to check on the shipping movements and he found that a sloop was sailing to Liverpool the next day. He saw the ship's agent, paid his fare and returned to the barracks. In his quarters he sat down and wrote out his resignation and the reasons for his decision. Then he went looking for Lt William Brown.

John knew William was in the barracks as he was the officer of the day. He found him at the stables checking his saddle buckle.

"William, I've decided to resign. I think it will be better all round, if I do. Will you please witness my letter?"

William agreed to but suggested that John write two more copies so they could each keep a copy. Thinking this a prudent suggestion, John went away to make the extra copies.

Later William witnessed the three letters. John gave him one to keep and he put a second copy in his own packet. Then he strode over to the colonel's office. He asked the aide to take him into the office and to remain while he was there.

The colonel had his head down and was working when they entered. Raising it, he asked, "Yes?"

John saluted. He placed the letter on the desk. "Please accept my resignation forthwith, sir." He heard the aide gasp.

The colonel froze and did not speak. He had not expected that Hall would do this. He thought he would fight the charge at a court martial as a serving officer. He now had a more serious problem. He dismissed the young lieutenant with, "Thank you." He needed time to think. He was going to Limerick within the hour and decided to let the matter rest for a day until he returned. He needed to consider the ramifications and then talk to Hall again regarding the charge against him.

John intended to leave the barracks quickly. He went to his quarters and began packing. He laid his issue uniform out on his bed and had them checked off by the quartermaster, who gave him a chit acknowledging everything was in order and handed the pay due to him. He located Trooper Miles and told him about his resignation and to write to the estate if he ever needed his help. He was in his debt for his loyalty.

After a few farewells, he left the barracks in the early evening.

William and Miles drove him by cart to the docks. They shook hands, wishing him a successful journey and headed back up the river road.

A ship's dingy rowed in to collect him and his baggage. After meeting the captain and introducing himself, he went to his cabin and promptly fell asleep. It had been a long and somewhat difficult day. When he awoke the ship was leaving the Shannon River estuary under half sail to Liverpool.

The next morning, the colonel felt in control of the situation. He had given plenty of thought to what he would say in response to Lieutenant Hall's letter of resignation. Firstly he would not accept it and secondly he would offer to transfer him to where he wished. He asked his aide to bring him to his office.

When his aide returned without him, Lang was advised that Lieutenant Hall had sailed for England on the morning's tide. Colonel Paul Lang, for once, was at a loss for words. He was dumbfounded and sat at his desk staring into space. God, what a mess he had created. What was to happen now? What should he do?

CHAPTER THREE

Voyage to the Colonies

—

ohn stood at the stern of the ship and looked across at the rolling green hills of Clare. He wondered if he would ever see them again. The ship heeled to port and headed south out into the Atlantic Ocean with all of its sails full. The sea was calm and he presumed they would make good time if the weather held. As the ship was sailing to Liverpool, he had decided to go to his father's home and write to the regiment's commanding officer to seek an appointment. If he had gone directly to Wiltshire Headquarters, he would have breached protocol. It was inappropriate to just 'turn up'.

The voyage was quick, as he had expected. The seas were calm and they had good south westerly winds. He wasted no time at Liverpool searching for a coach heading to Penrose. He boarded with his baggage and headed north up into the country he loved.

The hills and valleys were dotted with livestock and farmhouses with their smoking chimneys. The people they passed on the road appeared a contented lot. They did not have the hardship and misery the Irish were enduring. How different were the English and Irish worlds! He immediately thought of Maeve's words. The roads were winding through village after village, dropping off and picking up passengers. He dozed at times but woke up at each stop.

The villages had not changed for centuries with their church spires, cemeteries, inns, market squares and two story dwellings bordering the roads. He felt comfortable and yet sad as he would have liked to be coming home in different circumstances. Penrose was bigger than he though; perhaps some things had changed.

The coach bounced to a halt and John climbed out looking around seeking a face he knew, but to no avail. He left his baggage with the coach office and asked the clerk to forward it to Lazonby. After paying the clerk, he left to find a friend of his father's, who owned stables. He found him at the stables, had a quick chat, hired a horse and gig, and set off for home.

The horse trotted slowly along for about an hour before he stopped at an inn in Brockleton. He knew people in this village. His father had a large farm on its outskirts which employed several locals.

The innkeeper recognized him immediately and held out his hand in welcome. "And how would you be, sir? I thought you were in Ireland," he asked with a smile.

John shook his hand. "Time to come home for a visit. I'd like an ale and a bite to eat, if I may, and could your stableman see to my horse?"

The innkeeper quickly left to do his bidding.

John's father was one of the most influential men in the district, as well as being one of the most wealthy. John was sensitive to his social position and tried to treat everyone as equal. Sometimes other people were the problem, though, and not him. It caused him embarrassment when people treated him differently.

After the short stop, he remounted the gig and headed down the road to his father's home, just before the village of Lazonby. It was a pleasant drive with hedges of hawthorn lining the road and enclosing the rolling green fields.

He stopped at the farm gate and looked at the main building.

He was pleased to be back. He climbed from the gig and led the horse to the stables, handing the reins to a farm hand.

John went to his father's study and knocked quietly. A voice invited him in. He opened the study door and approached his father.

His father stood when he saw who it was. Naturally he looked surprised. "Well, to what do we owe the pleasure of your company?" He waved him to take a seat.

John sat and briefly explained that he had resigned his commission and that he would be seeking an audience with the regimental commandant.

His father stood up and walked around his study. "Is this the same Colonel Lang that Lieutenant George Russell spoke to Lord Russell about?"

"Yes," John answered.

"Do you wish to continue your military career?"

"Yes."

His father nodded. "Then you should go ahead and write an accurate statement for your defence. Keep it brief, but step by step of the events leading to your resignation. I'll make some enquires about another direction for your career. However, it is possible that you may never obtain another commission in the British Army, even if you are found blameless."

The dinner gong sounded and they left the study to dress for dinner.

John's room was as he had left it. As he dressed, his mind turned to his meals in Maeve's cottage and he mused at the difference in the social atmosphere between the two cultures. It was no problem for him but would, or could, she accept this change to her lifestyle and local customs.

He went downstairs and entered the dining room. He saw his mother immediately. She rushed to him and put her arms around him, kissing him on the cheek. She was delighted to see him again. His sister, Mary, also came forward and kissed him. She began asking question after question.

He put up his hand and said, laughing, "Stop. Not yet. Let's eat first." They dined and engaged in small talk. The subject of why he had returned was not discussed.

There was one person missing from their family dinner — John's brother, David, who was still studying at Manchester University. He had an uncle teaching mathematics there, who was monitoring his performance. John would have liked to have had a full family dinner but that would have to be another time. Instead he enjoyed the chatter of his sister and his mother. Both refrained from asking about his return.

Mary knew that he would tell his mother and her when he was ready.

At the end of the meal, John's father invited him to his study for an after dinner port and a cigar.

They sat looking out the window, across the fields towards the mountains. They sat in silence enjoying the moment. They were alike — both were ambitious and strong willed, and had similar mannerisms and physical features.

John's father started the conversation. "You will need to decide how you will answer the charge. Know your strengths and weaknesses. You must have your evidence itemized and in order. Your witnesses will need to be available during the hearing. Finally, ensure that you show an orderly and logical mind and have the support of a competent legal person."

His father's advice was basic common sense but John agreed with his logic. He would write to the commandant and start planning his defence of his charge the next day.

9

John knew that he must speak positively and accurately. Every word that he said would be examined in depth, not only from a legal point of view but also from a military perspective. If he wished to continue a military career, his presentation would decide his future.

John sat at his writing desk thinking deeply about how to proceed, pen in hand, paper before him. After deliberation he decided to state his defence as simply as possible, while ensuring that no relevant details were omitted.

This decided, he drafted out six statements:-

a) The orders he had received to secure the artefacts.
b) The security procedures he had instigated.
c) The change and reduction of the security procedures by the colonel.
d) The alleged involvement of the colonel's son.
e) Each of the above four points as witnessed.
f) Details of the names and addresses of the witnesses.

John forwarded his defence package, including a statement, to the office of the regimental commanding officer.

He received an immediate response advising him to present himself for a court martial tribunal at the regimental barracks within ten days. He was surprised at the short notification and he hoped that his witnesses would be able to be in attendance.

On the day of the tribunal John wore his personal dress uniform as his resignation had not yet been accepted. He was early. After reporting to the tribunal clerk, he took a seat opposite the court room door. When the door opened he could see the bench where the tribunal members would sit. He was nervous when he first arrived but was even more so now.

Colonel Paul Lang and his wife arrived and sat very quietly in a corner by themselves. His wife looked decidedly ill and extremely nervous. The waiting area was filling up with various uniformed personnel.

John was glad to see some friendly faces when both Lieutenant Brown and Trooper Miles arrived. They had travelled together from Kilrush.

Ten minutes prior to the hearing start time the regiment commanding officer and his other tribunal officers arrived in a group and entered by a side door of the court room.

On the hour an officer opened the court room door and called the named parties, witnesses and observers to enter. After rising for the tribunal to enter and be seated, the various parties and observers sat down.

The president of the tribunal declared the hearing open and asked for the charges to be read. He then asked if all the parties and witnesses were in attendance. The court officer advised that all were present except Frederick Lang.

The president looked incredulous. "He is a key witness to this case. This is unacceptable." He looked to Colonel Lang, who was white with worry.

"My son is studying in Rome and has taken ill. The situation is beyond my control."

The president lent over and spoke in a whisper to his tribunal panel. They conferred for several minutes.

When he sat back, John could see that he was very angry. He said, "Lieutenant Hall, please stand."

John stood; most concerned that something serious was to happen.

"Lieutenant Hall, the tribunal wishes to give you the option of proceeding with this hearing without the key witness or to defer the hearing. Do you need some time to consider your options?"

John stood silent for a short time, thinking that it would serve no useful purpose prolonging this ordeal. "Sir, I wish the hearing to continue."

The president replied, "Very good. Thank you, Lieutenant Hall."

Colonel Lang and his wife looked shocked; they had not expected Lieutenant Hall to proceed without their son as a witness.

"Please swear in Lieutenant John Hall," requested the president.

Taking the bible in his right hand, John swore to tell the truth. He looked at the Langs while taking the oath.

"Lieutenant John Hall, how do you plead?" asked the court official.

"Not guilty," John replied.

The president said, "As we have a written statement of defence from Lieutenant Hall I believe it would be appropriate to read this paper out. It may help to expedite this hearing." The court officer read through the statement.

Then the president summarised the statement.

"a) Colonel Lang delegated the security of the artefacts to Lieutenant Hall who secured the artefacts in the armoury with Lieutenant Hall having the sole key.

"b) Colonel Lang moved the artefacts to an ordinary cell to obtain more space for ammunition; the cell had more than one key.

"c) Lieutenant Hall implemented a log book to record the name of anyone who entered the cell.

"d) Frederick Lang is recorded as the last person to enter the cell and remove items. i.e. a saddle blanket.

"Lieutenant Hall, is this a fair summary of your statement?" asked the president.

"Yes, sir," replied Lieutenant Hall.

"Do you have evidence that:-

"a) Frederick Lang was the last person to enter the cell, and,

b) that Frederick Lang removed a saddle blanket from this cell in question?"

"Yes, Lieutenant Brown, who is here as a witness," replied Lieutenant Hall.

"Lieutenant Brown step forward and be sworn." The swearing was duly given.

"Lieutenant Brown, how can you prove these statements?" asked the president.

"Sir, I wish to table the record of the last cell entry on the day of the alleged offence."

Another tribunal member asked, "How can you be sure that the cell guard did not enter the cell?"

"The master cell key is held in the commandant's office, sir," Lieutenant Brown answered.

"Thank you," the tribunal member acknowledged.

"Colonel Paul Lang, Lieutenant Hall has tendered his defence to the court; do you wish to comment at this stage or take leave to answer when you are called?" asked the tribunal president.

Colonel Lang sat thinking, when all of a sudden his wife jumped up and shouted, "You are all trying to blame my son. He is sick because of this. He didn't mean to do it!" She stopped, suddenly realising what she had said and promptly fainted. The colonel sat there stunned. The president immediately adjourned the court proceedings until the next day.

The court was in an uproar, everyone talking and milling around. As there was now no reason for them to remain, Lieutenants Hall and Brown, together with Trooper Miles moved quietly to a door and left the building without saying a word. They adjourned to a nearby inn where they ordered a round of ale and sat there in amazement. What would happen now?

There was no doubt that the charge against Lieutenant John Hall would be dismissed, but what would be the aftermath? They did not stay for long. Each returned to their barracks quarters and had an early night wondering what tomorrow would hold.

§

They soon found out. The three of them were summoned to be at the commandant's office at noon. The commandant advised that he had closed the hearing in the morning. He spoke to Trooper Miles first and advised him that he was promoted to corporal and transferred to the Kashmir — far from Ireland. Although he had not been called to give evidence, the commandant wished to ensure that he was not seen to be involved in the hearing. He then dismissed Miles and spoke to Hall and Brown.

He spoke to Hall first and asked bluntly, "Do you wish to withdraw your resignation, or do you need time to make up your mind?"

John had already considered his options and had decided to leave the British Army and immigrate to Australia. "Yes, sir. With regret, I will resign my commission."

"I accept it with reluctance but I understand your position and I wish you luck in your future. I believe you would have made a good officer and would have had a long and successful career," said the commandant.

"Now, Brown, what do I do with you? I have an immediate position for an aide. It's yours if you want it. It will only be for twelve months but it will give you time to look around and decide your future."

Lieutenant Brown sat thinking. This would be good, he would not like to go back out in the field just yet. He would need more seniority to overcome any animosity that he may have engendered through this incident. "Yes, sir, I would be delighted to serve you."

"Good, report to me tomorrow.

"Finally, before you both leave, Colonel Lang has submitted his resignation. His wife is at their home under medical care. It appears that she has had a complete mental and physical breakdown. No penalty will be applied and we will close this infamous event in the regiment's history. No useful purpose will be served in attempting to locate the Irish artefacts."

When John Hall and Lieutenant Brown left the commandant's office, they found Trooper Miles waiting for them. He was both pleased and relieved with his promotion and his transfer. He had known the risks being a witness against a senior military officer but he had stuck by his principles and supported his friend.

They went back to the inn and enjoyed a large dinner and several ales. Three friends who might not see each other again — John Hall was going to Australia, Corporal Miles to join a regiment stationed in Kashmir at the Kyber Pass and Lieutenant Brown was staying in England at least for the next twelve months.

The next morning Lieutenant John Hall was no more. He was just plain John Hall. He bade goodbye to his army friends, who remained at the barracks, and headed north to Lazonby. He had not brought Duke with him so he had taken the coach to Leeds. He was travelling with only a valise. He had sent his army uniform on a separate coach.

He was dozing in the early evening when he heard the call of "Stand and deliver". The coach halted, brakes screeching. A dark figure loomed from the trees with two pistols in his hands.

The dark figure became a faceless man who motioned the

driver to step down and release the baggage in the rear pannier. The passengers sat quietly with a nervous calm, waiting for the highwayman's next move. The highwayman selected a few small parcels and then motioned the passengers to exit the coach.

The first two were women. He offered his arm and helped the first lady down. As he turned to help the next lady he placed one of his pistols in his belt. He bowed to the lady and offered his arm to her to help her alight. His head was level with the coach door. John kicked the door violently outwards. The door hit the highwayman in the temple and immediately knocked him unconscious. John and another man jumped out and grabbed a pistol each from the highwayman.

John looked at his captured pistol and saw that it was well made, and inlaid with ivory. The two pistols were a matched pair; they were the new American Navy Colt revolvers. The highwayman would have no further use for them where he was going so John and the other man, whom John later found was an Irishman named William McMahon, pocketed them; a small payment for subduing him.

They tied his arms and legs, and then lifted him up alongside the coach driver. There he stayed until they reached the next town where he was locked in a cell.

The coach driver kept the highwayman's horse.

John found out later that the captive was the notorious Gentleman Highwayman. He was eventually hanged for his many years of misdeeds.

John arrived home at the time of the local agriculture show to see Mary win her equestrian event. His father and mother won several prizes as well, so together with his return, it was a happy homecoming. That evening at dinner John related the events of the court martial and the results that occurred. His family sat and listened until he had finished.

His father spoke first. "What do you intend to do now?"

John replied, "As I am a former commissioned army officer I would like to use my qualifications. I intend seeking a commission in the Colonies. The father of an old school friend of mine, George Nickle, is the commandant of a regiment in the Colonies. I met him once. Perhaps he will remember me. I'm sure you know him, Father."

"Yes, I do. He and I are members of an association. He hasn't been home for several years but we are acquainted. I can attach an epistle of introduction to your application if you wish."

John's mother and sister had sat quietly listening to their conversation, both thinking of the distance of separation. John going to the antipodes, it was the other side of the world! It had been a long day for all and they retired, each with their own different thoughts.

Next morning John wrote out his application, detailing his education, qualifications and military training and experience but made no mention of the court martial. He addressed it to — *Colonel Robert Nickle, Commandant 12th Regiment, Melbourne — Colony of Victoria.*

John attached his father's epistle to his application and asked Jack Keane to take the package to his father's shipping agent for on-forwarding by clipper ship to the Victorian Branch of the Bank of New South Wales. The journey to Victoria would take around three months. He did not intend to wait for an answer; he would follow up the application within the month.

He wrote to Maeve and told her of his intentions and again asked her to marry him. He wanted her to go to Melbourne with him. He already felt he knew her answer as she would not leave her father or Aunt Jane. He must first settle in Melbourne and then plan to bring the three of them to Australia together.

When he received Maeve's letter he would then decide his

immediate future. He recalled Maeve's comment, "that she was only a simple farm girl". He went to see Mary and mentioned Maeve's comment.

Mary went to the family library in her father's study, extracted a book and handed it to John. "This is a present for her." The book's title was *Etiquette for Young Ladies*. John included the book in his next letter to her, hoping it would ease her concerns. He was unconcerned but after her comment, he felt he should give her more support in her future as his wife.

John enjoyed his leisure time at the farm. He helped the supervisor, Jack Keane, doing the normal duties of ploughing, clean up shearing and horse shoeing. He visited his relatives, old school friends and his father's other properties.

The time passed quickly. Soon enough he received Maeve's answer to his letter. It was as he expected. She would not leave her father and Aunt Jane but expressed her love for him and would wait for their time. He made up his mind to depart Liverpool within the week and travel via Ireland to see Maeve. He now sat with his father to seek his wisdom of age.

John was not daunted by his coming adventure but needed assurance from his father that he had considered all aspects of his future life. His father advised him to remember his upbringing, to trust his judgment and believe in God. These were the words of advice *his* father had given him and that advice had served him well.

John's parents arranged a farewell dance in the winter sheep barn. The barn had not been used for five months. The floor was firm and it smelt of lanoline from their shorn sheep wool. It was not an unpleasant smell. Most country people were aware of it and wouldn't be offended.

His mother invited nearly one hundred relatives and friends and John knew that it would be a very happy night. The two big fireplaces were burning brightly and soon warmed the chilly air. The cooks had prepared two long tables and had laden them with typical country food including vegetables, eggs, meats and breads of various kinds. They sat on hay bales and wool bales eating their meals. After dining, the band started with waltzes and reels which were popular in the north country. Couples paired and danced the night away. There was only one speech and that was given by John. He thanked his parents for the evening and then their friends for coming. He wished everyone a happy future and stood at the door to farewell the guests. He shook nearly fifty hands and received nearly fifty kisses. It had been a long night.

He left two days later, after a very tearful family goodbye. His father gave him a letter to be handed to the Bank of New South Wales in Melbourne to open a bank account. He shook his son's hand, turned and walked back into the house.

Jack Keane accompanied John, who was riding Duke for the last time, to the coach station in Penrith with his baggage. He asked Jack to look after his family, particularly his father. Jack was a trusted employee, almost a member of the family, and he both liked and respected the Hall family.

John shook Jack's hand and handed him Duke's reins. Then he quickly stepped up into the coach. He waved to Jack as the coach horses trotted away and headed to his destiny.

John's sea trip from Liverpool to Dublin was very quick with good winds and calm seas. He travelled from Dublin to Kilrush by coach, stopping nightly at inns.

The trip took several days to reach Kilrush. On arrival he hired a cart to drive him to Maeve's home. His arrival was a scene of pure joy for all. Maeve, her father and Aunt Jane were in Jane's kitchen and were absolutely delighted to see him.

After Jane served tea, John told them of his plans and asked the three of them if they would come to Australia at a later date.

Maeve waited until her father and Aunt Jane spoke. They would not stand in Maeve's way to marry John but were unsure about leaving Ireland.

Maeve wanted to marry John and go with him but John could see she was in a dilemma. John did not want to take her away from her family and have her feeling guilty. He suggested that they consider coming after he had settled in Melbourne and had prepared a new home for them. They all agreed that they would probably be happy with his proposal.

Maeve and John spent time walking on the cliffs, enjoying each other's company and discussing their future in a new and strange country. They were both excited with the prospect of starting a new life together.

John stayed for a week and went through another tearful farewell. Maeve was to write to him by way of John's father, who would send her mail to him in Melbourne via his shipping agent in Liverpool. He now had two families and he would miss them both. As John left Maeve gave him a letter addressed to her other brother, Patrick, who was a shipwright in Cork.

John headed to Cork by stagecoach, from where he would sail to Melbourne.

After a long but uneventful road trip he arrived in the centre of Cork. It was bigger than he expected and had a large harbour. He found Patrick's rooms down by the docks, close to where he worked in a ship yard. After Patrick read his sister's letter he greeted John and invited him into his rooms. He asked after his father, sister and aunt.

They enjoyed an ale and a humble meal together and spoke into the night.

John found Patrick a likable person who resembled his brother, Michael. Michael had not been mentioned during their mealtime conversation.

Patrick eventually raised the subject of Michael conjecturing as to where he might be now. Little did they both know that he was still in Cork Harbour on board a convict hulk ship, waiting to be shipped to Van Diemen's Land.

After being held in Kilrush for a month Michael had been sent to a Cork hulk. He had been on board for about a month. These ships were unserviceable naval ships, converted and stripped of rigging.

John thanked Patrick for his hospitality and left to visit the local shipping agent to finalise his booking to Melbourne via Hobart. The ship he was to sail on was called the SS Ventnor. It was anchored midstream, as it had eighty convicts on board who had been transferred from the prison hulk two days ago. There were also twenty Royal Marines aboard guarding them.

The next day he was at the dock at noon. A whaler collected him and the other seven passengers and their baggage and took them out to the ship.

The ship had been chartered by the British Colonial Office to deliver the convicts to Van Diemen's Land. It had been built as a cargo vessel and later converted to accommodate a few passengers with the main hold converted for transporting convicts overseas.

John looked up at the three-masted ship with its high quarter deck and small enclosed wheel house for its helm and binnacle compass. It looked like a fine ship and he looked forward to his journey.

John stood on the deck, getting his sea legs and familiarising himself with the vessel. The most obvious items on the main deck were a capstan for the anchor, two main hatchways, two whaler boats, rope lockers, barrels of water lashed to the gunwales and several small animal pens. The captain greeted the passengers and then they were shown to their quarters.

John's cabin was small but it would do him. He had learnt during his previous sailing trips not to leave things suspended in one's cabin due to the rolling and pitching of the vessel. Similarly, it was prudent to leave items in their cases or boxes and wedge the baggage at floor level whenever possible.

John was pleased to be advised that he had been invited to dine at Captain Marshall's table.

§

The convicts were positioned between decks in the main cargo hold. Prior to embarking on the SS Ventnor they had washed and been given new clothes. Many of them were Irish rebels and had been convicted of quasi-political crimes. Only a few were regarded as genuine criminals. Their crimes were mostly stealing goods to survive.

Michael's crime was probably seen as one of the worst offences, by the government of the day.

The convicts slept in double tiered berths, one above another in rows either side of the ship's side bulkhead. Each berth accommodated three convicts. Adjacent the hatchways were several hammock rails. Selected 'trustees' among the convicts were assigned these positions and provided with a hammock.

The trustees were generally from the ranks of the Irish rebels. They rarely gave trouble and some were even pleased to be on board. Here they had shelter, clothing, a blanket and basic food — broth, beef and potatoes, and sometimes bread or a biscuit and cheese. A far cry from the starvation they faced from the potato famine at home, which still affected their daily lives.

They were all issued with eating and drinking utensils and a small water keg. The trustees were given some menial tasks that allowed them to go up on deck; tasks such as collecting the food for their fellow convicts, filling the prisoners' water casks and emptying the sewage buckets.

Michael was classed as a risk. He had been involved in a violent act and was not given a chance of being classed as a trustee. He could not set foot on the main deck until Hobart Town was reached.

Fresh air was provided via the scuttles in the side bulkheads. At times during the voyage, vinegar was swept on the deck to help kill bugs and disinfect the hold. Heating was provided by a stove ventilated through to the main deck.

Inactivity was a major problem, especially for those who were not given the chance as a trustee. They sat around all day with only themselves and the bulkheads to stare at. This frustration often caused fights. However, some of them were articulate and would recite poetry while others would sing; a plaintive voice singing a ballad with words reminding them of home often brought tears to the eyes of the strongest convicts.

Daily the Royal Marines entered the hold with the doctor and did a walk through inspection to check the convicts. The Royal Marines were armed with fixed bayonets and had all been veterans of the Indian Wars; they were not to be tempted. The convicts sensed their no nonsense demeanour and gave no trouble. Such was Michael's introduction to his voyage to Van Diemen's Land.

¶

It was 23rd October 1852, when the ship headed out into the harbour on a beautiful sunny morning; a light swell and a south west breeze made a picture of perfect maritime splendour.

The sails were full, the decks clean, ropes cheesed and cargo stowed neatly. The chicken coops, sheep and pigs pens were on the main deck. They even had a milking goat. It promised to be a pleasant voyage, at least for the passengers and the crew. The convicts were stowed below the main deck and were lounging around wondering what awaited them at the end of this journey.

Their course steered towards the Canary Islands. After leaving the sight of the craggy cliffs of Ireland the seas began to increase. The wind freshened and white caps appeared on the wave tops more frequently. The vessel started to roll and pitch. To stand up was an ordeal for the non-nautical types. Walking required a firm handhold.

Only a few passengers appeared at the captain's table for dinner. When John arrived the captain had just sat down. He introduced John to the other passengers. A married couple from Limerick sat next to John. The table conversation was stimulating between catching sliding plates and holding cups of tea. The food was pleasant and well cooked. John wondered what the food would be like in two to three months' time. The dining finished promptly at 2100 hours. John went to bed immediately afterwards and promptly fell asleep; no doubt the few glasses of Madeira wine helped him.

The next morning the sea had abated a little, although there were still some white caps on the waves. He had walked around the deck and gradually become used to the sensation of stepping lightly and feeling for the deck with the rise and sink of the deck beneath his feet.

John had breakfast with some of his fellow passengers; one was the doctor supervising the health of the convicts.

Another diner was the Royal Marine captain, who was responsible for guarding the convicts. He and John became friends immediately. No doubt their military relationship was common ground. After they introduced each other, they sat chatting.

The Royal Marine was Captain George Walters and he was from Yorkshire.

"I have been in the military for ten years and have served in Ireland for two years and was glad to leave. I felt the politics being applied to ordinary Irish people was wrong and that few people in England know the full situation. This trip is my second voyage to Hobart. I may settle in the colonies one day." He spoke highly of the country he had seen. This greatly enthused John with his decision to go to the antipodes.

Two of the other passengers were land surveyors who were on their way to join the new Victorian Government. Their job was to survey the land outside of Melbourne for the planning of new towns in the surrounding country. The other passengers were a farmer and his wife who were heading back to Hobart after settling the sale of a property in Limerick. The final passenger was the wife of the ship's captain. Mrs Marshall and her husband were very devoted to each other and had voyaged together ever since he gained his command some ten years earlier. John found Mrs Marshall to be a most pleasant person. She was affable, intelligent and a good hostess.

Each week Mrs Marshall would invite the passengers to the captain's cabin to enjoy afternoon tea, weather permitting. Sitting in this cabin, balancing a cup of tea and not spilling any of the contents while maintaining a conversation, required considerable concentration.

The dinners were pleasant and the conversation covered a cross section of passengers' interests. The topics were wide and varied, with the discussions sometimes continuing late into the night, particularly with Madeira as a stimulant.

The voyage started with John viewing it as an adventure but it was gradually becoming monotonous and then downright boring. He had read all his books and written letters for handing over at the first opportunity. The ship was experiencing variable winds and these were causing the captain to tack his ship back and forth to make distance as they worked the ship southward.

He found sleeping at times was difficult due to the creaking and groaning of the ship's timbers working with the stress on the hull. The convicts were quiet and John only knew that they were on board when they started singing or there was a loud argument. Although it was difficult to ignore the stench from their hatches. John had expected to hear floggings but none had occurred so far during the voyage.

The captain had told the diners one evening that this might be the last convict voyage to Tasmania. He had read an article in the Times repeating a submission forwarded from Hobart representing a Peoples' Anti Transportation voice with Western Australia requiring more convicts.

The days dragged on and on. The ship passed the Canary Islands and Cape Verdes to check their longitude. With the captain's chronometer's accuracy and sextant shots of the sun he could obtain a position within twenty miles of his charts.

John sat on the deck in the bow watching the land slip by. He often sat there looking for other ships on the horizon. It was exciting when he saw one. Several ships did appear in the distance, but disappointingly did not come close.

Eventually one ship did approach them. The ship was viewed suspiciously until the Union Jack was seen fluttering in the wind. The ship's captain bellowed through a trumpet, "What ship are you?"

The captain of John's ship replied, "SS Ventnor out of Plymouth, and you are?"

"SS Colonist out of Liverpool." Mail was transferred. The captains exchanged their latitudes and longitudes, they bid bon voyage before continuing onto their destinations.

It had been a pleasant interlude. John returned to scanning the horizon for the next change to the maritime scene. He wondered what the captain would do if they encountered a privateer. Were there any in these times? Other than the marines, he had seen no weapons with which to defend the ship. He must ask the captain at a private moment.

The sea was often alive with various marine species. The dolphins' performance was always a pleasure to watch. John stood in the bow and could see below him. The fish dived and darted across the ship, sometimes only a few feet separating them from the bow strake.

The dolphins could make the sea boil with hundreds of them leaping into the air and splashing back into the sea. Then they would join up with their respective shoals.

Another fish which was much smaller, less than a foot in size, was the flying fish. It was a unique species and most colourful with their silver scales reflecting a blue glitter from the sea water. It had larger eyes than fish normally possessed and had wings which had a total wing span equal to half the length of their body. John marvelled at the flight of these fish. They reached the height of several feet; several times he saw them actually land on the ship's deck. They would flutter their wings on the water, lift and then glide like a bird for a considerable number of yards. Although he saw other marine life, the antics of these two species created the most interest. The sea life provided another diversion from his boredom.

The captain frequently invited one or two of the passengers to join him on the quarter deck. John accepted his invitation with delight. The quarter deck was the highest part of the hull.

When John looked down he was afforded a different perspective of the ship. He was intrigued by two sailors holding a rope over the stern rail. Captain Marshall explained that it was

called 'heaving the log' to enable the ship's speed to be calculated. A triangular section of wood was attached to a light rope,
which was marked with a knot at intervals of approximately two
and a half feet. One sailor would hold a half minute sandglass
which he turned over as the first knot, pulled from the coil held
by a second sailor, entered the water.

At the exact second when all of the sand had flowed out of
the top of the glass, the first sailor would call "Stop!" The light
rope running line was checked by the second sailor. The knots
which had entered the water were counted and that number
was the ship's speed in knots. The knots on the running line had
been positioned to indicate the movement of the ship through
one nautical mile.

It was inevitable that the ship would encounter bad weather
on such a long voyage. Twenty days out, the glass began to fall
dramatically with the cloud line south continuing completely
across the horizon. At the start of the forenoon watch the captain ordered the ship to be battened down and the passengers
to stay in their cabins. The ship's crew were all on standby duty.
The sailors had covered the animal pens with an old sail and
tied it securely. The marines locked the convict hold hatchways
covers and adjourned to their quarters.

The sails were reefed and the sea anchors readied for use if
needed. They waited and waited. In the distance the turbulent
waves could be seen. The sky darkened and the ship began to
yaw and roll and pitch. Then the rain started in squalls, followed
by gusting winds. The ship was not holding its heading and
the captain released the sea anchor; this immediately stabilised
the ship but the rolling continued. A sail ripped and its upper
yardarm snapped and began swinging from its ropes, to damage other sails.

Water flooded over the deck and entered the convicts' hold.

The convicts called out for help as panic set in. Michael stayed in the corner of his berth and lay on his back, his arms spread to attempt to reduce the ship's rolling effect on him.

His berth mates sat on the deck with their backs against a bulkhead in an attempt to stop them from being thrown about with the pitching and rolling of the vessel. Sea water was entering in through some of the scuttles and the hatchways and was flowing into the bilges.

The ship was in no immediate danger but with the convicts locked in the hold in such a violent storm, their panic was understandable. The captain ordered the hatch covers to be unlocked even though this was the responsibility of Royal Marine Captain Walters.

Captain Walters entered the hold with four of his armed marines and ordered the convicts back from the hatches. He said he would stay with them and open the hatch if there was any danger of the ship floundering. This was a dangerous ploy. As the convicts were mainly political activists Walters was not overly concerned for his safety. His ploy was successful; the convicts settled down and waited for the storm to run its course.

The winds suddenly stopped and an eerie silence surrounded the ship. It was the eye of the storm. The captain took the opportunity to have the crew cut away the torn sail, the yardarm and the ropes. It took half an hour to clear the decks.

Then the storm hit the ship again, just as fiercely. Another sea anchor was dropped and the ship did not yaw as much as it had previously, although the pitching still continued. The rain was squalling with violent gusting winds which stung the faces of the quarter deck crew steering the ship.

After two hours the wind and sea slowly abated, the sea anchors were hauled in. By sundown the ship, even with one broken yardarm, continued under almost full sail with a following northerly wind of around twenty knots. The captain and his marines left the convicts' hold and relocked the hatches.

The doctor inspected each of the convicts and found them to be bruised but generally uninjured. The ship's crew was checked too. Two sailors had been injured; one sailor had a broken arm and the other had severally gashed his arm when handling the broken yardarm. Nearly all the crew had suffered bruising from the violent motions of the ship.

The damage to the ship was assessed by the captain and his shipwright. The hull was in good condition after the battering from the seas; only a few timbers had sprung leaks. They were caulked with tarred oakum to fill the gaps. Crews operated the water pumps to empty the bilges of the storm water and re-stowed any cargo that had broken loose. The animals had survived in their cages and pens but were absolutely drenched. The sheep needed to be watched to see if they could last through any cold weather in the next few days with their soaked wool.

Mrs Marshall invited the passengers to tea and at the same time the doctor examined any injuries. He was kept busy. He was also having difficulty walking himself, as he had fallen down the gangway from the quarter deck when seeing to the health of the captain and quarter deck crew. Each passenger told their story of the time in their cabins during the storm with relief. When the storm eventually passed they were able to tidy up their cabins. The farmer and his wife had been sea sick; the farmer to the point of unconsciousness.

All the passengers had been badly bruised when thrown from their bunks during one particular heavy sea swell.

During the clean-up John got to know more of the tasks carried out on a ship and enjoyed talking with the busy sailors as they went about their tasks of clearing and cleaning the decks, tarring ropes, oiling the brass fittings, and setting the sails. He even stood alongside the helmsman and the binnacle, learning the art of navigating a ship. The blocks and the tackles were freed. The rigging was reset, running it through the blocks and bull's eyes to ensure it could do its job of trimming, hoisting or setting the sails.

The setting of the sails required considerable agility from the sailors who climbed the rigging to reef the sails in strong winds, and strength to hoist and set the sails. Their voices were heard calling — "Leggo! Watch below! Loose that! Belay that!" All this was occurring under the watchful eyes of the boatswain and the officer of the day standing on the quarter deck.

To see all the sails full and the bow wave high with slight seas was a picture to behold. The prime aim in setting the sails was to ensure that the ship was not de-masted in strong winds and secondly to catch each breath of wind. The broken yardarm would be replaced in Cape Town.

Mrs Marshall prepared a special dinner for the 'Crossing of the Line of the Equator'. The sailors had been fishing and had caught some splendid sharks. The flesh of these fish was delicious — white and fleshy with no small bones. This together with mashed potatoes, pepper and lime made an excellent meal. The cook had excelled himself and also produced a large split cake with jam between the two cake slabs. This was followed by a port which finished a memorable night. A simple ceremony was carried out by the boatswain and the 'fiery chariot' departed. This was actually a tar filled barrel set on fire and set free on the sea.

From this time on, until the ship reached Cape Town, very little excitement occurred. The meals had become very basic and with not much taste; the food stores were deteriorating rapidly.

The SS Ventnor had not approached land for several weeks until just after the ship turned east heading towards Cape Town.

Three days later land appeared ahead and the ship then turned to the south east. Giant albatross had joined the ship, gliding overhead. Their wing span was nearly four yards. The presence of the birds brought all the passengers and some of the sailors up on deck to watch their graceful gliding and soaring, with scarcely a movement of their large wings. Some sailors believed that the birds were past sailors reincarnated and treated the birds with respect by throwing them food scraps. But other sailors dined on their flesh.

As the ship sailed towards the land mass, Table Mountain soon dominated the landscape — a large flat surface several miles long, towering three thousand five hundred feet above sea level. It was situated behind Cape Town with Table Bay the ship's destination immediately over the bow.

Even with the loss of one sail, the ship had made good time from Cork. After fifty-five days, the ship sailed slowly into Table Bay, ready to drop anchor. The day was warm and the sea was calm, with only enough wind to make way. It was a pleasure for John to sit on deck and look at the foreshore and the buildings. The anchor was dropped, the sails furled, ropes secured and within the hour a whaler was launched. The first mate and the shipwright went ashore to meet the shipping agent to both hand over and collect mail and then to try to purchase a yardarm and some ropes. The ship already had spare sails.

The marines were on high alert. When a ship was in harbour it was potentially a time when trouble could occur.

Captain Marshall offered to ferry any interested passenger to Cape Town, when the ship's whaler returned. He said he expected to be in Cape Town for around seven days, but he advised them to watch for the 'Blue Peter' flag from the masthead. That meant that the ship would sail within twenty-four hours.

Captain Walters wished to visit the local military barracks as a courtesy as a transiting officer. He invited John to join him and John eagerly accepted the invitation. When the whaler returned, five passengers had decided to go ashore.

John climbed aboard with the farmer and his wife, the doctor and George. He sat in the whaler and savoured every moment of the short harbour trip, looking over the serene bay waters towards the town. He was particularly in awe of the flat topped mountain in the background.

Cape Town was unique. He could see why it was a world renowned landmark. They could see several other ships at anchor and still more moored alongside. It was a very busy port with many warehouses on the docks. Much activity occurred with moving cargo here and there. It was a splendid sight. The ships were mainly traveling to and from the Far East and the Orient, the so called 'Spice Route'. The ships stopped at Cape Town for fresh food supplies, water and trading goods.

The whaler came alongside a small rock stairway and the five of them disembarked and headed towards the main street.

Over the past fifty years the town had experienced a turbulent time under the administration of several different nations. The Cape was under British rule from 1795 to 1803 then returned to the Bavarian Republic. Three years later the Napoleonic Wars began. Seeing that Holland was no longer a British ally, the British took possession of Cape Town by force. With the defeat of Napoleon, the Congress of Vienna confirmed Britain's possession of the Cape and other entities for the sum of six million pounds. Although Cape Town was British, the Dutch influence was everywhere, from the language to the town buildings and countryside farms.

John and George walked the main street to get their 'land legs'. After a month or so at sea, a person has a tendency to walk softly or sway a little for the first hour or so on land again. They each purchased several books and some out of date newspapers from Sydney. They then went to a tavern for a local meal with fresh vegetables and a lager or two, and just sat looking down the street and at the people.

Afterwards they looked for an official office or government official and found a customs officer walking towards them. He was most helpful and explained the direction of the military barracks and offered to drive them in his 'two in hand'. He told his story during the drive. He had been the first mate on a clipper ship and after thirty years at sea he had decided to settle down in Cape Town. He had secured the position of Port Deputy Customs Officer and married. This was where he was staying for the remainder of his life. He was a happy soul and was enjoying life.

The barracks were built like an old time classic fort and had originally been the Dutch Military Headquarters and Stronghold. It had married quarters and shops inside the fort. It was different from the British concept of forts. The quadrangle was spacious and impressive with the duty office in the corner nearest the main gate.

Captain George Walters introduced himself to the duty officer, an army lieutenant. He requested him to advise the commandant that he was transiting Cape Town and he would be there for around seven days. The duty officer invited the visitors to the officers' mess to have tea while he went to advise the commandant of their arrival.

The mess was well presented with the regiment's Battle Honours proudly hanging from the walls. Various trophies were also on show, awarded for cavalry and shooting competitions. Rhino, lion, leopard and giraffe heads were mounted on the wall. Two lower legs of an elephant were being used as umbrella stands with a zebra and tiger skin wall mounted behind the bar. It was like no other military mess he had seen in his short career, George agreed, although he had seen some trophies in the Punjab years ago.

They turned at a noise behind them to see the colonel approaching with an outstretched hand. "Welcome to the 34th Regiment and Cape Town. I'm Colonel Winslow and you, Captain, are?"

"Captain George Walters of the Royal Marines, and this is my friend, John Hall, a former army officer proceeding to take up a position with a British Colonial Regiment." They shook hands and the colonel invited them to be seated.

He queried, "To what do we owe the pleasure of your company?"

George replied, "I have a detachment of marines and am escorting eighty convicts to Van Diemen's Land. On a more personal nature I have some newspapers and magazines which you may care to read. I know when I was serving in India I felt starved for news from home."

The colonel smiled. "Capital! Well done, Walters. Can you stay and dine tonight? Better still stay the night so we can have a good chat about what's happening back home these days. I have been away for nearly two years now and I'm looking forward to my leave. I like it here but one needs to go home for a while." He paused. "Of course you are invited as well, Mr Hall."

"Thank you, Colonel," John replied and looked at George.

George nodded. "Yes, we will stay the night. Incidentally can you see the harbour from here? We need to watch for the sailing flag."

"Yes, our signal tower will afford you a perfect view of the entire harbour. The Dutch planned this fort very well. Gentlemen, I must away now. I will see you at dinner. Walters, you will be excused mess dress as you are a transiting officer."

The first mate and the shipwright had run into a major problem. There were no yard arms available for nearly six weeks. A previous storm had used up their stock. The first mate sat on a seat at the docks and pondered his next option. He then noticed another ship in the bay with mast and sail damage.

A small boat was leaving the ship and he made to intercept the passengers as they disembarked at the dockside. The first person from the boat had an air of authority about him so he decided to talk to him first. He walked up to him and started the conversation by explaining how his ship, the SS Ventnor, had suffered a top yardarm loss.

"May I ask what damage your ship suffered?" He was talking to the captain.

The captain looked at him sadly and said that his main mast had a major crack that necessitated a new mast. The ship would be idle for three months at least. This captain had gone through the same storm as they had and had fared worse.

The first mate took a deep breath and asked, "Can we buy your foremast top yardarm?"

The captain thought for a moment and agreed. The first mate advised he would bring his captain over to discuss the deal. The first mate and the shipwright went back to the SS Ventnor and together with Captain Marshall went to the other ship. While the shipwright climbed the rigging and inspected the yardarm and the ropes, the two captains agreed upon a price. The money would be handled between their respective shipping agents.

The shipwright tackled the task of removing the sail and ropes. He was helped by the ship's crew. By nightfall the yardarm had been lowered into the harbour water and had being floated to the SS Ventnor. The yardarm had all the fittings needed already in place. Now the ship would only be delayed two or three days — not a week!

First light the next morning the captain decided to fly the 'Blue Peter' as he planned to sail on the next morning tide if, as he expected, the top foremast sail would be rigged by then. The shipwright already had the crew hauling the yardarm on board and then aloft. It was a slow laborious task and dangerous. The yardarm was heavy and difficult to position when standing in the rigging.

Slowly the blocks and tackles lifted it into position and the crew began to rig the ropes to retain the yardarm. By noon the first part of the task was completed and the captain was now supervising the loading of food and water.

¶

George and John strolled around the barracks and the outside town. John was unfamiliar with the local South Africans; he had only ever been associated with people of Anglo-Saxon origin and naturally eyed the locals with curiosity.

He noticed that the locally born people appeared subservient to both of them and he supposed it was because they had been employed by white people. This was only partly true; in some cases they had been made subservient by malevolent white people in authority. Possibly it was an aftermath of the colonial slavery trade which had been abolished in 1833, only twenty years previously. The people he saw now were happy and well fed and made him wonder what the local Australian people would be like.

The houses built for the Europeans were on larger blocks of land than those in England and had larger windows and doors with flourishing front gardens of green shrubs and multi-coloured varied flowers. No doubt the sunny climate and a generous rainfall helped make this cascade of colour.

They returned to the barracks in time to freshen up for dinner and were in the mess prior to the commandant arriving. They were introduced to the other officers and Captain Walters was invited to propose the Royal Toast. They were well received by the other officers. Lively and stimulating conversation continued throughout the evening. They obviously enjoyed meeting new acquaintances.

During the evening John listened to the conversation about merino sheep being sent to Australia for breeding. It appeared that a Scot, Colonel Robert Jacob Gordon, had commanded the Dutch garrison and owned merino sheep.

Captain John Macarthur, a retired British Army officer and now a New South Wales farmer, had asked two sea captains to buy him some sheep in Cape Town. They bought some from Gordon's widow. The origin of the sheep flock had an interesting history. They had originally been bred from a flock presented to the Dutch Government by the King of Spain. The Dutch Government sent them to South Africa but the farmers were not interested in the wool, only the mutton.

John paid particular attention to this conversation as he would write to his father about these sheep the first opportunity he had. Although he wondered if they would be suitable to breed in the damp English climate.

At 2200 hours the commandant bade goodnight. This signalled an end to the evening with a mass exodus of officers from the mess — George and John included. They were shown to their rooms by the duty steward who advised he would wake them at 0600 hours.

They slept soundly and were asleep when the rap on their doors occurred. After their toilets, in particular, a warm fresh water bath, they went for a half hour walk before breakfast and climbed to the signal tower to see the view.

The morning was clear with no clouds and the ships in the harbour were riding gently at anchor, casting early morning shadows on the water.

John suddenly said, "Am I seeing things? Is our ship flying the 'Blue Peter'?"

"You're right. Let's have a quick breakfast and head to the docks," George replied. At the earliest the ship would not leave for at least another six or seven hours.

Breakfast was better than any meal that they had had on board since they had left Ireland. They complimented the cook accordingly.

It would be several months before they would have breakfast ashore again. After the morning assembly of the regiment they paid their respects to Colonel Winslow and thanked him for his hospitality. They asked if they could provide him with any service. He handed over a parcel which he requested to be delivered to a friend at an inn in Melbourne. John replied that he would be pleased to assist in this task.

After shaking their hands and bidding them a safe voyage he presented them with a souvenir regimental mug as a memento of their visit. The colonel then provided a carriage to take them to the ship.

The dock was a hive of activity and it took over an hour to find the ship's crew of the SS Ventnor, who were loading the last of the supplies en route for Australia. They waited for the second whaler going to the ship before they embarked, sharing the whaler with several sheep.

They were pleased to be on board the ship again. They paid their respects to the captain and adjourned to their cabins with their reading material. Their fellow passengers had all returned aboard and all looked refreshed. No doubt they had all enjoyed the luxury of a bath. The ship even smelt better as the crew had swabbed all the decks above and below. What a difference it made!

Mrs Marshall had prepared tea and sandwiches for lunch and the passengers exchanged the stories of what they had done and seen in Cape Town.

The first officer had carried out a roll call of the ship's crew and was pleased to be able to report to Captain Marshall, "All present and correct." This was unusual — most ships lost a few crew at transit ports.

The captain nodded and continued to watch the flags on the tall buildings to the west of Table Bay. They showed a weak south westerly breeze. He judged that would be sufficiently strong enough for steerage towards Robben Island. Once clear of the harbour he would turn and tack south down the Cape Peninsula. The ship would then head east around the Cape of Good Hope and then out into and across the Indian Ocean. He finally called to raise the mainsails and the anchor to be weighed. The ship then slowly gained momentum heading across the bay and, after steerage was obtained, it then headed towards Robben Island.

All the passengers and sailors were on deck for the departure. The day was sunny with only a few clouds drifting over Table Mountain. It was a picture card scene. Table Mountain was definitely unique. Its flat top slowly vanished into the distance. The ship turned to port and continued south down past Hout Bay thence to Cape Point. As the ship turned east at the Cape of Good Hope, the vast False Bay appeared on their port side. Table Bay was only five miles wide whereas False Bay was over twenty miles wide. It obviously did not provide the weather shelter that the Table Bay harbour could.

The ship now had all sails raised and was clipping along at

a good rate. They would eventually be a month away from any major land mass in the middle of the Indian Ocean. The closest they would be to land would be Mauritius or Reunion Island. These two islands were often replenishment ports of call for vessels on the way heading west back to Europe. The head winds incurred much slower and longer voyages.

Two days out of Cape Town it was Christmas Day, 1853. The captain held a small religious service on the main deck for the crew and the passengers. They held a separate service in the convict quarters. This was followed by dinner as arranged by Mrs Marshall for the passengers and ship's officers. While it was a most pleasant meal it was rather subdued. The diners' thoughts were of their loved ones far away.

John stood up on the bow and wondered what Maeve was doing at this very moment. His mind wandered to his family in England and Maeve's family in Ireland. What was happening in their counties? No doubt it was snowing, whereas he was sitting in sunlight with a sea breeze in his face.

Christmas was not Christmas without family and the day was soon forgotten.

Below deck Michael was having similar thoughts of his family in Ireland. Momentarily, for some unknown reason, John Hall flashed into his mind.

¶

A month out of Cape Town the winds abated. The sails were flapping and the rigging slapping against the masts. It was difficult sleeping with the noise. The captain decided to head south to see if he could locate some better wind streams. This was a usual tactic employed by many captains in this situation. Over dinner he advised the passengers that the temperature would drop considerably and to unpack any warm clothing to air it. If the clothing had been packed since departing Ireland it would probably be damp and musty by now. Particularly after the storm two months ago.

After five days sailing south east, the temperature dropped suddenly and the waves began to rise. White caps appeared in the distance and the wind increased. The sails filled and the ship leaned into the seas.

The ship was making way again. The sea had developed a long deep swell making the ship pitch up the face of the wave and come crashing down the other side. This swell continued for two days and made sailing decidedly uncomfortable. Only the sailors ventured onto the open decks. The spray made the deck too slippery for the passengers and the marines with their leather shoes. The sailors wore coir rope soled slippers which provided some traction on the wooden deck planks but even so, they still had to hang onto the handrails and ropes for security. The captain ordered the ship change direction and head due east, sailing across the swell. It was less violent but the ship was still bucking around on its axis.

The temperature during the nights approached close to freezing. One morning John opened the lower quarter deck door and looked out onto the main deck to see a light covering of ice on the rigging. He did not venture out and closed the door. If there was ice on the rigging, probably the deck had some ice on it as well.

The convict quarters had their coal heater lit for two weeks now and the area was comfortable except for the motion of the ship in the swells. The continued good health of the convicts had been a pleasant surprise for the doctor. He had identified only a few cases of mild scurvy in convicts who had not taken their daily issue of lime juice due to its sour taste, and also two cases of boils. One marine had a bad case of stomach cramps while the ship's crew and passengers enjoyed good health.

The captain made another navigation correction to intercept forty-two degrees south latitude and followed that track continuing east. The weather gradually improved. The waves were more settled with the wind astern. The sails filled and the ship was making good time again.

When the new course was set, heading due east, the sea life appeared again. Shoals of sleek bonito fish between one and two feet long appeared around the ship for days at a time. The sailors caught some on baited hooks. They had the appearance of a mackerel with a bluish shimmering colour, their outer surface covering was smooth with the dorsal fin stowing into their spine. The sailors found them very difficult to land on the deck when the baited hook had been taken. The fish fought strongly and often jumped up clear of the water. They were a bloody fish and needed to be bled before cooking. Turtles were often seen floating near the ship and had been captured by the sailors by throwing a net from the ship. They were duly cooked but had only an average taste. The diners were of the opinion they would not go out of their way to eat one in the future.

When the weather was predictable, the sea calm with the ship steady, Mrs Marshall introduced the passengers to a game of shovelboard. This consisted of a three foot square divided into nine smaller squares marked one to nine. Each competitor had two wooden discs measuring four inches by one inch and called 'boards'. These boards were slid along the deck aiming to stop in the highest numbered square. The other competitors then tried to move a board into the next highest numbered square from that square, that is, shovel it out.

John and George were both eager competitors and enjoyed many close games. They also spent time reading the books they had purchased in Cape Town and exchanged them with each other. Time was passing quickly and there was a certain excitement in the air, although they still had several weeks of sailing to reach Hobart.

The captain advised his passengers that they were now south of and level with the west coast of Australia and that they were entering the Great Australian Bight but they would still not see land until they reached the west coast of Van Diemen's Land. This would be around another three weeks at their current rate of progress, if the winds continued with their same strength and direction.

Early one morning, the cry from the lookout, "Whales ho, on the port bow", brought both passengers and crew onto the main deck.

John and George went to the bow and saw immediately the spectacular sight of a large pod of whales heading east on the same course as the ship. They lay only slightly to the port and the captain had altered course slightly to starboard to ensure he was not sailing into their path. He counted twenty and called to the lookout to go to the topmast crow's nest and keep a sharp lookout for any whales removed from the main section of the pod. He was concerned about the possibility of a collision. The body mass of a whale could cause major damage to the ship.

The whales were sounding and blowing spumes of water high into the air, diving then surfacing with a large part of their bodies rising from the sea, twisting sideways and then crashing back into the water. The observers watched them for several hours as they slowly out-distanced them.

It was the talk of the dinner table that evening. Only the Marshall's were unimpressed. They had seen whales many times before.

Even the convicts were impressed. They were taking turns to view them from the scuttles.

The weather was deteriorating rapidly. The glass had fallen and John could see that the ship was heading into a rain squall. A large water spout formed to port and appeared to be tracking the same direction as the ship. The captain ordered the ship to batten down. All loose cargo on the main deck was tied down and the animal pens covered. Cupboards were locked. The passengers remembered the previous storm and made sure that they did this time what they did not do then.

When the wind increased John lay on his bunk on his back and tried to concentrate on his reading. Then the rain and wind struck. The rain could be heard above his cabin, striking the quarter deck, such was the volume. The wind was howling through the rigging and even though the sails had been furled the yardarms were swinging and swaying with the strength of the wind. Suddenly an enormous gust of wind struck the ship. It rolled violently and stayed over for fully twenty seconds before righting and heaving itself out of the sea.

All the passengers and marines were thrown from their bunks and the convicts all ended up on the floor against the port bulkhead. The ship steadied and kept its head. The wind had dropped but the dense rain continued for two more hours before ceasing completely.

Almost immediately the sun resumed and they sailed on into a sunny day.

The ship had survived the squall without any damage but many of the convicts, a surveyor and a marine were injured. The convicts fared the worst, suffering broken ribs, a broken nose and one broken arm. The surveyor had been knocked unconscious and the marine had a broken arm.

The doctor was kept busy for several hours and was ably assisted by the farmer's wife. John, George and, ironically, Michael each had their bunks on the port side. Consequently when the ship rolled they only rolled over towards the bulkhead and had been uninjured. The galley was a mess rather than a disaster. Food was everywhere. The main cupboard door had sprung open and allowed all the perishables to be released. However, it was small price to pay for the potential damage that could have occurred.

At dinner that night the captain explained what happened leading to the violent roll incident. The helmsman had been struck in the face by a loose halyard through the open wheel house window. It had temporarily blinded him and he was unable to see when to turn into the seas so the seas struck the ship beam on. The captain said he saw what had happened and grabbed the wheel. He managed to work the wheel to turn the ship into the seas.

¶

The ship sailed on and on, nearing the coast of Van Diemen's land. The captain suggested that it would be in view within the next day or so. The bow now became very popular with the passengers, each hoping to be the first to see the coastline. No doubt the sailor who was the duty lookout, would be the first to see land, as he sat high up on the main mast.

John and George started to discuss their futures; John in particular thinking of his application to Lieutenant Colonel Robert Nickle of the British Regiment, hoping it had been successful. George would not know of his next assignment until he reported to the Marine Regiment in Hobart. He reiterated his thoughts of settling in the colonies in the next year or so. Although he was unsure in what capacity. He felt he could obtain an administrative role with the new Government; George did not really want to continue his military career. He needed a new direction. They both agreed to keep in contact and hopefully their paths would cross again. George's immediate responsibility would cease when he transferred the convicts to the Port Arthur authorities. He hoped that he would have a few days free to see Hobart, its surrounding district and its unusual animals. He might even write a book about the voyage.

Their voyage was nearing its end with a new life on the horizon, for not only John Hall and George Walters, but also for Michael Keogh and his fellow convicts.

CHAPTER FOUR

Van Diemen's Land

 cry finally came from the lookout. "Land ho —
Port bow!" At long last — Van Diemen's Land. All
eyes on the main deck scanned the horizon, while
the convicts retreated into their own thoughts.

What did their futures hold? They'd all heard stories of the
brutality of the jailors and the privations that they might expect.
Although for most of them, the worst part of their sentences
was the distance from their kith and kin. However, one thing
was sure, at least they would not be locked in the hold of a ship
for much longer. Any freedom would be better than what they
had endured over the last four months. Eventual freedom and
possibly a better life was their hope.

The cliffs were getting closer. A small village could be seen
through Captain Marshall's telescope. Several small fishing boats
were visible off shore, no doubt earning a pittance. Elder Mountain
was identifiable with Mount Zeehan at its western end. Captain
Marshall judged his landfall was north of Macquarie Harbour. It
was the entrance to the waterway where the notorious convict
settlement of Sarah Island had been until 1823. He turned his ship
due south to sail parallel to the coast down past Port Davey, eventually turning due east. Port Davey was an estuary with dozens of
islands surrounded by a shoreline with several beaches. The land
was green for as far as one could see. It ranged from grasslands to
forests and rugged seaside cliff with a few sandy beaches.

After passing Macquarie Harbour no sign of habitation was seen — neither boats nor people.

A strong south-easterly wind with rough seas and a long deep swell greeted their turn east towards Maatsuyker Island. There were several islands close to their set course requiring the captain to post three lookouts, one at each mast head. The ship was pitching violently, causing most on board to suffer seasickness. Once he reached longitude one hundred and forty-seven degrees he altered his ship's heading to the north east. The ship entered the D'Entrecasteaux Channel at first light sailing between the mainland and Bruny Island. This course provided some shelter from the gusty winds and turbulent seas. They could see land on both sides of the ship and with the improved weather the deck was full of sightseers. The convicts pushed and shoved to have a look out of the scuttles at their new land.

Slowly settlements became visible. Small cottages sitting on the hills and on the foreshores with smoke lazily rising towards the scattered cloud. Fishing boats of all shapes and sizes were dragged up on the beaches. Their nets were stretched out on long poles drying in the wind. Ploughed paddocks and livestock were grazing on the lush grass. The country was a picture of serenity and apparent contented living. After leaving the shelter of Bruny Island, habitation became denser, more houses, with more substantial buildings appeared on the foreshore.

Finally Hobart Town appeared in the distance. A sense of excitement was in the air. Even Captain and Mrs Marshall were standing arm in arm on the quarter deck, talking happily to each other.

Slowly the harbour revealed its grandeur. It had impressive sandstone buildings, namely Government House, three large warehouses at Salamanca Place and the Customs House. These together with Mount Wellington in the background with a small layer of snow at its peak made a grand sight. The entire scene was bathed in sunshine, creating an excellent first impression of the town. Their first view of Hobart Town was a sight never to be forgotten.

The sailors dropped the anchor, furled the sails and secured the ship for a layover. It was Monday 2nd March 1854. The voyage had taken one hundred and twenty-eight days. The captain noted in his log that, "The voyage has been successfully completed. The ship and the crew are in good condition."

The customs' whaler came alongside with the harbour controller. He met with the captain, which was a normal requirement. The captain showed him his manifest. Some papers were signed and exchanged, followed by a chat over a glass of Madeira. They would meet later after an assessment had been made regarding taxes to be paid to the Crown.

After the controller departed, the captain called for his whaler and, together with Captain Walters, left to visit the Lieutenant-Governor, Sir William Thomas Denison. They walked to Government House which was a short distance up from the docks. The streets were busy with all sorts of citizens going about their business. The assortment of attire was surprising. They ranged from various colourful military uniforms to civil employed 'dandys' attired in the latest fashions, to those poverty stricken citizens clothed in rags.

The town had been built out for several miles and was no longer a bush settlement. There were substantial buildings over an area of some hundred acres to the north and west of the town. The eastern shore, which bordered the Derwent River, a large estuary of the D'Entrecasteaux Channel, had a ferry providing a service from the town across to Kangaroo Point, a distance of over a mile. The nearest bridge was some ten miles upstream, north up past the original Van Diemen's Land settlement of Risdon.

The Governor's aide, a young military officer, greeted them. After a short wait they were shown into the Governor's office. Introductions were quite formal and after the normal voyage reports had been completed, the Governor invited the two captains to a side table. The aide arranged for drinks and appropriate food to be served. The subject of the convicts was raised by the Governor. Captain Marshall advised that he had been told by an official of the Colonial Office, that this party of convicts would be one of the last destined to be sent to Van Diemen's Land. This was believed to be the decision resulting from the Van Diemen's Land Legislative Council submission. The convicts would now go to Western Australia as the farmers there had requested them. However, what he had been told was unofficial as Parliament needed to approve the change of policy.

The Governor said, "That is disappointing news to me. I am a staunch supporter of the supply of convicts to assist in the labour requirements of this colony. I would appreciate it if you could keep this information to yourself until it is confirmed from London."

"Captain Walters, what of your convicts? What background do they have and where are they from?" asked the Governor.

"They are predominately Irish activists with a few non-violent felons, burglary, theft etc. But there are several tradesmen amongst them and they will be an asset to the Crown and indeed the colony. They gave very little trouble on the voyage and I believe they could make a valuable contribution to the colony in the long term," he replied.

The Governor stood up, indicating the audience was over. The captains thanked him for his time, shook hands and left the office.

During their absence, the vessel owner's agent had rowed to the ship and met with the first officer. He advised him that he had a consignment of Huon pine and cedar timber. Also to keep a secure cabin available for a special consignment to be collected at the Williamstown dock in Victoria. This consignment would be collected by the Colonial Office in Plymouth and the timber by the vessel owners. The Governor's aide had informed the penal authorities of the arrival of the convicts. The authorities arrived at the ship at the same time as the two captains returned. The chief constable had the port doctor with him and two clerks. After the introductions were completed, Captain Walters and two of his marines opened the hatchways and led the group down into the convicts' quarters.

The convicts were ordered to undress and step forward when their name was called. They were examined by the port doctor with the ship's doctor as an observer. After the examination the convicts washed and donned a new set of clothes and then paraded on deck. For most of the convicts, this was the first day out of their quarters for around four months. They lined up and gazed around them like children, some fainted, others had trouble walking but all were happy to be out of their quarters.

They were shackled and then the chief constable's clerk called out their names. The convicts stepped forward and were asked to describe their work history. Initially, all would serve one month as a probationer at Port Arthur or Richmond and then be assigned as their behaviour dictated. The chief constable then decided their assignments, whether it be in a trustee position with the Government, a farmer, a tradesman or to stay in jail to complete their sentence.

Michael, as a qualified shipwright, knew that he would be in demand and was determined to keep himself out of trouble during his probationary period. It was late in the afternoon so it was decided not to transfer the convicts until the next morning. The Port Arthur authorities had a small sloop to transport the convicts from Hobart Harbour to the Port Arthur Gaol dock.

The following morning, the sloop came alongside and a ramp was made fast between the two ships. The convicts were told to transfer across to the sloop. Guards were at each end of the sloop and watched the convicts like hawks. They did not want any of them trying to swim to shore even though they were shackled. The convicts were herded into the cargo hold with the guards moving aft. The sailors released the lines, the ships separated, and the sloop slowly headed downstream south east to Storm Bay. The wind was still strong, and the sloop heeled to port with the bow spray increasing, stinging the eyes of the forward hands.

The spray entered the open cargo hold and many of the convicts, together with new clothes were soon drenched. This discomfort was a taste of things to come. Forty miles from Hobart Town the sloop reached Point Raoul, the southern point of the Port Arthur Peninsula. It then turned to port to sail up alongside the coastline of Maingon Bay. Within an hour or so Port Arthur Bay appeared on the port bow. The buildings were much larger than Michael expected. It looked like a reasonably sized town and somewhat forbidding.

❡

John Hall went ashore immediately after the two captains had gone to see the Governor. He stayed at a small inn in Macquarie Street for four days and carried out some sightseeing. He spent one day travelling with George to Richmond, which was George's new posting. Richmond had a small jail guarded by a military company and George had been promoted to Deputy

Commandant of Richmond Gaol. It was a small hamlet forty miles from Hobart on the Coal River. It had been a very early settlement with a dozen or so impressive sandstone buildings including the jail. The two friends dined together for the last time and bid each other farewell.

John caught a coach back to the harbour and called the ship for the whaler to collect him. The surveyors had returned to the ship in the morning.

John wrote some more letters to both to his family and the Keogh's, in particular to Maeve. He was looking forward to reaching Melbourne and hopefully receiving some letters for himself. Other ships would have reached Melbourne before them even though they had left England earlier. The captain sent John's letters ashore with the last of his paperwork and he was now ready to depart for Victoria.

¶

The sloop tied up alongside the Port Arthur dock. The convicts were then ordered off the sloop and made to form two lines. The commandant arrived with an entourage of six — a military officer, a senior constable and four supervisors. The convicts were given a lecture on the merits of conforming to the jail regulations and the disciplinary measures that were in place. They were also advised that their behaviour over the first twelve months in Port Arthur would decide the direction of the rest of their lives.

The convicts were divided into groups related to their education, skills and their offences. Michael was identified as one of five who were educated, skilled and was not a political activist. The other seventy-five were separated into three groups — one as unskilled and uneducated, another group of uneducated political activists and the final group of educated activists. The final group remained at Port Arthur for one month and afterwards were given positions in the government in both Hobart and Launceston, after they signed a pledge — not to attempt to escape!

Within six months the other uneducated political activists were assigned to various farms throughout Van Diemen's Land, under a similar agreement. The unskilled were retained at Port Arthur for the time being and would be employed assisting in farming and timber felling and carting. Only seven, who had carried out serious crimes, were jailed.

The five in Michael's group were marched to the supervisor's office. Michael was called first into his inner office. The supervisor eyed him without saying a word. Michael looked back at him for a while and then averted his eyes. He didn't want to be caught in a staring competition.

The supervisor sat down. "I have read your offence. Tell me what happened in your own words and don't lie. If I find out that you have lied to me you will be sent to the rock pile."

Michael told his story exactly how it happened.

The supervisor said, "You are said to be a shipwright. For how long and with whom and how long did you go to school?"

Michael replied, "I went to school for eight years and was a shipwright with my uncle's shipyard in Kilrush."

"What size ships did you work on?"

"All sizes from Indianmen and Ships of War down to river fishing boats," Michael replied.

The supervisor had heard enough. "Dismissed. Send the next man in." The orderly opened the door and told him to get back into line.

Michael was dumbfounded. He didn't know what to think. Had he said something wrong?

After the five of them had been questioned by the supervisor they were taken to a mess room for a meal and to collect a mattress, a blanket and pillow. Then they were taken to a large dormitory and allocated a bunk. The bunk was narrow but at least he was by himself and it was not pitching and rolling. The five of them were the last into the dormitory and were bunking close to each other. Three of them were from County Clare and they would get to know and rely upon each other over the coming months.

Seamus Lynch had been caught poaching. He had been doing it on and off for years. It was inevitable that he would be caught. He had been a roof thatcher, had hit his employer and that was his last job. He was five years older than Michael and also from County Clare. They had similar backgrounds and soon became friends. The other convict from County Clare was Thomas Byrne. He had been convicted of stealing two bottles of rum from a local tavern owned by an ex-British Army officer. Together with his barman, they had caught Thomas and handed him over to the constabulary. The three convicts had each been sentenced to seven years penal servitude and transportation overseas. Another thing they had in common!

Ten convicts from the SS Ventnor were assigned to the timber yard, including Michael, Seamus and Thomas. The work was primarily cutting and shaping timbers for the Port Arthur boatyard. After the first days sawing, all ten of the men had blistered hands. It took over a week for them to get used to the manual work.

Michael was soon noted to be experienced at the shaping of the timbers and was soon appointed as leader of the team. There were only two other workers who were shipwrights and they ran the shipyard. They had been there for twelve months and were due to leave very soon. The shipyard built small single mast fishing boats for local sale to encourage fishing for the local market.

The colony was having serious problems with food supplies due to the change in policy for the supply of farm labourers. Several years previously probation stations were introduced to help reform convicts. Unfortunately, it denied farmers of having assigned convicts to assist in the farming of their lands.

This policy had consequently created a food shortage for the entire colony. The convicts were reasonably well fed; porridge for breakfast with bread and water. Lunch consisted of soup, boiled meat, potatoes and sometimes cabbage. The last daily meal was a quarter of a loaf of bread and tea. They had to eat all of their food during their meal and were not permitted to hoard food. A different convict was selected periodically to represent their peers to see if the food had been prepared satisfactorily.

Michael was advised that previously, on Sunday mornings, the convicts were marched to the only church at Port Arthur. On arrival at the church the order would be given, "Halt, Roman Catholics fall out." The Catholics were then required to stand in their ranks until the service was completed — rain, hail or shine. Sometimes they were afforded a priest who visited from Sorell.

Michael was pleasantly surprised to find that Catholics now had their own service with a priest. No conversation was allowed. The convicts used church as a means to pass on gossip by replacing words in their hymns. It took Michael a while to pick up the replaced words and make sense of a conversation.

This could not be done by the more incorrigible convicts or those who had misbehaved in other parts of the prison and had been sent to the Model Prison. In this prison each prisoner was in a cubicle which made it impossible for them to see who else was in the church or be able to communicate with one another. When these prisoners were exercised they wore a full face mask with only eye holes. Michael had heard of the Model Prison and hoped he would not fall foul of the system and become an inmate.

On a Sunday they were allowed to visit the library and obtain a book. Times were changing as there had been a rumour since they had arrived that transportation would be ceasing for this colony. Clerks were exempt from manual labour and some even had their own rooms. The commandant was a firm man but also fair. Surprisingly he was respected by many of the convicts. The punishments of the early days no longer existed. Flogging was now almost non-existent, although some of the inmates were particularly vicious, mainly the ones who had been sent from Norfolk Island. Some were still jailed whereas many of the inmates were almost free men and worked on farms breeding sheep and cattle, growing hops, grains and vegetables. All were necessary agriculture products for the colony's survival. Others with an appropriate level of education were employed in various government offices.

Thomas performed his tasks well and was recognised for his good behaviour. He was to be released as a probationary constable and was to be sent to Launceston. Michael and Seamus were disappointed to lose a friend but acknowledged his good fortune.

Michael was further promoted to be in charge of one of the boat building crews. He enjoyed this position until he was advised that no replacement shipwrights had arrived in the colony. He then realised that if he couldn't be replaced he was destined to remain in the colony indefinitely. He had hoped his performance and good behaviour would assist him in being freed early.

The shipyard was several miles west of the neck of land which was the entrance to the Port Arthur settlement. It was guarded by ten or so dogs. The dogs were tied up in such a way that they were only separated by less than a yard. They were all different breeds ranging from hounds to fox terriers. Whilst there were guards positioned with the dogs, the main deterrent in attempting to escape wasn't the guards but the noise the barking dogs created when they saw anyone other than their handlers. With any easterly wind blowing Michael could hear the dogs barking when the horse teams came through with their various cargos.

Michael's dilemma had generated some vague thoughts of escape. He needed a plan for bypassing the dogs. Several escapes via the Eaglehawk Neck had failed. One attempt had been made by an escapee who tried to swim past the guards under a large headdress of sea weed. He nearly succeeded but he travelled too fast and a guard saw him and fired his rifle which caused the convict to surrender. The only successful escape from Port Arthur had been via Norfolk Bay north of the settlement. This was Michael's focus for an escape.

Seamus had been assigned to drive a wagon loaded with timber to Sorell escorted by two constables. They duly arrived after an uneventful trip and offloaded the timber. They were not due to leave until the next day so the three of them made a shelter under the wagon from an old ship's sail for the night's sleep.

Seamus left Sorell in the early morning with the team of four horses and a wagonload of barrels full of vinegar, wine and beer. He and the two constables rode on the high seat enjoying a good view of the surrounding countryside. The long, rolling, green flatlands leading to the low shoreline with its saltbush scrubs made for a peaceful scene. The only sounds were the clip-clop of the horses' hooves and the clinking of the harness. They expected to arrive in the early evening. It had not rained for a few weeks so the problem of being bogged by wet low ground was non-existent and there were no other difficulties expected.

They came to a steep road leading to a bridge over a creek at the base of the road and then there was a sharp turn to the right. The wagon wound down the road with Seamus riding the brake, suddenly the pivot pin on the brake pedal sheared and the wagon surged forward. The horses picked up their pace and slowly started to gallop. Seamus called to the constables to jump and the three of them jumped together and rolled off the side of the road. As the horses were approaching the creek bridge, the turntable pin sheared and the wagon and the horses separated with the horses galloping over the bridge and around the bend successfully and continuing on into the distance.

The wagon hit the bridge side and tilted. The load of barrels slowly slid sideways towards the bridge edge. The barrels spilled from the tray and rolled down into the creek bed thirty feet below, several of the barrels split on impact showering their contents into the air. The wagon was left hanging on the edge supported by several bridge uprights. The broken barrel panels floated down the creek eventually jamming into a narrow neck of the stream under a large and heavily foliaged tree which hid the barrels effectively. These barrels would be an eventual means of escape.

The two constables and Seamus were unharmed by their desperate jump and walked down to the bridge. Only two barrels appeared to be undamaged. One other barrel was lying on the bank and was split open, but otherwise intact. They climbed down and were pleased to find the split barrel on the bank contained beer.

They had two mugs in their packs and so decided to have a drink, 'On the house'.

The horses eventually arrived back at the Neck. They had travelled the road before so it was natural they would follow the road back to Port Arthur. A search team was organized the next morning and they found the three of them late that evening sitting under a tree sheltering from the light rain that was falling. The group was worse for wear due to exposure to the cold night air and wet weather. Beer was not mentioned! The search team pulled two intact barrels from the creek and dragged the wagon back onto the road, hitched up the horses, loaded the two barrels and headed back to Port Arthur.

Michael knew Seamus was missing and wondered whether he had seen an opportunity to escape and taken it. He would miss Seamus's company and hoped he had made good his escape. However when Seamus returned with the search party he was pleased but soon felt guilty that he did not feel disappointed that Seamus had not escaped. When Seamus told Michael the details of the incident, he immediately showed interest in where the creek flowed.

Seamus asked, "Why? What do have in mind?"

Michael said, "Perhaps the wood and the hoops can be used for a small boat." Michael still had visions of paddling across Norfolk Bay then traveling to Sorell, up past Richmond and then north to get passage across Bass Strait to Victoria. He had access to woodworking tools. All he needed were these materials and the opportunity.

Michael explained his plan. He thought he could reassemble five barrels and bolt four of them together in a square. Then cut two holes for Seamus and him to sit in. The fifth barrel would be connected to one side of the bolted barrels; this would stop the four barrels from rolling over. Paddles could be shaped from other barrel pieces. All he needed now was to locate the broken barrels and find the opportunity to build his 'boat'.

Michael made a mission of learning the topography of the Port Arthur area. He managed to plot the initial course of the creek to a spot about a mile from the bridge. He decided to explore this area whenever the chance arose. This chance happened sooner than he expected. He was assigned to a working party to locate suitable timber for a twenty foot fishing boat.

As the shipwright he was virtually leading the party with the guard only following. He led the party near to the creek and asked them to spread out and head north. He told them what type of tree and what height he wanted. He went to the creek and headed in the same direction. The creek widened as it got nearer to the coast and, looking downstream, he could see a narrowed section with several large trees across it. As he got closer he could see some of the broken barrels in a small backwater. He went closer and saw that there were over a dozen barrels trapped in the inlet. As a bonus he saw the area was quite close to Norfolk Bay. After an examination of the damage to the barrels, he was satisfied that he would have sufficient intact wooden barrel panels to be able to assemble his boat. He then decided to meet up with the rest of the party and find out if they had located any suitable trees, which fortunately they had.

This now gave him the perfect opportunity to build his boat when the trees were being trimmed for transporting to the ship yard. Over the next two weeks Michael managed to find an hour or two away from the work party to assemble the barrels. He found sufficient hoops to wedge the wood panels together. He then filled the barrels with water to allow them to swell and become water tight. After a week he emptied the water and bolted the five barrels together then wedged the boat at the top of a steep section of the creek. After hiding the boat under a covering of ferns Michael returned to his work party, full of anticipation of the future.

Michael and Seamus decided to wait for a night with cloud, no moon and a southerly wind blowing. Michael tracked the tides from what he had learnt on his previous trips to the creek.

He hoped the night would be an outgoing tide in Norfolk Bay. They intended to create a fire at the saw mill and if the smoke was dense enough it might blind the semaphore lookouts from seeing them. The semaphore lookout system of signals were relayed across the island settlement onto Hobart within five minutes. This advised of an escaped convict, or bolter, as they were commonly called. It was manned by convicts and was extremely efficient. Michael hoped to nullify their effectiveness during their escape attempt.

The saw mill had accumulated a large pile of sawdust, forty feet by twelve feet, adjacent the timber storage area. The sawdust was used in the manufacturing of mud bricks and was mixed with some adhesives to fill in gaps in woodwork. Over a period of two weeks Michael had assigned Seamus to work on the sawdust pile. To all intents Seamus was moving the pile of new sawdust from the saw mill onto the pile. However, he was, in fact, creating a one foot tunnel by placing half sections of tree bark upside down to form a hollow into the centre of the pile. Thomas had volunteered to light an oil soaked rag on the end of a long pole and poke the pole deep into the sawdust pile. This was to be done at the end of the work day just before the guards came to march them all back to their quarters.

Michael had moved two small dinghies near to the pile and the entry to the tunnel. A small hot coal from the steamer used to bend wood would be collected in a tin and taken to the pole and oil cloth which would be positioned between the dinghies. It was expected that the smoke would appear within two hours and the sawdust would be well alight internally and generate a considerable amount of smoke.

The plan was now in place but needed to be carried out before Thomas was released. They had already waited two weeks. Michael had been closely watching the weather patterns over the last three days and now was the time.

The next morning arrived and the three friends wished each other luck, hoping to meet again one day.

Michael took a team of workers, including Seamus, to collect some felled timber. They worked quickly and had all the timber loaded by late afternoon. The work party started back with the constable riding on the first wagon. Michael knew the constable from many previous work parties. He asked him if he and Seamus could mark some more trees, then they would head straight back to their quarters, as he didn't wish to come back tomorrow for only one hour of work. He knew the constable would agree and he did!

Michael and Seamus immediately ran to where they had hidden the barrel boat. They launched it by sliding it down the bank. They checked it for leaks, stepped in and started to paddle downstream. Michael noticed the tide was high but he was unsure how long it had been high. He needed the tide to turn within the hour as it would be dark by then and they would be in the bay. It would give them several hours paddling with an outgoing tide and a good speed. The craft was easy to handle and had plenty of freeboard so it could handle a small choppy sea. The southerly wind was blowing at around ten to twenty knots which would carry the saw dust smoke directly at the nearest semaphore station.

They had been rowing for nearly an hour when Seamus pointed excitedly to the sky. White smoke was blowing from the south. Thomas had succeeded in igniting the sawdust. Their plan was working. It was dark now and Michael was pleased to see the tide was running out.

The men paddled out of the creek entrance into Norfolk Bay hugging the shore. Seamus looked back and could not see the semaphore station; it was enveloped in smoke. The night was very dark with no moon and total cloud and it made hugging the shore line difficult. Seamus suggested moving out a hundred yards or so to head in a straighter line. Michael agreed and they made better progress.

They rowed for over two hours but then suddenly Michael heard the sound of oars slapping the water and voices. He steered into shore and hid under a large tree with branches that hung to the water. It was a patrol boat from Port Arthur. Michael knew that they had a boat which patrolled the bay and he also knew of the risk of being detected. They held their breaths as it got closer and closer. They could hear the crew talking but they did not appear to be searching for anyone; they were more intent at looking back towards the prison. Michael and Seamus waited for the boat to vanish into the darkness and the crew's voices to no longer be heard before they started paddling again. When they moved away from the shore Seamus looked back and could see the redness in the sky. The fire was well under way. The plan had worked.

They now had to cross the bay to reach the northern shore. The wind was stronger in the middle and there were small choppy waves. They both paddled silently, each with their own concerns — Seamus worried about the choppy seas and Michael wondering when the tide was going to stop running out of the bay.

They had been paddling now for around six hours. The lights of a farm house appeared out of the darkness and soon the shoreline became visible with a small beach to their right. The barrel boat touched the sandy bottom and both men had difficulty trying to stand up after squatting in their barrel for so long. After a good long stretch, they looked around but could see no sign of life. Where were they?

Michael guessed they were near a place called Carlton Beach, from what he had heard from convicts at the prison. He decided not to sink the boat but let it float back into Norfolk Bay. It would confuse the eventual search parties as to where they had landed. He found out later that it did. The search parties went south east as they believed that the escapees headed up the east coast of the colony. The fire had caused considerable confusion as the fire fighting facilities consisted of a bucket brigade and a team of not very enthusiastic convicts. The heat and the smoke were intense and the commandant was concerned that the fire would spread to the valuable timber ready for cartage to Hobart Town.

It took until dawn to get the fire under control. Three other convicts had tried to escape during the night but were caught in Port Arthur. Michael and Seamus were not identified as missing until breakfast roll call.

The commandant said of Michael, "I knew I shouldn't have told him that we had no replacement for him."

Michael and Seamus decided to walk as far as they could in the darkness and find a safe site to sleep during the next day. They walked adjacent the western coast line. They saw two homesteads and gave them a very wide berth to avoid their dogs hearing them. They stopped walking when the sun started to appear in the east. Michael was pleased he now knew that they had walked north as planned.

They found a wooded section with some ferns which they broke off to make into a makeshift bed. The two exhausted men slept until late afternoon.

Seamus showed his poaching skills by catching possums and kangaroos. The animals were plentiful and easily trapped in his snares. He sometimes snared a devil, which he let go. This small animal had a large head with sharp teeth and they were too vicious to handle and kill. It was a thickset furry animal which grew to around twenty inches long and was unique to Van Diemen's Land.

The creeks had eels and fish. The eels were difficult to snare but the fish were easily caught. Sometimes they managed to spear a fish and if they were lucky they would find swan eggs.

One morning Michael was sitting quietly on a creek bank looking into the water when he realised he was looking at an animal that he not seen before. It had a duck's bill, a body like a beaver and four webbed clawed feet and was swimming slowly along the creek, occasionally stirring up the creek bed with its bill. He had read a few articles on the unique animals of these colonies and guessed correctly that the animal was a platypus. He sat there mesmerised by the sight and the antics of the animal and did not move until the platypus vanished downstream.

They continued walking north avoiding farms and roads. The terrain was mostly flat and fortunately the weather was good with sunny days and mild nights. Once they saw a military squad in the distance and so changed direction to move east in the opposite direction.

After walking for four days, they reached Sorell and were fortunate that they arrived on the day of the weekly market. They went to the market at first light when there were few people around. They traded two kangaroo hind legs for two loaves of bread, a packet of matches and a flagon of milk. Michael and Seamus had had plenty to eat but had missed the luxury of having bread. Then they immediately left the town and quickly headed north towards Richmond, through the bush, avoiding the roads and bush tracks.

They were crossing a dirt track when they heard a woman talking. Skirting a row of trees they stepped out and came face to face with a farmer and a heavily pregnant woman. The four stood, startled, and looked at each other for a second or two.

The farmer moved in front of his wife and held up a shovel to protect her.

Michael could see that their wagon was bogged deep in a wheel rut mud hole. He spoke first. "We mean you no harm. Can we help you?" Michael's soft Irish voice allayed their fears.

"We have been stranded here since last night and I want to get my wife home quickly," said the farmer.

Michael and Seamus nodded and looked at each other. They moved to the wagon to see for themselves. The cargo had been unloaded by the farmer and he had dug a long trench in front of the wheel but the wheel was still sunk in the mud.

"Why not try to dig it out backwards?" suggested Seamus. They all agreed to give this method a try. They dug a long trench until the soil appeared less muddy. Then the horse was hitched to the middle of the back of the wagon and after a lot of shouting, pushing by the men and pulling by the horse the cart came free.

The woman was in tears of delight. The farmer asked Seamus where he had learnt the trick and Seamus told him of his farming and poaching days.

The farmer laughed. "I thought you might be thieves. I didn't think of you as a poacher. So that's why you were a convict. What about your friend?" He turned to Michael. "What did you do?" When Michael told him, the farmer said, "Good for you."

The farmer stood looking at them and after sizing them up he said, "I owe you for your help today. I need farm labourers and there are none available. Would you like to work for me? I live a fair way out from the towns and villages and after growing my vegetables and fruit I lose too much time traveling to markets to sell them. I can make more if I travel and you do much of the farming. I also have some sheep that need crutching and shearing once a year. Plus I need to extend the farmhouse. I'll pay you and give you board and keep and a change of clothes so that you can burn your prison clothes. Come with me now, rest up and think about my offer."

Michael and Seamus agreed to accept the farmer's offer to rest up, and to think about his proposition. The wagon ride took around four hours. During this time the farmer's wife was very quiet. Her face was drawn with worry. She wanted to be home safe and comfortable in her farm.

The farm was situated in a small valley close to a deep creek. The farmhouse was well built and surrounded by two other buildings and a small orchard. The land was well grassed and they could see sheep grazing on the hillside. Across the creek, via a sturdy wooden bridge, were several large vegetable plots. The vegetables ensured a constant income not like grain food which was not only seasonal but suspect to weather conditions.

Michael guessed the farmer had cleared around two hundred acres for cultivation and grazing. He felt a pang of sadness; the scene reminded him of home.

The farmer's name was Albert Alford and his wife was Heather. They were free settlers from Yeovil in Somerset and had come out with their parents thirty years ago. Albert's parents were farmers and lived near Orford on the east coast on a large sheep property. His father was also the Shire President and a leader in the local community.

"My parents often visit and will no doubt come to see the new baby," he said. "You will meet them if you accept my offer." Seeing the looks on their faces, the farmer laughed. "Don't worry; my father has no liking for the British system as it is now. He's a self-made man who received no help on his way up the ladder. Incidentally, my mother is Irish from Tipperary; her maiden name was Breen, so have no fear." He looked at the mantle clock. "Now let's get you sorted out with a bath and some clothes and then I'll see how my wife is faring. She is close to her time."

Albert continued, "I hope it is an easy birth. She refused to go to town or have a midwife. I did one year of medicine at university and she keeps telling me she has complete confidence in me."

One of the two buildings outside was the labourers' quarters. It was spacious and clean and had three small rooms. There was a bath at the end of the quarters with water heated over an open fire. After they had bathed Albert brought in some clothes and suggested that they try them on for fit and then burn the prison clothes in the open fire and to do a good job of burning them.

Michael and Seamus could not believe their good luck. They sat down to discuss the pros and cons of staying there as farm labourers. The biggest risk they faced was, the longer they stayed increased the possibility of discovery. On the other hand the longer they stayed gave them the chance to establish themselves somehow in the community as tradesmen. Michael came up with the suggestion that they stay long enough to learn how to shear sheep and grade wool and then travel between towns. While they were prisoners they had not shaved or had their hair cut. If they kept themselves well groomed and trimmed their eyebrows they would be difficult to recognise. He also suggested they wear high heeled American boots.

Seamus agreed to stay but needed to think about the suggestion of becoming an itinerant shearer, although he conceded that they could work anywhere in the colonies, by being shearers.

Albert was delighted that they had agreed to stay and work for him. They agreed upon a period of three months.

They started next morning furrowing for a new planting of vegetables.

The Alford's baby arrived early in the morning two days later. Albert called loudly for help from Seamus who had helped in the birth of his sister's first baby. The birth was uncomplicated and Seamus was more for moral support.

Heather was so grateful she named the boy Seamus. When Albert introduced himself and Heather, Michael and Seamus did not give him their family names. They had previously decided to call each other Mick and Jack respectively and that if challenged they would say that they were deserters from the SS Ventnor. It was not unusual for ships to have crewmen desert after a long voyage. They made an allowance with the Alford's by telling them their true story as they had helped each other in their hour of need and had now formed a common bond of trust.

For the next month they planted vegetables and they soon had results. Albert had extended the vegetable plots by over a third of the original plots.

By the end of the three months it was time to harvest the vegetable crops. It was so large it took three separate trips to the Sorell market. Michael went to market with Albert. With his close cropped hair, trimmed eyebrows, no beard and a deep suntan, no one even looked at him as other than a farmer.

The crop was a bumper. The prices exceeded Albert's expectations and he was delighted. Both Michael and Seamus were given a handsome bonus. Life was good.

At dinner one evening, Albert announced that his father and mother were coming to visit. Michael and Seamus froze and did not respond. Albert was surprised as he thought that he had gained their confidence and that they trusted his judgement of what his father's attitude to them would be.

Heather resolved the impasse. "Seamus, you should remember you helped in the birth of his only grandson; that surely must convince you that he will be supportive of both you and Michael."

It did convince him and although their three months were up, no one mentioned it and they stayed on to meet Albert's father. It was a good piece of advice that Albert had given to Michael and Seamus, to destroy their prison uniforms, as they found out after Alfred's family left for their home at Orford.

George Henry Alford and his wife, Mary, were obviously wealthy. Their coach was highly polished as was their coachman resplendent in his uniform. However, they were not pompous as one would have thought as a first impression.

Albert introduced Michael and Seamus and each felt the warmth in the firm handshake he returned. The women departed to the nursery Michael had made. The men went to the parlour.

Michael had been dreading this moment but George spoke first. "Albert has been telling me about you two. You certainly caused an uproar for a month or so." Looking at them closely he continued. "It's a pity the government at the time didn't give people in your predicament the opportunity to work for the colonies with the skills they possess. Although in your case I'm referring to your farming skills, not the other."

Seamus gave a wry smile.

The women returned from the nursery with baby Seamus, who became the centre of attention.

Mary Alford turned to Seamus. "It's nice to have a touch of Irish in Albert and Heather's family. Thank you for being there for Albert." Mary spoke with a soft but firm voice. She was no doubt a good strong woman to partner George. She had left Ireland as a young girl with her widowed mother, who had since died. She met George at a dance and they had been together ever since. They loved Van Diemen's Land, and even though they had travelled to England twice to see George's relatives, they had no intention of returning.

They only stayed at the farm for two days. The men folk walked around Albert's property, each giving a comment of what to and what not to do. Shearing was due and there were over three hundred sheep. This would be a learning curve for Michael and Seamus. Albert would prove to be a very capable tutor.

After dinner on the second night George called Michael and Seamus into the parlour and handed them each a letter. The letter they were handed stated that were personally known to him and to render any assistance to them that they might need.

Michael and Seamus were speechless. Two days ago they were fearful at the prospect of meeting this man and here he was giving them a letter of support. They were made out in the names of Mick Somerset Esquire and Jack Lodge Esquire. He signed the letters with his title of Shire President and Justice of the Peace. They all laughed at his name selections. The thanks that they gave him seemed inadequate for this extraordinary favour.

The women shed tears while the men gave hearty handshakes. As a final gesture, George Alford invited the men to visit them at any time at Somerset Lodge, his Orford property. The meeting was most memorable.

During the visit, the coachman had slept in the third bedroom in the labourers' quarters. He was a very reserved person who kept to himself and did not enter into any conversation whatever. On the day of departure, the men rose early as was the custom, leaving the coachman asleep.

After the visitors departed, Seamus went to his room and found several of his clothes had been moved. He immediately told Michael, who found a similar situation with his belongings. It was a wake-up call for them to be alert at all times, regardless of having a friend in high places.

Thank god they had heeded Albert's advice and burnt everything from the prison. They mentioned this incident to Albert to warn his father of his coachman's prowling.

Shearing had started and both Michael and Seamus soon realised that they needed, not only skills, but a strong back. For the first week they lay in a hot bath to ease their sore back muscles. By the second week they were becoming skilled and confident and the soreness gradually disappeared.

For a few days Seamus had been intrigued by an animal pelt on the back of the shearing shed door. It was the size of a medium dog but it had a large head. The pelt was mainly brown with dark stripes radiating from the middle of the back downwards; the stripes were more pronounced towards the hind quarters. He mentioned it to Alfred, who took Seamus into the house and showed him the skull of the animal and also a drawing of it. Alfred explained that it was called a thylacine or, locally, a wolf although some mistakenly called it a tiger. It was native to Van Diemen's Land. The skull had larger jaws than an ordinary dog and opened much wider. Wolves were creating problems for sheep farmers by the indiscriminate killing of their sheep and were now being shot on sight.

With the noise of the sheep dogs barking and rounding up the sheep it was a satisfying life. Their sheep were merino cross and produced quality fine wool, much in demand in the mills of Milan and Manchester.

By the end of the shearing, Albert announced with a flourish that they were now shearers. They knew how to shear and crutch, and separate the belly wool and scraps from the main fleece. They could grade the quality and roll the fleece ready for pressing. They would now be able to get a shearing job anywhere. The wool clip returned another handsome profit for Albert and a bonus for Michael and Seamus.

That night they all sat down to decide their future. Albert and Heather knew they would leave eventually but were secretly hoping they would stay indefinitely.

Michael and Seamus told Albert of their idea to go north as a shearing team, seeking jobs on the way.

Albert asked, "How do you intend to travel?"

"We intend to buy a small wagon, like yours."

Albert said, "You can have mine; I still have the big wagon." After much protesting, from both sides, Michael and Seamus became the proud owners of a wagon plus a horse and gear and a sheep dog.

Albert then told them of his plans. They had an offer to purchase their farm and also his mother and father had asked him to manage the Orford farm so that they could retire. They had intended to sell next year but a year earlier suited all parties.

The time for parting arrived and with a tearful Heather and some stiff upper lips and handshakes they each bid farewell. Seamus and Michael promised to visit the Orford farm and keep corresponding with them.

They first drove to Sorell to a coach repairer and had a sign painted on the two sides and the back gate. 'Shearing — We have a dog.' It was done quickly and they were away, heading to Richmond. They got their first job a mile out of Richmond on the Cambridge Road. It was only fifty sheep but they were now in business. They still had short haircuts, trimmed eyebrows, were clean shaven and smelt of lanolin from the wool. They decided to write down every shearing job they obtained, to use as references for future jobs.

After they completed this job they drove to Richmond and stayed at the Bridge Inn, next to the jail and court house. They stayed the night and early next morning headed out over the Coal River Bridge, up past the church and then east towards the coast. Two days later a horseman chased them, asking them to shear one hundred and fifty sheep. They were now shearing faster and completed the job in two days. The dog had got used to them by now and worked well following their commands. He was saving them hours with his efficiency at rounding up the sheep. Most sheep runs had poorly trained dogs. They could keep sheep moving in a mob but were incapable of moving a small flock to a pen.

When they reached Buckland, the men restocked with flour, sugar, salt and tea. They had cured meat from the previous farm where they had done some shearing. The next part of their trip took them over a rugged mountain range that separated them from the coastal plains. The tracks made by previous travellers helped them to keep moving but several times they had to dismantle the cart and carry it over a difficult ridge or waterway.

They searched for hours to find a way to lead the horse over a ridge. It took five days to reach the east coast flatlands, where they rested for a day before moving on. By the time they reached the coastline they had had three more jobs and now had money to spare. The scenery had changed. The sea could be seen through the low foliage bordering the coast and it was a pleasant change from the never ending inland gum trees they had been traversing through for the last two weeks.

The road sign said — 'Orford 2 miles'. The sea breeze was chilly but refreshing and the scene was impressive with its white caps dancing on the waves and the foaming surf crashing on the sandy shore. The blue sea stretched to the horizon, only a small schooner interrupting the skyline. Michael and Seamus truly appreciated their freedom at this moment. They turned north up the road towards the town. George Alford had provided them with a map directing them to the Somerset Lodge farm. Soon the farm sign appeared. They turned the cart and headed up the long driveway towards a row of buildings sited on the top of a low ridge about a mile away.

The paddocks had grazing sheep that were overdue for shearing. Michael and Seamus looked at each other and nodded in silence. They may be here for quite a while! They could hear several dogs barking from the direction of the buildings as they ran down to meet them. Their sheep dog started barking in return and together they created an almighty din.

A horseman rode down to Michael and Seamus and asked their business. He told them to continue up the drive to the big house, then he turned and rode off, the dogs following him.

They reached the end of the driveway and stopped in the front of the large English style manor house.

The front door opened and out stepped George Alford, beaming at them. "Welcome. Please do come in. It's good to see both of you again. My wife is away today but returns tomorrow and will be delighted to see you two again." George led them to his lounge room. He called his house maid to prepare them a bath each and said he had a 'Cow coming in' and wanted to ensure everything went smoothly. He would meet them here for dinner

They were shown to the west wing, each to their own bedroom with a separate bathroom. They enjoyed lolling in their respective baths and did not return to the lounge until late afternoon.

On arrival they were each offered a Madeira wine or a whisky. The men were in an environment with which they were unfamiliar but one they found enjoyable.

George arrived nearly a half hour late but he was smiling and advised that the cow had dropped an excellent young bull with no difficulties. Dinner was then served.

George immediately asked them to tell him of their travels from Alfred's farm and how their shearing work was going.

He listened attentively, asking a question here and there, and he was pleased to hear of the number of sheep flocks and the increase of crops in the districts through which they had travelled. Perhaps now the colony's food shortage would soon be resolved.

George's farm was a five thousand acre Government grant. The area was roughly a square with two sides bounded by the sea and its beaches, with the other two sides enclosed by a three feet dry rock wall along the main north-south road.

When they first arrived they had employed shepherds for their flock, but two years ago he had employed three Irishmen to build the dry rock wall. Mary had seen them in Tipperary and the walls had proved a resounding success. One beach had a small pier sheltered from the easterly winds. A small sailing boat completed the picture and this was used for fishing more for a pastime than a commercial venture.

They had an enjoyable dinner and each of them contributed to the conversation. Seamus surprised them with some of his stories of his poaching days. He had obviously been very successful in his endeavours.

During the conversation George mentioned that he had fired the driver who had entered their rooms. He'd had concerns about his honesty before their incident.

After bidding goodnight, they each went to their rooms, agreeing to meet at eight for breakfast. They had accepted George's offer to be shown around his property.

The breakfast was sumptuous — eggs, rashers of bacon, freshly baked bread and jam and a large pot of tea. Michael and Seamus could not recall having had a better one. George greeted them full of enthusiasm for his farm which thet could see was his pride and joy.

He and his wife had settled there some twenty years ago, soon after arriving in Van Diemen's Land. The farm consisted of three thousand acres of rolling grasslands separated into twelve paddocks. Half of the remaining two thousand acres had been cleared for crops, the rest consisted of a forest running along the coastline. He had left these trees intact, to form a windbreak and to provide the shoreline protection from soil erosion.

They rode around the road boundary down to the pier. The sea was calm and the wind from the west. It was a very pleasant scene with the small sailing boat bobbing up and down on the waves. The sandy beach was cluttered with seaweed together with some pieces of timber and other flotsam dumped up on the high tide line. Old seashells also littered the beach, and seagulls wheeled overhead completing the idyllic scene.

The cook had prepared a hamper. Michael lit a fire and boiled the billy and the three sat on the beach quietly looking out to sea, each with their thoughts.

Michael thought of bygone days at the Cliffs of Moher and suddenly felt extremely sad. His mind was suddenly crowded with questions, to which he had no answers. How was his family? Were they surviving? Were they well in mind and body? When would he hear from them? He got up and walked away by himself to hide the tears in his eyes.

They completed the ride around the remaining property and were shown the buildings. There were four buildings and all were built of bluestone rock. The homestead was the biggest with five bedrooms, lounge room, dining room, two parlours, a kitchen, servants' quarters and amenity rooms. The other buildings were a large stable with six horse stalls and parking for two gigs and a coach, a shearing shed with men's quarters, which appeared too small for his large flock of sheep. The last building was the combined farm equipment shed and milking bay.

As George and Mary were actively involved with the running of the homestead, she only had a cook and a general housemaid and he had only a farm hand and a general hand.

George's two men had been former convicts who had been convicted of poaching and sent to the Antipodes for 'being caught'! Other farm hands were shared between farms in peak workload periods.

George Alford was truly a self-made man. When they walked through the shearing shed, George turned to Seamus. "No doubt you saw the sheep and realise that the entire flock needs shearing. You two can have the job if you can plan to stay long enough."

Michael nodded to Seamus who replied for them. "Yes, we would like the job. Thank you."

Next morning they started rounding up the sheep. Using the dog and with the assistance of the two farmhands they filled up the shed pens each day. The weather was dry and overcast with cloud, ideal for shearing.

They had been shearing for three weeks and the end was in sight — only one pen of sheep remained. George had loaded twenty pressed fleece bales and two bales of pieces and belly wool onto two large four-wheeled wagons.

The wool wagons had been made by a coach builder in Orford. They were an ugly wagon but capable of carrying very large loads and were typical of the local farm scene. The wheels were nearly six feet in diameter with sixteen thick wooden spokes. The wooden wheel rim was encased in a nine inch wide steel band shrunk onto the wooden rim, after being heated and quenched in a water trough. The wagon itself consisted of a flat wooden planked platform made from eucalyptus gum trees, mounted on the axles for the wheels. The horse towing shaft was attached to the platform via a swivel pin and the shaft had two cross poles, one in front of and one behind the two horses. The horses were harnessed to pull from the rear cross pole. The driver could either sit on top of the load or walk beside the wagon, as the horses could only plod along when they had heavy loads.

The dry weather was a blessing. The roads were firm and George was confident that hauling the wool to Swansea would be successful. Two years ago a wool wagon had become bogged and it had taken them three days to extract it from the mud hole.

With the shearing finished and the wagons ready to roll, they prepared to travel to Swansea via Triabunna. George was going in a pagnel cart made of Van Diemen's Land blackwood with seven metal leaf springs which gave a better ride than most other gigs. Michael and Seamus would ride in their two wheeled cart, leading the wool wagons driven by George's farmhands.

The night before they were to leave, Mary prepared an excellent three course meal, complete with good wine. The four of them each made a toast to their futures. Alfred, Heather and young Seamus were also toasted. At the end of the evening George presented them with a pistol each as a going away present. He had purchased four pistols from the Colt Guns Stand at the Great Britain Great Exhibition held at the Paxton Crystal Palace in Hyde Park, during his visit to London in 1851. He had presented one to Alfred and had now decided to give Michael and Seamus one each. "Crime is bad here but worse when you get to Victoria. You will need to protect yourself and I regard you two as almost family, hence my concern for your safety and these presents." The pistols were 1851 Navy Colt percussion six shot .36 calibre revolvers. His gift would prove to be an apt present in times to come. Their thanks were profound.

After a quick farewell to Mary, the wool convoy headed down

the farm driveway, turned right at the road and headed north to Triabunna. The roads had some ruts from previous inclement weather but the wide steel rims of the wool wagon wheels handled them without difficulty. The gig and the cart often left the road and travelled on the grass edges of the road to protect the wheels from unnecessary heavy impact with the potholes.

They made good progress and the miles were quickly covered. Several times they stopped while George made some idle gossip with other farmers, catching up with the local news. They were advised to keep an eye out for strangers and treat them with caution. There had been several attempted hold ups over the last three months. Fortunately only a few of them had been successful. There were troopers and constables around but they did not know the country as well as the bushrangers and could not locate them. The only other news was the rumour that the transportation of convicts might cease and that the colony's name might be changed from Van Diemen's Land to Tasmania. George had been mooting for a year that the British Government should be giving more assistance to families who could contribute to the growth of the colony rather than convicts. A name change would help remove the penal colony image.

During their midday stop they watered and fed the horses and had a meal break themselves. The remainder of the day's travel was uneventful other than passing a small group of Aborigines who showed little interest in their convoy. It was a boring drive with only the plod of the horses' hoofs and the clinking of the harness shackles interrupting the silence of the bush. Michael amused himself by laying back in the cart admiring the eagles that flew overhead, circling, gliding and then soaring up into the blue skies.

They reached Triabunna mid-afternoon and George, Michael and Seamus found rooms in the Spring Bay Inn, which overlooked a small bay leading off Prosser Bay. After stabling the horses they had a meal and all retired early. The farmhands slept underneath the wagons which had been lined up. The dog was tied up to the gig; his bark would alert the farm hands to any intruders who might come near the wagons during the night time hours.

The next morning the inn's fowl run rooster advised all of the approaching dawn with his raucous crowing. The kitchen was warm and ready to feed them with a warm bowl of oats and a large pot of tea then eggs on bread. It was a good way to start the day.

They packed some bread and cold meat for the final run up to Swansea. They intended to stop at noon, boil the billy and have a meal break, then continue non-stop to Swansea. The farm hands had already had breakfast and fed and watered the horses and the dog, and were completing the harnessing of the horses to the vehicles. The sun was just rising. A low mist hovered over the road and the fields. There was no wind and it could take until noon before the wind would be strong enough to move the mist.

The whips cracked and the wagons rolled, the horses blowing moisture in the morning air from their nostrils, creating a typical winter farm scene. The small wool convoy rolled along, making good time. The mist lifted mid-morning and the sun slowly started to appear.

The driver of the first wagon called down from his seat on the top front bale. "I can see over the top of the rise in the road and there are three horsemen in the middle of the road looking this way." He slipped down into a gap behind the two front bales and placed his shotgun alongside his right side on top of the bale. George, Michael and Seamus each drew their revolvers. George moved his gig to the left of the front wagon while Michael moved his cart to the right side.

The horses continued to plod along with the cart and the gig now in a line with the front wagon, and the second wagon bringing up the rear.

As the convoy reached the top of the rise they saw that the three horsemen had heard the approach of the wool convoy. They now turned and moved towards it.

George ordered the front wagon driver to fire his shotgun high above the horsemen's heads. The three horsemen immediately stopped their advance and saw that George, Michael and Seamus each held a revolver in their hands.

The three horsemen spoke to each other and then turned as one and rode at a high gallop back down the road. They headed off over the fields to the distant tree line. As the horsemen had made no effort to converse with them, they all agreed that they had driven off some bushrangers and all felt a rush of pride in their action. What a story George had to tell his family!

The convoy stopped at noon and watered and fed the animals. They had a meal themselves with the two farmhands standing guard on top of the wool wagons. The remainder of the trip was without incident and they arrived at Swansea at dusk.

It was too late to consider unloading the wool so George called a stop. "We will go down to the wharf tomorrow mid-morning." He had to organise a barge through his agent.

There were several ships anchored off the foreshore sitting quietly in the still waters of the bay, with the sun setting slowly behind them. The ships' shadows stretched across the bay making them feel at peace with such a serene scene.

The next morning George went by himself to the agent. He expected to be away for an hour. Michael and Seamus went down to the docks and left the farmhands to keep an eye on the wool wagon. They turned a corner and walked straight into a constable talking with two men.

The constable turned. "Stay where you are!" He spoke to the other men and then handed some papers back to them. The constable said, "What are your names?"

They answered, "Michael Somerset and Jack Lodge."

He then asked, "Your papers please."

Michael and Seamus did as ordered.

He then asked, "How do I know that these papers are yours?"

A voice said, "Because I signed them." It was George, he had been told that the agent was at the docks and he had come here to find him.

The constable turned and saw George. "Good morning, Mr Alford. Are these your men?"

"Yes, they are," replied George.

Another voice said, "Good morning. What's going on here?"

Michael froze. He knew that voice! Another constable walked into the group. It was Thomas Byrne!

Each stared at each other for a moment but neither gave any indication that they knew each other. Each had a stoic countenance.

George spoke first. "Your fellow constable was just checking the identity of my shearers. There is no problem; I can vouch for them."

Constable Byrne nodded and walked away. The other constable gave them back their papers, nodded to George and also left.

George asked, "What was that all about?" He had sensed something untoward had occurred. When he was told, he burst into laughter. "Lucky I was there to ward off the first constable. He knows me from Council Chambers as the Shire President. You two solved the problem with the second constable. It shows you how risky it is for you to remain in the colony for too long." Michael and Seamus nodded their agreement. Exactly what they had been thinking!

George went off in search of the elusive agent, while Michael and Seamus went back to the wagon. They boiled the billy and sat drinking tea, thanking their lucky stars for their narrow escape and agreed that they must leave the colony at the first opportunity. They also agreed that if they possibly could, they would take the cart and horse, together with the dog, to Victoria. This would give them a reliable income as shearers and also give them some visual credibility and acceptance.

A voice said, "Meet me behind the inn stables in an hour." It was Thomas. He had walked along the opposite side of the wagon, keeping out of sight. It was best if he was not seen with them.

The stables were only ten minutes' walk away and they were early. Thomas walked over, smiling, and the three each shook hands and patted each other on the back. It was a happy meeting of old friends. They each told of the events they had faced after leaving Port Arthur.

Thomas had done a short practical training course at the Hobart Police Barracks and had been posted to Swansea. There was one sergeant and four constables to cover a semi-circular area from Bicheno to Orford and about fifty miles inland. He travelled often and widely and had met a young lady. He was enjoying the job and was happy to stay there for the time being.

Michael and Seamus related their experiences and Thomas listened in amazement at their luck at meeting Albert and Heather Alford. However, after this morning's scare they said that they were now going to leave the colony as soon as possible, but they were unsure how best to attempt their escape.

Thomas said, "The port of Bicheno is notorious for transporting illegal passengers and cargo by ship. Mostly the customs officers are tied up with handling ships arriving and departing Swansea. The police are more interested in maintaining law and order, rather than being involved with illegal shipping activities. If I had to leave I would try to ship out of Bicheno. It should be fairly easy to find contacts in the port; they're everywhere."

The port of Bicheno was north, only a day's travel away. Thomas had to leave, so they each wished each other good fortune and safe travel for the future, not knowing if they would ever meet again.

Michael and Seamus accepted Thomas's advice and decided they would leave for the port as soon as the wool was unloaded and George was heading home with his farmhands.

George returned around midday and advised they would start unloading the wool immediately. They drove the wagon under a large swinging arm crane. The winch rope had four separate ropes with a hook attached to each. The winch rope was slackened and the four hooks pushed by hand into the four sides of the wool bale. The winch was then operated and lifted the bale clear of the wagon. The swinging arm manoeuvred the bale out over a barge moored along the wharf. The rope was slackened dumping the bale onto the barge deck. The hooks pulled out and the process was repeated until the wagon was emptied of the bales, all before nightfall.

The last night they spent together was both a celebration and a farewell dinner. The wool cheque was better than he expected and George gave Michael, Seamus and the two farmhands a bonus. The farewell consisted of an excellent meal and quality wines. Everyone was toasted, starting with their families down to the dog and everyone in between. They had formed a genuine affection for George and he treated them as blood relatives. They promised to keep in contact now that the mail service had been organised throughout the colonies. After the drink had taken its toll, they each decided to retire for the night.

¶

The next morning, after a quick good bye, both parties departed, going their separate ways. George headed south in his gig leading the wagon being driven by the farmhands. Michael and Seamus headed north in their cart with the dog sitting under the seat.

The road north was in reasonable condition with very few pot holes and the land in the immediate vicinity was flat, closely following the shoreline. To the west the mountains were shrouded in low cloud. Their greenness belied their carpet-like denseness and the extreme danger of becoming lost for the inexperienced traveller.

After ten hours driving with a few breaks in between, a small rise appeared in the distance. Upon reaching the top of the rise they could see the sea and the small port of Bicheno about two miles away.

The port was in darkness when they arrived with very few shops open and even less people around. Several ships were lying idle at anchor with a few more tied alongside the wharf. An old sailor appeared from the dock and began to walk in front of them. He turned and asked for a lift to a pub in the distance. They agreed and he climbed in beside the dog, who looked at him and then promptly went back to sleep.

Michael asked, "Do you know of anyone needing a crew to Melbourne?"

The sailor replied, "I own my own boat and I sail anywhere at any time. Tell your friends to ask for China Jack if they need to go somewhere; no questions asked."

"How big is your boat? Would it take our cart and horse?" asked Michael.

China Jack answered, "Yes, but I need to arrange some more cargo from this port first." They dismounted at the pub and entered a small smoky bar room filled with all types of people, some well-dressed and others with extremely dishevelled attire.

In the light of the room China Jack appeared even smaller than before. He was strongly built with a small beard and had a cap perched on top of a mass of grey hair. His grim expression showed that he was not a man to be trifled with. He stood by himself in the corner looking around the room.

Michael watched as several people approached and spoke to him. He nodded to several and said a few words and then walked towards the entry door.

He whispered to Michael, "Meet me here tomorrow morning at eight."

Michael said, "How much?"

"You can afford my price," China Jack responded.

Michael and Seamus stabled the horse, tied the dog to the cart and took a large room to enjoy a good night's sleep.

At eight the next mornimg they were outside the pub after having had a large breakfast and feeding the horse and dog. They were unsure when they would eat again. China Jack arrived on time.

He said, "Take the coast road east for around one mile and you will see a small road to the right. This will take you to a single wharf situated between two buildings used by the whaling ships for cutting up the whales and extracting oil. I will be there at 0900 hours. Be there on time; do not be late. I will load the cart and horse first and then some other cargo. I want the cart to be dismantled by you and the horse blindfolded. It must be done quickly. I don't want interference from the two local customs officers. They are busy at the moment in Swansea as two boats are docking now. It will take several hours to be checked and for the officers to arrive here, but I prefer to leave nothing to chance."

Michael and Seamus arrived on time and true to his word the dismantled cart and horse were immediately loaded on board a pontoon by his two crewmen. The pontoon was thirty feet long and twenty feet wide but really was only a glorified raft. Four large tree trunks formed a square with heavy twenty feet long planks bolted to the two thirty feet long trunks. Four metal rings were bolted to each corner. In the following twenty minutes, twenty barrels of whale oil were rolled onto the pontoon and upended around the horse. The pontoon was towed out to the ship by a large row boat from the whaling ship.

Michael, Seamus and the dog went on board the ship first. The ship's crew immediately swung out a boom and lowered a sling large enough to lift the barrels, the horse and finally the cart. The barrels and the horse were lowered into the hold and placed in a sling and the cart tied down on the main deck.

The small ship was named the SS Eliza and it was anchored close to Governor's Rock opposite the wharf. The high tide was due to turn within the next two hours. This, together with the assistance of a weak off shore breeze, had the ship under way by ten o'clock.

The ship was very basic. There was a small cabin for the passengers and a wheel house for China Jack. Michael looked at the sails and the ropes and was surprised to see that they were all in good condition.

China Jack saw him looking and invited him to the wheelhouse. "Am I right in thinking you are a sea going man?"

Michael told him of his experience at sailing and his shipwright qualifications. China Jack told Michael that he kept a good ship. He had clashed with a particular customs officer over bribery payments wanted by the officer and was now being harassed by him, forcing China Jack to resort to move in dubious circles and assignments, and into carrying persons wishing to bypass the formal departure procedures.

The SS Eliza sailed well. China Jack was a good mariner.

He kept his small ship close to shore along the Van Diemen's Land coast. Michael enjoyed the smell of the clean cool sea air as much as that of the smell of freshly cut green grass. They sailed up past the Bay of Fires, often mistakenly thought to be named after the orange lichen on the rocks but really they had been named after Aboriginal fires.

China Jack told Michael he was going into Western Port Bay as it was shorter than sailing up to Port Phillip Bay. It was also easier to enter as he would not have to negotiate the notorious Heads. China Jack advised them that this would be a safe port for them to enter Victoria. The customs officers were all at Williamstown near Melbourne.

He thought their idea of entering Victoria with a ready-made and popular business was the best idea he had heard yet. Their secret would be safe with him, he said. He laughed at their audacity. The voyage cost was twenty five pounds and it was reasonable. He would still make money, as, strangely enough, he had some people to smuggle back to Van Diemen's Land.

The SS Eliza pitched and rolled as it headed north along the coast for a day before turning to port into Bass Strait and onto the Victorian coast. The winds in the Strait were strong and gusty and made for unpleasant sailing. For Michael and Seamus this was no ordeal as this voyage was taking them to a new life full of hope.

CHAPTER FIVE

Arrival in Victoria

—

he *SS Ventnor* sat calm on the still Hobart waters. It had been riding at anchor in the harbour for six days. The sailors had been busy dismantling the convicts' berths and had tied them to the main mast in the cargo hold, plus the main cargo hold planks had been removed to allow the loading of the timber. It had taken two days to load the consignment, replace the main deck cargo and for the hold access planks to be made ready for sailing. During this time, the harbour master had completed his duties assessment and had cleared the ship for departure to Williamstown harbour in Victoria. The ship's victualling had been completed and the crew had all returned, which was unusual as one or two normally deserted after they were paid. A cabin had been selected for the secure consignment and locks fitted. Captain Marshall was now ready to sail to Victoria on the outgoing tide.

It was 1854. A lot had happened since both Michael and John left their homelands in early 1853.

John Hall was awakened by the clanking of the anchor chain. He looked out of his porthole and could see that it was still dark. He dressed quickly and went up on deck. It was a hive of activity with sailors hauling ropes, sails being raised and the bosun shouting orders.

The ship drifted south, the sails gradually filling with a

gentle breeze. The lights of Hobart and the western shore residences gradually faded into the distance.

Captain Marshall invited John to join him up on the quarter deck for a better view. A few lights could be seen on the side of Mount Wellington with the early morning sunlight shining on its escarpment.

The ship tacked down the channel with a good westerly wind off their starboard quarter. First light was appearing and one could see the white caps of the sea all around them. By mid-morning they were clearing land's end. They continued south for half a day, turned and then headed east. The wind was behind them and the ship pitched in the troughs but it was no longer rolling. The sails had been shortened due to the wind's strength.

John stood on deck until the land mass disappeared from his view behind low cloud. He then went below and started to write some letters; the first to his father. He wrote quickly relating the events since his last letter.

The letters he wrote home basically were his diary and his father treated them as such and kept them in calendar order in his desk. He would sit in his study late at night, enjoying a wine, rereading the letters and visualising John's travels.

John's letters to Maeve took much more thought and time. He spoke of his memories of her and the hopes he had for their future in a new land. He sat there for hours, when far out to sea, dreaming of what he hoped he could achieve in the future as a family man, and make her proud of his profession and the possessions he might acquire along the way.

When the ship headed north it was under full sail. The wind was still from the west so the captain considered it was safe to steer the ship closer to land, where the scene changed constantly.

There were small bays with golden sandy beaches and

grasslands. Small columns of smoke often appeared in the forests, as did mountain peaks in the distance and then only the sea as a bay disappeared in the distance. Some of the bays were quite large but the captain steered a straight course and was not tempted to 'have a look'. Islands were dotted on the ship's course. Maria Island was the largest well-known penal settlement.

Most of the coastline and the bays had not been surveyed and caution was required. There had been many ships wrecked all around the colony.

After the ship reached Schouten Island they steered due north keeping the coast in sight on the port beam. The rest of the trip up the east coast was uneventful with moderate weather. The wind was from the west at ten knots and the seas calm to slight. They were now heading towards Banks Strait which was between Clarke Island, the Cape Barren Islands and Flinders Island of the Furneaux Group of Islands and the northern tip of the colony of Van Diemen's land.

Banks Strait was dotted with islands and the wrecks that had fallen foul to the tides and westerly winds. It made tacking any course, between the islands and reefs, fraught with danger.

Captain Marshall timed his entry into the Strait to be just after first light. Only a few of the crew had sailed this trip before and were apprehensive about what the weather would be when they turned north-west into the Strait. However, they were satisfied that they had a good ship and a competent captain. Breakfast was served early for both passengers and crew, then the ship was battened down. Portholes were closed, decks cleared, ropes stowed and all loose items below decks stored. The passengers had been advised to pack all items in their cabins and be ready for rough seas. The precautions taken were just that, precautions. It was best to be prepared before the ship turned to the north-west and started to tack through the Strait.

Bass Strait appeared in the first morning light, white caps curling in the distance. The waves could be seen dashing on the low cliffs of a small island off on the starboard bow. The ship began to pitch and roll but the seas were only moderate. The ship was tacking and holding its head. They had a turning tide astern which helped them steer a direct course in the middle of the strait. For an hour all was well.

Suddenly, they had a wind shift from the south. The captain immediately turned to port and shortened sail. They were holding their course but the ship was being pushed north towards Clarke Island.

The lookout suddenly called down, "Reef, distance near, two points off the starboard bow." Everyone on deck heard his call and nervously looked in that direction. A small row of waves different to the rest of the sea became visible and showed the reef line. The captain had no choice but to turn about and sail back down the Strait. He headed further south this time and then turned northwest, again keeping close to the north coast of the colony. This time they ran straight and true and cleared the danger area. They then headed out of Banks Strait into the notorious Bass Strait.

The SS Ventnor sailed out into Bass Strait which was living up to its reputation. Gusty westerly winds and choppy seas greeted them. The sails were straining, the yardarms creaking and the hull groaned with the pitching and rolling action in the seas. The seas were washing over the decks and only essential crew ventured onto the main deck and the quarter deck, with the passengers confined to their cabins for the day. The ship tacked west into the 'Roaring Forties'. Progress was slow but steady; they were making about eight knots.

The passengers eased their boredom by reading and savouring the small hot meals being delivered to them by the galley crew. A low cloud hung over the coast of Victoria as it appeared on the horizon. Eventually the coast separated, revealing the entrance into Port Phillip Bay, leading up to the town of Melbourne. With this weather, the entry into the bay between the two narrow headlands would require considerable caution. The riptide at the headlands was fierce, both in the volume of water and its turbulence, as the sea poured into or out of the bay.

Captain Marshall decided to sit outside the Heads and select a favourable tide as signalled by the new Queenscliff Bluff system of signals. These signals were a new innovation of a retired sea captain. Selected flags were suspended on a mast on the foreshore and gave updated riptide information.

When he headed the ship towards the bay opening the seas were still rough with a westerly wind. The signal station had just changed the flags to indicate a 'high tide'. The ship was making good way and the captain kept it sailing in the channel middle, between the two headlands, ready to turn to starboard immediately he was in the bay, to avoid the mud flats off Queenscliff.

A long swell was developing. It was a little unpleasant but the ship was under control and holding its head. All hands were on deck. John and the surveyors stood in the bow eager to see the ship enter the bay through the two headlands, which could be clearly seen either side of the ship. The long swell continued. At times the colour of the sea changed from dark blue to a light sandy blue, as the depth of the entry channel changed.

The wind increased and began to push the ship easterly towards Point Lonsdale. Captain Marshall reefed the topsails; this reduced the cross wind effect. It might take longer to clear the headlands but the ship would ride in on the incoming tide. His decision was correct. The incoming tide came with the expected turbulence and volume of water and, together with the wind, the tide pushed the ship into the bay well clear of the danger areas. It entered a very large bay with another smaller bay off to the west. The ship turned to starboard and followed the coast up past Sorrento.

The size of the bay surprised John. Standing on the bow he could see no land on the horizon to the north. It was many hours before the horizon scene changed. A haze appeared first, then the shape of buildings and ships at anchor. They passed two ships heading outbound but they were afar. Residences became visible to the east and to the north at the top of the bay. Captain Marshall anchored in Hobson's Bay just off the Williamstown docks and waited on board for the harbour controller to come alongside. In the meantime he sent the first officer ashore to contact the owner's agent.

John Hall was on his own now; in a foreign country in all but language. His first task was to locate the Melbourne branch of the Bank of New South Wales. He was advised that Melbourne was over the river some six miles away. After booking into a hotel, he located the river ferry and then shared a hansom cab to be driven to the centre of Melbourne. It was a disappointing town although the streets had been surveyed and blocks marked. The progress of completing any civil project seemed to have stalled. The Bank of New South Wales was a commanding building when compared to others in the vicinity.

John was duly welcomed and shown to a private room where he deposited his father's cheque of three hundred pounds. Following the finalisation of the paperwork, he was presented with a large envelope containing twelve letters.

He only opened the official looking letters. He wished to enjoy reading the others in the solitude of his hotel room. The first letter he opened was signed by Lt Col Robert Nickle. The letter was an official invitation to visit his office at John's first opportunity. This response gave John some confidence regarding his future in the colony. The second letter he opened was from the Bank of New South Wales allowing him credit to the limit of one thousand pounds.

The third letter was from his friend, Lt Brown. He had made a success of his move to headquarters and had become a staff officer with a promotion to major. John replaced all the letters into the large envelope and returned to Williamstown. Tomorrow he would seek out the headquarters of the 12th Regiment. He sat out on a small balcony attached to his hotel room and looked out across Hobson's Bay.

He arranged Maeve's letters in date order and started to read them. A feeling of warmth and desire almost overwhelmed him as he read the tenderness in her words. It was almost as if she were there reading to him. Each letter was from the heart and when he read the last of her six letters he was beyond speech. What a surprise! The Keogh's had decided to come to Australia but only Maeve and her father. Aunt Jane had decided to remain in County Clare. This was the news for which he had been waiting, for nearly a year. While it was great news, there was no time mentioned. He would write and ask her tonight. Perhaps she was already on her way. It would take around four months to receive an answer to a letter. If only Michael could be with them. Where was he? He wondered how he could find out.

Maeve had received a letter from Michael but she had told only her father. She did not mention him in her letters to John, for fear her letters may go astray. She would tell John when they were together again.

He dressed smartly for his meeting with Sir Robert Nickle. He hoped that by the day's end he would have a new career in the military service. After travelling to Melbourne again he located the regiment east of the town. The officer of the day recognised a fellow officer and afforded him the courtesy of a visiting officer by inviting him into the officers' mess while he located the commandant.

John could hear Lt Col Sir Robert Nickle coming up the hall well before he saw him. He still remembered his resonant voice.

"Welcome, John. I've been wondering where you were and when you would arrive." He shook his hand. "Come with me," and led him to his office.

He closed the door and motioned to him to be seated. He started with, "I have your application and I also have your history. Now don't look shocked, we at the top know all and, between you and me, you did the honourable thing. Now let's put that behind us. I offer you a commission in the 12th Regiment. After three months in Melbourne I will post you to an outlying town. Your experience in Ireland will be invaluable here. Some of my officers have been nowhere and lack skills in handling different cultures. You can help change their thinking by example. The Government is honest and they have some skills but they have a steep learning curve to surmount. It is a good colony with good people and I hope you find life as satisfying as I do. That's all for now. See me here tomorrow at eleven sharp." He opened the door. "I'm looking forward to having a good chat with you later."

After his meeting the next day, he was told to have a look around Melbourne for a day or so. Two days later John was invited into Sir Robert's private quarters and they sat down and spoke of days gone by. John told him of his father's success with his farming ventures and his sister's top performances in the district horse shows. Sir Robert reciprocated by telling John that George had nearly completed his legal studies and intended to specialise in criminal law. Sir Robert's wife had died and the old soldier was rather lonely and far away from his native country. However, he stated he would settle in Australia as he preferred the milder weather in Victoria to the extremes of the Cumberland climate.

He spoke of the problems he'd had in the past. He mentioned the miners' Eureka Stockade rebellion at Ballarat over their gold mining licence fees and the involvement of the 12th Regiment. His men had quelled the rebellion but he felt the action would never have happened if the Government had been more professional and had listened to the miners sooner.

John could sense his interest in the future of the colony. They spoke for nearly two hours and then John departed after forging a common bond with his mentor.

John was duly sworn in as a Lieutenant in the British Army 12th Regiment on the 1st of December 1854. He was issued with his red and yellow trimmed uniform, given an office and handed the book of Regulations and Rules to read and digest. He was put on the duty roster and finally, to refresh his skills, he travelled to a firing range. He had some practise with a pistol and rifle and later with a field gun. He then felt competent enough to oversee some practise for the new junior officers.

He was comfortable in his role and looked forward to some challenges. Apart from some trouble with a drunken mob and some convicts who refused to work, he had not had much to do. John paraded the platoon every second Sunday, past the gardens, when the local band was playing. He attended several official functions, which required him to escort a debutante to a pre-dance. Other than dinners with high level government officials, his social life was somewhat reserved, even boring. He wrote to his father and Maeve each fortnight and went to the bank weekly hoping for letters. It would be sometime before letters started to come to the barracks.

The regiment had been told that with the increase in bushranger activity they would be required to provide escorts for the gold shipments as the current security system was not working. Gold was in every conversation due to its importance in the colony's economic future. Gold had first been found at Bathurst in New South Wales in 1823 and again in 1839 and 1841. Payable quantities were discovered in Victoria at Clunes in 1850 and 1851.

The gold field had attracted people from all over the world including the people of Melbourne. Homes were deserted; shopkeepers and their assistants left town, including skilled persons, and sailors deserted their ships. Some captains refused to allow their crews to leave ship for fear of being short of sailors and unable to leave the port. A few gold miners became wealthy but many became destitute and lawless. The dramatic increase in costs of food also contributed to social disharmony in the colony.

John was assigned a military gold escort duty. This was to be his first trip outside of Melbourne town and he was eager to see some of the local unique wildlife and fauna. He had not even seen a kangaroo.

He led a troop of twelve troopers with a sergeant to Bendigo to escort the gold shipment back to Melbourne. They had two carts, driven by two of the troopers. He intended to travel only in daylight and to stay overnight at small towns on the main road to Melbourne. The trip was planned to take four days. Each cart had two horses and it was mostly downhill, so the travelling was not arduous. They made good time from Bendigo and the troopers were alert. Some had fought in India and were not frightened of a gun fight. John advised his men what he wanted done if there was a roadside ambush. His plan was to dismount and attack, not to defend against any bushrangers, and only to fire at a clear target.

The convoy left the small town of Woodend and was trotting down the Black Forest Road at around noon with a cliff on their left and a dense tree line on their right side. As planned, John and the sergeant were in the lead with three troopers. Two more were riding adjacent each cart and the last three riding at the rear. John called to his men to be alert. After travelling for a half an hour, the terrain had not changed. Suddenly the trooper in the first cart shouted, "Ambush". A second or two later, sporadic gunfire erupted from the tree line.

The drivers of the carts slid down into the cart's foot well. However, the first driver was hit by a bullet in the shoulder and dropped his reins. The troopers alongside the carts immediately returned fire from their sheltered positions while the sergeant jumped up onto the first wagon and got the horses trotting faster. The driver of the second cart followed his example. The troopers in front of the convoy immediately entered the bush on the same side as the bushrangers and the rear troopers rode in and entered the tree line similarly. The bushrangers kept firing but only one other trooper was hit by a bullet and sustained a wrist injury.

John's plan had the effect of confusing and panicking the bushrangers as they had expected the troopers to go to the other side of the road. The bushrangers were now the hunted.

John had ridden alongside with the sergeant and the gold carts and they now stopped the carts and left them a hundred yards down the road. He checked that the driver was not too seriously wounded then he and the sergeant rode back to the gunfight, leaving the two troopers to protect the carts. John left two troopers minding the road to stop the bushrangers from escaping from the front and down the road, reminding them to fire at only clear targets and not towards the rear troopers who had moved forward up the road, moving from tree to tree.

He took four troopers with him and crept into the bush for about fifty yards. He turned towards where he could hear the bushrangers talking as they tried to decide which way to go to get away. When John and his troopers were in position, they could see that they were behind them and to their left only forty yards away and had not been noticed.

John called, "Surrender!"

The bushrangers turned and started to fire at them. The troopers immediately returned fire and brought down five of the bushrangers in two volleys. Three others immediately surrendered, one continued to fire and John shot him in the shoulder, stopping him from escaping on his horse. Another of his troopers was hit in the side but fortunately the bullet went through his flesh just above his hip.

When John returned to the road he saw his other troopers had captured two more. They had captured five bushrangers, wounded one and shot five dead. After catching their horses, John sent a trooper back to Woodend for the police to come and take away the bodies. He then had the prisoners shackled and taken to Melbourne for trial. While the three wounded troopers and prisoner were driven back to the Kyneton Hospital.

The bushrangers were swiftly judged, tried and hanged in the Melbourne Gaol within six months. The incident slowed down the number of robberies in the notorious Black Forest area and a period of peace existed for several months.

When the news became known of the attempted robbery being foiled and a major bushranger gang captured, the 12th Regiment became in demand for all gold shipments. Both John and the sergeant were awarded medals for Devotion to Duty.

Sir Robert was delighted and immediately promoted John to captain. John was only involved in the next three gold shipments. Junior officers were now charged with that responsibility and these officers followed John's strategy plan in case of a similar ambush.

That was a good week for John. He also received a welcomed

letter from his father and a letter from Maeve, giving a possible departure date of July 1855 from Cork.

It was now time for John to ask Sir Robert where he might be posted. John wanted to prepare for the Keoghs' arrival. He explained that his fiancé was on her way and that he wished to buy a home for them. Sir Robert said he wished to keep John close to the regiment headquarters and that the closest posting would be in a town called Kyneton and was around a two day ride from Melbourne. John knew of the town as he had passed through it en route to Bendigo. Sir Robert wanted only a small garrison of around twenty troopers kept there. John would command the garrison and would be supported by Lieutenant Caly, a sergeant, a corporal and twenty troopers. They would be sited alongside the agricultural showgrounds. John agreed that his assignment would be acceptable to him and thanked Sir Robert for the posting. They had become friends. Without crossing the line, they would often sit and have a chat during his future visits to Kyneton. Sir Robert was always the commandant. John felt that he was seen as a link to Sir Robert's family in Cumberland.

John moved his platoon from the Melbourne Barracks within the week and they rode into Kyneton late the next day. He agreed the area adjacent the agriculture grounds was an excellent site for his camp. It was treed and on high ground. The Campaspe River was two hundred yards away and also the site was on the edge of the township. While the camp would be comprised mainly of tents John decided to build two wooden buildings. One building would be for a general multi-use office and the other for a mess and dining facility for the soldiers. This was well received by them.

Meanwhile John started to search for a house or a farm to prepare for Maeve's arrival. He had little to do other than to parade the platoon through the town at different times,

particularly on local festive occasions, such as building open-
ings and Vice Regal occasions. Kyneton was a quiet town, en
route north — the centre of an agriculture district, with many
successful farmers.

From a social point of view he was required to represent the
Queen at official occasions and make speeches and cut ribbons
commemorating an opening of a building or a bridge.

A major fire occurred at the height of the summer season
and he took charge of the fire fighting, as members of the local
brigade were arguing with each other.

Yes, it was a quiet town. He continued his policy of parad-
ing the platoon when outdoor functions were being conducted
in the gardens, agricultural showgrounds or racecourse. The
crowds would cheer them and the children would run alongside them for miles. His platoon had become part of the local
scenery.

Sir Robert arrived unannounced on his way to visit Bendigo.
He only stopped for an hour and during that time he advised John
that he had been promoted to the rank of major and that the role
of his platoon would be increased in the immediate future.

John's leisure hours were now occupied with riding around
the town and the district looking at houses and land sites. He
would have preferred to buy a house with land but very few
were available. Finally, he started to concentrate on the town
area. He had also advised Mr Carroll, the Kyneton land agent,
of his interest in a house or an established farm. Mr Carroll said
he would put him on his list. The current house demands were
higher than the supply. John pondered his next move. It might
be better to buy land and build a farmhouse using itinerant
labourers. He had brought a drawing of his father's farm in
Lazonby. The drawing was very detailed and John hoped the
drawing was good enough for builders to use for his farmhouse.

He continued to keep looking while checking on the availability of workers. He had made several friends in the town and had mentioned to them his interest in establishing a home in the district around Kyneton and Malmsbury.

Informing his friends of his intentions finally paid off. John had returned from a 'Show the Flag' exercise in Woodend and found a note from William Eden. He was a local businessman with whom John had dined several times. The note requested John to contact him as soon as possible.

That evening John rode to William's home, full of curiosity. William invited him into his parlour, poured drinks for them and motioned to John to be seated. He started with, "I might have a farm for you. It has eighty acres of land and a farmhouse. A relative of mine passed away the day you left on your trip to Woodend and his wife wants to return to London where the rest of her family are living. I told her you were an interested buyer and she agreed to give you first choice."

John said, "Thank you. When can I see the property?"

William laughed at his enthusiastic reply. "Is tomorrow too soon?"

William arranged to collect John the next morning at the barracks office. They rode out of Kyneton and headed north in his gig. The country was relatively flat with scattered stands of gumtrees. Sheep and cattle grazed on the lush green grass. Wildlife was abundant with kangaroos and colourful birds in the gumtree stands.

As they headed north a large hill appeared. William said that it was called Black Hill and that the property was at its base.

They drove up a small incline on the road. At the top William stopped and pointed ahead to a long wooden building. "That's the farmhouse. The land starts here and continues for the same distance on the other side of the farmhouse."

John was not immediately impressed. He was looking for a farmhouse as a home. It did not compare with his father's home in any way. The fencing consisted of a combination of dry rock walls and Hawthorn shrubs with a ditch inside the line of shrubs.

He could see sheep and some cattle, and a dog ran down to greet them. Soon a woman appeared on the veranda. She recognised William's gig and gave them a wave. John was introduced to Mrs Blair, who as per local custom, immediately invited them in for tea.

The kitchen was a large room with a real farm feeling. It was combined as a dining room as well. Mrs Blair was quite affable and kept the conversation going. In particular she described the farm in total.

John could see that she was very proud of what her husband had achieved in the few short years they had been in the district. The farm house was a long building over one hundred and fifty feet long and forty feet wide with walls made of wooden planks and a roof covered by hundreds of shingles. A twelve foot veranda surrounded the entire building and provided weather protection during both the hot and the rainy days. John was surprised to find that the building was divided. Half of the building was used as a farm house and included the kitchen. It comprised two large parlours, five bedrooms and a utilities room for laundry. The rest of the building was divided into four horse stalls, fodder storage, a tack room, farm equipment, a small shearing stand, a workshop and a two bunk labourers' room.

He was concerned that the property did not have a river or creek frontage. However, he was surprised to find three ten feet high water barrels that collected the rain fall that ran off from the roof and verandas. It provided the house and the feed troughs with sufficient water for all. The land had been divided into several large paddocks separated by dry rock fences; two larger paddocks had natural spoon dams.

Mr Blair had blocked the rain water run off at the bottom of two adjoining gullies and had created two reservoirs which captured the rain water running off the higher land. This water supplied the livestock.

John asked Mrs Blair and William if he could walk by himself and have a think about the property. He walked to the highest point on the farm and looked around the surrounding countryside. It was green for as far as the eye could see. Even Black Hill was deep green with its forest of trees. He could see the two spoon dams in the distance and the farmhouse sitting on a small rise, with smoke floating lazily from the kitchen chimney. The north east paddocks had several acres of corn growing with an adjacent ten acres still timbered. The sheep and the cattle completed the picture. John's only concern was that the house was very basic and did not have the trimmings he had been used to. He sat on a tree stump pondering. Was this what Maeve would expect?

In the distance he could see a mob of kangaroos grazing, bent over on their fores and strong tail, with their young joey's climbing in their mothers' pouches. These kangaroos were much larger than the Van Diemen's Land animals, up to five feet tall. They had strong hind legs and jumped long distances with their tail balancing them. Their two small front legs could hold a dog and disembowel it with the toes of the two large hind legs. The big male roos were very dangerous if they were cornered.

His thoughts drifted back to the reason why he was here. He began to consider that they could live in the current farm house and later build the bluestone home which he eventually wanted. Not having running water was now no longer of concern and he had to agree the farmhouse was suitable to be lived in. It was solid and dry and had ample accommodation. He made up his mind.

He walked back, looking everywhere to ensure he had seen all he needed to see, both good and bad. He hoped he had not missed anything considered important.

Mrs Blair and William were talking when he walked in and both looked up; Mrs Blair with an apprehensive look.

John looked at her and said, "I really wanted a bluestone house but if we can reach a suitable price, I would consider buying your property."

Mrs Blair nodded. "I can understand your thinking. I have been advised by Mr Carroll that the land is valued at two pounds per acre and the house at around forty pounds. I believe the price of two hundred pounds is fair and I hope that is your opinion also."

John still had his father's two hundred and fifty pounds in the Melbourne bank and thirty pounds in a Kyneton Bank. He could afford to buy the farm outright.

During John's previous property searching he had acquired a reasonable knowledge of the value of land and buildings. He could see that the price Mrs Blair suggested was fair. He took a deep breath walked over to her, offering his hand. "I agree two hundred pounds is fair and I accept."

Mrs Blair stood up and shook his hand. "I hope you will be as happy as my husband and I were living on this farm." She sat down and cried.

William went to the stove and made a pot of tea to celebrate. John and Mrs Blair discussed the method of payment and she decided on a bank draft to be cashed in England. She had other funds in the local Bank of New South Wales. John also purchased the livestock and farm equipment for forty pounds. This left him very short of ready cash but he believed with frugal living he would not have to draw on the credit he had in Melbourne. Hopefully he would make the farm profitable within six months with the corn crop, wool return and selling some young cattle.

John and William bid Mrs Blair farewell and drove back to Kyneton. John could not thank William enough.

William brushed off his thanks saying magnanimously, "That's what friends are for."

John would not forget his friend William Eden.

John decided to name the farm 'Sunny Lodge'.

His immediate concern was to find a farmhand he could trust. He asked Mr Russell if he could keep an eye open for him and find a person who had lived and worked in the district and had a reference from his previous employer.

Two weeks later, the corporal on the gate knocked on his office door and advised him he had a visitor. John invited the visitor into his office and, after greeting him, the visitor informed him that Mr Russell had sent him for the position as a farmhand. He was a free settler and had been working the district building dry walls but had injured ligaments in his elbow and now had trouble lifting the large rocks. He could chop wood and dig soil, heavy lifting was his only restriction.

He had been a farmhand in Limerick in Ireland. His name was Connor Scanlon. He had a stocky build and was of medium height and he enjoyed talking with the normal soft Irish brogue. John liked what he saw and asked him for references. Connor handed over six pages. He recognised some of the names. John hired him and told him to be at the barracks the next day and he would drive him to the farm.

John and Connor, together with his dog, Blackie, arrived at midday and he showed Connor around the property. There was plenty of water and the paddocks were all well grassed with only four of the seven paddocks being grazed at one time. There were sixty merino sheep and twenty cattle. Rotating the paddocks would ensure the animals would maintain their quality in their meat value and wool standard.

John allowed Connor to do the talking and he soon realised that he was an experienced farmhand. Connor suggested that he concentrate on maintaining the vegetable garden and the small orchard and that John purchase a milking cow and a few fowls. This would ensure that the farm would be virtually self-sufficient, except for bread. John knew that Mrs Blair used her kitchen oven to cook bread so John said he would obtain a recipe and the bread ingredients for Connor to try his hand at baking some bread.

Connor would have the run of the house but he said he preferred to set up in the labourers' quarters with Blackie. John agreed to his suggestions. They shook hands. John advised him that he would be back at the weekend. He then returned to the barracks.

John was confident that he had hired a reliable farmhand and was optimistic that his farm would be in profit within the year. His next project would be to build the new homestead ready for Maeve and Edmund's arrival.

The SS Eliza struggled into a head wind and it was getting dark. The Victorian coastline appeared out of the gloom. There was some moonlight but it was still difficult to pick out landmarks. Suddenly China Jack found the landmark he wanted. It was a hill with an unusual double peak at the western point of the Western Port Bay. He now relaxed and swung the wheel to bring the ship around and to keep the point around five hundred yards off the beam.

When they entered the bay the choppy waves ceased and the sails were reefed. He sailed to the end of the bay and anchored. It was low tide. A light flashed from the shore and soon another pontoon appeared out of the gloom, towed by a whaler and crew. The barrels were unloaded first then the horse and finally the dismantled cart and the pontoon was ready to return to shore. Michael paid China Jack and they shook hands. Together with Seamus and the dog they climbed into the whaler and headed for shore, returning a farewell wave to China Jack.

On a small beach they soon assembled the cart, repacked their goods and chattels and the dog and headed north-west to Melbourne. They drove for a few miles looking for somewhere to rest for the night and wondered where the ship's cargo had gone. They never found out! After selecting a small clearing they bedded down for the night, anxious to be travelling at first light. They were glad of the dog for he was very alert and would warn them of any strangers prowling around. They were both armed with pistols and had a shotgun, but the dog was an extra comfort. It was August 1855.

The next morning was a dismal day, mainly cloud with misty rain, although looking to the west it was possible that the weather would clear later in the day. The track they were on gradually improved. It was a pleasant drive and birds were everywhere with plenty of warbling and screeching. The kookaburra was beautiful to hear with its unique sound, just like a laugh! The flowering gumtrees and wattles were in bloom. Their reds and yellows and deep green leaves made for a scene of total tranquillity, making them feel at peace with the world and themselves.

The dog started barking loudly and both men reached for

their revolvers. They could see several Aborigines appearing from the trees about twenty yards from them.

Seamus kept the horse trotting along while watching to see if the Aborigines intended to do them harm. The leader waved his spear in the air and began shouting loudly.

Michael raised his pistol and fired it into the air and then he pointed the pistol straight at the leader. The leader stopped shouting and looked puzzled. Another Aborigine ran forward and grabbed him, pointing to the pistol. He said some words and pulled the leader away.

Seamus kept the horse at a trot while Michael kept watching the Aborigines. Meanwhile the dog was going berserk with its barking. They all eventually relaxed, and wondered if they would have been attacked if the pistol had not been fired.

They reached a road which followed the shoreline north around the bay veering in a westerly direction. Several inns and residences began to appear frequently the further they travelled north. They stopped at a village called Sorrento and had an ale and lunch. They fed and watered the dog and the horse, and began chatting to the inn owner, an ex-sailor. He saw the sign on their cart and asked where they were from. They told him they lived in the Gippsland area out east. He nodded and said, "You'll get plenty of work north of Melbourne right through to Bendigo. You may get some jobs this side but if I were you I would go to the north out through Keilor and Kyneton where there is good land at a good price." He drew them a rough map of the Melbourne district and the outlying areas.

This map was to be their guiding light and away the two went again getting further and further away from Van Diemen's Land and, in particular, Port Arthur.

They chatted as they drove along.

"What do you say to buying some land if we can find some

at a good price, and starting a farm?" suggested Seamus. "We could continue to work as shearers, until it could sustain us."

Michael jumped at the suggestion. "That's a great idea. We can have that as our objective; let's aim for it." Michael had written to Maeve several times and she had written back to him inside a letter addressed to Heather Alford. He would not receive them until he had arranged an address for himself in Victoria.

They reached Melbourne on the seventh day and decided to rest the horse. It was six years old and fit but they always kept an eye on its health. They did not push the animal; indeed they looked after the horse and the dog. They were always well fed and watered and washed down. Finding a farrier, a Mr Brinkhuis from Holland, Michael had their horse reshod and the condition of both animals checked. They were fine.

Melbourne was a shambles compared to Hobart. Its streets were rutted and there were puddles everywhere. Some buildings were made of solid bluestone but then next door there would be a hovel or tent. The town site had been surveyed, marked out and the blocks auctioned several years earlier. Churches had been built and several government buildings completed. Hotel accommodation varied from reasonable to mediocre and dining was in a similar vein. The Yarra River docks were busy with small vessels, although the main docks were at Williamstown on Hobsons Bay and Port Melbourne, a short distance south west of Melbourne at the top of Port Phillip Bay.

They did not stay in Melbourne for very long and soon headed north out towards the Moonee Creek and then west through Keilor. Some nights, to save money, they slept under the cart and wrapped an old sail around the base of the cart to keep out the cold wind and rain.

Michael and Seamus started to look for work and stopped

at each inn to ask around. They still had some money but they needed to increase their cash to buy some land and improve their status from humble shearers to landowners. There was land available cheaply as many farmers had walked off their properties and gone gold digging at Castlemaine, Bendigo and Ballarat and the banks had foreclosed on many of them. Some farmers made good finds but not all were successful gold diggers. Michael and Seamus had been advised that there was some good grazing land available around the Malmsbury and Kyneton district.

They both had agreed not to go mining and would endeavour to succeed as farmers and shearers with their own properties by pooling their resources initially. They began to find work outside Keilor, picking up a run with four hundred sheep and another at Toolern with one thousand sheep. Heading north to Sunbury they had a flock of five hundred and another of one thousand. Michael and Seamus were gaining a reputation as good and honest shearers with the jobs offered on the way from Melbourne. It had taken them nearly two months to get to Kyneton, during which time they had accumulated over a hundred pounds cash including the money left over from their Van Diemen's Land shearing jobs.

Michael and Seamus arrived in Kyneton and stayed at the Commercial Hotel. Tomorrow they would go land hunting.

9

The Land Sales Office was unimpressive and deserted when they pushed open the door. They waited a few minutes and were about to leave when in rushed a rather flustered man who apologised profusely. The mail had been late and he had been forced to wait for a package containing land ownership documents relating to several cancellations due to default of payment. He introduced himself as Mr Russell Carroll, sat down and began to relax. As he asked them their business, he began opening the package.

Michael advised him that they were interested in purchasing eighty to a hundred acres of land suitable for grazing and cultivation between Kyneton and Malmsbury. They wanted to buy now!

Mr Carroll continued rummaging through the documents he pulled from the envelope. He looked up, suddenly realising what Michael had said.

"You have good timing. I have six sections of eighty acre blocks for sale right here in my hand, in the district you're interested in. I can show you now, if you are free." He showed them on his map where the blocks were and then they headed out of town, due west in his gig. They selected two of the four and put down a deposit to show their confirmed interest. They would return tomorrow and advise which block they would buy. The two blocks that they examined had both main road frontages and a river water access. The block they preferred had the Campaspe River flowing through the property and had a small bluestone house on the top of a rise in the middle. Most had been cleared. A previous storm had uprooted a gum tree and the tree was lying on the roof of the house and the roof had collapsed under its weight. The other property was between the river and the main road and had been fully cleared. Michael and Seamus preferred the block with the house.

The next morning they walked to the Land Sales Office and were surprised to see a large queue had formed. They walked past the queue and into the building to see the queue started at the desk.

Mr Carroll saw them enter through the glass window of his

office and waved them to come in. He was escorting a man out and, after saying good bye to him, he asked them to be seated.

He said, "I had over twenty blocks for sale from that envelope yesterday and I've sold ten already. I don't know how they found out so quickly. Incidentally, I have sold one of the two blocks you were interested in but I have kept you the other one." He saw the look of dismay on their faces and said quickly, "I have a business to run, and I sell, first come first served. Also the other buyer already owned the land next to the block I sold to him. I felt that it was the right thing to do."

Michael interrupted, "Which block did you keep for us?" hoping it was the block with the house.

He replied "The block with the house on it." They breathed a sigh of relief. They had got the block they had wanted. The price was agreed at two pounds an acre, balance payable annually over ten years.

They paid a deposit of fifty pounds and had the Title Deed listed in the names of Michael's sister Maeve Keogh and Mary Kirwan, who was Seamus's widowed sister. Mr Carroll would do the conveyancing for them. The deed would be ready within thirty days for collection. They agreed that the deed could remain in his care locked in Carroll's safe. After they had celebrated by having lunch and a few ales at the hotel, Michael and Seamus collected the horse and cart and, together with the dog, headed to their newly acquired farm. It was now December 1855.

The road between Kyneton and Malmsbury was reasonably direct but did a large S-turn down a hill to the Campaspe River Bridge mid-way between the towns. This was where their block was situated, about seven miles from Kyneton, on the hill overlooking the bridge.

When they arrived at the block they began to have a detailed look at the property. The house walls were solid and it had three rooms. They were not overly concerned at the condition of the roof as it could be repaired without too much trouble. Michael had the skills to do it.

Over the next weeks they made six paddocks with dry rock fences and marked out a large area adjacent to the house for a vegetable garden and orchard. The boundary did not require fencing as Hawthorn bushes had been planted around the entire block and with their denseness, made both a hedge and a fence. The hedge would require trimming and cutting back every few years to ensure it maintained its denseness.

The second week they purchased a plough, some seedlings, timber for the roof and a few geese to act as watchdogs when Seamus was away with the dog. While Michael repaired the roof, Seamus prepared the vegetable garden. Water was no immediate problem for the garden although the water barrels needed to be dragged by the horse on a skid, from the river. Although the rainfall was good, a reserve of water needed to be kept near the house for themselves and the garden. They would purchase a large water tank later and use the water runoff from the roof to fill it.

After a month, Seamus decided to go shearing to earn some money for their coffers and it was agreed that Michael would continue improving the house and maintain the vegetable garden and orchard.

Two weeks after Seamus departed, Michael was awakened during the night by the geese making a racket. This was joined by a heavy banging on the door. A voice called, "We need some help." Michael's revolver was in a holster behind the door. As he opened the door he had his hand touching the butt, but he withdrew his hand when he saw the first man with a revolver and the second man with a shotgun pointed at his midriff. He pushed the door wide open and stepped back as two men entered his home.

The taller man introduced himself. "I'm Captain Irish and I mean you no harm but we need food. Help me and we will be on our way. Our pack horse fell down a ravine and we lost all of our tucker." He handed Michael a gunny bag.

Michael made no comment but walked to the larder and removed half of all he had including tea, sugar, salt, meat and some damper; it nearly filled the bag. He handed the bag to Captain Irish.

"What's your name?" asked Captain Irish.

Michael said, "Michael Somerset."

Captain Irish looked at him, noting an Irish accent similar to his own and just said, "Umm I will remember it. I bid you goodnight and I am in debt to you for your food. We will meet again." He nodded and shook his hand and thanked him. Both he and his partner turned and walked out the door, mounted their horses and galloped off into the night.

Michael had noticed that Captain Irish had been holding a magnificent new type revolver, heavily engraved with ivory. After they left Michael sat down with a cup of tea. It was only then that he noticed that his hand was shaking. He was sure that if he had pulled out his revolver he would have been shot. It had been a nerve racking experience.

Seamus returned after nearly six weeks. He said he'd had plenty of work and he had brought home several lambs and a ram.

Michael laughed. "From small things, big things grow." He suggested that as the grain season was approaching they should plant some corn. With their farm produce they were now becoming self-sufficient. All they needed was a cow or two and maybe a few pigs.

Michael had built a barn and a few pens for the day when they would be shearing their own sheep. They had named the farm 'Woodlea' and had the name printed in white paint on the main gate which had been painted emerald green. They now had an address and could communicate without using their names. He wrote to Heather Alford advising her to address his letters from Maeve, simply as: 'Woodlea' Kyneton, Colony of Victoria.

However, little did he know that this letter arrived after Maeve had left Ireland.

They were almost living a normal life but they were both aware that a simple slip could be their downfall and could result in them being sent back to Port Arthur. Michael Keogh and Seamus Lynch were still runaway convicts, no matter how successful they were.

They continued to be clean shaven, with short hair and trimmed eyebrows. They decided they needed another horse and a larger cart. Seamus had made good money on his last shearing venture and they could afford to buy not only another horse and cart but also a water tank at the house. They were a good team.

Their crops had good yields and vegetables and fruit were bountiful. They also had some sheep to slaughter. They decided to load the large cart and go to the goldfields to sell their goods. They travelled to Malmsbury and joined the main road to Bendigo which started south on the outskirts of Melbourne at the town of Keilor. The road was notorious for bushrangers robbing travellers after dark, particularly on the Black Forest Road near Woodend. Malmsbury was well north of Woodend so Michael and Seamus felt reasonably secure, armed and with the dog to warn them of approaching strangers. The road trip was tedious as they could only travel at a slow pace due to both the heavy load and the steep terrain they encountered several times. The road was good on the higher sections but rutted in the lower sections, sometimes full of water. They were careful and eventually reached the Bendigo goldfields without any damage to the cart, horses or themselves.

The goldfields consisted of hills and valleys with thousands of people from all walks of life endeavouring to find their El Dorado at the end of their pick or shovel. They lived in tents, lean-tos or under a tree, some even in the pits. The roads were only tracks and ablution facilities were non-existent.

Michael and Seamus set up a stall from the side of the cart between the end of Bendigo and the goldfields. Business was slow for the first two days but within six days they had sold all the produce they had brought with them. It had taken them over a week to get there but it had been worth the effort and time. They decided to stay in a hotel for the night before they returned home, as they felt they had earned some type of luxury.

As they headed out of town, an armed military squad halted them and an officer walked over. They feared the worst, but when he stopped alongside the cart he saluted Michael and said, "Be on your guard, you have probably made some money from your sales and the word may be out to the bushrangers to rob you. I am unable to provide you with an escort today but if you can wait for the gold shipment next week, you would be welcome to travel with my squad."

Michael thought for a second and decided it was better to keep clear of the soldiers in case one of them made a slip of the tongue and gave themselves away. Michael thanked the officer for his kind offer and warning. He touched the horse with the whip and they headed south to connect with the main road to Melbourne. If they were bailed up they would tell the bushrangers they were only workers.

They each then put a few pounds in their pockets and then hid the rest under the horse blanket. The horses would be of no interest to them as they were just work horses, hardly mounts for bushrangers!

They had travelled for two days mainly downhill and expected to be home within two more. That night they set up camp and put the horse out to graze on a long line. Michael hid the money and the pistols in a hole in a tree about one hundred yards away. The two of them could not win a shoot-out if ambushed by bushrangers at night; they would be killed. Daylight was a different matter.

Early in the morning the dog started barking furiously. Michael and Seamus awoke to see three men riding straight at them. They dismounted quickly and drew their pistols at them before they were fully awake.

The leader said, "Money or your life, what is it to be?" As ordered they each emptied their pockets and handed over the few pounds they had kept.

The leader laughed at them. "I am not joking, where is your money?"

Michael said, "We are only drivers, the money we gave you is our wages for delivering the cargo to Bendigo; the boss has the money."

The leader turned to his men. "Search everywhere. They may be lying!"

Michael and Seamus were tied to a tree while the search continued for over an hour. The bushrangers looked everywhere, under the cart through their sleeping bags, even the horse blanket which was lying on the ground, the harness and finally stripped them naked to search their clothes. Finally, the bushrangers gave up and without a word rode off, leaving them tied to the tree, naked. They were soon able to release themselves, made a brew and had a good laugh at their successful ruse.

When they arrived home they sat down and counted the

money and were pleasantly surprised to find they had collected two hundred and fifteen pounds. This was enough to pay off the bank loan, buy seed and some more young lambs.

Michael decided to pay off the loan the next day and as he prepared to leave Seamus asked him to put an advertisement in the Guardian newspaper about their shearing business.

They had placed a shingle outside the gate letting other farmers know of their capabilities, but it hadn't got them any shearing work locally. Michael went to the bank and paid off the debt. With a letter from the bank manager, he then went to Mr Carroll and requested that the deed be noted that the property was now debt free.

He had to search for the Guardian newspaper as it was not in the main streets. He found it set back off a side street. As he opened the door he caught sight of a man entering an office and vaguely recognized him. But from where?

The desk attendant asked, "May I help you, sir?"

Michael explained his business and paid for the advertisement. He paused and then asked, "What is the name of that man in that office?"

She answered, "Oh, that's Mr Brendan, the new owner."

"Could we be introduced, please?" The attendant came back with Mr Brendan.

"How may I help you?" They shook hands and Michael asked if they could speak privately. He agreed and they went to his office, and he closed the door behind them. He invited Michael to be seated.

Michael looked closely at him. He was Brendan Devine, the famous Irish rebel. Michael said quietly, "Do you remember Galway Bay and the *SS Nantucket*?"

Brendan's face did not change; it remained expressionless. After a second or two he said, "Could you explain that comment?"

"Yes, I was one of the two crew on the boat that sailed you to Galway Bay. I wore a sheep skin bonnet and had a short beard," Brendan replied.

"Should I remember you as such? But I do have a name that I have not forgotten."

Michael said, "I am Michael Keogh."

Brendan smiled broadly. "Yes, I remember you and your father. I have never forgotten your help. What a small world we live in. To meet you again is unbelievable." He stood up and hugged Michael. "Your help allowed me to escape to America and establish a branch of the Free Ireland Party called the 'The Fenian Brotherhood of America'. I am now doing the same here." He looked up at the clock on the wall. "I must apologise for now. Do you mind? I have an urgent appointment. Could we meet later and talk again?"

Michael invited Brendan to dinner at the farm within the week. He was delighted to meet this man again and looked forward to seeing him for dinner.

9

The dog started barking causing Michael to look in the direction the dog was facing and in the distance he could see a rider approaching. He could not help but be amazed at the extraordinary hearing of the dog. The rider was nearly a half mile away!

It was Brendan. He dismounted, smiling. They shook hands and he presented Michael with a bottle of Irish whisky. Seamus walked up to them and offered his hand and introduced himself, welcoming him to Woodlea.

It was an evening that none of them would forget. After dinner the three of them sat and told each other their life stories. It was probably the only times in their short lives that they had completely considered their previous deeds and the reasons they were now in Victoria. They each considered what they would do differently if they had another chance.

Both Brendan and Michael said they would still have done the same deeds again, as they believed they were morally right in their actions and were satisfied with their current positions in life. However, Michael made the point that he would consider his life a failure if he did not recover the stolen sword and cape, the Irish treasures taken from his father by a British Army officer named Colonel Lang.

Seamus thought for a while before he made a comment. He had been an apprentice roof thatcher in Limerick for a year before he fell afoul of his employer's vicious temper. His employer drank from noon until dusk leaving Seamus to do the majority of the work. His last job was required to be completed on time. It ended up needing two more days work to satisfy the house owner. His employer was penalised and was not paid the full amount of the original agreed price. The employer blamed Seamus and struck him with a paling. Seamus retaliated by throwing a stone at him and hit him in the face. The employer then sent for the constable. Seamus had no option but to run away and left the town forever. He was only able to obtain menial jobs and eventually this resulted in him becoming a poacher. He said he had enjoyed being a roof thatcher but having not completed his apprenticeship and having no money to start up this employment, this situation lead to him ultimately becoming a convict and fortunately now a farmer.

Seamus laughed and summed up saying, "I think my employer did me a favour by hitting me."

Michael asked Brendan about what had happened when he boarded the SS *Nantucket*.

Brendan started, "Well, I picked a bad time to board the ship.

The ship's captain was entertaining some British officials. The two seamen who met me at the ship's side took me below into their quarters in the bow and that's where I stayed until the ship sailed for New York two days later. They said that the captain was an American and often carried Irish passengers, legal or otherwise."

"However, as I thought, there were Irish crew members on board and they went ashore to meet with my contacts in Galway and returned with a small box for me. With the two Irish crew members keeping watch, I opened the box in the seclusion of the rope locker and found several brochures, a list of names written in Gaelic and a quantity of money in various denominations."

Brendan continued. "After giving the crewmen a token payment, I hid the box in the shipwright's timber store. With a great sense of relief I felt the ship get underway. My next concern was that the crewmen took me to the captain. I hoped that this would not be a problem. I knew he would not turn back to Galway but also I didn't want to be in the brig for the entire voyage.

"We waited outside the captain's room until a voice called, 'Enter'. A tall middle aged man sat behind a desk studying a large navigation map. Another man stood alongside him with dividers and a pen in his hand. I found out later that he was the first mate and navigator. One of the Irish crewman explained that I wanted passage to New York. Captain Stevenson smiled. He agreed to my passage provided I kept to myself, and to keeping me off the manifest provided I did not make any trouble. Then he asked me my name. I gave him the name I was told to give — Brian Boru and he laughed. Apparently, the name is popular because I was the second one to use it that year. We agreed that I would pay the normal passage price. I gave my word that I would adhere to his rules Then Captain Stevenson told the Irish crewmen to take me to a small cabin on the main deck. After retrieving the box, I paid for my fare and began to inspect the contents in depth. The brochures were similar to the ones that I had got into trouble with in Kilrush. I presumed correctly that they would be used as a basis to write an appropriate American brochure to support 'The Fenian Brotherhood of America.'

"The list of names — fourteen in all — were of Irish origin. Some names were familiar and I looked forward to meeting with them. I had heard that the Irish in New York were more Irish than those living in Ireland.

"The voyage was uneventful, with the ship tacking continuously into the westerly winds, the pitching and the rolling became monotonous, up then down, over and back with the seas smashing into the bow and spraying the fo'castle. The top sails had been reefed to reduce the stress on the masts from the wind strength. We passed a few ships and saw little sea life. All in all it was an extremely boring trip. The coastline of America appeared at dawn, with the sun rising behind us, shining on the shores, a calm sea and I was full of anticipation for my future crusade. This day was memorable as the last day of my voyage of escape from Ireland."

He continued to tell them how the SS Nantucket was positioned alongside the wharf by two small boats and tied to the wharf bollards. After bidding farewell to Captain Stevenson, Brendan went ashore with the two Irish crewmen, who took him to a popular Irish pub frequented by well-known Irish businessmen. Brendan ordered three meals for them while they asked the barman and patrons, who were their friends, if they knew any of the names Brendan gave them. By the time they had completed their meals, two men had approached them and introduced themselves. They were on his list. The Irish crewmen bid farewell and wished him success in his venture and departed.

Mick Hogan and Will Badger introduced themselves as New York policemen. Brendan was to learn that seven of the men on the list were policemen, three of the others were city officials, one a lawyer and the other three were dock workers who held influential positions.

Each of them was in a position of influence either political or industrial and they were well organised.

Thousands of Irishmen lived in America and most of them were in New York. Mike and Will knew of Brendan and his escape and subsequent mission. They arranged accommodation and meals at the home of a prominent businessman and then took him shopping as he had arrived with virtually nothing. Over the next month he was taken throughout the city. He was indoctrinated with the district, its history, local customs and politics, meeting people, identifying problems the Irish had in New York. Brendan was most interested in what was being done to raise money and how they highlighted the problems of the Irish people in Ireland, to the people in Europe.

The committee of the Fenian Brotherhood of America was in its infancy when Brendan arrived in New York. After he felt he had a feel for the New York way of life and the Irish interface, he asked to meet with the committee. The committee consisted of ten of the fourteen names he had been given in Galway. They all had one thing in common — a fierce Irishness and had left Ireland determined to help recruit members and improve the lot of their countrymen, either by returning in armed conflict or to provide material support with money, arms or both.

The first meeting he attended was basically a discussion, with an open agenda and loose discussions, without seeking policies, actions or plans. Brendan could see that some committee members would not be team members and could be difficult to keep focused on a task however well-meaning their intentions might be. He found Mick, Will and Lionel Jamieson, the lawyer, to be the most logical thinkers who did not lose their trend of thought on important issues. He listened to their comments and made notes on their reasons and possible solutions. There was considerable discussion on minor problems which were of no interest to Brendan and his mission. He decided he would give tacit support to these problems to keep the other committee members on side but he would be focusing on the acquisition of arms and money and getting the 'Irish Message' to Europe. The meeting ended cordially with the members patting each other on the back for their contribution, no matter how important or menial it had been. It was decided to have a formal meeting within the month with a set agenda to identify priorities and with suggested solutions. They then proceeded to open the bar and drink, somewhat to excess in Brendan's opinion. He knew it was the Irish way.

Brendan began work on the wording of the brochures for the Fenian Brotherhood of America. He wished to emphasise the horrors and the deaths from the famine and the barbaric British rule. The wording was factual, accurate and pointed, aimed at having the maximum impact on the reader. The brochures would have large lettering and could not be more than eight inches by twelve inches, to fit on the gas lamp poles and be easily handed out. He focused on disputing comments made by the Times newspaper whose editor was a known bigot and critic of the Irish population.

After a week he had decided on the wording and approached Mick, Will and Lionel for their comments. He was more interested in Lionel's opinion from a legal point of view because he did not want to cause any local animosity towards the Irish or end up in a law suit in New York. He needed the Americans' support to be able to carry out his mission.

They all agreed that the wording was suitable. The final judges would be the public. The response was much better than even Brendan expected, with recruits and money literally pouring in.

The Fenian Brotherhood of America was delighted and they could and would continue their attack on both the English government and their press, using Brendan's methodology and would now deal directly with contacts in Dublin. He had done his job in New York quicker than expected. He had originally planned to be in New York for three months but had done his task in two. He was then off to the colonies of Australia, funded by The Fenian Brotherhood of America, arriving in Melbourne in January 1854. Since then he had established himself as a prominent member of the local society, despite some bias against the Irish.

Michael and Seamus had sat listening to him, totally absorbed in Brendan's story.

Suddenly he yawned, stood up and said he must be away. "I'm travelling to a meeting in Melbourne on the noon coach."

They agreed to meet frequently. Each shook hands and Michael and Seamus walked out to his horse with him. Brendan mounted, gave a wave and headed back to Kyneton. It had been an incredible evening of revelation.

Michael and Seamus had now been in Victoria for nine months and during this time they had continued to keep a low profile. Generally, they were self-sufficient and if they did need goods they drove the shearing cart into town. It gave them an image of respectability as journeymen. They had planted the vegetable seeds, pruned the fruit trees, cut wood for the approaching winter months and had built another room onto the house. This was the time to improve the property and plan their produce as shearing would not start until the end of winter, several months away. They had succeeded in their objective to establish a farm. The only wish Michael still had was to receive a letter from Maeve.

Her last letter told him of his father's and her decision to travel to the colony but it had no local address or date of arrival. He had received an answer from Heather Alford acknowledging his request to use the Woodlea address in future but nothing further from Maeve. Why had he not received a letter?

CHAPTER SIX

The Keoghs Emigrate

dmund Keogh patted the dog. "Let's go for a walk." He headed out of his cottage and strolled down the path towards the cliffs. The day was cloudless and the sun shining made for a pleasant stroll. He never tired of the view he had known from his earliest years — the birds, the flowering lichen, the rabbits and the rugged cliffs with the seas continually spraying upwards as they smacked into the cliff face. The smell of the salt water spray, the wind in his ears and the noise of the waves completed the scene. Such serenity!

He was under pressure from his family to make up his mind whether to go to Australia or to stay in Ireland. If he did go, he would miss visiting this setting. What to do?

His brother, Sean, had returned from his gold prospecting in America and now intended to stay home. Both Sean and Jane needed to be together after all of the years of separation. Maeve had moved back to be with her father two weeks ago, and had taken Michael's bed.

She had broached the question of leaving Ireland and going to Australia. Edmund did not answer immediately and just sat there looking at her. He looked out of the window for several minutes. Finally he said, "I think it is a good idea. The future of Ireland is not promising — it may even get worse — so you should look to your future. You have John waiting for you in a new country. Yes, you should go."

Maeve interrupted. "No, I mean we both go."

Edmund waved his hand in the air. "No, it's your future that is important, don't worry about me."

Maeve replied and tried a bluff. "We both go." She then got up and started to prepare the evening meal.

Edmund shook his head, stood up and walked out of the cottage. He knew she would raise the subject again and soon. He would like to be with her but he was getting on in years, with health problems and he was comfortable with his lot in life. The fear of the unknown, at his age, concerned him and there was also the cost of the passage. He had some money but not a lot.

Aunt Jane knew that Maeve wanted to go to Australia and encouraged her. She also guessed that Edmund would be reluctant to leave Ireland and go to a new country.

She invited Edmund and Maeve to dinner with the express purpose of helping to solve the impasse. Sean had returned to Ireland and had become very interested in farming again. When he found out that Maeve intended to go to Australia, he wondered if Edmund would accompany her. If so, he would like to add their farm to his and Jane's farm.

During dinner, Sean asked his brother, "If you go to Australia, we would like to continue farming your land. We would pay you a reasonable amount and it would help you and keep the land under Keogh control."

Edmund appreciated the concerns of his family, for him, but he knew that Sean and Jane did not have much money to spare. He had only made wages in America and their farm produce sustained them but they made little profit. However, Sean believed that with Edmund's land they would gradually save some money. The dinner finished without Edmund giving an answer either way.

A week after the dinner meeting, Sean went to the Kilrush

market, and like all farmers, joined with a group. They started talking and discussing local news. One farmer made the comment that he and his family were off to Australia as Government Assisted Immigrants.

Sean was fully attentive and, after asking a few questions and making further enquiries, he went and obtained an application form from the customs office at the docks. If money was Edmund's main concern, Sean hoped that this offer of a free passage to Australia would help him make up his mind.

On his return Edmund listened to Sean explain the Government Assisted Passage terms and he had to admit it did appeal to him. The money he had and what he would get from Sean and Jane would give him some independence. He knew that Maeve and John would want him to live with them and he accepted that situation would not be debatable, nor need it be.

Edmund, after his stroll to the cliffs, with Maeve in tow, walked to Sean and Jane's farm. They all sat down and dramatically Edmund stood up and said, "I will go to Australia with Maeve." Then equally dramatic he sat down.

The women both kissed Edmund, and Sean shook his hand. Sean opened a bottle of whisky he had been saving for an important occasion such as this. They toasted each other, the Australian colonies, Ireland and when somewhat inebriated, even the dogs, while they all absorbed the implication of Edmund's decision now that it had finally been made.

Edmund and Maeve walked home in silence; Edmund with his thoughts of travelling to a new land and leaving Ireland possibly forever, and Maeve with her thoughts of seeing John again. It was over a year since they had parted and now they would meet again.

The Keoghs needed to apply to be listed as Government Assisted Immigrants. This arrangement was handled by

Edmund's brother, Jack. As a businessman he was held in high regard; even the British conceded that he was a valuable citizen. The paperwork took nearly two months to be completed and Maeve and Edmund were advised that their ship would be leaving from Cork Harbour in the first week of November 1855.

The final weeks, prior to travelling to Cork for their departure, were difficult. Both Maeve and her father decided to only take family mementos and clothing. The furniture had no real value either as heirlooms or in money. They would take some books, prints, letters, ornaments and bric-a-brac, including Mary's gift, *Etiquette for a Young Lady*. They would only take two sea chests as personal belongings. One of the chests was almost as old as the one which had contained the stolen sword and cape. Sean gave them the second chest which had accompanied him during his wandering years. The letters, 'KEOGH', on the lid were starting to fade now.

Their friends dropped by more often now, as they had appeared to have increased their image in the local community by their decision to make the trip to the antipodes. Many jokes were shared as to what they might expect from the weird and wonderful Australian animals and what the Aborigines might be like! Edmund and Maeve enjoyed the good natured jesting. They had made up their minds to go and they would not be deterred, no matter what comments were made. They even decided to accept Jack's invitation to stay in Kilrush for a week with his family.

It was difficult leaving the farm and the animals, particularly the dog, man's best friend! They left the furniture and tools in the farm and took the bedding and clothes they did not want to Aunt Jane's farm. It would not get mildewed there. Patrick had indicated he would visit Kilrush occasionally and would stay at his father's farm. Sean was satisfied he could manage the extra workload and had settled back into country life again with Jane.

Edmund and Maeve left the farm without fanfare. Tears were shed and promises made by both parties to write often, kisses all round and away they went down the road for the last time. Aunt Jane gave Maeve a wedding veil as a farewell gift. Maeve looked back from the top of the road and in the distance she could still see Aunt Jane waving goodbye. They had left the farm forever.

Sean had borrowed a large cart and drove both of them with their two chests to Jack's home. He needed to get the cart back so didn't linger. After a quick wave to them he turned his cart around and headed back home.

Edmund and Maeve had accepted Jack and Anne's invitation for them to stay a few days. James was still living at home and worked with his father at the boat yard and seemed as excited as Edmund and Maeve about their voyage. He had bought them a book and a map of the Australian Colonies as a going away present, after reading them himself. He was enthralled by the description of the unique animals. Perhaps he might travel there himself one day! Edmund and Maeve had a daily walk into Kilrush and down to the docks, taking their last look at town. They would both miss County Clare and their acquaintances but they balanced this with the optimism of a voyage to a new life in a new land together with meeting John again and possibly locating Michael.

Two days before they were scheduled to leave Kilrush, walking up past the barracks to Jack's home, they heard a voice call, "Mr Keogh, sir." Looking around they saw a British officer waving to them from the barracks' gates.

Edmund recognised Lieutenant William James. He had been introduced to him by John Hall when they were on a military deployment to Galway and stopped at his farm.

He walked over to them. He saluted Maeve and shook hands with Edmund. "Good afternoon to you both. I have heard you are leaving for the Antipodes, namely Melbourne."

Edmund replied, "Yes, we leave here the day after tomorrow and sail from Cork next week."

"Have you heard from John?" he asked.

Maeve replied, "Yes, he is well and serving in the military in Victoria."

He thought for a moment and then replied, "We are having an Open Day at the barracks tomorrow for selected local identities. Would you care to come as my guests? I should like to hear more about John's life in Victoria."

Edmund looked at Maeve and, seeing no visual objection, he turned to him and said, "Yes, we would be delighted. Thank you."

"Good I'll meet you here tomorrow at noon. I must go now; I'm the duty officer. Good bye for now." He saluted, turned and marched back to the gates, passing a hawker selling caps and scarves.

Maeve was surprised at Edmund's acceptance, but Edmund felt that as Lieutenant James had been a very good friend and also supportive of John during his tribulation, he felt quite comfortable about discussing his voyage and his life in the regiment in Victoria with him.

The Open Day was a pleasant day. The sun was shining and, after having their credentials checked by the guards, Lieutenant James escorted them to a table shaded by an old tree. The new commandant made a short speech and drinks were served together with sandwiches. Edmund and William chatted away with questions and alternating answers. Edmund showed him some drawings of John's farm and the farmhouse. With all of William's questions, Edmund began to wonder if William was contemplating going to the Antipodes himself. They did not socialise with the other guests and as soon as the conversation slowed they bid their farewells with the colonel and William and walked out the gates. Edmund noticed that the hawker was still at the gate selling caps and scarves. He nodded to him as they passed.

They both were nervously looking forward to their voyage. They had an early dinner that evening and after packing their belongings ready for a noon departure next day, they went to bed.

After a fitful night's sleep, Edmund and Maeve both arose to a bleak overcast sky and had breakfast in near silence. Jack had arranged the coach to pick them up at his home. This saved them all a considerable amount of inconvenience. Edmund thanked Jack and Anne for their hospitality. The coach arrived on time at noon, with the jingling and creaking of leather and wood. Again with kisses all round; even James seemed overwhelmed with their departure. They boarded the coach with a packed lunch and a bottle of drink, courtesy of Anne. Away the horses went, with the crack of a whip and a few verbal urgings, up the hill heading for Cork. They looked back, waving, seeing Kilrush slowly disappear behind the hill. Would they ever see the town again?

The coach was clean with comfortable seats and they were not cramped. The horses were changed each hour with the coach stopping for a short break after four or five hours, for a meal and a nature break. The journey was monotonous with very little conversation between the few passengers but they were making good time. They continued into the early evening heading for Ennis and then onto Limerick.

The coach was rocking from side to side rhythmically speeding through the night with the passengers either dozing or sleeping. Suddenly, the coached lurched forward, waking them all.

The driver was shouting. "Get out of the way!" The coach

drew to a stop, the driver sitting back in his seat pulling tightly on the reins. In the full moonlight he could see a line of men across the road.

Two of the men walked forward, carrying arms. The leader said, "All of the passengers are to leave the coach!"

The passengers lined up on the road.

The smaller of the men walked along the line and pointed to Edmund and Maeve. "That's them."

The other man told them, "Come with me, you two, and pull out your baggage."

Edmund put his arm around Maeve who was shaking with fear. The other men carried their baggage to the side of the road and told Maeve to sit down. She refused and stayed with Edmund. The passengers and the driver were made to stand in a group near the coach.

The second man came forward. "Do you know why you have been taken from the coach?"

"No," said Edmund.

"We have reason to believe you have been associating with the British army and that you are passing on local information to them. Don't lie; this man saw you," the second man said as he pointed to the smaller man.

Edmund retorted angrily. "I would never collude with the British; I am a loyal Irishman."

Edmund suddenly recognised the smaller man as the hawker at the barracks gate. Edmund hesitated unsure how to explain the day at the Open Day at the barracks.

A voice said, "You will be shot if you can't explain to our satisfaction why you were in the barracks."

A young man stepped forward and walked around them. He continued to circle them and their luggage. He stopped and looked at their luggage closely. "Is your name Keogh?"

"Yes," replied Edmund.

"Are you related to Michael Keogh of Liscannor?" the questioning continued.

"Yes, I'm his father and this is his sister," Edmund answered.

"Where is he now?" was the next question.

Edmund told him. "He was been transported for seven years to Van Diemen's Land."

It was Jaime Neyland, who had become a member of the Free Ireland Party and been active in seeking out Irishmen who were pro-English. When he saw the coach pull up he stood back and watched the event unfold. He felt sorry to see a young woman involved but they had been identified by the hawker from their attendance at the Kilrush Barracks Open Day. Their group had a technique; several persons would take turns questioning a suspect. This often caused confusion with the alleged offenders and generally the group obtained the answers they expected. However when he saw the name 'Keogh — Liscannor' on the trunk, it brought back memories of Michael and he taking Brendan Devlin to Galway Bay. Thank God he saw the sign! Edmund would have had trouble explaining John's letters being shown to a British Army officer.

Jaime shook Edmund's hand. "I'm Jaime Neyland. I knew your son very well. He was my friend and is a loyal Irishman. He and I helped Brendan Devlin to escape to America." He paused and queried, "To where are you travelling now?"

Edmund replied, "We are immigrating to the Australian colonies and, hopefully, we will meet with Michael again. We know where he is."

The others of the group had gathered around and had heard what Jaime had said and all now stepped forwarded and shook his hand.

The tall man ordered, "Load their baggage back on the coach." Turning he said, "Please accept our apologies. I hope that you can appreciate our objectives. Enjoy your voyage." He quickly walked away with the group following him.

Jaime escorted Edmund and Maeve back to the coach, bidding them a safe trip. He asked to be remembered to Michael, and then waved good bye to them. He walked off into the roadside shrub, quickly vanishing from sight.

The coachman took charge and helped the remaining passengers on board.

Maeve was still shaking and snuggled close to her father. Edmund would probably never realise how close they had been to being shot as collaborators. The coach continued rocking its way through the night while the passengers sat in silence, each unsure what to say about the hold up. They changed horses at Ennis and continued to Limerick, reaching it well into the night.

There they stayed overnight in the Irish Arms Hotel. As they had arrived over an hour late they decided to have a quick meal and immediately go to bed, hoping for a few hours of good sleep ready for the next day's travel to Cork.

The trip to Cork was due south from Limerick. The roads were better and the coach only rocked slightly. Each coach seat was occupied and these passengers were now conversing. They seemed friendlier than those on the trip from Kilrush. No doubt their previous coach companions had become unsure of them after the 'hold up' incident.

During the course of Maeve talking with another passenger, Mary Cooney — a young Irish lass from Limerick — they discovered that they were both voyaging to Melbourne on the same day. Perhaps they would be on the same ship! Mary's father was in the British Army with her mother in Victoria; she was joining them.

While the two young ladies chatted, Edmund started to have doubts about the voyage. It was not so much about going to a new land, indeed a new life; he was worried he would not find the contentment he had enjoyed on his farm.

The green lush fields of County Cork rolled by monotonously. Edmund could see labourers building stone fences and clearing the road edges and laying new tracks. Sheep and cattle grazed contentedly, idly looking at the coach. The milking cows were responsible for Cork's major export produce, its butter. Cork even had a Butter Exchange where butter was graded, indicating its importance. Various crops had been sown. They would not be harvested for a few more months yet and then would only benefit the landlords and the English markets. The efforts of tenant farmers would go unrewarded again. He wondered, would Australian fields be green like Ireland's? County Clare seemed to have castles over every hill and dale, although they were picturesque, many seemed to be in a sad state of disrepair and many uninhabited.

The coach rolled on and on until small groups of houses eventually increased in density to become the city of Cork. The centre was situated on an island between two channels of the River Lee. The city was much larger than both Kilrush and Limerick, the main roads lined with small shops supplying all of one's needs. Large warehouses and Government buildings completed the picture.

The coach rolled to a stop with plenty of creaking wood and leather and jingling from the horses' harnesses. The coach driver helped the passengers alight and then unloaded their luggage, bidding them good bye. Maeve said good bye to Mary Cooney; both were hoping they would be travelling to the colonies on the same ship. They would know in three days' time when they were scheduled to sail.

Edmund and Maeve were in the centre of Cork outside the British Arms Inn, a large limestone building within walking distance of the wharfs. Both channels had ships lining the docks. They were very impressive with their tall masts and extensive rigging. Porters were hurrying to and fro pushing carts laden with all types of cargo and food products.

A voice called, "Father." Turning, Edmund saw Patrick waving to them as he hurried to join them. Father and son embraced. They had not seen each other for nearly twelve months. Patrick then hugged his sister and gave her a brotherly kiss. He had borrowed a friend's hand cart to help with their luggage. After loading it on he led them to his abode two streets from the docks.

Both Edmund and Maeve were enjoying the walk through the streets after their two days on the coach. Patrick was giving a running commentary of the city during their walk. It was obvious he enjoyed living in Cork and no doubt had a wide circle of friends due to his affable nature.

Patrick's rooms were on the first floor of a large building. Although the rooms were small they had a homely feel about them. Pictures on the walls, mats on the floor and a table cloth with a flower arrangement in the middle of the table completed the main room. Patrick had made two beds on the floor for his sister and himself and gave his single bed to his father to sleep in.

Edmund accepted the offer thankfully but he would have slept on the floor if necessary.

It was now evening. Patrick had prepared a meal of broth followed by a meat and turnip dish. Edmund and Maeve retired immediately after dinner with Patrick leaving to return the cart to his friend. They had agreed to stay up and have a family talk the next night. No one knew if they would have another chance.

Next day Patrick took them to see the shipping agent to collect their travel documents and find out which ship they would travel on. Also, importantly, where the ship was moored. Patrick knew you could walk for several hours trying to locate the vessel if you didn't know the port. However, as luck would have it, it was directly opposite the street leading to the British Arms Inn. After sorting out the travel arrangements, Patrick became a tour guide and showed them around the fair city of Cork.

The city of Cork derives its name from the marshy land of the rivers banks. Corcaigh means marsh in Gaelic. The city had several imposing buildings including churches and monuments. These buildings together with the city setting on the river made for a memorable tour. The most famous landmark was the church of St Ann's Shandon sited on a hill overlooking the river and the city. Adjacent was the butter market which was an important commercial concern.

The three enjoyed the long walk but were glad to return to Patrick's abode. That night they sat around the table and talked for hours about the past, the present and what they wished for in the future. Each was comfortable with their lot in life but was still looking forward to the future. For Edmund and Maeve it would start tomorrow on the outgoing tide.

¶

The ship had been partially rigged ready for sailing and was being loaded for the long journey to the antipodes. The farewells were painful for them all — Patrick because his family was travelling to the other side of the world, Edmund and Maeve, because they were leaving the land of their birth and neither party may see each other again.

The two of them stood on the deck opposite where Patrick stood on the dock.

The bosun called, "Release the lines," and then signalled the row boats to start rowing and towing the ship into the river channel. Once into the river the ship slowly gained speed under half sail.

They continued waving to each other until they vanished from each other's view.

The day was cloudy and chilly but both Edmund and Maeve were unaware of the weather. They were wondering what lay ahead for them. Edmund was wondering if he would see Michael again and Maeve was eager to see John again. Had he changed? What was their house going to be like? Would she like the colony?

The ship slowly made its way south down the Cork Harbour passing Cobh with its convict hulks and the coastal towns of Whitegate and Crosshaven, through the estuary and out into the open seas, turning onto a heading of south-south-east. The captain raised the topsails. They soon filled with the twenty knot westerly wind. The ship heeled and ploughed on through a four foot wave swell. It was not overly uncomfortable but Maeve was pleased when she was able to lie down on her bunk.

The ship had been named the SS Ocean Maid and had six cabins for private passengers and fifty individual bunks separated by canvas drops for the fifty Government immigrant passengers. Edmund's and Maeve's bunks were adjacent. Privacy was at a minimum but it was adequate. The private passengers would dine at the captain's table while the Government passengers' meals would be served in a community mess.

As the sun was setting, the Government passengers were called to dinner. Edmund and Maeve went forward to mid-ships to the mess room. As they were sitting down Maeve heard her name called. She turned to see Mary Cooney walking towards her. She was pleased to see Mary. They would be good company for each other. They hugged then sat together and started chatting about nothing and everything.

Mary had been billeted with an elderly married couple sharing their double cabin. She had seen Maeve coming on board but had lost sight of her. She knew she would find her at dinner time.

The ship made very good progress down the west coast of Africa. The seas were relatively calm and the sun was frequently shining. The girls sat on the main deck enjoying the sun and read to each other. This helped Maeve conquer her feelings of inadequacy due to her limited schooling.

The trip was generally uneventful. Few ships were seen on the horizon and sea life was limited. They arrived in Cape Town surprisingly on schedule. Most ships were late. After a two day stopover they headed east out into the Indian Ocean. The trip was now to become eventful, changing weather and seas making the voyage uncomfortable.

The wind speed increased and was gusting. The topsails were reefed and the main deck hatches closed and passengers confined to below decks. The sea spray from the bow periodically covered the entire main deck from the pitching of the ship. The thumping of the hull crashing onto the sea and the creaking of the timbers were difficult to ignore. Even though the hull was sound, the noises were disconcerting to first time passengers on a sea voyage. The captain changed course to find some calmer weather. First he sailed south for a day but after encountering some ice on the decks and not finding any improvement in the rough seas and high winds, he headed due north. After two days sailing north the winds abated and the seas became calmer together with the sun shining through the clouds.

Most passengers had only been eating one or two meals a day for about a week due to the weather. That night the mess was full and all had an ample meal. Life on board the ship was more comfortable. Although the seas still had a long swell and the wind was around thirty to forty knots.

The first warning of danger was an enormous crash, the ship rose up and then the hull came crashing down to the water, wallowing and yawing. The ship had struck a large whale. The passengers were dining when the collision occurred. They could hear the captain and the bosun calling out orders to the sailors. The passengers were told to stay where they were.

After about half an hour the captain walked into the mess and advised that the whale had stove in two large planks amid ship at the waterline. Although the ship was safe they had to proceed to Port Louis on the island of Mauritius for repairs. He did not wish to continue the long voyage to the Australian colonies with a less than fully sound ship. His crew was in the process of hauling a sail underneath the ship to cover the damage and the shipwrights were attempting to place other timbers over the damage. The bilge pumps were pumping out more water than was flowing in, so the ship was safe.

Surprisingly there was little panic among the passengers. The captain's prompt communication about the situation and his intended action had a calming effect. His confident demeanour and strong personality contributed to reassuring the passengers.

The trip to Mauritius was slower. The captain was taking advantage of the winds to keep the ship heeled over from the side the whale hit to reduce any water leaking into the hull where the damage had occurred. The only obvious change to life on board was that all were required to hold onto ropes and rails when walking on the sloping deck.

The seas were relatively calm so Maeve and Mary continued their deck readings. Edmund was content to sit and gaze into the distance from a position in the bow with the breeze in his face, and allow his thoughts to wander.

Mauritius, or Ile de Maurice as the French called this island in the middle of the Indian Ocean east of Madagascar, appeared as Edmund and Maeve stood in the bow watching for the southern tip of the island to rise on the horizon. The southern area of the island had a small steep mountain named Le Morne Brabant from which a hilly spine continued running north through the centre of the island.

The ship continued north and west of the reef which surrounded the sandy coastline. It then turned east half way up the coast into a small natural bay which sheltered their destination.

The town of Port Louis was the idyllic scene. Maeve marvelled at the palm trees, the lush shrubbery, and the golden sands bordering the light blue sea water. On Mary's insistence, she had purchased a large hat in Cape Town to protect her face from the sun. Maeve now appreciated this good advice as the sun's rays were intense and would have reddened her skin within an hour or two.

The captain addressed the passengers and off duty crew. He advised that they could disembark but must return on board before sundown each day. He did not know how long the repairs would take but he would sail immediately they were completed. They had been warned!

Edmund, Maeve and Mary went ashore in the third cutter and strolled around the town. It was mainly a shipping port with ships' chandlers on every corner and streets of warehouses for storing their main export, sugar cane and its by-products. Mauritius had been a French possession prior to the defeat of Napoleon, after which the British took possession of the island.

The population intrigued them. There were creoles from South Africa and Indians providing the labour in the sugar fields. The minority white population consisted of mainly locally born French speaking civilians and a few British civil servants and businessmen. The people were content, well fed and living in a pleasant environment; it was very different to Ireland.

The ship planned to leave within the week so it gave Edmund, Maeve and Mary a chance to have a day trip inland in a four wheel horse drawn cart. They travelled into the hills where the foliage was even denser and the climate cooler. Standing at a vantage point in the hills they had a grand view of the entire northern coast looking over the treacherous reefs which had claimed ships for hundreds of years. The scene was magnificent and they would never forget it.

They visited a small museum with paintings of the extinct flightless dodo bird which had been hunted down by the dogs of the early settlers.

The visit was enjoyed by all the passengers and they avidly discussed their adventures during the evening meals in the ship's mess. The ship was repaired on schedule and sailed on the tide, one week later.

The SS Ocean Maid headed out of Port Louis Harbour with a slight south westerly breeze, turned north and, after clearing the northern reefs, the ship headed east towards the Australian colonies. They were on their last leg of a long voyage with the next port of call, Melbourne in the Colony of Victoria.

The three of them sat watching an albatross wheeling and circling overhead in the clear sky. Its effortless movement was a grace to behold. They had seen some beautiful sights during the voyage but nothing surpassed the splendour of the gliding albatross. The seas were choppy with the intermittent spray annoying the enjoyment they had from walking along the deck. The girls had read all their books and had exchanged them with the other passengers.

Maeve was a quick learner and now had an excellent command of the English language, although she would always have her Irish accent. Her association with Mary had been most beneficial. They had formed a mutual bond of respect and friendship which Edmund hoped would last. They would both need friends in the new country.

The ship made good time with the strong westerly winds that prevailed at this latitude — the 'roaring forties' as the old salts called it. Fortunately the winds were steady and the ship kept an even keel for several weeks. It wasn't until they were well into the Bight that the weather changed, but even then it allowed passengers to walk on deck.

The westerly wind changed to a southerly and forced the ship to tack more frequently and hence delay their arrival. When they reached the Port Phillip Bay Heads they were four days late. Luckily the ship arrived on the high tide and managed an immediate passage through the entrance into the bay where Melbourne was located.

John had left a message and money, with the shipping agent, to be handed to Edmund upon their arrival in the port of Melbourne. The letter instructed the agent to hire rooms for Edmund and Maeve Keogh at the Travellers Inn at Williamstown and for them to wait there for him. The agent had also been requested to send a letter to John's barracks in Kyneton advising of their arrival.

On arrival at Hobson's Bay, the agent found out about their arrival by locating their names on the ship's manifest. He was most helpful and helped them settle into the inn, then he wrote to John as requested.

The Keoghs found the hustle and bustle of Williamstown a bit disconcerting after the quiet Irish village lifestyle they had enjoyed. Mary Cooney was met by her father and mother and she gave Maeve their address. After a few tears and hugs they departed, promising to write to each other. Maeve had invited Mary to be her bridesmaid for her forthcoming wedding.

The great day was getting closer. John and Maeve had not

seen each other since October 1854 and it was now March 1856. They had poured out their hearts to each other, sharing their wishes, desires and hopes. They both worried if they or the other had changed. They need not have worried.

¶

John left Kyneton well before daylight in a four-in-hand cart with Connor Scanlon accompanying him. He had received the advice that Maeve and Edmund had arrived in Melbourne the previous evening. John had been anticipating this news for nearly a month and finally he was to see her again.

The trip took until noon with several horse changes en route. The sun was overhead as they drove up the main street of Williamstown.

Maeve was standing by the window and glanced at the four-in-hand that stopped outside the inn. Two men alighted and suddenly she realised that she was looking down at John.

Her John! She did not move but simply watched him. John looked well. He was tanned and smartly dressed. He was magnificent!

Edmund was standing alongside her and saw John walking towards the inn. He took Maeve's arm and led her to the stairway. They had been expecting John since they arrived and for two days they had dressed ready to welcome him.

John was in the foyer talking to the porter when he looked up and saw Maeve descending the stairs, followed by Edmund. John just stood and looked at her. She seemed more mature and confident. She was indeed beautiful. Her face lit up when she saw him and a magnificent smile appeared. John walked to her and held out his arms to enfold her. He kissed her on the brow and they hugged each other without saying a word.

John stepped back. "I seem to have waited an eternity for this moment. I thank God for your safe arrival." He gently kissed her. Turning to Edmund he offered his hand. "Welcome to the colony, sir."

He called Connor forward and introduced him. "Connor will see the porter and collect your belongings. We will travel home as soon as we can. If we get delayed or are running very late, we will stop at Woodend."

John and Maeve sat in the back of the carriage while Edmund sat up front with Connor, who soon had the horses clipping along at a good rate. John guessed they would arrive at Sunny Lodge late evening.

While Edmund and Connor chatted to each other and exchanged their histories, John and Maeve sat holding hands. Maeve told him of her voyage. He was content just to listen to her lilting Irish voice. The story of the voyage had taken second place in his priorities.

They stopped three times to change horses and to take refreshments. At Macedon they joined with four other carriages to travel through the dangerous Black Forrest at Woodend. The convoy had a safe trip and at Woodend they each went their own way with Connor continuing towards Kyneton and Sunny Lodge.

The sun had well set when they arrived in Woodend but the sky was cloudless and the night would enjoy a full moon, so John decided to continue home. Edmund was dozing up front and the rocking of the carriage had caused Maeve to fall asleep in John's arms.

It was another two hours before Connor turned up the long driveway and headed to the house. Connor's dog, Blackie, ran down the drive barking and jumping around the carriage. With the reins pulled back and the brake applied, they stopped at their future home.

Maeve was now awake and sat up, looking around. The moonlight was shining over the fields and had cast shadows around the house. She could hear cattle in the distance and see some sheep standing at a nearby fence looking at them. It was a picture of serenity. Maeve felt that she had arrived at her destiny.

John sat in the carriage looking at her. She turned with tears in her eyes and kissed him. They left the carriage and together walked hand in hand into the house. John showed them to their rooms. It had been a long day and they immediately went to bed.

Maeve slept deeply. The next morning she dressed quickly and wandered through the house, finding her father sitting at the table in the kitchen waiting for the pot to boil. He had risen over an hour ago and had gone for a walk with Connor and had just returned to have breakfast. It was the country habit to keep the large wood stove alight all day and night in the winter months. Wood was plentiful and had been cut and stacked by Connor under the adjacent veranda.

Edmund said John had been called on by a trooper and had immediately dressed and ridden out. "Tell Maeve I'll be back by nightfall."

Connor was available for the day and after breakfast he walked with Edmund and Maeve around the farm. Maeve was delighted and Edmund was impressed with the layout, the facilities and the stock. He could see that it was almost self-sufficient. He would enjoy living here.

John arrived at dinner time and both he and Maeve sat at the end of the table and talked animatedly. They could not get enough of each other's company and it was very obvious.

The next four weeks soon passed and they had settled into a comfortable relationship born from their love for each other. During this time Maeve sat and wrote a letter to Michael c/- Heather Alford in Van Diemen's Land and gave him John's address. Her father constantly spoke of Michael. He was in his thoughts all the time.

¶

The wedding had been arranged to be held in May. Caroline Eden, the wife of John's friend William, had befriended Maeve and had been invited to be her maid of honour with John's deputy, Lieutenant Caly, John's best man. Naturally Edmund would be giving the bride away.

As Maeve was a devout Catholic, John agreed to have the marriage service in her religion. John was not a Catholic, so the Kilmore district visiting priest had suggested that they hold the wedding and the celebration at Sunny Lodge. This arrangement was satisfactory; indeed it would help resolve some potential transport problems for guests during the wedding day. The music would be provided by a local trio consisting of a soprano accompanied by a piano and a violin.

The day duly arrived. It was sunny but cold, a typical Kyneton day for this time of the year. The guest list consisted of businessmen and most civic leaders and several soldiers of the 12th Regiment including Lieutenant Colonel Sir Nickle.

The two parlours had the unnecessary furniture removed. One room was prepared for the ceremony and the other room was laid out for dinner. They had borrowed the tables and chairs from the Kyneton Mechanics Institute. Connor had cleared the farm shed and whitewashed the interior walls ready for the overnight guests' horses to be stabled. The two cooks had started cooking the day before and the serving staff would arrive one hour before the dinner was to be served. All was now organised.

After meeting Mary Cooney at the coach station, John drove

her to Sunny Lodge and returned to Kyneton to stay at the barracks for the night. The wedding was scheduled for noon.

John rose early and went to his office to check the mail. Then he carried out the daily inspection of the stables and the men's dormitory. As the wedding was on a Saturday, only a guard and a duty officer remained at the barracks; most of the others were at leisure in town. The soldiers who had been invited to the wedding had left the barracks at ten o'clock with John and Lieutenant Caly left an hour later.

The two were resplendent in their red and yellow trimmed dress uniforms and white shoulder belts, together with the sun glimmering on their black polished hats, riding boots, saddles, bridles and chrome sword scabbards. They were a fine example of British Army officers mounted on their two jet black horses. They rode quietly, listening to the birds. In the distance they could hear a laughing kookaburra.

As they came over a hill John looked down on his property and he could see the carriages of the guests and people milling around the farm house. The time had arrived.

Maeve had risen early and had breakfast with her father and Mary. She was naturally excited and was pleased she had Mary to comfort her and Caroline to help and advise her. Maeve began dressing at ten o'clock. She wore a long white dress and the others wore light pink dresses, all made by the local seamstress. Her veil was the one Aunt Jane had given to her on her departure from County Clare. The wedding room flowers, bouquets and table floral arrangements were from the farm gardens. They were simple but colourful. Caroline pinned Maeve's hair and tied ribbons in her tresses and did the same to Mary's hair.

John had bought Edmund a wedding outfit including a suit, shirt and shoes. He walked to Maeve and kissed her lightly. "If only your mother could see you now." He turned and walked away. As John and Lieutenant Caly dismounted, the priest and Connor stepped forward. The priest shook their hands as Connor took the reins of the two horses and led them to the stables. He smiled and asked, "Are you ready?" They took off their hats, placed them under their arms, took a deep breath and nodded.

The music started and they followed the priest down the hall into the temporary chapel. The guests were standing, facing them and smiling. John nodded to all, stopping when the priest stopped, turning to face them.

The music changed and John turned to see Maeve entering the room on Edmund's arm, followed by Mary and Caroline. She walked slowly towards him, in step with the music. John turned as she arrived at his side and they both faced the priest.

The ceremony went smoothly but was a blur to Maeve. She later said all she could remember was saying, "I do" and the priest's final words, "I now pronounce you man and wife." John kissed his bride gently. They turned and walked out of the room arm in arm and then from the farm under a military guard, their swords raised forming an arch. They stood side by side accepting the congratulations from their friends. Lieutenant Colonel Nickle came forward and congratulated John, not only on his marriage but the standard of dress and presentation of his command.

The reception dinner was well organised by the local chef with speeches comfortably fitted between the meal courses. John was an eloquent speaker and enjoyed receiving some good natured banter from his military comrades. He entertained the guests with comical comments and finished the dinner with a comment at the 'toast' to missing friends.

"Our day has nearly been perfect but some of our family members are not here. They are remembered and are not forgotten." He raised his glass. "To absent friends."

The guests responded, "To absent friends."

The violinist entertained the guests with medleys of popular tunes and reels. John and Maeve performed the bridal waltz, compliments of Maeve's tuition from Caroline. Their dance started a rush, with most of the guests taking a turn around the floor, even Lieutenant Colonel Nickle danced with Caroline. After dancing, refreshments were available for their parched throats.

Around five o'clock John whispered to Maeve, "It's time to go. I'm going to change now. I'll meet you in the kitchen when you're ready."

Maeve asked Mary Cooney to help her change. John asked Lieutenant Caly to tell the guests they were leaving and to ask Connor to bring a gig around to the front door area.

As Maeve and John came out the front door they received a loud round of applause. The couple moved through the crowd; they shook hands or were kissed and received best wishes for their future. John helped Maeve into the gig and, with a quick wave, they were off down the road as man and wife at long last.

John had been granted a week's leave and they decided to drive around the local countryside at leisure. The first night they stayed in Kyneton and the next day drove to the nearby village of Lauriston where there was a large water catchment. They stayed there for two nights and tried some fishing. They proceeded on to Malmsbury for a few days.

It was a wonderful week that would stay with them forever. It was a time when they could share some inner most thoughts.

Maeve opened her soul one night when she said, "I am very happy but it would be more complete if I knew where Michael was."

John had wondered why nothing had been heard of Michael. He knew he had escaped custody, but he was unaware Michael had provided Maeve with a contact address through the Alford's in Van Diemen's Land. She now told him that she had written to him at this address. John was surprised at this news but was happy for her and he hoped that something would eventuate from her letter.

They headed back to Kyneton up past a bluestone farm-house on a hill by the Campaspe River and on to home. They had enjoyed the time by themselves and looked forward to the future with anticipation.

¶

Michael stood at the back of the coach station, waiting for the mail to be sorted. The coach had arrived late and he knew that the mail would not be sorted until the out-going passengers were loaded and the horse team changed over. Maybe Brendan was in his office. Perhaps he had time to chat as he waited for the mail. He had not seen him for over two weeks. He walked to the office door and knocked.

"Come in, Michael. I saw you through the side window", called Brendan.

"Bring two teas, please," he instructed his clerk.

Turning to Michael he shook his hand. "To what do I owe this unexpected pleasure?"

"It's mail day; I'm still anticipating a letter from Maeve. Is there anything of interest happening around town?"

The tea arrived as Brendan answered. "I feel sure you will receive your letter in time. Regarding local news — make sure that you avoid the new District Police Inspector. He's out to make a name for himself."

Michael laughed. "I avoid authority like the plague."

They chatted some more before Michael took his leave from

Brendan and returned unsuccessfully again to the coach station mail room.

There was a letter requesting some shearing to be carried out in Kilmore. Over fifty sheep had been missed during the summer muster and had now been located in a gully and they badly needed to be shorn. They agreed Seamus would go as Michael was more suited to working the farm and extending the farm house. The following day Seamus loaded the shearing cart and together with the dog barking Seamus gave a wave, and headed down the road off to Kilmore.

CHAPTER SEVEN

Auckland to Kyneton

—

fter resigning his commission in the British Army, Paul Lang wrote to the Colonial Office offering his services to the Empire's colonies. He was advised that both New Zealand and the Australian colonies were seeking 'men of position' to assume roles to maintain law and order. He was further advised to proceed to the colony of his choice and present his credentials to an appropriate official. He had decided New Zealand would be his choice as it was not tainted with convict origins as were the colonies of Australia. His wife, Virginia, was happy to leave England and start a new life with new acquaintances, while son, Frederick, would continue his studies in Rome.

After an uneventful voyage from England and a two day stopover in Sydney Town, they arrived in the port of Auckland in June 1854 and took rooms at a small inn overlooking the large harbour. The settlement was spread out around the port and seemed to be progressing with many skilled shopkeepers and farmers developing their land. Their immediate impression was one of optimism. It could be felt in the air.

Paul had seen indigenous natives in South Africa and Australia but was surprised when he first saw the Maori natives. They carried themselves with a dignity far above the other races. They dressed differently, with wrap around flaxen mats; favourite adorned coverings were reserved for special days. He was to learn that the Maori had an extensive vocabulary, having names for all animals and plants. They were tattooed with various symbols, the more tattoos the higher the status in their society. He soon became aware that they were a warlike race with no fear. Prior to a battle they would perform the Haka war dance which was designed to put fear into their opponents — and often did.

Paul had several letters of introduction supplied by fellow officers and local government officials from his home county. He approached the office of the relatively new Local Provincial Government Council which had only been formed since 1852. From them he obtained the names and addresses of senior military and judicial officials. He wrote letters of request for interviews stating his former position and his inclination of the preferred position he was now seeking.

Paul received invitations to meet with a senior official of the military garrison, the local militia and the police magistrate's office. He made some discreet enquires and finally decided he would prefer a position in the militia. The militia had been formed as an armed force responsible to the Provincial Council in matters relating to civil disturbance or disorder.

It was not a police force and not an arm of the British Army. It had only recently been formed and was based in the town. He believed he would regain his confidence in such an environment. He accepted their interview first.

He duly arrived in his colonel's uniform, with his letters of introduction and was immediately ushered into the commandant's office. He was greeted by a younger man, Lieutenant Colonel James Stephenson, who exuded enthusiasm. They shook hands and the lieutenant colonel indicated for Paul to be seated.

They had some idle chatter initially as the lieutenant colonel summed up Paul.

Paul soon sensed that the commandant was alert and intelligent.

After reading the letters of introduction, he asked Paul, "What will you be bringing to the militia if you are successful in obtaining a position?"

Paul answered carefully, as he knew he must not be seen to be undermining this younger man. "Experience, support and credibility — experience in the field, a deputy for you and increased credibility for the militia by hiring a former British officer of rank."

The lieutenant colonel laughed. "I was most curious to know how you would answer that question. I have received a variety of unusual answers."

Paul was aware he gave a gasp when he realized he was not the only candidate.

The commandant continued, "I believe in quick but calculated decisions." Paul shifted uncomfortably. "I am prepared to offer you a position as my deputy as a Major. The salary will be advised to me by the Provincial Council. Do you wish for some time to think about this offer?"

Paul rose from his chair and walked to commandant's desk, extending his hand. "I accept."

"Good. Meet me here next Monday morning and we will finalise arrangements," replied Lieutenant Colonel Stephenson.

Paul felt a sense of satisfaction. Here was his chance to vindicate himself.

Major Lang and Virginia moved into officers' quarters and settled into their new life in a new country. They both had a contentment that they had not known for many years. The major's role was primarily training the militia to handle civil disorder problems with discretion initially and only use force as a last resort.

Life was easy. The troops were well trained after three

months but had little to do. However, the Maoris were unhappy with some aspects of the British rule as agreed at the Treaty of Waitangi in 1840 by the assembly of native chiefs.

The influx and spread of immigrants was bound to happen but the abuse of some of the terms of the treaty by some immigrants was causing some civil unrest. The major's baptism of fire with the Maoris was destined to happen one day. It happened with a simple stupid action of a European settler.

Sheep were being grazed in unfenced pastures. Owners were aware of the potential for sheep to wander away from the main flock. Most hired shepherds to reduce the problem. Five miles south of Auckland a sheep owner had been losing sheep and had accused a local Maori tribe of theft. The chief came down to see what the argument was about. During the ranting of the sheep owner he pushed the chief who fell on his back. The tribe did nothing at the time and the sheep owner continued his abuse as he mistook the lack of action as meekness.

That evening the tribe had a meeting and decided that the sheep owner must be punished. Two days later the tribal warriors descended on his farmhouse. The owner saw them coming and, together with four farm hands, decided to challenge the tribal warriors. The five of them stood outside the farmhouse with single barrel shot guns. The warriors stopped fifty yards from them and commenced to do the Haka war dance and were soon agitated. The sheep owner soon realized that they were going to attack regardless of his guns. The five hurried inside, bolting the doors and windows.

The Haka lasted nearly a minute and the warriors were all now at fever pitch of excitement. The dance stopped and the warriors charged the house. Shots were fired and two warriors were wounded but they continued up to the house, determined to break in through the doors or windows. They eventually

forced open the rear door and grabbed the sheep owner, drag-
ging him outside and killed him. The others were left alone to
live another day.

Three days later the news of the sheep owner's death reached
Auckland. The immediate reason for his death was unknown
as there had been no witness to the previous incident, other
than the Maoris.

After lengthy discussions it was decided to send in the militia to attempt to apprehend the culprits. There was no positive
description to identify the individuals and it was unlikely the
warriors involved would be handed over by the chief.

Lieutenant Colonel Stephenson gave the task to Major Lang
who immediately thought this was an opportunity to show
his value. Major Lang quickly assembled a lieutenant, two sergeants and twenty troopers, armed with guns and swords, and
marched to the district.

The tribe lived in a village or pa which was on a steep hill and
was surrounded by dense palisading of strong stakes fronted
by a ditch. It could be difficult to enter if the tribe wished to
defend itself from intruders.

Major Lang knew of this pa and, as he rode out, he pondered
the dilemma of how to gain entry. He knew he must first negotiate as he had been ordered by his commandant in no uncertain
terms. They neared the pa and the village gradually came into
sight.

The closer they got the more difficult their task appeared.
When they were about two hundred yards from the entrance
a young warrior walked down to meet them. The major and
Sergeant Mitchell dismounted and, handing the reins of their
horses to a trooper, they both walked to meet him.

The warrior could speak a little English and said, "No! You
stop here."

Major Lang responded, "I wish to speak to the chief." He pointed to the sergeant and himself and said, "Him and me speak to chief. Others stay," pointing to the platoon.

The warrior said, "Come." The three of them walked slowly up the steep hill, climbed over the wooden barrier and then headed towards the biggest of the huts.

There were Maoris everywhere. Lang did not realize that the pa contained so many people. They entered the large hut and were confronted by ten senior Maoris seated in a semi-circle. Their escort motioned them where to sit and he sat behind them. The scene was solemn; the Maoris were not happy. Lang would have a difficult, if not impossible, task in front of him.

The chief gave a welcome sign and then spoke. Their escort translated. "Why are you here?"

The major said, "We have come for the men who killed the sheep man."

The answer came quickly and directly. "No." Generally the Maoris were very verbose but not this time.

The major asked, "Why?"

"We have decided," he was told.

The major then made a direct statement. "If you do not hand them over to us, we will have to come and find them and take them." The looks on the faces of the ten Maoris gave him his answer. Immediately the major knew there would be no more discussion.

The escort said quietly, "Come, you go now."

As they rose to leave the major said quietly to Sergeant Mitchell, "Remember all you see on our way out and walk slowly." They then returned to the platoon, mounted their horses and headed back to the Auckland Barracks.

He immediately reported to his commandant who sat quietly and listened intently.

When he had completed the verbal report, Lieutenant Colonel Stephenson asked, "You said there were ten Maoris sitting in a semi-circle, were they dressed similarly?"

The major responded, "No, they had different coloured wraparound cloaks and had different tattoos. They were all senior and had a commanding appearance. They could have all been chiefs; it appeared to be a major meeting."

The commandant thanked him for his report and asked him to immediately put the report in writing and get it to his office. When he received the report he went to meet with the Provincial Council. Lieutenant Colonel Stephenson was most disturbed by the ten chiefs being at a pa meeting.

During the meeting he was advised that there was to be a meeting with the Paramount Chiefs within the next ten days and that his presence together with Major Lang was required. There was a possibility that the chiefs were meeting early prior to this meeting to discuss their own concerns to be raised. It was decided to await the meeting outcome before any further action regarding the killing of the sheep owner.

The meeting was held in the town hall. The two militia officers arrived on time in day uniform and were shown seats behind the Provincial Councillors. The chiefs filed in, in order of seniority, and sat opposite the councillors, completing a circle. The Maoris sat with a quiet composure, both dignified and proud, exuding strength.

The major had a good look at them and then wrote on a piece of paper — 'These are the chiefs I met at the big pa.' He handed the paper to the commandant who handed it onto the Presiding Councillor who nodded acceptance.

Stephenson turned to Major Hall, and said quietly, "The centre chief is one of the chiefs who signed the Treaty of Waitangi."

The meeting went smoothly when dealing with the

administrative matters and several issues were resolved quickly between the two parties. When the Presiding Councillor started addressing local issues, the chief sitting to the right of the paramount chief rose to his feet majestically. This indicated that what he was about to say was important in his opinion. Everyone could sense a change of mood in the room. The Provincial Councillors became most alert, ready to absorb his every word.

The chief was the second most senior of the group and spoke the English language slowly and deliberately. "Our Paramount Chief has been insulted by your sheep man and your soldier." He pointed to Major Lang who gasped at this comment being levelled at him. The chief then resumed his chair.

The Presiding Councillor said, "Please explain what happened to cause the death of the sheep owner." The same chief rose again and spoke. The councillors and militia men listened in silence as the chief detailed, accurately, the incident leading to the chief being pushed to the ground. The councillors realized that a serious impropriety had occurred to one of the most important chiefs in the country.

The chief was then asked to explain the second insult involving the major.

The chief said, "This soldier said he would come into our pa and take our warriors. We will not allow this." The chief sat down.

No one spoke. For a few seconds the room was quiet. It was now noon. The Presiding Councillor saw this as an opportunity to call a halt to the morning proceedings. He also wished to have discussions with the other councillors and the militia officers to come up with, not only answers, but also some solutions. He acknowledged the chief's statement, thanked them for their attendance and requested that they all meet again the next day to discuss these matters further. The Chiefs left the building while the others adjourned to the dining room. It was to be a luncheon discussion.

The tables were formed into a circle which allowed a group discussion, face to face. During their meal the councillors spoke freely in front of the militia officers. The first subject was regarded as serious by all and surprisingly each of the councillors agreed that the Maori story of the incident was probably correct. But what was the best way to handle the insult and the murder allegations? The Treaty of Waitangi guaranteed certain rights to the Maoris implying a spirit of fairness to them.

Lieutenant Colonel Stephenson suggested that an apology in writing could be considered and that the murder would remain unsolved as no witnesses would ever be found. This would ensure that the incident and the murder could be closed to the benefit of both parties with no loss of face. After several minutes of debate this suggestion was agreed unanimously by the councillors. Lunch was completed and port and cigars were handed around. The second issue of the insult was now raised. The Presiding Councillor called for the scribe to come to the room.

The scribe was asked to read back the words the chief had said regarding Major Lang. Lang was then asked to comment on these words.

Major Lang said, "Sir, I choose my words carefully. I did imply armed force. My words were to show the importance we attached to locating the culprits who committed the murder. It was merely a bluff and not really warranting military action. Frankly, I agree with the Lieutenant Colonel. We will never identify them."

The Presiding Councillor said, "Yes, I can see where you were coming from and I agree we need to show the importance of our efforts to maintain law and order to the Maoris. They must assist us with these efforts. Even though we will not locate these culprits I shall stress this requirement at tomorrow's meeting."

The following morning the meeting re-assembled. The Presiding Councillor first spoke at length about other matters and then broached the issues of the insults. He spoke for a short time and then handed over a paper with the written apology for the insult to the Paramount Chief by the sheep owner.

Regarding the murder, he stated that murder was unacceptable for any reason under British Law and hoped in future that the chiefs would convey this message to their people. Also that it was expected that the chiefs would assist in identifying people who did not observe the British Law. He said that the Maori Law would be respected. Regarding the major, he stated that he was performing his duty to apprehend the culprits who committed the murder and he was making the point that he had expected the chief to help. No offence was intended to him or his position.

The Maoris were happy with the apology and the response to their perceived insult by the major. After the meeting the Maori chiefs headed back to their pas throughout the north island. The Presiding Councillor congratulated both of the militia officers on their contribution during the meeting and, after shaking hands, they both headed back to the barracks.

Major Lang had been disappointed that no further action was to be taken against the tribe harbouring the culprits but could see that it would not take much for a Maori uprising. His introduction to the councillors opened a few social doors for he and his wife. They were now enjoying their life to the fullest.

§

Lieutenant Colonel Stephenson was unsure of Major Lang's intentions. Recently he had taken two months leave and had Major Lang act in his position. He was surprised that while Lang had had many meetings reviewing militia policies and procedures, none of the meetings were recorded. Tasks such as these were part of the military yearly progress and action reports were written up daily in the office diary. When he challenged Major Lang, he became somewhat embarrassed and did not give a straight answer. He found out eventually that Lang was having them rewritten by Lang's personal clerk. The clerk had originally worked for the Lieutenant Colonel and was still loyal to him. The Presiding Councillor was verbally advised and the matter was then left in limbo for a later day.

Major Lang and his wife were now firmly entrenched in the Auckland social scene and mixed with the cream of the colony's residents. All seemed cosy and they appeared to be set to stay and retire in Auckland.

In December 1854 a small band of Maori warriors began to terrorise the area east of Auckland. The warriors had distinctive tattoos that would identify them if they were caught. At first, little concern was shown by the authorities until two women were raped and a male companion slaughtered. This prompted a call for action from all quarters. After a meeting with the Provincial Council, Lieutenant Colonel Stephenson assembled two platoons of twenty troopers, one lieutenant and two sergeants. Stephenson would lead one and Lang would lead the other. They were to be armed with rifles and swords. Stephenson addressed the men and ordered that firearms were to be the last resort but they were to respond if they felt threatened.

The two platoons separated and headed west, keeping around ten miles apart. Major Lang's track took him to a small pa not far from the last reported sighting of the rebel warriors. As he approached the pa he could see activity. All the Maoris entered the pa and closed the bracken gates. His platoon could not get in but the Maoris could not get out of the pa to obtain water. He decided to sit outside. His men took positions around the pa and waited.

After three days the gates opened and the chief invited him in. Major Lang told a sergeant to take four men with him and watch the back of the pa. He then told the chief why he was there and he politely asked him to line up all his people, which the chief did.

The troopers then searched every hut and storage area in the pa while the major inspected the Maoris. None had the distinctive tattoo. Angrily the major thanked the chief and left the pa. He headed his platoon on to the coast. He met the commandant heading back from the coast but he had neither seen nor heard of the rebel warriors. They decided to continue over each other's previous track. When the lieutenant colonel arrived at the pa, he also decided to search the pa and examine the people for the tattoo. He had the lieutenant check the Maoris while he and Sergeant Mitchell searched the area.

After a few minutes Sergeant Mitchell lent over and said quietly, "I think I know where they are. I'll get the men." The pa had a long walkway built up on soil. This path allowed warriors to look over the wall and to defend the pa. The walkway was covered in flax matting supported underneath by cross branches.

The sergeant positioned five men at each end of the walkway and then told four others to start pulling up the flax matting in the middle of the walkway. Within two minutes a hole was opened revealing a trench which went from one end to the other. The chief was called and he was told to call the rebels out or the troopers would fire into the trench. After a short wait five rebels came out and were immediately handcuffed. Their tattoos confirmed that they were the rebels. They waited for another five minutes, and then all of a sudden a warrior appeared, his club raised above his head. He charged at the lieutenant colonel from ten yards away. When he was within two yards of him the lieutenant colonel coolly drew his pistol and shot the warrior dead. After a search of the trench for any other rebels, the troopers assembled with their prisoners for their ride back to the barracks.

Although unnecessary, Stephenson thanked the chief for his help. He felt that the chief may have had no choice but to hide the rebels.

On the ride back he asked Sergeant Mitchell, "What made you think of their hiding place?"

He answered, "When the major and I were at the big pa, I saw a Maori come out of a covered trench. I thought that would be perfect hiding place for the rebels, as few Europeans would have seen one."

"Well done, Sergeant." A trooper had been sent to find and tell the major of the capture of all the rebels and for him to return to barracks.

The platoon arrived back in Auckland to crowds gathered to greet them for their successful mission. Mrs Lang watched from the upstairs' room of the officers club.

The militia had performed the task for which they had been established and now they were being acknowledged. Lieutenant Colonel James Stephenson had reason to be pleased with the day's outcome. The militia had not had total support when it was first suggested and it was only because of the Presiding Councillor's casting vote that it had been formed. He sat and wrote out his report, including that indirectly the idea for the search of the trench came from Major Lang via an order to Sergeant Mitchell when leaving the pa during their first visit. He requested that both his Lieutenant and Sergeant Mitchell read it and agree its contents were true and correct and sign it.

He took it personally to the Presiding Councillor, who read

it and showed his delight at the successful mission. He noted only one injury had been sustained albeit an unfortunate Maori rebel. The commandant then declared the next day as a recreation day for his platoon.

9

Major Lang was sitting on his horse on top of a ridge overlooking the sea. It was a cold but clear day and the view was excellent in all directions. He had decided to return the next morning. He had no luck. None of the settlers had seen or heard any news of the rebels. He heard a call and looked back down the track to see a militia trooper riding up the hill towards him.

The trooper brought his horse to a halt and saluted him. "The rebels have been captured. Five alive and the commandant shot one dead. He said for you to return to the barracks, sir."

Major Lang said, "Good," but inwardly he was seething. He had wanted to capture them so badly, to show his capability. The sergeant assembled the platoon ready for his command to ride. He waited ten minutes before the major nodded to him to proceed.

It was a quiet ride back. The platoon could sense the anger in Major Lang's mood. No one wanted to incur his wrath so no one spoke.

When they arrived at the barracks the duty officer handed him the note suggesting a recreation day for him and his platoon. There was also a package in his office. He passed the note to his lieutenant. "See to this."

He asked, "Where is the commandant?" He was advised he would return the day after tomorrow and had gone inland. The major did not go to his office; he went straight to the mess and immediately downed two whiskies. He had missed his big chance all because the commandant went on the mission.

Lang mused that the commandant had shot and killed when he had stressed that was not to happen! He would complain directly to the Presiding Councillor. Yes! That's what he would do first thing tomorrow morning.

Mrs Lang did not help his frame of mind when she told him of the crowds that lined the street and cheered the platoon. He stayed in the mess too long and consequently drank too much.

He awoke in a foul mood the next morning. He dressed carefully but seemed unaware that he still smelt of alcohol from his late night drinking. The Presiding Councillor greeted him and congratulated him on the success of the militia's mission. He motioned him to a chair and eyed Major Lang curiously, wondering why he was there.

Major Lang shifted uncomfortably in his chair and said, "I think that there is something of which you should be made aware."

"Please continue," was the reply.

"We were given strict instructions to avoid the use of firearms and here we have the commandant killing a person. This is a bad example to the troopers. I feel he is undermining my authority with the troopers."

The Presiding Councillor asked, "Have you read the report."

The major answered, "No, I haven't got one."

"Then please read this one of mine and come back this afternoon. You are listed at the end as having a copy of the report. Good day to you."

The major now realised that he had over-reacted and had not done his homework. He went directly to his office to read the report. However the first thing he saw when he entered was a large sealed envelope containing his copy of the report sitting on his desk. He now remembered what the duty officer had told him about a package being in his office.

He started to read the report and, all of a sudden, he realised that the commandant had acknowledged his contribution in locating the rebels and that the shooting was fully justified. It had been witnessed by the entire platoon.

However, he also realised that this was the same pa that he had previously searched and found nothing. Could they have been hiding in the trench then? At the end he read of Sergeant Mitchell's idea to search the walkway, which resulted in them finding the trench and from where the idea came. So this was his contribution! His over-reaction was now serious. How would he explain his 'complaints' this afternoon?

That afternoon Major Lang walked into the Presiding Councillor's office and took the indicated chair. Then waited.

The Presiding Councillor came straight out. "After reading the report you will have seen that your commandant has been supportive of you regardless of you not locating the rebels during your search. There is a possibility that they were not there then, but it is highly probable that they were. The subject of the shooting was justified and set a good example of coolness under threat of violence for responsible and prompt action. Your complaint is not in writing so I think it was spontaneous and somewhat irresponsible from a man of your training and experience. I suggest we adjourn any further discussion until Lieutenant Colonel Stephenson returns tomorrow."

The next morning both the commandant and the major were given notices to attend a militia inquiry in full uniform at 1100 hours.

The major did not go to his office.

He went directly to the Provincial Councillors' office building. The lieutenant colonel was completely in the dark as to why he was being summoned. On arrival he saw the major and asked him why were they there. Before he could answer they were called into the council chamber by the clerk.

Both stood to attention in front of a large table where five councillors sat. This was when the major noticed that the lieutenant colonel was wearing several medals. He recognised one as a bravery award and another as a campaign medal. This was the first time he had seen his awards and now realised that he had misjudged the younger man. He was not just an administrator; he had seen active service as a combatant.

The Presiding Councillor spoke first with authority. "It has come to our attention that a state of personal conflict exists between two officers of the militia. This must be resolved and now. Lieutenant Colonel Stephenson, Major Lang has accused you of undermining his authority. What do you say?"

He responded, "I am surprised that I was given no warning to prepare myself for this enquiry. However, if I am accused of undermining Major Lang's authority, I believe I should hear some examples."

"Major Lang, how do you answer? Please, we want definite examples, not vague comments or feelings."

Major Lang stood there for a while. Finally, "I need time as well to prepare my case; I did not expect an inquiry so soon."

"Major Lang, you came to me with these accusations and I want this situation resolved today not tomorrow or the next day. Do you understand?"

"Yes," he answered.

A second councillor asked, "Major Lang, while you are pondering that question, could you advise if you are, or have been, negotiating with persons in the South Island to form a militia and that you have forwarded documents concerning policy and procedures to them? I should add that these types of documents used by the North Island Militia are confidential and have information regarding control of civil disorder."

The major went white. He had been uncovered. He answered, "Yes, that is true."

The Presiding Councillor asked Major Lang to leave the chamber and wait outside.

Lieutenant Colonel Stephenson still stood to attention and he was now told to take a chair. He was still none the wiser and decided to wait for an explanation. The councillors sat huddled, talking animatedly. Some were very angry and he heard one say he had served his purpose.

The clerk was called to bring in Major Lang. He walked in, slowly, fearing the worse.

The Presiding Councillor spoke from the shoulder. "Major Lang, we have found your behaviour unbecoming an officer in the militia and consequently your commission is withdrawn forthwith. We acknowledge your contribution to the training of the troopers and your performance in the field."

The major saluted, shook hands with the councillors and the commandant. Lang then turned and left the chamber. His military bearing was obvious to all.

Turning to Lieutenant Colonel Stephenson the Presiding Councillor said, "Now we owe you an explanation. However, we will only tell you what you need to know. The major's clerk knew what was happening and two days ago, while you were in the field, he accidently found a letter concerning our militia policies, procedures and other confidential documents being copied by Major Lang, for use by an outside body. This confirmed your previous suspicions. That is why we wanted this resolved today. The 'conflict' inquiry was a red herring. Forget about it. It won't be documented. "However, regardless of his action, we can be grateful for his training of the troops, as he did an excellent job. The militia is in good shape and we will advertise for a replacement to his position for you." Lieutenant Colonel Stephenson thanked him, saluted, then turned and left the chamber.

Surprisingly, Paul Lang felt a sense of relief with the withdrawal of his commission. While he had enjoyed his time with the militia he felt he needed to reach a higher position in a military or similar Government body. As he rode back to the barracks he felt pleased with himself that he had previously, not only applied for a position in the South Island's Provincial Council, but had also written to the Colony of Victoria Constabulary and the newly named Tasmania Prison System. Paul had changed his mind about settling in Victoria or Tasmania. Victoria did not have convicts and Tasmania had ceased convict transportation in 1853. He had been told the last convict ship was the SS Vincent which had arrived in Hobart on 26th May 1853.

Only last week he had an offer from Victoria and had written back accepting it. He had not told his wife of his search for another position. He would have to now! He had to admit to himself, being discovered copying and changing confidential documents was a bad error of judgment. He was an embarrassment but if his idea for a militia in the South Island had been accepted he would have had a flying start in establishing the militia with the stolen documents. But, for an officer and a gentleman, he had gone about it the wrong way.

When he told his wife that he was no longer with the militia, she was bitterly disappointed, as she had made several good friends. She was enjoying her social status and now she would have to start all over again in another foreign land.

He received a letter from the commandant offering him their current accommodation for a month, which he gratefully acknowledged in writing. He avoided the commandant and the other officers, mainly from his embarrassment and not being able to think of an adequate response for his foolhardy action.

They began packing their clothes, valuables and selected furniture and visited the Bank of Australasia to consolidate their money into a bank draft. He had accumulated a considerable sum during his military career and still owned their home in England, which he had always intended to sell when he finally decided to retire.

He enquired at the shipping offices for the next ship destined to sail for the port of Melbourne and found that the SS Carlene was due to sail in four days' time via Norfolk Island. He paid for their cabin and made arrangements for their personal effects to be collected on the morning of the day before their departure. They would stay at an inn for their last night in New Zealand. They would leave quietly without any farewells. Virginia accepted this decision stoically. What else could she do?

The morning of their departure arrived. It was cold and misty. A carriage drove them to the docks. They both walked up the ship's gangway to be greeted by the captain. After their cabin bags were stowed, and when the ship was under way, they went up on deck to see the town of Auckland slowly disappear in the harbour mist astern of the SS Carlene with the ship making good speed assisted by a following strong south westerly wind.

After sailing for sixty miles with land on either beam, they were soon in the open sea and the ship turned north past the tip of the North Island and into the Tasman Sea en route to Norfolk Island. There was no land close for the entire voyage. The captain had stood off the coast as these waters were uncharted. Indeed, after heading north- west, the next land fall would be the isolated Norfolk Island. The navigator had good weather to take sun shots and, in the evening, star shots, with his sextant.

With excellent accuracy the isolated island appeared on the horizon dead ahead, after a voyage of eight days.

Virginia stood alongside the first officer and watched the ship's longboat lowered to the water. The sea was calm and the longboat sat comfortably as the sailors lowered their oars and then rowed towards the Norfolk Island shore. She waved to her husband, Paul, who sat in the bow with a ship's officer. The captain had agreed for him to go ashore and visit the chief constable.

The main reason for the ship's stopover was to disembark some missionaries and food supplies. The ship anchored about a mile off shore in some twelve fathoms of water; a weather watch would be kept at all times while they were at this anchorage. It was early morning and the captain wished to be under way by nightfall, as the winds were unpredictable and several ships had been driven onto the rocks before with loss of life.

Captain Cook had discovered Norfolk Island in 1774 and it had been a penal settlement since 1788, eventually being administered from Van Diemen's Land. Its convict days were now over. Two months ago, an order in council had been issued declaring New Norfolk a District Settlement under the Governor of New South Wales. The history of this penal settlement was one of brutality and inhumanity, both from a British Government policy and its administration by incompetent and unfeeling commandants. Paul Lang was aware of this history and, as he had the opportunity to visit this infamous island, he now took the opportunity to see for himself.

As the longboat neared the shore, they could see the magnificent forests of pine trees. These trees were already being used as ships spars and were being transported to New South Wales and England. The coast line was rugged and very few bays were safe to attempt a landing. Only one was deemed to be acceptable and even it required considerable small boat handling skills.

There was a reef at the entrance to Sydney Bay and the tides needed to be observed prior to lining up for the run to shore. Fortunately the bosun had been to Norfolk Island before and had the necessary local knowledge to effect an accurate passage through the reef and up to the beach.

A crowd had gathered at the beach. Obviously this would be an eventful day for the islanders, as few ships passed this way.

The chief constable stepped forward and introduced himself to the ship's officer who in turn introduced him to Paul as Colonel Lang late of the British Army. Many other residents stepped forward and introduced themselves to the boat crew seeking news from anywhere.

The ship's officer handed the chief constable some old newspapers. No doubt they would be shared by all residents over the next month or so. The chief constable arranged for the local long boats to visit the ship and bring back supplies and the missionaries. The unloading needed to be completed by early afternoon before the winds increased causing subsequent rough seas.

The chief constable invited the ship's officer and Paul to join him in a short tour of the Kingston prison facilities. The town had been laid out on the flat land adjacent the beach area, with buildings that were substantial and made of handmade brick blocks. Obviously many of the prisoners had stone mason skills.

The prison was impressive with its grand entrance and three story barracks building. They did not convey the horror of what the inmates suffered but Colonel Lang could see the anchor points in the walls to which the prisoners would have been chained. They saw the cemetery where the 1834 mutineers were buried. It was sited looking out over the bay — at peace at last.

A short ride in a four-in-hand cab took them into the centre of the island. The scenery was delightful with trees, large bushes and colourful plants. It was hard to imagine that only a few miles away some of the most barbaric treatment of convicts had existed.

It was now nearing noon so they returned to Kingston and, as had previously been arranged, dined with a large group of local residents. They spent the next hour answering questions between meal courses. The chief constable escorted them to their longboat and, after shaking many hands, they bid good-bye. Together with a large bag of letters they departed the shores of Norfolk Island. The supplies had all been landed so as soon as the longboat had been hoisted aboard and stowed, the captain hoisted the sails and raised the anchor, setting a south easterly course for Port Phillip Bay.

Virginia had retired for the night and Paul sat in a sheltered corner of the main deck. He looked out over the sea. A few clouds drifted slowly by, covering the stars for a short time before reappearing. The sea had a slight swell and the sails were full with the ship holding its head. Ever since that fateful day of the court martial he had experienced a loss of confidence in his ability to be an effective leader. He often sought a secluded place to calm his frustration. Virginia had recovered from her mental breakdown and was much calmer. She appeared to have put the whole incident behind her. Frederick had not been told what had happened at the court martial. It would have served no useful purpose.

"Standby to reef the topsails!" The call from the quarterdeck brought Paul back from his New Zealand memories. The bosun came running from below decks and the duty crew climbed the riggings.

The order came, "Reef the topsails." The deck lines were slackened and the crew aloft reefed the sails, furled them and tied them secure. The wind had shifted and was now a nor'wester. The seas were choppy and the ship pitched and rolled as they changed course from due west to a southerly direction, looking for the best of the wind. The captain was looking aloft at his sails. Seeing they were all full he told the helmsman to hold and steer this course. They had left Norfolk Island five days ago and were now well south in the Tasman Sea.

Paul Lang enjoyed the sea. He had wondered in the past if it would have been better for him to have chosen a Navy career other than a military one. The battle with the elements may have been more satisfying than having to handle the differences in personalities he had encountered in the past. He was now finished with his military career and looked forward to a position in the new Colony of Victoria Constabulary. He was now fifty-six years of age and had been in New Zealand for two years. He would settle down and retire in Victoria. He had made up his mind that he would travel no more. The information he had on the Colony of Victoria was all good. His wife seemed content to retire with a few acres and his son was due to finish his education at the end of the year and would be joining them. Perhaps they would remain in the colony.

The ship continued further south for several days, turning due west straight into a strong westerly and heavy chop. The ship didn't roll excessively but it pitched heavily making the timbers creak continuously and the deck sprayed constantly with the cold and stinging sea water. It was a miserable week as they slowly made way up the Bass Strait to Port Phillip Bay.

The captain stood off for twelve hours waiting for the Queenscliff signal station flags to signal the tides. Then it was full sails spread and the ship was headed into the middle of the entrance, with the tide running with them, between the headlands and into the large bay and up the dogleg channel to the Williamstown docks.

The weather during the trip up the bay was warm with little

wind. Both Paul and Mrs Lang spent most of the day on deck looking at the shoreline, the hills and the surrounding green bush land. At times they sailed quite close to the sandy beaches with small settlements and smoke from fires in the wooded areas. It was not as hilly as New Zealand and the bay had large flat coastal plains vanishing into the distant hills. At one stage the first officer approached Paul and handed him a telescope and pointed to a stretch of low lying land close to the ship. Paul put the telescope to his eye and saw, for the first time, a kangaroo.

Indeed there were several kangaroos grazing near the shoreline. He was intrigued by the way they sat on the lower part of their hind legs while they grazed; their small front legs seemed of little use. One kangaroo stood up and looked around. At that very moment a small baby kangaroo — he was told it was called a joey — jumped from a pouch in front of her body. He was mesmerised by the sight of these unusual animals. He would see many of them in the days ahead. After a few minutes the kangaroos moved away. Bounding on their long hind legs, they quickly covered the distance of half a mile and then started grazing again. He handed the telescope to his wife who greatly enjoyed seeing them.

It took nearly a day to sail up the bay due to the light winds, to see the main settlements spreading across the top of the bay with the hills of Macedon to the north. The ship then headed into Hobson's Bay, to the west of the built on areas, and anchored close to the shore alongside many other ships swinging at anchor. Warehouses and small houses dotted the dock area which was a hive of activity. Carts and horses and people milled around, loading and unloading cargo. Small boats were being rowed to and from the many ships, some were towing barges to the ships. The Langs decided to remain on board for the night and disembark in the morning.

The following morning they were approached by a customs

agent with whom they spoke at length. He advised them how best to travel to Melbourne. They made arrangements with him to stow their personal effects at the Williamstown docks until after Lang had met with the Victorian Constabulary and found out when and where he was destined to start his new career. After thanking the ship's captain they found accommodation in a Williamstown inn.

After settling in, Paul proceeded by ferry to Sandridge and walked the remaining distance to Melbourne via the single span bluestone bridge crossing over the Yarra River.

He went first to the Australasian Bank to open up an account and deposit his bank draft. The sum that he deposited rated an immediate meeting with the bank manager. Paul felt content because, upon banking the draft, he was now regarded as a man of means.

During the informal discussions with the bank manager Paul asked for directions to the Constabulary Headquarters. The bank manager not only offered him his gig but had his driver take him there. Paul appreciated this offer as he had seen the condition of the streets with their pot holes and puddles. The footpaths were not much better. The drive took less than ten minutes and the gig stopped outside an impressive bluestone building on the side of a hill looking down to the Yarra River.

Although Lang's visit was naturally unexpected, the commissioner made time to meet with him within the hour. This made Paul feel comfortable as he was eager to know the details of the offer to be made to him as soon as possible. The offer had not explained his duties other than it would be a senior position. The Victorian Police Commissioner Zane was an old soldier who had served nearly all his service life on the Indian frontier and had not returned to England when he resigned his commission. He preferred a warmer climate.

The commissioner walked in, shook his hand and they sat down alongside each other. He did not place a desk between them as was the normal practice with interviews. He had Paul's application in his hand and asked him if he had anything more to add to his submission.

Paul said, "No." He saw no value in relating his reason for leaving the militia.

The commissioner said, "As you are no doubt aware I am short of senior officers and have several areas in the Victorian country that need strong and forceful men. I believe a military style of leadership is necessary to maintain law and order in the colony. The country men are energetic, and enthusiastic in their endeavours to succeed but generally act as responsible individuals. Many arrived here as impoverished Irishmen, most from County Clare where I believe you once served. A few are ex-convicts who are now free men as are some of their wives. The majority are employed and are law abiding but in many cases they are resentful of authority. You will need to exercise your diplomacy skills constantly. I can give you a position in Melbourne but I would prefer you to accept a country position as an inspector in charge of a district. You would be answerable directly to the Deputy Commissioner, who unfortunately today is in Ballarat."

He continued, "The district I propose is north of Melbourne and three days drive by gig. It is called Kyneton and it is the centre of a rural area. It sits on the Campaspe River and has less than a thousand persons in the area. The district covers over a thousand square miles and comprises mainly flat rolling plains suitable for grazing and crops. The town is well served with a variety of shops and agriculture, services and tradesmen. Suitable town accommodation would be arranged for you and your wife. Also, the British Army 12th Regiment has a presence in the centre of the town. I think that's enough for now. Do you have any questions?"

Paul thought quickly and then said, "No, but I believe I might like that posting. Could I visit the town prior to finally agreeing?"

"Yes, certainly. You can go tomorrow. I can supply you a horse or we have a weekly gold escort guard positioning to Bendigo via Kyneton tomorrow morning. You can travel with them if you wish. Be here at 0900 hours. You must now excuse me, I have another meeting." The commissioner rose quickly, shook hands and was gone from the room while Paul was still trying to digest what he had been told.

The news that the 12th Regiment was based in Melbourne concerned him a little but he dismissed it as being of no consequence. What had happened in Ireland was in the past and probably forgotten by all and sundry. He believed that he would be unknown here.

On his return, Virginia was standing at the window of the inn room looking out over Williamstown. She turned and looked at him expectantly. He was smiling, so she relaxed and went to make tea. They sat together while Paul told her all that he could remember from the commissioner's description. She yearned for stability in their life and she thought that maybe living in a rural environment could be the answer. When Frederick arrived she would have him to talk to and hopefully with some tame farm animal around the house, she would have another interest other than reading and sewing.

It was still dark when Lang left the inn the next morning. He arrived at the constabulary stables on time and was greeted by a sub-inspector who saluted him even though he was not in uniform. He then handed him a letter from the commissioner to pass to the sub-inspector in Kyneton. He obviously knew why Lang was taking this trip up country.

The gold escort guard mounted and formed two lines. They headed out at exactly 0900 hours. Their course headed due north for four hours to the village of Sunbury where they stopped, fed and watered the horses, then sat down themselves for a meal.

They resumed riding and continued on, veering roughly in a north westerly direction to the western side of the Macedon hills and up through the Black Forest. After another three hours riding they enjoyed another short break and arrived at Woodend as darkness was falling. They had a ready-made camp in the village on the village creek. They had previously built a small camp here when they first took over the gold escorting responsibility. It consisted of twelve bunk beds and a wood stove. It was primitive but it was better than sleeping outside in the cold and damp weather typical of this area.

Lang had been informed that the Kyneton district started at the southern part of the Black Forest, which they had just travelled through. He was to learn that the Black Forest area was notorious for 'robbery under arms' or as they called it in the colonies 'bushranging'.

The call of the kookaburra awoke the camp at daylight. Its raucous laugh was exhilarating to hear even though it was a bit too loud when sitting on the roof of the camp. The stove fire had been kept alight through the night by the duty guard and the hut was warm. A breakfast of bacon and eggs with bread and tea was enjoyed by all and made for the start of a good day. The horses were fed and watered.

Lang was pleased. It was good to see the constables treated their horses as well as the military. He noted that some of the men did not look each other in the eye when they spoke. He was later to find out that some convicts had developed this habit from their time at Port Arthur Gaol. They were punished if they looked a guard in the eye. It was regarded as insolence by the guards, so now he knew that some of his constables were ex-convicts. He would need to keep an eye on their trustworthiness and reliability.

They rode out of Woodend and headed north. The country was flat with a constant gradual incline all the way to Kyneton. Farm houses dotted the countryside. Their farmlands covered between one hundred to two hundred acres; some holdings were even larger. Paul recognised the Irish influence when he saw the dry rock fences while the English had contributed the thorny hawthorn bushes as fences. Sheep were everywhere with a few horses and cattle, corn, oats, barley and wheat crops flourishing, with only a few paddocks lying fallow in this fertile area. The area looked prosperous. This was a good sign as it indicated high employment with few idlers.

After two hours they crossed the Campaspe River at a ford and, upon reaching the top of a small hill, they could see the small town of Kyneton a mile away in front of them. Paul stopped to look around and saw bushlands and other farms in the distance. He thought, *This is where I will settle.* He had made up his mind.

The gold escort was continuing on to Malmsbury for the night so the sub-inspector had taken his guard via the constabulary building to introduce Paul to George Evans, the temporary Kyneton sub-inspector, soon to be relieved.

He then shook his hand, bid him goodbye then joined his men and left on his journey.

The Kyneton sub-inspector eyed Lang curiously as he opened the letter from the commissioner. He read the instructions in silence and then handed the letter to Lang to read. They had both sat down in the main office. The instructions were — 'to assist Mr Paul Lang in his every request, to show him around the town and to provide detailed answers to all his queries'.

Lang started by asking the sub-inspector if he could see the constabulary facilities.

There were three buildings. The main administration building was divided into five rooms with a counter in the entry area and a separate jail building behind it, with six cells capable of holding four persons at a time comfortably. There was also a large ten-horse stable and fodder store at the rear of the main building, with sleeping quarters above the stable for twenty constables. The two sergeants had quarters attached at the end of the administration building with an acre paddock adjacent to the buildings. The sub-inspector lived privately with his wife, four houses from the constabulary barracks. Some of the constables also lived close to the barracks in private residences with their wives and families. The buildings were clean and well kept. The stables were swept and there was adequate feed and water for the horses, with the paddock fencing in good order. Lang was more than satisfied.

He then asked to see the office records for the last three months. He found that they were neat and legible but he was surprised at the lack of entries of offences, town visits or field trips for the last month. He wondered how much of a presence the constabulary had in the eyes of the community. The sub-inspector then handed him the list of the constables and their records without being asked. Although it was not hard for him to anticipate that he would be asked for them eventually.

Very few words had been spoken between the two men, other than, would he care for some tea. An elderly constable brought a pot of tea to them both. Paul sat down in a back office and read the files of the constables; most were uneducated from the country either here or England. He found that there were none from Ireland; he made a mental note.

Three were ex-convicts convicted of minor theft, civil order disturbance and poaching. Two were ex-sailors, no doubt deserters, while the two sergeants had some education and were married with school children.

The older sergeant was William Macleod. He had been a farmhand in England, and travelled to the colony where he settled in Kyneton. His employer had gone to the New South Wales goldfields and had not returned, leaving William unemployed. He had been a sergeant for four years and was well known in the district.

George Evans, the sub-inspector, was the son of a doctor. He had got into trouble at a major English public school and had been sent to Australia, 'to grow up' as his father had said. George had married a Melbourne born girl and now intended to stay in Australia. He had been a sub-inspector for a year in Melbourne prior to being sent to Kyneton last month to cover the position until a new inspector arrived.

After a ride around the town and through the two main streets he identified an inn that he and Virginia could stay in temporarily. He then returned to the barracks. Lang had learnt enough and he could now return to Melbourne and accept the position.

Deputy Inspector Moore arrived in Kyneton the next day to assume the upgraded sub-inspector position, replacing Evans, and had missed meeting his new senior officer.

Cobb and Co. had started a coach service there in 1854 and they now had five coaches passing through Kyneton to Melbourne each day and return — three coaches during the day and two during the night. It was now late afternoon so Paul decided to take the next coach which would arrive in Melbourne at daylight the next day. The coaches were large and capable of carrying up to twenty persons, albeit only ten were inside the coach which was drawn by six horses. The drivers were mainly experienced Californians, bearded, in brightly coloured shirts, scarves and wide brimmed hats, carrying revolvers in their belts.

Sub-inspector Evans accompanied him to the office of Cobb and Co., saluted him, and bid him a comfortable trip before heading back to the barracks.

His coach only had eight passengers when they left Kyneton so they were all comfortable inside and out of the elements. The stages to Melbourne were each about one hour's duration and covered ten or so miles between stops. The coach swayed and rocked with the small passenger load on the dirt roads but it was a pleasant ride. The moon was full and the skies clear. He could see for miles; lights from the farmhouses glimmered in the distance. The first stop was at Woodend where two more passengers climbed aboard, but they sat outside at the back of the carriage. On to the next stage and the next and the next with monotonous regularity, until Paul lost count of the number of stops while he dozed on and off. He estimated that they had stopped seven times.

The coach arrived in the centre of Melbourne as dawn broke. It was now full. He had not left his seat and had enjoyed a comfortable trip and although a bit stiff in his joints he soon recovered and walked up the hill to the Constabulary Headquarters. It was still early so he stopped at a small inn where he ordered breakfast and began planning his departure from Melbourne.

On arrival at the headquarters he was advised that the deputy commissioner had now returned and wished to meet with him. The deputy commissioner was Thomas White, an ex-London police inspector and while he did not have the military bearing of the commissioner he was an impressive person. He wore his authority 'on his sleeve'. He was affable and had an enquiring mind. He was a man to be respected.

Paul advised that he would accept the position.

The deputy commissioner said, "Excellent. I will arrange for you to complete the paperwork formalities and collect your uniform. You will need to stay in Melbourne for two weeks training with our legal advisor on colony law, crimes regulations and the constabulary policies after which you can proceed to Kyneton and assume your new position." The deputy commissioner also suggested that perhaps he and his wife might wish to stay in the constabulary married quarters. They had several for visiting inspectors who came to Melbourne with their families from time to time for some long court cases.

Paul gladly accepted this offer. "Could we have assistance to move our personal effects to the barracks?"

The deputy commissioner replied, "See the duty officer of the headquarters barracks of your requirements, where and when, and he will arrange everything for you."

Virginia was looking out the same window when he entered their room. She said she saw him arrive. She listened intently as he told her of his impressions of Kyneton and his acceptance of the position. When he said they were going to stay in Melbourne she was delighted. She had felt claustrophobic in the inn and had not yet ventured outdoors due to the inn being so close to the docks. They packed their clothes and waited for the police cart to arrive. After the vehicle left, loaded with their personal effects, they travelled to the Melbourne barracks and their new accommodation.

District Inspector Paul Lang found the legal training interesting. He was already aware of some of the requirements as they had been adopted by the New Zealand North Island Militia. The policies had been developed from the London Constabulary. He had a head start with his previously acquired knowledge. The two weeks passed uneventfully.

Mrs Lang visited the shops and arcades each day with

another inspector's wife whose husband was in Melbourne as a witness in a court case from their district. She was content but apprehensive about going to Kyneton. She had only her husband's briefly acquired knowledge on which to rely. She hoped his enthusiasm had not clouded his objectivity.

¶

The training was completed. All was being prepared for their departure to Kyneton. Their personal effects were already on their way to the Kyneton barracks for storage until they could arrange a residence. The deputy commissioner was at the Melbourne Cobb and Co. office for their departure. With salutes, handshakes and hand waves the coach headed north out of Melbourne. There were eight passengers including the Langs. They did not engage in any conversation with the other passengers; several of them had gone to sleep or were dozing.

Virginia Lang had a seat inside the coach on the right hand side and had an uninterrupted view of the countryside. For a colony only settled twenty years ago she was surprised at the size of Melbourne and the number of people going to and fro.

The coach trip was further educating her in the growth of Victoria. During the trip's first stage, shops and inns were clustered together every few miles. The second stage headed out into the countryside with its wide open spaces. Small forests existed between the cleared paddocks. The trees were different; some were various shades of grey with sparse foliage and others with dark trunks and deep green leaves. Paul pointed out kangaroos. They were in view either side of the coach and were travelling at a very fast speed with their hops covering around ten feet each time. The long Macedon Hills were gradually getting closer revealing their different heights and dense forests.

After two more stage stops they headed into the Black Forest up a long steep road. The other passengers were now awake and for the first time Virginia realised that all of the men carried pistols. Paul knew the reason for their pistols, but did not say anything to her. He did not want to alarm her unnecessarily. The driver kept the coach to the centre of the road and kept looking around nervously. He had a double barrelled shotgun alongside him. He had used it before when 'bailed up' by bushrangers. They continued in this state of alert for an hour before arriving safely at Woodend. The other men promptly dozed off again.

The last stage into Kyneton was through treed flat land with some areas cleared or being cleared for paddocks to graze live-stock and sow grains. Virginia was now dozing. The coach rolled to a stop in front of the Royal Hotel and the Langs were helped from the coach by the driver. After a cheery wave from him, they entered the hotel, and retired to their room, tired and dusty. Virginia rested while Paul went down to the bar and had two whiskies before he too went upstairs for the night.

The following morning he went to his office and met Sub-inspector Moore, requesting him to fall in the station troopers with their horses. District Inspector Lang introduced himself and asked the troopers to introduce themselves. He then asked Moore to show him through the station. As they walked through buildings Lang made mental notes of areas where he believed there should be improvements. He was aware that Moore had only been there for two weeks and would, quite correctly, have waited for him to arrive before deciding any changes. Lang was reasonably happy with the station and decided to wait a month before implementing the improvements.

That afternoon he visited Russell Carroll's office to start his house search. There were several available houses in the centre of Kyneton and they were in his price range. Russell was very persuasive and he had made arrangements to collect Mr and Mrs Lang in his best carriage the next day. He then drove them around town to view these houses. They soon made up their minds and the relevant papers were signed within the week. Their furniture had already arrived in Kyneton and Mrs Lang and a servant immediately set out arranging the house interior for them to move into their new home.

District Inspector Lang soon settled into a routine with his home life and his position as the District Inspector of Police. He began to travel widely throughout the district. He met all and sundry and was welcomed by the town fathers. He had several invitations to official functions and was looking forward to becoming a person of note in the community.

The first functions were primarily dinner evenings with a small select guest list, primarily shire councillors. Virginia particularly enjoyed these smaller informal gatherings and she soon established a circle of friends in the so-called social elite.

ℊ

The Shire Ball was the event of the year and every senior citizen and community leader in the district were invited, including Major Hall and Lieutenant Caly of the 12th Regiment. The whole town was involved in one way or another — caterers, musicians, decorators, doormen, stable men, the list went on. The main street was decked with colourful flags and buntings. Several shops joined in the festive occasion by painting their shop fronts and the shire contributed by painting the horse rails and park seats etc. The town was ready for the great day.

CHAPTER EIGHT

Changed Lives for All

istrict Police Inspector Lang and Mrs Lang dressed formally. Paul was attired in his police uniform and Mrs Lang in a new ball gown. She was content in her new role as a new socialite and felt flattered with the attention being afforded her. The shire president had invited the Langs to stand alongside him and his wife to welcome the guests and also for the Langs to meet the local district identities.

Major Hall and Lieutenant Caly arrived in full dress uniform, with their red jackets and highly polished black boots. They stood out in the crowd. The only people who did not see them were the Langs. As the guests shuffled forward and John Hall saw Paul Lang, he stopped momentarily and Caly following closely, bumped into him. John stared at Lang, who was shaking hands and was standing side on to him. Gaining his composure he continued walking forward.

John stepped forward and shook hands with the shire president and his wife. The shire president then turned to Lang. "Major John Hall, this is District Police Inspector Paul Lang."

John offered his hand but held it short. Lang looked up sharply and was speechless with shock. He gazed into John's piercing eyes. He then offered his hand but was forced to step forward to reach John's. They momentarily touched hands and then both withdrew. He nodded then he faced Mrs Lang who looked at him and nearly fainted. John bowed slightly to her and walked away without speaking. The shire president and Lang both moved forward to support Mrs Lang and led her away to a side room.

Lieutenant Caly followed him, non-committal. He looked back and saw that the Langs were no longer standing with the welcoming committee. He could see that John was in a strange mood, both angry, yet subdued. He decided to leave him with his thoughts and wandered off to go dancing.

John obtained a drink and stood quietly in a corner, shaking his head as he found it hard to believe. He had just met the man, who had caused him so much trouble; who had nearly destroyed his military career. He would avoid him but, if they did meet again, this time things would be very different. He would be meeting him as an equal, not as an underling.

¶

Of all people — John Hall in Kyneton! It was difficult for the Langs to comprehend. Virginia retired to her bed for two weeks, only leaving when necessary. In all, she did not leave their home for four weeks.

The doctor prescribed sedatives and a tonic but really her illness was more mental than medical. The shock of seeing John Hall had brought back the devastating memories of the trial. Over the past years she had finally managed to handle her demons. It was like a bad dream.

Paul Lang had quickly recovered from the initial shock of, not only meeting him, but also shaking his hand and looking into his eyes. He had become instantly angry and concerned about his future. The Langs avoided official functions for over a month and were selective, not wishing to be confronted by John Hall's presence again.

¶

Seamus had finished shearing and was returning home from Kilmore over open paddocks. There were sheep and cattle grazing in the distance. As he crested a hill he saw smoke below the ridge in the trees. He stopped and tied his horse to a tree. He moved down to some scrubs to see if it was a camp and who was there. He was concerned that they might be bushrangers. But he was surprised and somewhat relieved to see it was an Aboriginal camp with a large group sitting in a circle around a fire. They appeared to be having a conference. Seamus could see many mia-mias made from tree branches with bark sections bent over a horizontal centre branch. They slept in these when the weather was inclement.

The Aborigines were a race of nomads and changed their camp sites often but remained in their own tribal district; often hundreds of square miles. They had a distinctive language consisting of hundreds of different dialects. These Aborigines had dark brown skin and were naked. He had seen some Aborigines before in town dressed in old shirts and trousers. These Aborigines were taller than the Van Diemen's Land Aborigines but like them were lightly framed. Seamus knew little about them, except that they were skilled at spearing fish and throwing spears with a woomera. They fitted the spear into a notch in the woomera and threw the spear from the woomera to give them greater distance. This, together with their favoured weapon, the boomerang, which was a curved carved wooden branch also used for throwing, and their extraordinary eyesight, made them formidable hunters. Their only other weapons were nulla nullas — wooden clubs made from a tree branch with a knobby end or a knoll, and, finally, an axe with a stone head.

He had seen an Aborigine corroboree dance ritual several

months ago. It had become common knowledge that the Aborigines were gathering for a celebration. They sent out a message stick — a stick around ten inches long which allowed the holder safe passage through other tribal districts. The message was delivered verbally that a corroboree was to occur, telling where and when. The dancers covered their bodies in emu fat and ochre designs.

The women had opossum cloaks stretched across their knees to use as drums and a male leader rhythmically struck the two sticks together. Their other musical instrument was the didgeridoo. It was a four foot long, two to three inch diameter hollow tree branch, blown like a trumpet with puffed out cheeks to make a prolonged droning sound.

The dancers moved side to side and then forward and back, increasing their tempo with the drumming. They bent over, stamping their feet and raising dust then suddenly leapt into the air and finished the dance. After a short time they started again with a different tempo and the women's voices increased to a shrill. The dance order suddenly became chaotic with the dancers doing different steps. They shouted, jumped, stomped and turned. The leader struck his sticks and the dance was over. It had only taken a few minutes but was exciting to see. Seamus had been impressed at seeing this side of a different culture of a primitive people.

He watched the camp, wondering whether to turn back or continue on. His mind was made up when his dog barked. He quickly turned and saw three Aborigines approaching him from only fifty yards away. He mounted his horse and started to ride away when he saw one throw a spear which hit the ground in front of the horse. The horse reared and nearly threw him from his saddle. The other Aborigines then threw their spears. He dodged the first spear but the second spear hit him in the back.

He felt an excruciating pain under his left shoulder and fell from the saddle. He blacked out, his vision failing. Seamus died within the hour.

When Michael realized that Seamus was overdue and had not returned, he rode to Kilmore and found Seamus's dog walking along the road. When he was told he had left the sheep station over two weeks ago, Michael feared the worst. He rode back to Kyneton to report Seamus's disappearance to the police. He knew he would not be recognised by Inspector Lang but was secretly delighted to find that Lang was in Melbourne meeting his son and taking two weeks leave. Sub-inspector Moore was the senior officer. He quickly assembled a search party which included an Aborigine tracker. Michael and Seamus's dog accompanied the party.

They went to Kilmore and headed back to Kyneton. They started a two mile wide search from the sheep station. The Aborigine and the dog were out in front of the search party and generally headed in the direction taken by Seamus. They travelled through bushland and over cleared land stopping at the various farmhouses on their path. They asked farmers, "Have you seen Seamus?" Each time the search party received a negative reply.

As they were crossing a large open paddock, the dog started barking. It ran ahead to a hill top and stopped and sat down. The search party stopped and looked at the tracker, who had jumped off his horse and walked to where the dog sat. He then walked around in a large circle. The dog did not move. This was the place where Seamus had been speared.

A constable called out, "There has been an Aborigine camp down there," pointing down the hill. The tracker went to the camp and started walking around the centre of it where some mia-mias were still standing. He bent over low to the ground. After about five minutes he looked up and said, "Dig here, Boss."

Sub-inspector Moore organised his team to start digging. After about five minutes' toil, Seamus's body was found.

It was in the exact spot the tracker had indicated. Later when Michael asked him how he knew exactly where to dig, he pointed and replied, "Plenty blow flies longum ground dere, Boss."

Michael looked closely and also saw the flies on the ground. Two constables were detailed to take Seamus's body back to Kyneton.

The sub-inspector called the tracker to him. "Lokum this fella tribe plenty quick time." The tracker mounted his horse and, leaning to one side, circled the camp before heading north into the nearby mountain range. The tribe was large and easy for the tracker to follow. Within two days they had located the tribe which was waiting for them.

The police drew their swords but it appeared they would not have to use them. An elderly headman approached them with three young men walking behind him. The remainder of the tribe watched in silence; none of them had weapons in their hands.

The tracker and the elder sat on the ground and spoke quietly for a few minutes. Sub-inspector Moore stood immediately behind the tracker looking down at the elder. He sensed that the three Aborigines with the elder were the culprits. None of the Aborigines made eye contact with him. He was later to learn that this was normal for the Aboriginal race.

The tracker stood up and pointed, "That fella killum white man. Long spear belongum him." He identified the tallest of them.

Sub-inspector Moore ordered his constables to arrest and handcuff the tall Aboriginal.

The tracker pointed to the other two. "They missum spear longa dem." Sub-inspector Moore thought for a moment and could see no useful purpose being served by arresting all of them. He decided that they could go back to their people. Turning to the elder he asked the tracker to thank him for his action in handing over the culprit. The search party returned with the murderer who was held in jail in Kyneton to await trial.

The local people cheered the party as they rode back into town. The shire president made a brief speech of acknowledgement for their quick and decisive action bringing immediate success in apprehending the culprit.

Seamus Lynch's funeral was simple with only twenty people attending. Michael felt his death most deeply. They had enjoyed good times and had suffered the bad together. He would be missed. Jack Lodge was no more.

He sat on the porch looking out over the hills, reminiscing over their experiences, and suddenly realised that he now had a dilemma with Sean's share of the farm. Where was Mary Kirwan? She now owned half of the farm. He knew she lived in Limerick but that was five years ago. He decided to write to Patrick to see if he could help locate her. That very night he wrote to his brother and forwarded some money for her boat fare — if he could find her!

§

District Inspector Lang and his wife were enjoying his leave. Frederick's ship was due to arrive the following day and they both looked forward to seeing him again. As he sat in the hotel breakfast room he glanced at the newspaper and was stunned when he read of the murder near Kilmore and the involvement of the Kyneton Police in the discovery of the body, and the apprehension of the culprit by his sub-inspector. His mood quickly turned to anger. Why had they not contacted him? The same day he received a note and a copy of the report. This did not satisfy him. He would sort his sub-inspector out when he returned. His jealousy knew no bounds.

Frederick Lang's ship arrived on a dawn high tide and he was one of the first passengers to disembark. His mother had assumed a vantage position on the pier and immediately saw him. She loudly called out his name above the noise of the hustle and bustle of the workers and their carts.

He waved to his mother and ran forward, laughing. His mother responded by opening her arms to embrace her son. Paul Lang stood alongside her unsmiling and summing up his son. Frederick had grown taller but was still lean. He had grown a large ginger moustache and was dressed in dandy clothes. Paul could see already that he would not be suited to the Kyneton lifestyle.

After stepping back from his mother's embrace, Frederick turned to his father, offering his hand. He could sense that an embrace with his father was not forthcoming. The hand shake from both was purely a gesture.

His father had been unable to forget the Irish incident and Frederick knew it. Paul said, "You look well! We look forward to hearing of your voyage. I will find a porter to collect your trunks and travel to Kyneton today. We will arrive around sunset." He walked to a group of porters standing idle awaiting a job. His mother held Frederick's arm as they walked to where the baggage and the cargo was being unloaded.

The coach ride to Kyneton was uneventful. Frederick sat by a window area comparing the colony's countryside with England. He was unimpressed by the rawness of the colony, the unmade roads, the hovels, the casual dress style and the emerging accent through the multiplicity of languages of the many emigrants from all over the world. He was used to the lifestyle of the upper middle class and wondered how he would handle this new environment.

The coach rolled into Kyneton and stopped at his parents' new home. The driver helped Frederick with his trunks and, with a crack of the whip, headed his coach down the main road. His room had a comfortable and clean feeling and was overlooking Main Street. He only unpacked the large trunk. The other smaller trunk was double locked and he had the maid cover it with a table cloth and place a few ornaments on it. He said it made the room look neater and he did not want to put it in the storeroom.

District Inspector Lang's return coincided with the magistrate's hearing of the murder of Seamus Lynch. The next morning he went to his office and immediately called Sub-inspector Moore to report to him. Moore had just completed his court briefing papers ready for the hearing. These papers summarised the final report.

Lang ordered him to stand. "Explain your reason as to why you did not inform me of your search for the murderer."

Moore was astonished at this question. He replied, "You were on official leave and off duty. I did give you the courtesy of sending a preliminary report to you in Melbourne. I planned it to arrive on the day you were due to finish your leave to ensure you were up to date when you returned on duty in Kyneton."

Lang retorted, "I will be charging you with dereliction of duty — not keeping your senior officer advised during a capital crime investigation. Dismissed." After Moore left, Lang also headed for the door and noticed an envelope marked for 'Immediate Attention'. He picked up the envelope then, looking at his watch, he realised he had very little time to reach the courthouse on time.

A shocked Sub-inspector Moore left the police station and headed to the court house for the hearing. His final report was the main document regarding the murder summation, for which he had been required to attend today. As he sat waiting to be called, District Inspector Lang arrived. He was the senior officer and was called into the court first. In his fury, Lang had neglected to realise he only had a preliminary report and quoted from this document. He had not had time to read the envelope on his desk. This mail had a copy of the final report.

On arrival at the court house Lang was the first person called. The magistrate asked him several questions for which he did not have the answers, such as the autopsy report and witness statements from the other members of the search team.

Moore was called next and asked what he could add as he was the investigating officer. His briefing papers held the answers to all of the magistrate's questions and he was soon dismissed. After three more witnesses were called the magistrate quickly made a ruling for the accused to stand trial for murder. He thanked the court and stated that he would put on record the manner and professionalism of the search team and in particular the leadership of Sub-inspector Moore.

He turned to District Inspector Lang. "Sir, you are to be complimented on your choice and quality of staff."

Lang returned to his office, seething from his misfortune at his lack of involvement in the murder case. It would be in all the newspapers tomorrow, together with the compliment to his junior officer. He sat at his desk and then realised he still had the large envelope marked 'For Immediate Attention' in his hand. Opening it, he became aware that this was the final report which he had needed to read prior to attending the court case. His anger had clouded his professionalism and had alienated his deputy. He wisely decided not to proceed with his threat of charging him with dereliction of duty and did not raise the issue again.

District Inspector Lang decided to stamp the authority of his office on the community. He inspected his team each morning, together with their mounts and their horse stalls, set arrest targets for each of the troopers and increased the work hours of their supervisors, including his deputy.

At first, the changes were accepted without question; the team did need an improvement in their performance and attitude. However, the arrest targets ran into trouble after two months. There was insufficient crime for the troopers to reach the targets. It got to the stage that false charges were being laid by the troopers and this soon became well-known around town and in particular in the hotels and inns.

The hoteliers began to complain to the shire president's office about the troopers waiting outside their establishments, selecting patrons to be arrested. The troopers intimidated and provoked the patrons. The troopers pushed and shoved patrons, pulling on bridles, until the patrons retaliated. Some drunken patrons were thrown into the back of a cart and were driven from the town precincts and dumped miles from home. The next morning the arrested patrons would be brought to court, battered and bruised, clothing torn and generally looking most disreputable.

The district inspector, by alienating his deputy, was not made aware of impending trouble and continued to think his arrest target policy was a success and welcomed by all.

The increase in arrests from the previous three months figures was over three hundred per cent. The shire president became interested in these figures and the relevant complaints. He decided to invite the district inspector to dine with him at the Royal Hotel.

Lang arrived at the hotel delighted to be invited by the civic leader.

The luncheon began pleasantly with only small talk and

discussion on minor civic matters. After the table was cleared and coffee and refreshments served, the time had arrived to discuss the policy of arrest targets and subsequent complaints. The shire president started the discussion by asking Lang to give an update on this policy.

Lang began, "I am delighted to report an increase of one hundred per cent of arrests for civil disorder over the last three months, with weekly arrests figures remaining steady."

He was surprised when asked by the shire president, "When would we expect to see a decrease in these figures? The populace should be seeing the light by now and I would have expected to see a reduction in the number of weekly arrests by now."

Lang thought before he answered, as he was unsure where the conversation was heading. "I believe that my policy is making a safer town and I have no doubt that this would also be an objective of the shire council."

"Yes, you are correct but I have been receiving complaints about the methods your troopers are employing to obtain these figures. Particularly the extra force being employed," responded the shire president.

"Sir, you should be aware that many of the culprits being arrested need to be restrained and sometimes injuries will be incurred. However, to allay your concerns I will personally accompany the troopers on some patrols and observe their arrest procedures," said Lang.

The shire president stood up, indicating the luncheon was now over and offered his hand. "Good, I like that idea. We will dine again soon. Good bye."

Lang returned to his office, wondering from where these complaints originated. He did not believe that they were coming from the offenders that had been arrested. More likely they were from influential businessmen, particularly the hoteliers.

He would need to be careful, but first he would check the arrest procedures of his troopers.

He did not have long to wait. That very night his troopers arrested Edmund Keogh as he left the Kyneton Hotel and charged him with being drunk and disorderly. Keogh was taken to jail. During the arrest he was pushed heavily into a bluestone wall and suffered lacerations to his face. As an old man the troopers thought he was an easy target. They were unaware he was the father-in-law of Captain John Hall of the King's Own 12th Regiment.

Edmund had been to the hotel to deliver an invitation to William Eden at his office. William was invited to join John Hall at Sunny Lodge farm for dinner. Edmund Keogh had not had a drink. He had only been inside the hotel for five minutes, waiting in the foyer for Eden.

This event contributed to the final downfall of Paul Lang. Edmund planned to stay at the barracks with John for the night and ride back next morning. When John realised that Edmund had not returned he rode to William's office at the hotel. Fortunately William was working late and advised John that Edmund had delivered the invitation but had left the hotel over two hours earlier.

This worried John as the distance between the hotel and the barracks was only one mile. As John was leaving the hotel he saw Sub-inspector Moore riding back into town with a police squad of four troopers. John hailed him.

Moore dismounted and they shook hands. They knew each other to nod to but had not met formally. John told Moore of his concern for his missing father-in-law and asked him to keep an eye out for him. John and some of his soldiers rode around town searching the streets until failing light made further searching impossible.

In the morning the cells were cleared and the arrested men were lined up to be marched to the court for their appearance before the magistrate. Lang had started to take more interest in his target arrest policy and began to read the list of names of the previous night's arrests, when he saw the name — Edmund Keogh.

He walked to the window and looked out at the men in the line up and saw him. He also noticed the injuries to his face. He immediately knew that he had a predicament, considering the shire president's comments about complaints of excessive force. This man was elderly, had injuries to his face and was the father-in-law of the popular military commander. Bringing him before the court on a charge of drunk and disorderly would bring further complaints from persons with authority. He thought for a while then vindictively decided to extend the charge to possession of stolen goods.

Two months ago an overseas visitor attending the Kyneton Agricultural Show had had an engraved watch stolen. This same engraved watch was later posted to the Kyneton Police Station and had arrived when he was talking to the duty constable. Lang took the envelope into his office and on opening the envelope found the missing watch. He had placed it in his drawer, intending to hold it for a few months on the possibility the visitor may return to Kyneton. Lang now had Edmund Keogh removed from the line up and sent back to the cells.

After the morning's court session, Lang returned to the barracks and called Moore and the two constables who arrested Edmund, into his office. He then sent for Edmund Keogh. When Keogh entered the room he saw in front of him the man he most hated in this world. He could feel the anger surging into his body and he could not speak. Lang sensed this fury and felt a fear he had not possessed before. Lang looked away and then asked the troopers if they had searched him when he was arrested. They answered in the negative. When he asked them why, they just shrugged their shoulders.

Lang cleared an area of his desk and ordered Edmund to remove his jacket, shirt and boots and place them on the desk.

Edmund had still not spoken but did as he was ordered. He removed his boots first, then his coat which he placed on the desk. Lang picked up the jacket and appeared to drop it. It fell on his side of the desk out of view of his men. As he bent down to pick it up he slipped the watch into the inside pocket. He stood up and then placed it back on the desk. He then ordered Moore to search the clothing. Moore looked at him, wondering what this was all about.

As Moore picked up the coat in one hand, he held it at arm's length. He had an uneasy feeling and sure enough with his other hand he found a watch and a crumpled piece of paper in Edmund Keogh's coat pocket. He handed the watch to Lang, who looked at it closely.

"This is the missing watch from the agriculture show; I recognise the engravings from the owner's description," said Lang.

"Edmund Keogh, I am charging you with possession of stolen goods. Do you have anything to say?" Edmund did not answer. "No? Return him to the cells," ordered Lang.

From the time the search began the only person who spoke was District Inspector Lang. After the others left the office he knew he was on his own. Moore had looked at him with disdain and the troopers had ignored him. At no time did Edmund Keogh speak; he just looked at him with hatred. Lang knew that the arrest of Edmund Keogh would be circulated around the entire district within the week.

Moore immediately rode to advise John where his father-in-law was and what had happened. John sent one of his men to inform Maeve and to find Edmund's horse which was still at the back of the hotel. He sat quietly listening to the full story. At least he had been found; that was the main concern satisfied. Now, how to handle the impending court hearing. He felt it was best if he kept a low profile until the court case.

Another ally of the Keogh's, Brendan Devlin, immediately began to investigate Edmund's dilemma. He back-tracked the arrest to the hotel and William Eden and began seeking witnesses to the arrest. Several men came forward when they knew whom and why their statements were required. Brendan started to follow up the story of the watch. He even approached Deputy Inspector Moore who volunteered, discreetly, the events in Lang's office.

A preliminary hearing was held a week later with the police magistrate. The small courtroom soon filled. All seats were taken and the remainder of the persons allowed in were leaning against the walls. Brendan Devlin and the Observer newspaper reporter were seated along the side wall adjacent to the magistrate near the evidence desk where the stolen watch had been placed and then covered by a gauze cloth. John arrived and sat upstairs in the balcony, out of the view of Lang. The hearing began with the clerk of the courts reading the charge of 'Possession of stolen goods, namely a watch.'

The Magistrate asked Edmund, "How do you plea?"

Edmund responded, "Not guilty, Your Honour."

"District Inspector, please present your case."

"The defendant was found to have a stolen watch in his possession when searched at the Kyneton Police Station."

"Why was he in the police station in the first place?"

"He had been arrested on a drunk and disorderly charge."

"What penalty did he receive for that offence?"

"I decided to drop the charge."

"Were there other persons arrested the same day as Mr Keogh? Were they all charged?" the magistrate asked.

"Yes."

"Did Mr Keogh have both of these charges laid the same day?"

"No." Lang was feeling a little uneasy.

"Was the search conducted the day of the arrest or the next day?"

"The next day," he answered.

"What prompted the search of his clothing the next day?"

"The troopers had forgotten to search him the previous day."

The magistrate was not satisfied with this answer and repeated the question. "What prompted the search, and who was in attendance when the defendant was being searched?"

"Myself, Sub-inspector Moore and the two arresting troopers."

"Who searched the clothes?"

"Sub-inspector Moore."

"Sub-inspector Moore, please take the stand.

"Please explain the search procedure."

"The district inspector asked me to examine the coat and as he picked up the coat he dropped it as he was placing it on the desk. He then picked it up and placed it on the desk. I then picked up the coat and found the watch in the pocket."

"Did anyone else touch the jacket?"

"No — not that I saw."

The magistrate began, "It seems to me that the defendant had in his possession a watch. Two senior police officers were the only persons to handle the jacket and I am obliged to accept their evidence. However, I wish now to call Mr Keogh to the—" He stopped mid-sentence.

Shouting was heard outside the court doors, which suddenly burst open with two men throwing punches. Other men tried to stop them, but then a melee formed. All eyes were on the confrontation. Brendan Devlin rose from his seat and, as he walked past the evidence desk and behind his fellow reporter, he was momentarily hidden. He quickly lifted the gauze covering, picked up the watch, slipped it into his briefcase and kept walking towards the door.

The magistrate called, "Court adjourned for one hour," while banging his gavel on the desk.

The police soon had control of the crowd and moved everybody out. The courtroom doors were locked and guarded.

Brendan Devlin walked to the toilet pit at the rear of the court-house. After checking that no one was looking in his direction, he dropped the watch into the pit where it vanished from sight forever. He walked to his office and had lunch. On the hour, he returned and found that the courtroom had filled again.

The magistrate commenced. "We have established that the defendant was found with a watch in his jacket pocket. I would now like to establish if this particular watch was stolen and how its identity was confirmed." He looked towards Lang.

Lang stood up. "We know it was the watch stolen from a visitor during the Agricultural Show this year. The watch has distinctive engravings as recorded on the statement from the owner." Lang handed a copy of the statement to the clerk to pass to the magistrate.

"It's time we looked at the evidence. Pass me the watch please," the magistrate asked the clerk who lifted the gauze cloth. He stood looking at the desk which was now devoid of the watch.

He looked at the district inspector who returned his look, wondering about the delay in the clerk presenting the watch to the magistrate. To his horror the watch was not on the exhibit table. Lang was speechless. Behind him he could hear muffled laughter.

The magistrate sat surveying the persons in the court with an expressionless face. He had had concerns regarding this case and they were now being confirmed. The fact that the accused had not been searched until the following day and had not been charged with drunk and disorderly seemed unusual. Without the evidence being available, the magistrate had an easy solution. Without the watch there could be no case to answer. He did not elaborate his concerns in the court summary.

He asked the district inspector if the missing watch could be explained as it was under his care. Lang stood up, glaring at the constable standing near the table. His face was red with anger and his hands were shaking. He shook his head and abruptly sat down again.

The magistrate then read his findings. "In so far as the charge is unable to be substantiated as the evidence is no longer available, the defendant is free to go. However, there are unusual issues in this case and, even though this is a minor offence I will be noting my concerns surrounding this case to Melbourne, for further investigation. The court is dismissed." The court erupted in cheers and Edmund was carried from the room and deposited in his cart where John sat, smiling, ready to drive him to Sunny Lodge and peace again.

John had been ready to appeal the case if Edmund had been sentenced but now there would be no need. Brendan Devlin stood by the side of the road and gave Edmund a short wave which Edmund guessed was his indication as to his involvement in the brawl and the 'losing' of the watch. Edmund waved back.

¶

Frederick lounged around the house for a few days and then

began to look around Kyneton. He soon found a few locals of his own age and ilk and began joining them for regular drinks in the front bar of the Royal Hotel and some gambling upstairs. He travelled to Melbourne several times to look around the new city but he was not overly impressed after living for a few years in a European society. Boredom gradually set in.

His father encouraged him to look for employment but this was received with, "Yes, I will when I make up my mind as to my calling."

The drinking and gambling began to become a habit. He had not become associated with any women as he seemed more interested in establishing friendship with his male friends.

The gambling during the day time was only social cards with small bets, but he soon developed the urge to join in the serious betting that occurred in the evenings.

The inn keeper, Tim Doolan, was a tough, no-nonsense man. He and his wife ran a good house and suffered fools lightly. Drunks and persons behaving in a rowdy manner were soon ejected by him or his staff. There were two bars and a ladies lounge, which was used mainly for dining. He tolerated the card games as they brought in customers who would drink and sometimes dine. His establishment was rated the best in Kyneton and frequented by civic leaders and farmhands.

Paul Lang was supplying Frederick with a weekly allowance, as he had no money of his own. This money rarely lasted the week and he was soon approaching his mother for more.

The evening gambling sessions had been successful at first as he had some substantial wins. However, after a week of losses he began to borrow from an Irish friend who was the local tailor and had a profitable business. His fortunes see-sawed but Frederick eventually found that he owed his friend nearly fifty pounds and he was being pressed to pay. With no means to borrow further he was in trouble; he was worried his father would find out.

Frederick paced back and forth in his room wondering what to do. When he hit his shin on the small trunk, he stopped and cursed. Of course — the sword! Could he sell it? What was it worth? He decided to mention it to his tailor friend the next day.

Frederick had received his weekly allowance and in the evening he strolled to the Royal Hotel and walked over to his friend. "Can we have a chat?"

They moved to a quiet corner of the room. "I have a very historical Irish sword for sale. I can sell it to you for a very reasonable price. Would you be interested?"

His friend shocked him by saying, "What would I do with a sword? I'm a tailor."

Frederick did not answer for a second or two, trying to quickly think of another sale angle, but he could see his friend was not in the least interested. Frederick nodded then walked away into the bar.

He sat at a side table looking down the street, wondering what next to do about his gambling debts. Perhaps he should go to Melbourne and offer the sword for sale in an auction room. He continued drinking alone and began to feel depressed and then angry. He was now in an aggressive mood, and went to the bar. He banged his fist down and shouted for another drink.

Tim was in the bar at this time. He looked up. "You have had enough. Goodnight, sir."

Frederick launched into a tirade of abuse rarely seen in the Royal Hotel.

Tim said, "Please leave, sir," walking to the door to open it. He had his back turned to Frederick who picked up a chair and swung it at Tim. It struck him in the back of the head and Tim immediately collapsed to the floor. Four other patrons then attacked Frederick, bringing him to the ground.

Sub-inspector Moore was in the police barracks when a rider ran in, calling out, "There is trouble at the Royal Hotel. Come quickly." On arrival he found Tim being treated by his wife. He had come round but had serious head injuries. A patron led Moore to the stables where a struggling and vocal Frederick had been tied to a hitching rail.

Moore stopped. *Good God, not the District Inspector's son.* He sent a constable to tell his father of the situation and, after talking to witnesses, his constables took Frederick to the police station. Moore spent the next hour taking witness statements, and there were plenty. By now, Tim had been attended by a doctor and prepared to be hospitalised.

When Moore arrived back at the police station, Paul Lang was in the cell talking to his son. Frederick was still agitated and walked round and round the small room.

Moore waited in the front office for his senior officer. The district inspector immediately asked, "What are the charges?"

Moore responded, "Aggravated assault, and drunk and disorderly."

"Witnesses?" Lang asked.

"Six," Moore replied.

Lang did not ask for his son to be bailed as he knew he was still drunk. He walked out of the office without another word. When he arrived home he sat Virginia down and told her what Frederick had done.

She sat there without saying a word. *First Major Hall and now this,* she thought. *Why me?*

¶

The tailor entered the Guardian Newspaper office and waved to Brendan through the door. He was there to place an advertisement.

Brendan waved him in. "What happened at the Royal last night?" After hearing the story he asked, "What set him off?"

The tailor replied, "Well he offered to sell me an historical Irish sword to clear his debt to me and I refused to buy it. Maybe that was it."

Brendan froze. Could this be the stolen sword Michael mentioned? They spoke some more, then the tailor rose and left to return to his shop. Brendan sat deep in thought. What should he do? If the sword was in Frederick's house, what was the best way to recover it? As a reporter and also as an Irishman he had made the acquaintance of several people on or over the fringes of the law; some he knew quite well. One such person was the renowned Captain Irish, the bushranger. His real name was William McMahon and his family had married into the Devlin's many years ago.

Captain Irish had several hiding places. One was the well-known landmark called Mt Diogenes named by the explorer Major Mitchell who was a Greek scholar. It was an unusual rocky outcrop situated between Woodend and Kyneton with a lookout at the top, affording views on all sides for many miles. It was ideal for persons who wished to avoid the long arm of the law. Brendan had not been there for over a year, but knew he could leave him a message. He saddled his horse and left early in the morning heading south. He reached Mt Diogenes at noon, dismounted and hobbled his horse. He walked between two large rocks at the base and started climbing.

He had not travelled fifty yards when a voice calling from above. "Hello, Brendan."

Looking up he saw Captain Irish smiling down. They sat down together. Brendan told his story.

Captain Irish asked, "I presume that you want me to retrieve the sword for you?"

Brendan replied, "Well, not for me but for a friend of mine, Michael Somerset."

Captain Irish replied, "I met him once in unusual circumstances; I owe him a favour. Yes, I will do it."

¶

Frederick had been bailed and had obtained a lawyer from Woodend, a Mr Johnson, to defend him. Their defence would be that he had been grossly insulted and he had been provoked into losing his temper.

The court case was two weeks later. The morning of the court case, the Lang family drove to the court house. District Inspector Lang and his wife sat together in the front seat. Frederick had presented himself at the police station. Sub-inspector Moore was to act as prosecutor. He was not happy with this onerous duty of prosecuting his senior officer's son as he was in a no-win position. Brendan was in his seat at the court as normal but that was the only thing normal for him that day.

The clerk called, "The court will rise."

The magistrate walked in, bowed and then sat down. He said, "Be seated. Please read the charges."

The clerk commenced his address. "Mr Frederick Lang you are charged on the said date with: the first charge being drunk and disorderly; the second charge — aggravated assault on the person of Mr Timothy Doolan.

"How do you plea?"

Frederick answered, "Guilty on the first charge and not guilty on the second charge, Your Honour."

The Magistrate ordered, "On the charge of drunk and

disorderly you are fined two pounds and costs. We will now proceed with the charge of aggravated assault causing grievous bodily harm."

Mr Johnson stood up. "We wish to submit a signed written statement, Your Honour." He handed the one page document to the clerk and a copy to Sub-inspector Moore as the prosecutor.

The clerk handed the document to the magistrate who immediately read through the page before looking up at Frederick Lang. "Is this your writing and signature on this page?"

Frederick answered, "Yes, it is, Your Honour."

The crux of the statement alleged Frederick had consumed several drinks and had wanted another. He had only shouted at the barman, Timothy Doolan, to attract his attention. The barman had spoken abusively to him and forced him to leave. Frederick stated that he had become frightened and he had only defended himself with the chair as it was known that the barman was an ex-prize fighter. Frederick had only meant to hit the door and frighten him. He also apologised and stated it was not usual for him to be aggressive.

After ten minutes of legal discussions the magistrate asked Prosecutor Moore for his comments regarding the statement. He responded, "The crown does not accept the accuracy of the defendant's statement. It does not agree with the prosecutions' witnesses statements. There are six witnesses and I would like to start the prosecution's case by calling them one at a time."

The magistrate nodded and asked the clerk to call the first name on his witnesses list.

A young carrier driver was the first witness called and after being sworn in he was asked to relate the events of the evening in question. He stated that he had just walked into the bar with two friends, when he heard shouting from the defendant. He saw the barman walk to the door telling the defendant to leave.

The barman turned to open the door and the defendant picked up a chair and hit the barman in the back of the head. He and his friends tackled the defendant, and with the other patrons, they carried him out and tied him to a hitching rail at the rear of the hotel.

Mr Johnson said he would not cross examine the carrier driver until all of the crown witnesses had been heard. The witnesses were all duly called and related their recollections of that evening and their stories were virtually identical.

The prosecutor then called the doctor who attended Tim Doolan and asked for his medical report. The doctor advised that Mr Doolan was still in hospital and had suffered a fractured skull. However, he did expect he would fully recover over time.

Mr Johnson knew he had a difficult, if not impossible, case to win. Frederick had lied to him. He asked Frederick to change his plea to guilty and allow him to focus on an excuse of, an irrational act out of character, and that he was now remorseful and regretful of his dastardly deed. He would offer compensation and pay for his victim's expenses. It was time for the lunch adjournment. Frederick said he would think about the change of plea during this time.

Frederick pondered what would be the advantage of changing his plea. Could he be found not guilty? He realised the witnesses statements appeared irrefutable, as was the medical evidence. Was there a possibility the witnesses could be found to be colluding and/or be declared not fit and proper persons, i.e. disreputable persons? This would destroy the creditability of their witness statements and could create doubt in the mind of the magistrate. He decided not to change his plea.

His lawyer said, "I think you are making a big mistake."

Frederick turned to him angrily. "Do you want to represent me or not? Make up your mind, now!"

Mr Johnson looked at his client and sensed that this day would finish in trouble. He wanted no part of it. He had his reputation to consider. Fredrick's lawyer answered, "Good afternoon, Mr Lang, and goodbye." He stood up, grabbed up his briefcase and walked out of the court house.

The clerk had been watching this exchange and asked Mr Lang if there was a problem. Frederick advised that he would be representing himself. The clerk advised the magistrate of this change in the court proceedings.

District Police Inspector Lang was surprised that his son had decided to represent himself. He knew he had some legal training and hoped his son knew what he was doing. Frederick rose and addressed the court, asking to interview the witnesses one at a time.

The first witness was recalled.

Frederick asked, "What is your permanent address?"

He was answered, "I have no permanent address other than my mother's home in Hobart. I am a travelling shearer going through to Morton Bay."

Frederick continued, "And your acquaintances — do you all work together?"

The witness answered, "Yes, we are all shearers and we travel together."

Frederick felt, here was his chance to discredit the witnesses.

He asked the witness, "Did you at any time discuss the alleged offence with your friends?"

"Yes, of course," the witness answered.

"Then we can assume that the statements you made were decided after your discussions with each other. Thank you. I have no further questions," Frederick stated.

Prosecutor Moore stood up. "I would like to ask the witness one question, Your Honour." The magistrate nodded.

"On the evening of the incident, I questioned you first. When you were questioned, where were your five friends?" asked Moore.

"You had the six of us in the main bar. I sat with you and my friends were at the other end of the room."

"Did you and your friends speak with each other?" Moore continued.

"No, you told us not to," the witness replied.

"Thank you," responded the prosecutor.

"You may step down," said the magistrate to the witness.

The magistrate looked to Frederick Lang and asked, "Are you ready to present your defence?"

"Yes, Your Honour," he replied and continued.

"Yes, I did pick up a chair but I only meant to hit the door. The evidence of the witnesses is in question. Not only is it inaccurate but I believe there has been collusion. They are itinerant workers from Tasmania and who knows what their history is. I submit their evidence should not be admissible. Yes, I admit I did commit an irrational act which is completely out of character for me for which I blame on an excess of alcohol served by the barman. I will pay for any costs for Mr Doolan and already have written him a letter of apology. I am remorseful and truly sorry for my action. Thank you." Frederick then sat down.

The magistrate asked, "Does the prosecution wish to speak?"

"No, Your Honour. I believe we have submitted the facts and that they substantiate the charges."

The magistrate said, "The court will adjourn for one hour."

Promptly on the hour the magistrate walked into the court and assumed his seat. "Mr Frederick Lang, please stand."

Frederick stood up. His mother and father looked at their son, and then at the magistrate, holding their breath.

"Frederick Lang, I have considered your statement

concerning your remorse and sorrow for your act. While I believe they are genuine, I find you guilty as charged of aggravated assault on the person of Timothy Doolan, with extenuating circumstances due to being served alcohol when inebriated. However, assault is a most serious crime and cannot be condoned under any circumstance. I hereby sentence you to six months jail suspended conditional upon your leaving the colony within four weeks, plus that you pay for all costs incurred by Mr Doolan's incapacitation." The Magistrate then stood up and left the courtroom.

Frederick sat still, not sure how to feel. He turned, as his mother who sat alongside him, put her arms around him. His father stood over them, silent and depressed. The sentence could have been worse, but it was still a conviction. They climbed into the gig and returned home. They sat there in silence until Paul Lang decided he would return to the police barracks and do some paperwork. He wanted to be alone and think of how this event would influence both his and Virginia's standing in the community. He did not even consider how Frederick felt or would react.

Frederick sat outside in the garden listening to the birds with his mind blank and stared into space. His mother's call brought him awareness when she asked him if he wanted tea. He went into the house and sat next to his mother. He held her hand and asked if she was feeling well. He still cared for his mother and now felt enormous guilt as to what he had done. While talking to her he decided to leave immediately. His mother agreed to give him the money to pay Mr Doolan's current costs and she would pay any other future bills.

¶

William McMahon alias Captain Irish rode slowly past the district police inspector's home. Brendan Devlin had briefed him well and, together with the map of the property, he had devised a simple plan. He would search Frederick's bedroom first as he believed that he would keep the sword close to him. It would be in the house; he could not imagine anyone leaving a valuable relic in the stables or other outhouses. The house was on a corner surrounded on three sides by a large continuous hedge and a low stone fence along the front. He knew the maid would not be home as she always accompanied Mrs Lang whenever she left the house.

McMahon made his move an hour after he saw the Lang's leave to go to the court house. He tied his horse to a tree in the back street, walked alongside the hedge and ducked into the Lang's garden through a small gap hidden by a large tree.

Inside the garden he went to the back door and found the door unlocked. This was common in the larger houses in Kyneton. He ran through the house and soon found Frederick's bedroom. After searching for ten minutes he began to think he had planned the search wrongly. He sat on the bed thinking and was looking around when he saw the base of the trunk beneath the cover near the window. He had thought it was a small table at first and had ignored it. He quickly pulled the cover off and looked for the best way to open it. He ran to the kitchen and returned with a meat cleaver and a small hatchet.

Captain Irish wedged the cleaver between the wood adjacent the hinge. He soon forced the cleaver in to pry the hinge off the wood side. He did the same to the second hinge. Inside was a large tray fitted into the top half of the chest packed with expensive items of clothing and various papers. Captain Irish lifted the tray up and out to check the contents of the lower half. Lying at the bottom was a linen wrapped package. With excitement increasing he unwrapped the linen wrapping and revealed the stolen cape and inside the cape, in an oil cloth, was the magnificent sword. This really was a treasure. He wasted little time. He replaced the tray and re-laid the clothes on top back in position, hammered in the hinge screws then put the cover over it, leaving the bedroom to all intentional purposes, untouched. He returned the kitchen articles, closed the back door, went to the hedge and, after a quick look, stepped out and mounted his horse. William McMahon, alias Captain Irish, rode casually out of town with the cape and sword in an empty worn wheat bag.

☙

After Frederick's trial, life slowly returned to normal for the Lang Family. With Frederick gone Virginia felt a sense of relief. However, their circle of friends had diminished and Virginia found that she now received fewer invitations. Paul felt that Frederick's case had caused him to be less comfortable in the Kyneton community and he now had doubts about his immediate future. Mr Doolan had left hospital and was back working with all his medical costs having now been paid.

The rate of arrests had decreased to a level where no further complaints of over-zealous police were received by the shire president's office. The police constables were now well presented and patrolled the town regularly. They had become accepted as an essential part of the community and not a necessary evil as they had been in the past. The Lang's attended selected functions although they were still cautious about meeting the Hall's at any soiree.

Two months after the Keogh trial, District Inspector Lang received advice that an Inspector Dawson and his aide from

Melbourne Head Office would be visiting Kyneton to investigate the anomalies in the Keogh case. Lang was not overly concerned at this investigation as he considered the case was of a minor nature and the investigation would be purely for show.

Lang was wrong, very wrong. Inspector Dawson was a tough no-nonsense ex-London policeman with a nose for procedural abuses and had been investigating complaints against the police for two years. Immediately on his arrival he stated that the investigation would commence at nine o'clock the following day. He submitted to Lang a list of names of persons he required to attend the investigation.

Lang immediately sent his troopers out to contact the names on the list and advised them of their requirement to attend, including Sub-inspector Moore who was also the police prosecutor, the two constables and Edmund Keogh.

Inspector Dawson opened proceedings by stating that it was an informal hearing and no decisions would be made by him. He would record the statements made during the proceedings and submit a transcript to his superiors. It would be up to them to make any judgements. He stated that he would ask general questions relating to the transcripts first and then go over the court case in detail.

The aide read out an abbreviated transcript of the Keogh case and placed several complete transcripts on a table for the use of whoever wished to read them.

The first person called was District Inspector Lang. He had a complete transcript in his hand.

Inspector Dawson asked, "Is this transcript of the Keogh case a true and accurate record of the case in question? Do you wish to make any comment?"

"Yes, it is correct and, no, I have no wish to make any comment."

Sub-inspector Moore was called next and asked, "Could you relate your involvement in this case?"

"My only involvement was in District Inspector Lang's office the day after his arrest when the clothing was searched and I found a watch in the jacket pocket," Moore answered.

"Could one of the constables step forward?" requested the aide.

A tall solid trooper stood up.

"I would like you to tell me what happened on the night Edmund Keogh was arrested," requested Dawson.

"Constable Rogers and I were passing the Kyneton Hotel when we saw Edmund Keogh stagger from the hotel. He slipped and hit his head on the bluestone wall. We arrested him and walked him back to the police barracks and locked him up," he answered.

"Thank you. I would now like to hear from Edmund Keogh," said Dawson.

"Mr Keogh, I am unable to find a statement from you in the transcript. Would you tell me what happened on the night you were arrested."

Edmund was nervous but replied, "I went to the hotel to deliver an invitation to Mr William Eden. I waited in the foyer for him to come down from his office and then left. It was pouring rain and I had my head down when I was pushed into the wall and fell onto the ground, and then I was arrested. I was walked back to the police barracks where the sergeant asked my name and address, and charged me as being drunk and disorderly. The constables took off their capes and the sergeant took off my coat. I was drenched. Then the constables locked me up."

"Please continue with the events of the next day," said Dawson as he made notes of Edmund's words.

"The next morning I was taken with the other prisoners to a courtyard. Shortly afterwards I was led away from them and sent back to my cell. I was only in my cell for a few minutes and then taken to his office—" indicating Lang, "and searched. They found a watch in my pocket." Dawson noticed the anger Keogh directed to Lang and wondered if there was more to this case.

"Thank you, Mr Keogh. If the sergeant is here, please bring him in. I was unaware of his involvement," said Dawson. Sergeant McLeod walked in and was asked to relate his contact with Mr Keogh.

He started, "Mr Keogh arrived with a bleeding face and drenched from the rain. I wrote down his particulars and removed his coat; it was dripping wet. He then went to the cells. During the next morning's parade of the previous night's persons arrested for drunk and disorderly, District Inspector Lang ordered him to be removed from the parade and to have him taken to his office. Keogh looked a bit scruffy so as he went in I gave him back his coat."

"Stop there!" said Dawson. "Are you sure about what you said about the coat? What made you remember that detail?"

"As I gave it to him a very crumpled piece of paper fell from his pocket onto the floor and I picked it up and put it back in the coat pocket," the sergeant answered.

"Which pocket?" Dawson asked.

"The jacket only had one pocket," the sergeant responded.

Lang knew what the next question would be. He had not considered that the sergeant would have handled the coat. Only three people had handled the coat and he had been one of them.

Inspector Dawson said, "Sergeant McLeod, now think carefully before you answer this question, could there have been anything else in this pocket?"

The sergeant knew a watch had been found in Edmund

Keogh's clothing but not where. He thought for a second or two and replied truthfully, "No, nothing else was in his coat pocket."

Sub-inspector Moore's jaw dropped; he realised his predicament. He stole a look across at Lang, who was sitting there stone faced. Moore began thinking of the incident when the coat fell to the floor behind the desk. Had he unwittingly become involved in a set up?

Inspector Dawson looked at each of them in turn and Moore wondered what he was thinking. Dawson lowered his head and started making notes again.

Edmund Keogh was still glaring at Lang with open hostility.

Dawson said, "Mr Keogh please contain your anger; your trial is over."

Edmund replied, "My trial with this man will never be over."

"Please explain that comment," requested Dawson.

"This man had my son transported to Van Diemen's Land for fourteen years," indicating District Inspector Lang. Except for the ticking of the clock on the wall, the room had gone silent.

Dawson sat looking at Edmund Keogh. He saw an angry elderly Irishman of peasant stock, who stood straight and proud.

Lang suddenly realised who this man was, even though it had nothing to do with the watch incident, it would not be seen that way. It could be construed as a personal issue.

Inspector Dawson decided that no useful purpose would be served by continuing the investigation further in Kyneton. He made a short summary, finishing with the comment, "Further investigations will be carried out in Melbourne and selected witnesses will be required to attend there."

He thanked the witnesses for attending, then stood up and left the room.

Edmund left the room and walked out into the sunshine

feeling content that he had his say, at long last. He waved to John who drove the gig over to him and they headed home.

Inspector Dawson went back to his hotel to write up his report. He wished he had the opportunity to talk with Sub-inspector Moore before he left. No doubt the Melbourne office would accept his advice and re-interview them both. He believed the sergeant, as he had nothing to gain, but Mr Keogh's comments made him wonder.

The next morning he went to Lang's office and bid his farewells. Dawson boarded the coach and headed back to Melbourne.

On arrival in Melbourne Inspector Dawson went immediately to Deputy Commissioner White's office. His knock on the door was followed by "Enter."

"Back already, Dawson. Was your trip successful?"

"Yes and no," he replied. "I still have some questions to be resolved and I am concerned the results will not be beneficial to the image of the force," Dawson answered.

"Sit down and brief me," ordered White. Instead of dialogue he handed Deputy Commissioner White, a one page summary of the investigation.

White read the paper twice. "Yes, I see. One — Why was the first charge withdrawn? Two — What instigated the search the next day? Three — How did or who put the watch in the coat pocket? Four — What was Lang's involvement with Keogh's son's arrest? This clouds the issue of the watch. Five — Is Moore involved in the placement of the watch?"

White commented, "I have watched Moore's career for five years. I believe he is a good officer. What would he stand to gain by fraudulently placing the watch in Keogh's pocket?

"Also, I have received a letter from the shire president who has expressed disquiet over the Lang family after their son's court case. I read between the lines that they would like Lang transferred as they see his image tarnished and they appear to have lost confidence in him.

"I think your recommendation that both Lang and Moore be interviewed in Melbourne as soon as possible is correct. Please see to it. Well done and advise me when you have arranged the interviews. You and I will perform the interviews." Dawson stood up and left the room.

Lang and Moore both left the room with concerns about the investigation. Lang wondered if he would escape a censure for his handling of the case. Moore wondered if he would be blamed in some way over the watch search.

§

Dawson moved quickly and he sent letters to Lang and Moore the following day to attend the Melbourne investigation hearing at their first opportunity. Sub-inspector Moore was to be interviewed first as a courtesy to allow Lang to respond on any dubious points arising from the interview. Sub-inspector Moore left on the next morning's coach for Melbourne.

The interviews were held in Deputy Commissioner White's office. After the normal pleasantries, White advised that the interview was being held to get to the bottom of the 'watch search and locating' incident. He explained that a magistrate had queried the police evidence and a resolution must be reached. He would chair the meeting but Inspector Dawson would conduct the interview. White would query as necessary and sum up the interview at the completion.

"You have a copy of the transcript in front of you. I would like your comments on the search during which you found the watch," Dawson said.

Moore read the document and replied, "I can only reiterate what I said in the transcript. I cannot add any more."

Dawson then asked, "Did you know the history of the missing watch?"

Moore replied, "No."

Dawson said, "Keogh obviously knew Lang from Ireland. Has he ever indicated to you that he knew him?"

Moore said, "No, but when Keogh saw District Inspector Lang on the day of the search, there was obvious dislike towards Lang. But Keogh never said a word during or after the search."

Dawson turned to White and asked, "Do you have any questions, sir?"

White replied, "Yes. Were the two constables near Keogh at any time in the room?"

Moore answered, "No, they stood together in the far corner of the room."

White continued, "Think carefully before you answer this question. Did anything out of the ordinary occur from the time Keogh entered the office until the watch was found in his pocket by you?"

Moore knew he had to say what he saw regardless of the outcome; his career was at stake. "The only thing that was unexpected was that District Inspector Lang dropped the coat behind the desk onto the floor."

"My final question to you is, how do you think the watch got into Keogh's pocket?" asked White.

Moore was ready for this question and said, "As a police officer I can only deal in facts."

White and Dawson both smiled. It was a good answer.

White stood up and extended his hand to Moore. "Thank you. You may return to Kyneton. Have a good trip." White turned to Dawson, nodded and then left the room. White went to Commissioner Zane's office to relay the events of the Keogh case to date.

It was late in the day so Moore stayed overnight and caught the early coach back to Kyneton, arriving mid-afternoon. He immediately went to Lang's office to report back. He knocked on Lang's door and entered. Lang looked up from some papers on his desk and nodded.

Moore spoke first. "I'm reporting back, sir."

Lang asked, "How was the interview? Is there anything new I should know about?"

Moore answered truthfully, "No, they just went over the transcript again."

Lang said, "Good. I'll go down on the first coach tomorrow. Dismissed."

¶

District Inspector Lang arrived at Police Headquarters. He was not in the best mood. Virginia had been asking him when they would be returning to their home in England. Frederick's folly had unsettled their confidence in their image in Kyneton and they were arguing constantly. Perhaps this meeting would decide their future.

Deputy Commissioner White greeted him and walked to his office where Dawson was already seated. Lang and Dawson shook hands and White invited them to be seated.

The meeting was conducted in the same manner as for Sub-inspector Moore.

Dawson started with, "You have the Keogh case transcript in front of you. Do you have anything more to add regarding the watch search?"

Lang quickly scanned the document and said, "No, I believe the transcript is a true and accurate record of the case."

Dawson asked, "What do you know of the history of the watch?"

Lang replied, "The watch was stolen at the Agriculture Show several months ago. It had very distinctive engravings which the owner supplied to us as a drawing."

Dawson continued, "It seems obvious that Mr Keogh knew you in Ireland. Would you care to tell us how?"

Lang knew that his answer would cloud the Keogh watch case but he had no choice. He decided to keep his answer as simple as possible.

He started, "It wasn't until Keogh mentioned, during Inspector Dawson's investigation, that his son had been transported as a convict that I realised he was a Keogh from County Clare where I had served with the British Army. Prior to that outburst I had not associated him with my service in Ireland. I do recall an incident where his son, Michael Keogh, interfered with a constable's horse during an eviction I attended. But I recall little else."

"My last question to you — Can you offer any further explanation as to how the watch was found in Keogh's pocket?" asked Dawson.

Lang answered, "No, I have given it much thought and can offer no explanation."

Dawson looked inquiringly at Deputy Commissioner White, who said, "Thank you, Dawson."

"Lang, I need to raise another issue. I have received a "letter from the shire president, signed by all councillors. The letter expresses concerns as to whether you should continue in the position of district police inspector following your son's conviction. This letter and the Keogh case anomalies are of concern to me." White stopped and continued looking at Lang.

Lang knew he was expected to answer White's statement. He thought for a while. Were they expecting him to defend himself, ask for a transfer or offer his resignation? "Sir, may I have time to consider my response to your comments?" asked Lang.

"Yes that's a good idea; it's time for a break. We will meet again in one hour's time."

White stood up and left the room. He already knew what the deputy commissioner wanted.

Lang left the building and walked to a nearby hotel, ordered a drink and sat in a quiet corner. How should he respond? Was this to be the finale of his career? He was independently comfortable. He owned a working farm and had a reasonable bank account in England. Would he enjoy being an English gentleman, a man of note in the local village? Perhaps he could become a justice of the peace and act as the local magistrate. What could he expect if he stayed? Obviously he would be encouraged to transfer. He could not remain in Kyneton if the leaders of the shire had expressed concerns about him continuing in his role as district police inspector. Others in the community could also be of the same opinion. Possibly his senior officers may have lost confidence in him.

Then there was Virginia to consider. He knew she wanted to return to their home. Suddenly he decided. He was too old to have to tolerate any further situations as this. He would resign forthwith.

He walked back to the police building and requested a pen, paper and envelope from the duty officer. He wrote his resignation without any explanation being mentioned. He realised the irony of the fact that the mention of his involvement with the Keogh's had now indirectly forced him to resign and ultimately finish his career.

Lang knocked on Deputy Commissioner White's office door and entered. White and Dawson were idly discussing the Melbourne weather.

White indicated to Lang to be seated.

"Gentlemen, I believe that the result of this investigation will involve my future in the force. I have given this matter some thought and, to cut matters short, I have decided to submit my resignation effective forthwith and I trust that you will accept it."

White accepted the envelope handed to him by Lang. After reading the letter he handed it to Dawson without comment.

Dawson read the letter and asked, "Do you want more time to consider your resignation?"

Lang shook his head. "No, I have had sufficient time and I know my wife wants to return to our home in England. My decision is final."

White and Dawson both stood up and shook his hand.

White said, "I wish you well and a safe trip. Could you join us for dinner before you return to Kyneton? We will sort out the administration of you resignation tomorrow."

Lang said, "Yes, I would be delighted to have a farewell dinner with you. I have enjoyed your command." Little did Lang know that the commissioner would have requested his resignation if it had not been offered.

Lang returned to Kyneton the next day as a civilian. He went to the barracks to clean out his office and hand a letter to Sub-inspector Moore which advised him that he was now the acting district inspector. This letter, in effect, exonerated him of any misdoings in the Keogh case.

Paul Lang returned home as soon as he cleared his office. When he told Virginia that he had resigned she started crying with delight. Within two days she had all their personnel effects packed ready to return to England.

Michael's week had begun well. He had received two letters; one was from Patrick telling him he had located Mary Kirwan through a friend he worked with from Limerick. Patrick had forwarded Michael's money and his request for her to visit Kyneton. Michael was delighted. He opened the second letter, the contents of the first one still on his mind, to find the second letter was from Mary herself.

She wrote a good letter. It was both interesting and informative. Yes, she would come to Victoria and if she liked the country would consider staying. This was good news; perhaps they could share the farm and keep it intact.

She had been living in Limerick since her husband had died, and her only relative was a married sister-in-law. Michael could read between the lines of her loneliness. Perhaps she could find happiness in a new land. He wondered how long it would be before she arrived.

¶

Brendan received a note from William McMahon to meet him, at the Carlsruhe Bridge four miles from Kyneton, with Michael Somerset. Brendan and Michael arrived early and were sitting on the ground throwing stones in the river and chatting. Brendan said he had a surprise for him but did not elaborate.

A horseman cantered towards them. They both stood up, warily eying the incoming rider.

Then Brendan relaxed as he recognised the rider. "Here is your surprise."

The rider dismounted and walked towards them. He shook Brendan's hand and turned to Michael. "We meet again."

Michael recognised his face but couldn't place him.

"I'm William McMahon but you met me as Captain Irish."

Michael laughed. "Yes, I remember you now. What is this all about?"

William went to his horse and returned with the old wheat bag. "I believe that this is your father's property." He placed a linen wrapped package on the ground at his feet.

Michael knelt down and opened the linen covering and after seeing the cape and the enclosed sword he rose and stood speechless. Was this a dream?

"I have repaid my debt to you," said William.

"Yes, a thousand times over. I won't ask how you did it, but you have done Ireland a great service."

Captain Irish turned, mounted his horse waved. "Remember me." He rode off south towards Mount Diogenes.

The meeting had lasted about ten minutes. Michael had trouble believing his dual good fortune for the week. But his good fortune was to continue. On their way back to town, Brendan told him how the sword had been found and his involvement in its recovery. Michael had a good friend in Brendan. He would be forever grateful to him.

The next week a letter from Maeve arrived, who wrote that she and their father were in the colony and that she was now married to John Hall. The best news was that they lived near Kyneton. What an extraordinary month! He soon found out where their farm was and decided to visit Sunny Lodge on the coming Sunday.

On that morning, he collected flowers from the garden and dressed in his best clothes. He even polished his boots and saddle. He had groomed the horse the previous day. He headed off down the road mid-morning and expected the trip to take about an hour.

¶

Michael sat on the hill and looked down at Sunny Lodge. John's father had taught him well as he had selected a good site. Lush green grass abounded with stands of large gum trees on a hill. It had good water with the dams all full. White smoke was curling into the clear sky and he could see two people walking back to the farmhouse. He allowed the horse to set his own pace while he took in the farm sights — the sheep, the cattle and the crops; it looked profitable.

The two people walking to the house had stopped and were looking towards him. He could now see they were a man and a woman. His mouth was dry and his heart was beating faster as he recognised Maeve and John. He waved to them and urged his horse to a trot.

Maeve shouted, "Michael," and started to run to meet him. He stopped his horse, jumped to the ground and hugged her for a long time. She was crying for joy as Michael kissed her on the cheek.

Stepping back he said, "You look lovely. Victoria is good for you."

John stood back smiling at them and their happiness. He took the horse's bridle and gave it to Connor to lead the horse to the stables.

They walked to the house together without speaking. Michael released one hand and greeted John. Inside the house the three of them started talking at once. Then Maeve looked at the doorway and saw Edmund standing there, crying.

Michael kissed his father on the brow and sat next to him.

John said, "I'll tell the cook we have a guest for lunch." When he returned he said, "Michael, you talk first. Tell us your story of your experiences."

Michael started with the voyage from Cork and stopped only when he was going to tell of the sword. He excused himself and went to the stable to collect a parcel for his father.

When Michael returned he asked a table to be cleared. He then unwrapped the linen covering and laid out the cape and the sword. Then he stood back from the table, looking at his father and then John. Neither his father nor John said a word.

John eventually picked up the sword and said to Michael, "You have had an exciting life. I'll be interested to hear how you recovered these treasures."

Michael said, "That is a secret that will remain with me for the rest of my life." His father had picked up the cape and was holding it reverently. He could not believe that the treasures were back in his care. He carefully wrapped them in the linen covering and went to his room with them. He stayed there until lunch was called.

Michael completed his story telling them of the possibility of Mary Kirwan coming to Victoria. Lunch time had arrived. He sat between his father and Maeve and listened while they spoke of their voyage, and his father's court case. They spoke affably with laughter. He could see that they were both happy here with John and that they enjoyed their new lifestyle.

John was the next to talk. He was reluctant to go into depth but generally he conveyed the story of his court martial, the voyage and his time in Victoria. He did not mention his meeting with District Police Inspector Lang; it would have achieved no purpose.

By this time it was late afternoon, the table had been cleared and drinks had been served on the veranda. They all agreed it had been a reunion never to be forgotten. Maeve invited Michael to stay the night, which he accepted. He had a few drinks and was in no hurry to return to the farm. He was content to just sit with his family and chat. He also told them of his new name, Michael Somerset; Michael Keogh was no more. He would return to Woodlea tomorrow. When he told John where Woodlea was located, John laughed and said, "Maeve and I passed your place when we returned from Malmsbury. We know where it is."

❡

Frederick started to pack his belongings the day after his trial. The housemaid's husband helped. He had the job of wrapping the small chest in canvas and sewing the seams. The chest would not be opened for four more months. He would be home in England when he discovered that the Irish treasures were no longer in his possession. He had sailed from the colony within three weeks of his trial, to return to England and the family home, where he sat at an upstairs window for the next twelve months before depression eventually overcame him and he committed suicide.

❡

Paul Lang felt no emotion on leaving the Victorian Police. He had accepted his fate and would be his own man from now on. He would become a retired gentleman and would use his old military rank — Colonel Lang, retired — on his visiting card. His wish to retire to Victoria was now dashed forever.

Virginia was pleased to be going home. She'd had enough of Paul's career disasters and Frederick's dishonesty. All she wanted was to have her window seat and her garden in England. She could not understand how Paul could have been so totally oblivious to the turbulent effect he had had on peoples' lives. Paul just moved on never looking back.

Others around Paul were waving, crying or gazing at the now distant port. The ship's sails were filling with a northerly breeze, increasing speed and creating a symmetrical bow wave. The teak decks were creaking and groaning but he enjoyed the sounds and the smell of the tarred ropes and the sea air. He stood on deck watching the town of Melbourne disappear and finally the Macedon Hills.

Paul retired for a few hours at noon before coming back up on deck in the late afternoon. Virginia remained asleep and did not join him. The ship sailed down the east coast of Port Phillip Bay to avoid the sandbanks and the shoals, eventually turning to a westerly heading to prepare to enter and sail through the notoriously treacherous seas of the Heads. The sea started to churn and the ship pitched and rolled uncomfortably.

The captain had furled the topsails due to the strengthening north wind. The waves were choppy and spraying over the main deck. Paul was soon drenched but he was determined to see the ship exit the bay and set course for England. He could see the line of foam from the hidden reef line, and then all of a sudden they were out into Bass Strait. The pilot was lowered to his boat to return and perform the same service for the next ship to arrive at the Heads. Paul stayed on deck until dinner time when he went to his cabin and changed. He was now on his way home. He pondered — should he write his story telling all or just enjoy the remainder of his life and dwell on his successes as a retired gentleman?

§

Michael was mending the shearing shed door when he heard the geese and the dog loudly advising the arrival of a visitor driving up the farm road. He walked out to see who it was. It was a gig with two people — one who was Russell Carroll, the other a lady about his own age.

Russell waved. "Good morning, Michael. You have a welcome visitor. Guess who?"

Michael nodded to them and stepped forward to help the lady alight. "Welcome and good morning to both of you." The lady was slim and dressed in country attire. He could see she was a country person by her complexion.

Russell said, "Allow me to introduce Mary Kirwan."

Michael could not believe what he was hearing. He stood there with his mouth open.

Mary laughed. "Yes, it's me."

Michael stepped to her and gave her a hug. "At long last. It is good to finally meet you."

Russell interrupted, "I took the liberty of bringing her luggage as I know you have plenty of rooms."

"Yes, of course, the farm is half yours," answered Michael. "Please do come in." He took Mary's arm. Russell declined, pleading urgent business in town.

Mary could see that the farm was productive by the condition of the crops and livestock. Her late husband had been a farmer and she had spent plenty of time in the fields. Michael had impressed her within those first few minutes. He obviously had been genuinely pleased to see her.

Michael took her on a tour of the farm. They had plenty of time to talk about their lives and, in particular, Seamus, at a later date. The farmhouse was now completed with a large parlour and separate kitchen, four bedrooms and a study.

It was twice the size of her house in Limerick and had a veranda surrounding the entire house. She was happy with her room and delighted with the view from her window which overlooked the river. They spoke for hours, about everything and nothing, until Mary started to show how tired she was, it had been a long voyage. Michael showed her to her bedroom and she retired early.

The next morning she awoke early and decided to go for a

walk. She headed down to the river. The dog followed her, running to and fro chasing the plovers hiding in the lush green foliage. The day was fresh and cloud covered but she enjoyed the walk in the long grass near the river. Suddenly she heard a gunshot and looked back towards the farm. Michael was waving her back. What was wrong?

He ran down to her, shouting to come away from the river. Mary was to have her first lesson in the colonies about its wild life. Don't walk near rivers with long grass because of the snakes. Victoria had some of the most deadly snakes in the world and they were most prevalent near rivers and creeks.

Mary decided to have Michael with her whenever she went outdoors again. They had formed an immediate friendship and enjoyed each other's company, talking about their past lives. Whenever Seamus's name came up Mary would cry at his memory.

They made a good team. The farm was being constantly improved by them. Mary was a good cook and had a green thumb regarding the orchard and the gardens. Michael was good with the livestock and farm repairs. They both helped with the sowing of the crops.

Three months after Mary's arrival, Michael realised he had developed a deep affection for her and had tried to pluck up courage to ask her if she felt the same way. His answer came after having Sunday lunch at John and Maeve's. They arrived back late at Woodlea and as he was helping Mary from the gig when she slipped and fell into his arms. Looking up into his eyes, Mary took the initiative and kissed Michael. He put his arms around her and kissed her in return. They said not a word but walked to the veranda. Mary sat with Michael's arms around her, both looking out into the moonlit night. Michael proposed that very night and Mary happily accepted.

The next morning Michael walked up their farm road, by himself, still not believing how his life had turned around. Even though he was still technically an escaped convict, he had beaten the odds to become a successful married farmer in a new country. Together with his father, his sister, Maeve, lived nearby, happily married to John Hall, a military officer, and another successful farmer. How all their lives had changed!

Without Paul Lang's involvement in their lives, Michael wondered where each of them would have been now — in particular he and John.

A convict and a soldier.

THE END

Historical Notes

i. The Popery Act of the old Penal Law had allowed Catholics to divide inherited land between sons but all knew what the all-powerful local landlords would stoop to, if they wanted the land. On the eastern side of the coast road from Liscannor Bay to Galway Bay, the landlord had obtained title for as far as the eye could see, all the land and all the tiny cottages, some being only hovels.

ii. The Potato Famine of 1845 to 1848 was a disaster for the people of Clare. It was worse than the famine one hundred years before when the potato crops failed due to extreme cold and wet weather for two successive years. Over the course of the five or six years, millions either died or immigrated. Many tenant farmers were evicted by their landlords.

iii. One of the distant Keogh families risked their lives and sailed the dangerous and long voyage to Australia. Another family immigrated to New York, with the third family obtaining work at the local town of Kilrush, as caretakers of the property of an absentee English landlord. Fortunately they had had basic education and obtained employment. Only around one in ten persons of County Clare could be considered literate. Very few ever had the opportunity and many accepted that to be uneducated was their destiny.

iv.   In 1646 General Owen Roe O'Neill led the Irish Army
        into battle at Benburb County Tyrone against a superior
        Scottish Army led by General Monroe. O'Neill drew up
        his army between two hills with a river one side and a
        marshland on the other. The Irish routed the Scots who
        fled across the deeper part of the river "that one might
        have crossed dry shod on the bodies". General Monroe's
        hat, cape and sword were amongst the spoils.

v.   The Potato Famine of 1845-48 was the worst period in the
        history of Ireland. Amid the horrors of 1847 the Irish lay
        dead in hundreds on the highways and in the fields. There
        was food in abundance but the Government said it could
        not be touched, unless in accordance with the teachings
        of Adam Smith or the "laws of political economy". The
        corn exported from Ireland that year would, alone,
        have sufficed to feed a larger population. Over 2 million
        persons died or immigrated. The west coast was most
        affected. Complete settlements vanished.

vi.   The original Hall family settled in Kyneton in 1849.
        Joseph Hall owned the Windmill Farm, the White Hill
        Farm (now Sunbury Lodge) and the Park Hall Farm, all on
        the Metcalfe Road. In 1836 Major Mitchell, the explorer,
        crossed the south-west boundary where White Hall Farm
        was established some thirteen years later.

vii.   Cork sits on the Lee River and is divided by two water
        ways. In the 1800s, the harbour side was lined with
        warehouses, shipping agents' offices and their residences.
        It was a major port for all points of the compass.

viii. The name Van Diemen's Land was changed in 1855 to Tasmania. The name was more in keeping with the discoverer, Abel Tasman, and to delete its reference to its convict past.

ix. Macquarie Harbour (1821-1833) contained the Sarah Island Prison and was remote from civilization. The most notorious of prisoners were sent here. The narrow opening to the harbour was called Hell's Gates and was surrounded by dense forests and snow covered mountains. Escape to freedom was almost impossible. Gruesome stories of murder of fellow prisoners and half crazed men were plentiful. The costs eventually outweighed the value of the prison and it closed in 1833.

x. Cessation of transportation of convicts to Australia occurred in 1840 in New South Wales, Queensland 1850, 1853 in Tasmania and 1868 in Western Australia. Victoria was trialled with exiles and prisoners were kept in hulks for several years in the mid 1840's, but Victorian did not have a penal settlement nor did South Australia.

xi. Port Phillip Bay is a drowned basin with Melbourne sited around thirty-five miles, at the northern end. The entrance is S shaped and is only twelve hundred yards wide and forty-five feet deep. With a tide run of about eight knots, it is renowned for its extremely turbulent eddies and has claimed many sailing ships.

xii. The Eureka Stockade was the site of Australia's only armed rebellion. In 1854 the incompetent administration and excessive costs of miners' licences caused the miners to riot. They armed themselves with a motley collection of weapons and assembled behind a stockade consisting of slabs and pickets. The army defeated them in a matter of minutes. The eventual consequence was that the miners received cheaper licences, franchises and better administration.

xiii. Bushranger is the Australian term for Highway Men (English) or Outlaws (USA). The Bushrangers fell into four categories:

- Escaped convicts (Bolters). Mainly in Van Diemen's Land in the first part of the 1800s.
- The Gold rush period 1850s in Victoria, many were ex Van Diemen's Land convicts.
- The sons of convicts or poor settlers in New South Wales. All through the 1800's.
- In Victoria 1878-80 – The Kelly Gang – they transplanted hatred of the Irish Catholic for the English Protestant.

The last bushrangers were the Governor Brothers who, in 1900, murdered nine people. They were half caste Aborigines goaded by racial prejudice.

xiv. Brothers Joseph (Jnr) and John Hall were awoken by bushrangers when returning from Bendigo, but had hidden their money in a tree. This is a true story.

xv. In the 1850's, the gold rush period, Victoria's population rose from 400,000 to 1,100,000 in ten years. The British Government provided assisted passage for countless thousands of Irish from the west coast of Ireland such as County Clare where the famine was worst.

xvi. The employment of ex-convicts was necessary, as manpower was short. Many proved of value, particularly those with skills in farming, stonework, blacksmiths etc. and they helped Australia to get started. However, some without skills found their way into the police force and caused untold damage within the community. The Kelly Gang saga was caused by one constable who was later sacked.

xvii. The Australian Aborigines are renowned hunters and have exceptional bush skills. One is their incredible tracking skills either by eyesight or observance of disturbed environment, i.e. broken or bent grass.

xviii. Mt Diogenes (locally named Hanging Rock) was named by the explorer Major Mitchell. He was a student of ancient Greece. He also named Port Phillip Bay, Alexander Road and Mt Macedon, to name a few.

About the Author

John P. F. Lynch has written several
local history books and the history of
his maternal ancestors. His mother's
great great grandparents all settled
in the Kyneton area of Victoria in the
1840-50's. He is a member of both the
Kyneton and Romsey Historical Societies, both of which helped with his
research for his books.

John is a member of the Order of Australia, a Knight Hospi-
taller of the Order of St. John of Jerusalem and a Justice of the
Peace. He is also the former President of the Romsey/Lancefield
RSL Sub Branch, President/Secretary of the Romsey Football/
Netball Club as well as Chairman of the Macedon Ranges Leg-
acy Group.

Also by John P. F. Lynch

- *Joseph Hall (1804-1871) Kyneton Pioneer: Including Park Hall, Windmill Farm & Sunbury Lodge*

- *Celebration of the Catholic Parish of Lancefield and Romsey Centenary 1906-2006*

- *History of the Romsey Football/Netball Club, founded 1879: Remembering 120 years of Competition (1888-2008)*

- *Romsey-Lancefield RSL Sub-Branch: 75 years (1933-2008)*

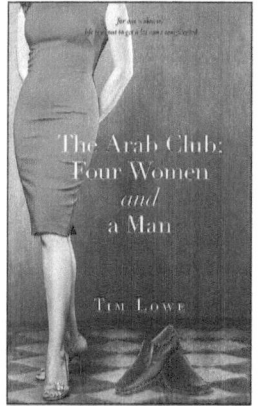

Best-selling titles by Kerry B. Collison

Readers are invited to visit our publishing websites at:
http://sidharta.com.au
http://publisher-guidelines.com/
Kerry B. Collison's home pages:
http://www.authorsden.com/visit/author.
asp?AuthorID=2239
http://www.expat.or.id/sponsors/collison.html
email: author@sidharta.com.au

Purchase Sid Harta titles online at:
http://sidharta.com.au

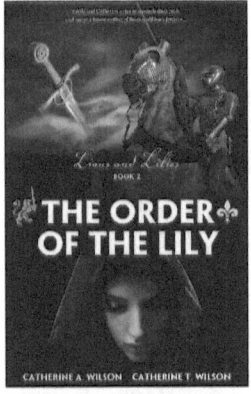

www.ingramcontent.com/pod-product-compliance
Lightning Source LLC
Chambersburg PA
CBHW030919260626
47169CB00002B/322